STORM

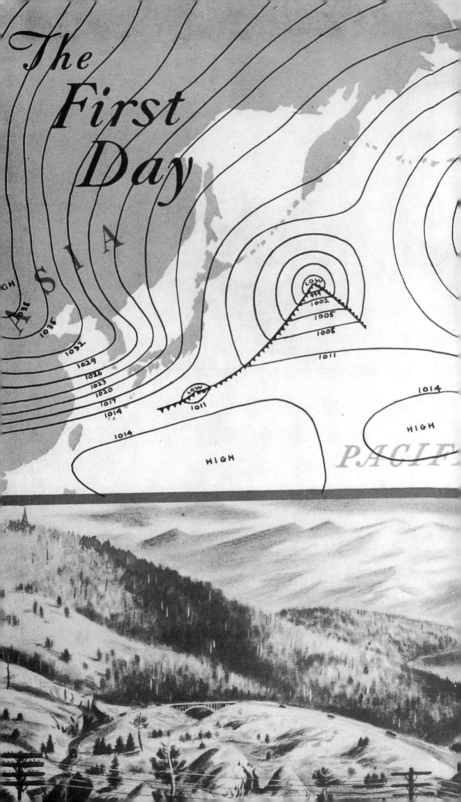

The First Day

ORM

GEORGE R. STEWART

FOREWORD BY ERNEST CALLENBACH

SANTA CLARA UNIVERSITY, SANTA CLARA, CALIFORNIA
HEYDAY BOOKS, BERKELEY, CALIFORNIA

The characters of this book—including Maria—are imaginary.
Whenever, as with the Chief and L.D., the title or office seemed to
suggest an individual, a characterization of the present incumbent
has been avoided. Although the scene is largely California, the
story is not a local-color study, and for simplification a few alter-
ations of setting have been introduced.

© 1941 by George R. Stewart
Foreword © 2003 by Ernest Callenbach

Library of Congress Cataloging-in-Publication Data
Stewart, George Rippey, 1895-
  Storm / George R. Stewart ; foreword by Ernest Callenbach.
    p. cm.
  ISBN 1-890771-74-0 (pbk. : alk. paper)
  1. Storms—Fiction. 2. California—Fiction. I. Title.
PS3537.T48545S7 2003
813'.52--dc22
                                    2003015860

Cover Art: Ruth Sorenson/Illustration Works/Getty Images
Cover Design: Rebecca LeGates
Printing and Binding: McNaughton & Gunn, Saline, MI

Orders, inquiries, and correspondence should be addressed to:
        Heyday Books
        P.O. Box 9145, Berkeley, CA 94709
        (510) 549-3564, Fax (510) 549-1889
        www.heydaybooks.com

Printed in the United States of America

10 9 8 7 6 5 4 3 2 1

FOREWORD

by Ernest Callenbach

When it first appeared in 1941, *Storm* gave readers a frisson similar to what we much later felt on seeing the first photo of Earth from space: a breathless realization that the planet was a working, living whole. *Storm*'s stunning effect came from its being a synoptic novel—"synoptic" as a weather map is, displaying what's happening all over the world at once. Human drama unfolds in stories that are intricately organized into successive days—or rather, many small dramas unfold, some of them intersecting. There's also meteorological drama and geological drama and even corporate drama. Like a filmmaker, Stewart cuts quickly from scene to numbered scene, giving a driving energy to the book. Yet the overall effect is not linear, but a sort of vast California mural.

This sense of simultaneity is sometimes global, sometimes minutely regional. And it is what enables the book's unique tone, its feel of poetic realism, and indeed its claim to classic status. We had never seen the world like this before, or the California landscape, or the lighthouses along the coast that first meet the book's central character, a great storm, as it approaches. Because of *Storm,* we saw the world differently, even if we had never set foot in California. And *Storm* showed us, as the world plunged into World War II, a society that made sense—a panorama of lives in touch with vast global realities, lives whose humdrum events turned out to be important. To readers today, some of Stewart's ordinary folks may seem unduly so. But Stewart *wanted* them to be ordinary: that was the point. Nor were they noticeably "Californian" types—

perhaps one reason the book was immediately popular throughout the country. It was chosen for the Book of the Month Club and soon reprinted in the Modern Library series. It was even made into a so-so film by Disney. Over the years it has probably sold a million copies, huge distribution for a serious novel.

Curiously too, *Storm* changed readers' lives in concrete ways. I am by no means the only one who, after reading it, decided to go into meteorology—though gradually I came to realize that it was Stewart's writing about meteorology which moved me, and not the study of weather in itself. Nor am I the only one who, having become fascinated by California in the novel, ended up migrating here. Even now, passages from *Storm* echo through my mind whenever I travel through landscapes crucial to the story: Donner Pass particularly, where not only the original legend but Stewart's modern story "brood still," as he writes, "over peak and canyon"; San Francisco, "set upon hills, pearl-grey in the winter sun"; the levees precariously guarding Sacramento and the Central Valley towns. And my memory is not the only one where this takes place: once, when Cody's Books in Berkeley invited local authors to try to stump listeners with a mystery paragraph from a favorite work, I chose *Storm,* thinking it obscure by then. Hands shot up in recognition after a single sentence.

In its complex, lovely sense of simultaneity and complexly interlinked causes, *Storm* was in fact far ahead of its time. Now, sixty years on, we know that causation does not follow the levers-and-gears model of mechanistic physics—a model that once governed the structures of virtually all novels. (In many ways, the novel reached its peak in the nineteenth century, when mechanics was king.) Especially in biology—and human affairs, a subsidiary realm—causation is multiple and operates in elaborate networks and feedback patterns. Stewart delights in what he once called "the infinite divisibility of time"; *Storm* is a distant precursor to the recently fashionable idea that the flapping of a butterfly's wings in China can lead to a hurricane in the Caribbean. But Stewart's butterfly is never a solitary creature. When a chipmunk hollows out a shelter under a decaying log that, snow-weighted, will later slide and crush a crucial transcontinental telephone cable, Stewart makes us see that this is part of a great pattern—of storms, erosion, forest evolution—in which humans play only a small part.

Because of this global, indeed cosmic, perspective, *Storm* is a humbling book to read. In his almost Biblical prose, Stewart reminds us of our modest role on the planet: "Four times in the known history of the earth have the mountains risen like a tide. Three times have the forces of air and water made head against those mountains, eating away the towering granite peaks into little rounded hills. Two hundred and fifty million years is the period of that cycle—majestic among earthly rhythms."

Following this passage comes a brilliantly compact survey of the major erosion mechanisms, in language any thirteen-year-old—as I was when I first read it—can easily grasp. It ends with a characteristic Stewart flourish, echoing the ancient rhythms of Ecclesiastes: "On hillsides the adobe soil grew heavy until great sections settled and slid, leaving behind them wide crescent-shaped scars of raw earth. And always the movement was downward, from the hilltops toward the sea." I have never been quite sure why, but such passages give me shivers, as a long rumble of thunder does, or Mozart's *Dies Irae*. I love the sound of this formal language, the elegant roll and sonority of it, the author not afraid to go for Big Effects.

The sweeping historical perspective of *Storm* adds to its power; Stewart is magisterial in relating our current concerns to those of far distant generations—the vanished

Mesa Verde people, the builders of Westminster Abbey, Galileo and others who first began to understand the workings of the atmosphere, even Ben Franklin, who first grasped the idea of a rotating and traveling storm. Stewart's historical connections still reverberate in my mind: when Vizcaíno sailed north along the fogbound California coast, giving the points their Spanish names, Stewart says, "the old queen lay dying, and *Hamlet* was a new play at the Globe."

Like any good novel, *Storm* has a deep and detailed sense of its primary setting—the California landscape. Stewart was a grand figure on the faculty during a brilliant epoch at the University of California at Berkeley, when departmental divisions were less sharp. He must have often lunched in the Faculty Club with the geographer Carl Sauer, who was laying out the lines upon which cultural geography would evolve for generations; with the anthropologist Alfred Kroeber, striving to understand how California Indians inhabited the region so successfully; with A. Starker Leopold, dean of American wildlife studies; with Woodrow Borah, the pioneering student of the Western Hemisphere's original populations; and with his hiking friend Charles Camp, a paleontologist. (It was one of Stewart's passions to hunt for old trails.)

And Stewart of course lived in the region that had given birth to the Sierra Club, that had already begun to preserve redwood forests and other natural areas for posterity, and that had sustained Joaquin Miller and John Muir, writers to whom California was a great human and spiritual drama, not just spectacular landscape. But to their appreciative reverence for the natural world Stewart added something much more modern. With Steinbeck and Dos

Passos, who had sketched the problem-beset nation as a whole, and with Michener, who would later portray whole cultures in novelized histories, Stewart created fiction of a truly sweeping scope. But his work is distinguished by a unique sense of ecological and social connections: almost as if they comprise an unfamiliar culture, he shows us humans inhabiting their special landscape.

Stewart knew the winds, the myriad creeks and the rivers they feed, the patterns of forest, meadow, and alpine rockscape, the points along the coast. I once asked him how he had learned so much about the state. He was not a loquacious man. Well, he said, he had traveled around a lot. He evidently followed Sauer's dictum, "Locomotion should be slow, the slower the better; and should be interrupted by leisurely halts to sit on vantage points and stop at question marks." Stewart knew the road over the Sierra Nevada as well as the old coyote in *Storm* does, the coyote who finds a car that has slid through the snow wall and crashed over a cliff—an episode based on an incident Stewart learned of while hanging around Donner Pass. Once Stewart accompanied a lineman assigned to repair some wires on a pole. Like the lineman in the book, this one fell, though not fatally.

An English department colleague once asked Stewart, who was a best-selling author and thus a curiosity on campus, how he remembered it all: did he have a special filing system? "It's all up here," Stewart replied, tapping his head. And indeed it was: the geography, botany, zoology, geology, history, and of course climatology and meteorology of the state—a huge interconnected wealth of knowledge of what and who lived here and how they survived.

Younger readers may be puzzled by one human feature of the book: the evident solidarity among most of its people. In the face of the storm, they cooperate in a complex regional dance of resistance and persistence. They are generally helpful; they are not obnoxiously competitive or acquisitive. They believe their society makes sense, and they are loyal to it, though it seems to be dominated by vast impersonal corporations. Can these be our recent American ancestors? Well, yes. *Storm* is situated near the beginning of World War II. Stewart probably finished writing it during the Battle of Britain, well before Pearl Harbor. In American perspective, it is thus a prewar book.

The country was coming out of a long, devastating economic depression. People felt lucky if they had food and a roof—everybody knew others who did not. Stewart writes somewhere that the great storm's rain fell on rich and poor alike: meteorology become morality. We were all in it together, and we had better look out for each other. This may seem quaint in our morally tattered times, but it is ancient and perennial wisdom: a people imagines at its peril that greed and profit-making can suffice as compass points for living.

Moreover, the California of *Storm*'s epoch was not yet caught up in the maelstrom of American life as a whole. It still had a small population; the immense growth set in motion by the war industries lay dimly ahead. Silicon Valley was still agricultural, magically afloat with plum blossoms in the spring. Cut off from the eastern centers by two thousand miles of mountains, deserts, and plains, California seemed almost a country to itself. Eastern goods were priced "slightly higher west of the Rockies." The 1940s exoticism of California may indeed account for some of *Storm*'s appeal to easterners like myself: it was another country, where things were done differently. Doubtless the book had a strong appeal to Californians, too, relatively unaccustomed to seeing their home portrayed in fiction.

Storm was pathbreaking in other ways, of course. The naming of tropical storms is now a commonplace of television weather news; when Stewart's Junior Meteorologist first did it, it was daring and charming, an important part of his becoming an adult, finding a meaningful role to play in the world. Stewart himself felt that the major achievement of the book was to make Maria, the storm, a dramatic "heroine"—appropriately somewhat inscrutable, since the forecasters in *Storm* had no satellite images to aid them, no syndicated forecast service, not even knowledge of the jet stream. Like the forecaster I once worked for after school, they pored over the map, went up on the roof, looked at the clouds, checked the wind with a wet finger, and then winged their regional forecasts. And no, they were not less accurate than today's high-tech forecasters.

Storm made Alta California, as the bioregionalists call it, seem like home, and ultimately it did become home for me. I had first read *Storm* as a schoolboy in rural Pennsylvania and, identifying with the Junior Meteorologist, set my course to become a forecaster too. I went to the University of Chicago largely because it had the country's leading meteorology department. And when opportunity offered, I hitchhiked to California to spend a summer with a roommate who came from Los Angeles. One July Thursday I called in "sick" and took the overnight Greyhound north. I remember riding drowsily at dawn through the unearthly rounded hills near Livermore, feeling I must be dreaming. After debarking into the crisp clean Bay Area morning (relishing Stewart's saying that we humans are "creatures of the air"), I took the yellow Key train across the bay, seeing San Francisco sparkling in air so brisk and invigorating as to seem almost a new element after the smog of Los Angeles and the muggy, enervating heat of Chicago.

I phoned Stewart, to whom I had earlier written several fan letters. He graciously let me descend on him in his battered, wartime wood office building on the Berkeley campus. He proved to be a kindly professorial type, trim and a little distant; he listened to my ambitions, advised me that writing entailed a great deal of hard work but had its compensations, and wished me well. I went out onto the campus, sniffed the famous eucalyptus, admired the lithe young women in their summery blouses, and felt lonely and a little sorry for myself, so far from home. But somehow, along about there, I decided this would be a good place to live.

A couple of years later, I came back and stayed. The California landscape is still inhabited for me by Stewart's words. They hover over it, history and legend; they have given it an organic body, known and loved, so that when I began to think about writing of an ecologically healthy society, Ecotopia, it seemed inevitable to situate it in this territory. And when I wrote a "prequel" to explain how Ecotopia came into existence, I adopted *Storm*'s multi-strand structure for *Ecotopia Emerging*.

On balance, and I am inescapably speaking quite personally, Stewart's contribution to how we see California thus seems to me immense. I literally cannot envisage California without awareness of how he saw it, dramatized it, loved it. In *Storm*, however, we are so far from contemporary media-ized California that the timespan seems almost geological—far from freeways, from megapopulation, from sprawl, from beach TV, from stress, from gunfire in the streets, from road rage. But we are in touch with a much deeper reality, of land and water and weather, of humans huddled together on the planet in a dark universe. As the official in charge of protecting Sacramento from flooding muses near the end of *Storm,* "Yet other storms would come; again the brown water would rise against the levees. In the end the levees would go down—a hundred years, a thousand years; but in the end they would go, and the men who built them." The particular legacy of *Storm,* what Stewart gave us that we must live with from here on, is nothing less than global consciousness.

CONTENTS . . . .

STORM

ENVELOPED in the gaseous film of the atmosphere, half-covered by a skim of water forming the oceans—the great sphere of the earth spun upon its axis and moved inflexibly in its course around the sun. Continuously, in the succession of day and night, season and season, year and year, the earth had received heat from the sun, and again lost into space that same amount of heat. But this balance of the entire sphere did not hold for its individual parts. The equatorial belt received yearly much more heat than it radiated off, and the polar regions lost much more heat than they received. Nevertheless the one was not growing hotter while the others sank toward absolute zero. Instead, at once tempering cosmic extremes and maintaining equilibrium with the sun, by a gigantic and complex circulation, the poles constantly cooled the tropics and the tropics reciprocally warmed the poles.

In this process, cold currents bore icebergs toward the equator, and warm currents moved poleward. But even these vast rivers of the oceans achieved only a small part of the necessary whole.

In the stupendous work of transport the paramount agent was the atmosphere, thin and insignificant though it was in comparison with the monstrous earth itself. Within the atmosphere the chief equalizers of heat were the great winds—the trades and anti-trades, the monsoons, the tropical hurricanes, the polar easterlies, and (most notable of all) the gigantic whirling storms of the temperate zones, which in the stateliest of earthly processions moved ever along their sinuous paths, across ocean and continent, from the setting toward the rising sun.

2

Early in November, had come "Election-Day rains." Chilling after the warmth of October, low-lying clouds blew in from the southwest, thick with moisture from the Pacific. The golden-brown hills of the Coast Ranges grew darker beneath the downpour. In the Great Valley summer-dry creeks again ran water. Upon the Sierra the snow fell steadily. The six-month dry season was over.

Between drenching showers the sun shone brightly, warming the earth. Thousands of hillsides were suddenly green with the sprouted grass. In the valleys, overnight, the square miles of summer fallow became fields of new wheat and barley. Stockmen talked jovially to one another—a good year! Farmers in irrigated districts thought comfortably of rising water-tables and filling reservoirs. In the towns the merchants gave larger orders to wholesale houses.

November ended with two weeks of good growing-weather. The grass and the grain sucked moisture from the soil, and spread lush blades in the sunshine.

December came in—days still warm and sunny, nights clear, with a touch of frost in the valleys and on the higher hills. Farmers began to look more often to the south—but there were no clouds. Stockmen no longer went about slapping one another on the back; instead, they went secretly and inquired the price of cotton-seed meal at the Fresno mills. As the weeks passed, store-keepers grew chary about granting credit.

By Christmas, the green of the pasture-lands and the wide grain fields showed a faint cast of yellow. In favored spots the grass was six inches tall; but the blades were curled a little, and at the edges were brownish red. Where cattle had grazed, the ragged ends still showed.

The city-folk went about congratulating themselves on the fine weather. The tourist trade was flourishing. On New Year's Day the sports experts broadcasting the football games talked almost as much about the fine weather as about the passes.

But just after the first of the year pessimistic crop-reports from California helped send the price of barley up a half cent on the Chicago exchange. That same day, six great trucks with trailers, heavy-laden with cotton-seed meal, plugged up the highway from Fresno; the richer stockmen had started to buy feed.

So, in the first weeks of the new year a winter drought lay tense upon the land.

3

From Siberia the wide torrent of air was sweeping south-ward—from death-cold Verkhoyansk, from the frigid basin of the Lena, from thick-frozen Lake Baikal. The great wind poured over the Desert of Gobi. Even the hardy nomads winced; the long-haired northern camels stirred uneasily; the rough-coated ponies shivered; all sound of running water was hushed. High in the air swirled the dust blown up from the desert. Over the mountain-jagged rim of the table-land the wind poured forth; through all the gaps and passes of the Khingan Mountains, down the gorge of the Hwang-ho. As in centuries past, it stormed across the Great Wall, asking no emperor's leave. Swifter than Tartar, more terrible than Mongol, more pitiless than Manchu, it swept down upon the plains of China.

Descending from the plateau and entering a warmer region, the air lost some of its arctic coldness; nonetheless, in the ancient northern capital the chill struck into men's blood. By day, a sun like tarnished brass shone without warmth through clouds of yellow dust. By night, the eyes saw nothing, but the dryness and smell of dust pinched the nostrils. The fur-coated foreigners (as was their birthright) blasphemed at the weather; the thin-clad, shivering coolies moved stoically about their business. Nightly in hovel and doorway, huddling in corners, some scores of the poor froze slowly to death.

Southward along the coast of China ran that river of air. Among the hills of Shantung it was still an iron-cold blast, but on the plain of the Yangtze its power was less. In Nanking and Shanghai the ice formed only in quieter, shallower pools.

The air at last swung away from the coast, and moved out over the sea; with every mile of passage across the water it grew more moist and temperate. Through a

thinning yellow haze the sun pierced more warmly. Now
the wind was no longer a gale, scarcely even a strong
breeze. The polar fury was spent. But still, east by south,
the river of air flowed on across the China Sea toward the
far reaches of the Pacific.

4

In mid-afternoon the front of the Siberian air-mass was
pushing slowly across the island-studded ocean which lies
east of China and south of Japan. Its cold heavy air
clung close to the surface of the water. Advancing thus
as a northeasterly breeze, it forced backward the warmer,
lighter air ahead of it, and occasionally pushed beneath
this air vigorously enough to cause a shower.

This opposing and retreating air had lain, some days
previous, over the tropical ocean near the Philippine
Islands. A storm had taken it northeast, shedding rain,
clear to the Japanese coast; it had then moved slowly
back before the pressure of the cold wave. By this northern foray it had lost its extreme humidity and warmth,
and become temperate rather than tropical. Nevertheless it still remained warmer and more moist than the
air which had swept down from Siberia.

The advance of the northern air and corresponding
retreat of the southern were related, like all movements
in the atmosphere, to conditions existing concurrently
over the whole earth. The conditions of this particular
day were such that the advance was losing its vigor and
becoming slower.

An hour before sunset, one section of the front reached
a small island—a mere mountain-peak above the ocean.
A dead-tired man may stumble over a pebble and fall;

but his weariness, rather than the pebble, is the cause. Similarly, a vigorously advancing front would simply have swept over and around the island, but now the obstruction caused an appreciable break, and a hesitant eddy, about a mile in diameter, began to form—weakened—took shape again. At one point the southern air no longer yielded passively to the northern, but actively flowed up its slope, as up a gradual hill. Rising, this air grew cooler, and from it a fine drizzle began to fall. This condensation of water in turn further warmed the air, and caused it to press up the slope more steadily with still further condensation. The process thus became self-perpetuating and self-strengthening.

The movement of this advancing warm air was now a little southwest breeze, where previously all the flow of air had been from the northeast. With this new breeze, air which was still warmer and more moist moved in from the south along the near-by section of the original front, renewing its vigor and causing a little shower. All these new and renewed activities—winds, drizzle, and shower—were now arranged in complex but orderly fashion around a single point.

As from the union of two opposite germ-cells begins a life, so from the contact of northern and southern air had sprung something which before had not been. As a new life, a focus of activity, begins to develop after its kind and grow by what it feeds on, so in the air that complex of forces began to develop and grow strong. A new storm had been born.

5

The ship's course lay almost due west. Her position was about three hundred miles southeast of Yokohama, but her port was Foochow on the coast of China, still fourteen hundred miles distant.

At seven that evening when the radio-operator came on deck, he found that the weather had changed. He noted breaks in the high cloud-deck beneath which the ship had been moving for several days. The air seemed both cool and dry, in comparison with the former half-tropical suavity. Automatically, he looked at the smoke-wisp trailing behind; knowing the ship's course, he estimated that in the last hour the wind had veered from about two points south of west to an equal angle north of west.

Since one of his duties was to read the instruments and report to shore stations, the radio-operator felt more than the usual seafaring-man's interest in the weather. He stepped in to look at the barometer; it had fallen slightly, but not enough to matter. In January a typhoon was unlikely; and besides, the international reports showed no disturbance in the region which they were now traversing.

Nevertheless, about eight o'clock a light drizzle began. This increased to a steady gentle rain; but the air was warmer than before. The light wind had backed sharply, and was now from the southwest. The smoke rose almost vertically. After a few minutes the rain ceased, but the ship still moved beneath the low cloud-deck. The air was again warm and oppressive as it had been on preceding days.

A quarter of an hour later, the weather changed again. A gust of wind, not enough to be called a squall, raised a few white-caps. Along with it but scarcely of ten seconds' duration, a sudden shower spattered the deck with large raindrops. The temperature seemed to drop immediately at least ten degrees.

"Queer weather!" remarked the radio-operator to the second officer, at the same time noticing the smoke. It was trailing off to port, again indicating a northerly wind; moreover, instead of rising, the smoke lay close to the surface of the ocean.

"Something getting ready to begin," said the second officer. "Hope it's not for us."

There was, however, no further marked change. At nine o'clock—noon by Greenwich time—the radio-operator began to make his observations, preparatory to reporting to the nearest shore station. He recorded the barometer at 1011, slightly higher than at the time of the shower. He noted the Fahrenheit temperature at 55, fourteen degrees cooler than on the preceding evening. The wind was a steady breeze from the northwest. The cloud-deck was breaking, and a new moon, low in the west, shone over the ocean-surface.

West toward the Chinese coast the ship plowed on steadily. "Whatever we ran through back there," said the radio-operator, "we're done with it." Then he sniffed curiously. "Funny thing—hundreds of miles at sea, and I'd swear I smell dust!"

6

The new Junior Meteorologist ($2,000 a year) was working at his table. The telephone rang and he answered it mechanically. "Weather Bureau. . . . Fair tonight and Wednesday; no change in temperature; moderate northwest winds. . . . You're welcome." He clicked down the receiver with unnecessary vigor, showing his irritation. In the five weeks since he had come to work in the Bureau, the weather had been inane. Sometimes he wanted to take up the telephone and shout into it: "Blizzards, lightning, and hurricanes!" But as he bent over his table again, irritation oozed away. Instead, there swelled up within him the joy of the workman, of the scientist, even of the artist. For, as he often told himself, his present task was the only one of his daily assignments over which he could work with some degree of calm and detachment. It was not like the hurried preparation of the early morning map upon which the forecasts were based. His present work had its uses, but they were a little removed from the immediate present.

On the table lay a large map which he had almost finished preparing. It was large not only by its own dimensions but also by its coverage of about one half the northern hemisphere. At its top were the Arctic regions; from these the two continents slanted down— to the right, North America, to the left, the eastern portion of Asia. In the center of the map stretched the great spaces of the North Pacific Ocean. The outline of land and sea, the parallels and meridians, the names and numbers of weather stations formed the printed background. Upon this the Junior Meteorologist had entered the current weather data as they had been reported by radio and telegraph, internationally, some hours earlier.

Visitors to the Weather Bureau found such a map

confused and unintelligible. But to its maker it was simple, beautiful, and inspiring. Now he was giving it the final revision; with the care of a poet polishing a quatrain, he erased an inch of one line and redrew it with slightly altered curve.

He laid aside his eraser and colored pencils, and sat back to look at the work. Involuntarily, he breathed a little more deeply. To him, as to some archangel hovering in the ninth heaven, the weather lay revealed. Suppose that the telephone should ring and some voice inquire the weather in Kamchatka, upon Laysan Island, or at Aklavik in the frozen delta of the Mackenzie. He could reply not only as to what the weather actually was but also with fair assurance as to what it would most likely be in the near future.

The first sweeping glance assured him that nothing exceptional or unforeseen had happened in the twenty-four hours since he had prepared the last similar map. Antonia had moved about as he had expected. Cornelia and the others were developing normally. Not at any price would the Junior Meteorologist have revealed to the Chief that he was bestowing names—and girls' names —upon those great moving low-pressure areas. But he justified the sentimental vagary by explaining mentally that each storm was really an individual and that he could more easily say (to himself, of course) "Antonia" than "the low-pressure center which was yesterday in latitude one-seventy-five East, longitude forty-two North."

The game, nevertheless, was beginning to play out. At first he had christened each new-born storm after some girl he had known—Ruth, Lucy, Katherine. Then he had watched eagerly, hoping in turn that each of these little storms might develop in proper fashion to bring the rain. But one after another they had failed him. Of late the supply of names had run short, and he had been relying chiefly upon long ones ending in -*ia* which suggested actresses or heroines of books rather than girls he had ever known.

Upon the present map four such storms stood out boldly—concentricities of black-pencil curves about centers marked LOW, the curves sharpening to angles as they crossed certain red, blue, or purple lines. Sylvia was a vigorous storm now centering over Boston; it—or she—had just brought heavy snow-fall to the northeastern states and was now moving out to sea, leaving a cold-snap behind. Felicia was a weak disturbance over Manitoba; she had little past and probably not much future. Cornelia was a large mature storm centering four hundred miles at sea southeast of Dutch Harbor. Antonia, young and still growing, was moving out into mid-ocean some two thousand miles behind Cornelia. In spite of their distances apart, the storms overlapped, and a curved belt of disturbed weather thus extended from Nova Scotia clear across to Japan.

In the western United States, however, and over the adjacent part of the Pacific Ocean the black curves nowhere crossed colored lines or sharpened to angles; they lay far apart and were drawn about points marked HIGH. To the Junior Meteorologist these were all obvious signs of clear calm weather. In the jargon of his trade, this region was covered by "the semi-permanent Pacific High." He looked at it malignantly. Then he smiled, for he noticed that the High had today accidentally assumed the shape of a gigantic dog's head. Rising from

the Pacific waters it looked out stupidly across the continent. The blunt nose just touched Denver; the top of
the head was in British Columbia. A small circle over
southern Idaho supplied an eye; three concentric ovals
pointing southwest from the California coast furnished
a passable ear.

Dog's head or not—the Pacific High was no laughing
matter for California. While it remained, every storm
advancing in boldly from the Pacific would sheer off
northeastward. A drenching rain would pour down upon
the south Alaskan coast and Vancouver Island; a steady
drizzle in Seattle and Portland. But San Francisco and
the Great Valley would have only cloud, while still
farther south Los Angeles would continue to bake in the
sunshine. In its actuality, invisible to man's eye, the
Pacific High lay upon the map as clearly as a mountain
range—and not less important than the Sierra Nevada
itself in its effects upon the people of California.

Far away from the American coast, in the upper left-
hand corner of the map, long lines which were close
together and almost parallel ran from the interior of
Asia southward to China and then curved eastward into
the Pacific. To the Junior Meteorologist this too was a
commonplace—the visible sign of that great river of
wind, the winter monsoon, at work pouring out the cold
air from Siberia. He noted in passing that the temperature at Peiping was eight below zero Fahrenheit. With
more professional interest he let his eyes follow along
those curving lines which ran into the Pacific.

Here and there in this region as elsewhere in the ocean
he saw a little cluster of notations representing the
weather reports furnished by radio from some vessel.

Over one of these he paused. The ship, three hundred miles southeast of Yokohama, had reported a barometric pressure of 1011, but by its position on the map it should have reported about 1012. A difference of one millibar, he realized, was inconsiderable and might easily result from an inaccurate barometer or from a careless reading of the instrument. For these reasons he had at first permitted himself to neglect this particular report. But now he reconsidered.

The ship's position was about half way between the island weather-stations of Hatidyosima to the north and Titijima to the south, about two hundred miles distant from each. But the temperature of the air at the ship was only two degrees warmer than at Hatidyosima, whereas it was twelve degrees colder than at Titijima. This was clear indication that the ship had already been engulfed in the cooler air which was sweeping out with the monsoon, and that somewhere between the ship and the southern island the cooler air which had come from the north would be pushing against the warmer southern air. He himself had already recognized this fact by drawing a blue line, indicative of a "cold front," from the center of Antonia westward and southward clear to the Chinese coast. Along such a boundary between cool and warm air a new storm was almost certain to form somewhere.

No other ships reported from that vicinity. Glancing at the wind-arrows of the two island stations, he saw that they tended to contradict rather than confirm the reading of the ship's barometer. Hatidyosima had a northeast wind instead of northwest; Titijima a west wind instead of south or southwest. Practically, he realized, the whole matter was of no importance, but he felt the twinge of scientific curiosity and the challenge of a difficult problem.

Methodically he checked back over the maps of the last ten days, and determined that there had never before been an occasion to doubt the accuracy of the reports from this particular ship. He paused a moment with eraser held above the blue line. The ship's barometer-reading, he considered, along with the general probability of the whole situation indicated an incipient storm. The failure of the island reports to confirm would mean only that the disturbance was as yet too small to have affected them. This in itself lent a piquancy, for seldom was it possible to spot a storm so close to its beginning.

He erased a little section of the blue line, and drew in a red line at such an angle as to indicate a shallow wave. Then around the crest of the wave as center he drew a black line in the shape of a tiny football; this he labeled 1011, and inside it he printed, in minute letters, LOW. So much accomplished, he again surveyed his work, and smiled.

As a baby possesses the parts of the adult, so the baby storm displayed as in caricature the features of a mature storm. The red line symbolized the "warm front" along which the southern air was advancing and sliding over the northern; the blue line symbolized the "cold front" where the northern air was advancing and pushing beneath the southern. The black line shaped like a football was an isobar, indicating a barometric pressure of 1011 around the center of low pressure, symbolizing also the complete circuit of winds around that point. As a baby is without teeth, so also the storm was lacking in some attributes of maturity. But just as surely as a baby is a human being, so also was his new discovery a storm in charming miniature—provided always that he had rightly analyzed the situation.

For a moment he looked contentedly at his creation, and then glanced over the Pacific, considering the future. The general set-up seemed to indicate that in the next twenty-four hours the new storm would move rapidly eastward. As it moved, it could grow both in area and in intensity; its winds becoming stronger, its rains heavier.

Suddenly his fingers itched for a slide-rule. He remembered his training under professors who considered weather a branch of physics; his own thesis—almost entirely complicated equations—had won him High Honors. Such equations now flashed into his mind with photographic exactitude; they dealt with velocities and accelerations, with the Coriolis force, and frictionless horizontal rectilinear flow. They contained such delightful terms as $\frac{1}{2}A_i t^2$, $\Delta T^{0,0}$, and $2mv\omega \sin \phi$. To a well-trained mathematical meteorologist they were more beautiful than Grecian urns.

He shrugged his shoulders. The local Weather Bureau had to deal in immediate practicality; there was little need and no time for mathematical abstractions. And besides—he was forced to admit—with data supplied by a single ship and by weather stations two hundred miles from the center of activity, the application of highly refined methods was hardly warranted.

With resignation he again turned his attention to the map, and considered the lonely cluster of notations in the ocean. That particular ship, he presumed, had just passed through the area of disturbance. In a few hours it had probably crossed the boundary between warm and cold air more than once, and had experienced changeable but not very pronounced weather. The ship was moving west; the storm, like all such storms, was moving easterly. Ship and storm would not meet again, and yet for a moment the two lingered together in his thoughts. Doubtless the ship would be of interest to sailors, but to him it seemed wholly dull and mechanical. It might be one of twenty built to the same specifications, indistinguishable from the others unless you were close enough to read the name. But the storm! He felt the sudden rise of feeling along his spine. A storm lived and grew; no two were ever the same.

This one—this incipient little whorl, come into being southeast of Japan—would live its own life, for good or for bad, just as much as some human child born the same hour. With the luck of favorable conditions it would grow and prosper to a fine old age for a storm; just as possibly it might languish, or be suddenly annihilated.

There remained one other detail, and this called for no marks on the map. He must name the baby. He considered a moment for more names in -ia, and thought of Maria. It was more homely than Antonia or Cornelia; it did not even sound like them. But it was a name. And, as if he had been a minister who had just christened a baby, he found himself smiling and benign, inchoately wishing it joy and prosperity. Good luck, Maria!

As a crab moves on the ocean-bottom, but is of the water, so man rests his feet upon the earth—but lives in the air. Man thinks of the crab as a water-animal; illogically and curiously, he calls himself a creature of the land.

As water environs the crab, so air surrounds, permeates, and vivifies the body of man. If traces of noxious gas mingle with it, he coughs and his complexion turns deathly gray. If it becomes overcharged with water-droplets, he gropes helplessly in fog. If it moves too fast, he becomes a pitiable wind-swept creature, cowering in cellars and ditches. Even for rain he is dependent on air. If actually removed from air, he dies immediately.

Physicists describe the air as tasteless, odorless, and invisible. It could not well be otherwise. But these are not so much its qualities as adjustments of man. For if the air impressed the senses, being at the same time all-pervasive, it would necessarily obscure all other tastes, odors, and sights.

Air is so bound up with man's life that only with diffi-

19

culty can he realize its existence as something in itself. To a savage it is as much an abstraction as consciousness; a child can conceive wind, which is air in motion, but not air itself. In our own language, *wind, mist,* and *rain* are ancient words, but *air* is a late and learned borrowing of a Greek word, which itself originally meant *wind.*

In his pre-natal months, indeed, man is aquatic. But thrust forth into the atmosphere—small and red—he sucks in a first breath spasmodically, and owns his allegiance to air. Seventy years later, a nurse stands by an old man's bed, waiting for what is known as "the last breath."

Even among the so-called land-animals, man is less than most bound to the earth. His tree-dwelling ancestors may have descended to the ground furtively, as to a foreign and hostile region; in civilization people spend most of their time upon raised platforms called floors.

As individual men move in a too well-known land-scape without noticing its features, so man—fallaciously—takes for granted the all-pervasive air. His historians deal in lands and seas. But most movements of peoples have been not so much quests for better countries as for better atmospheric conditions. "A place in the sun" explains much of history more exactly than we usually realize, except that just as often we should say, "A place in the rain." A thunderstorm in hay-time may overthrow a ministry, and a slight average rise or fall of temperature may topple a throne; a shift in the storm-track can ruin an empire. In the twentieth century a temporary variation of rainfall put Okies upon the highway by the hundred-thousand, just as in the third century a similar shift might in a single year hurl the Huns against the Chinese frontier and set the blue-painted Caledonians swarming at Hadrian's Wall. In the mass as in the individual, man is less a land-animal than a creature of the air.

2

At five minutes to four on January mornings there was never any sign of dawn. Few buildings showed lights, and the Chief, still sleepy, felt himself steering from street-lamp to street-lamp like the captain of a coastwise steamer laying his course from one lighthouse to the next. An occasional truck passed by, showing that even at that hour the city did not entirely give over activity.

One advantage of getting to work so early was that at least you had no parking troubles. As he walked across to Tom's All-Night Coffee Shop, he took a professional survey of weather conditions. No moon, stars bright everywhere, cloudless; fresh breeze from the northwest; temperature safely above frost; a typical winter morning for San Francisco.

"Fair and warmer," said Tom.

"If it doesn't rain," replied the Chief, completing the formula begun so many years back that they had forgotten the original joke.

"Orange juice, coffee, snail."

"Right, Chief," said Tom, putting a morning paper on the counter.

The Chief glanced at the headlines without enthusiasm —rumbles of war, labor crises, political strife. He felt a stirring of pride at his own international profession in which you were pitted against natural forces, not your fellow-men. By association of thought he glanced out of the window. A row of electric lights now shone brightly from the flat roof of the Federal Building just across the street; one of the boys must just have gone up to read the instruments. Tom's clock pointed at four—but that meant noon, Greenwich time. At this minute, everywhere, observers in weather stations were peering at thermometers and barometers and scanning the sky to see how much of it was cloud-covered.

He had a sudden thought of the whole world and all those observers. In London and Paris they would read the instruments and have plenty of time left before lunch. In Rio it was nine in the morning; in New York, seven. Here on the Pacific Coast men turned out sleepily at a very inconvenient hour. But Alaska was even worse off. By the time you got around to New Zealand, the observer most likely stayed up till he read his instruments and went to bed afterward. The Japs had an easy time of it—about nine in the evening. In Bombay it might be sundown; in Athens and Cape Town, early afternoon. Ships at sea changed hours as they moved. And what about the Arctic stations? There it was night all winter anyway, and perhaps a man arranged his private life by whatever time was most convenient.

He came back from his survey of the world as Tom set breakfast before him.

"What'ya goin' t'give us t'day, Chief?"

"Hn-n? Nothing much today, Tom, I don't believe."

"Time y'were scarin' somethin' up for us. Sure could use a rain."

Tom moved off to a new customer. The drought was really getting bad, the Chief reflected, when the proprietor of an all-night-restaurant began talking about it.

Down the counter Tom was obviously telling the newcomer who the other fellow was. The Chief had long known that he was Tom's most treasured exhibit. He could hear the not-too-well-muffled voice.

"Yessir, that's Old Weather Man himself."

"Yu-don't-say!" The Chief caught the tone of mingled surprise and awe. A lot of people, he knew from experience, never quite sensed any difference between predicting weather and making weather.

Tom's coffee still warm within him, the Chief walked along the lighted corridor on the top floor of the Federal Building. On the right were the Administration offices; on the left, the Climatological Division. Both were still dark. Only ahead could he see light shining through a glass door; it bore the words: *Forecasting Division*. At that point the Chief felt his regular tingle of professional pride. Administration—that meant stenographers and mailing-lists and pay-checks, just what you found in a thousand other offices in the city. Climatology—that was only endless statistics about dead weather. But Forecasting—that was the battle-line.

"Hello, Whitey. . . . How are you, boys? . . . Any reports in yet?"

"Nothing yet, sir," said Whitey.

In the chart room stood a long table divided into four sections, a draftsman's stool at each. On the nearest stool sat the new Junior Meteorologist; he had almost finished the plotting of air soundings taken at various Pacific Coast stations that night. The Chief looked at the graphs. Phoenix, San Diego, Burbank. The lines ran upward and inclined off to the left; here and there they showed angles; a definite reversal of direction marked the point at which each balloon had entered the stratosphere. Oakland, Medford, Spokane. In a minute his practiced brain had summarized what was happening in the upper air over the district.

The next chart displayed the winds of the western United States at two-thousand-foot intervals from the surface up to fourteen thousand feet. Upon the first map the arrows pointed in many directions, for at the surface local relations of hill and valley were often the determining factors. The two- and four-thousand-foot maps were largely blank, for the mountain stations were actually above that level. At six and eight thousand the map filled in, and a fairly simple wind-pattern began to appear. At ten thousand and higher all the winds were strong and from the west.

Just as the Chief was finishing his survey, the sudden click of a teletype-machine sounded from the next room. Involuntarily, he smiled. It was like a bugle-call. During the next hour his life would move at its fastest.

"Who's chart-man this morning?" he said.

"I am, sir," said Whitey.

"Good."

The Chief turned from the long table to the smaller one which stood in a windowed alcove. His own chair was in the alcove facing inward. Opposite it, across a large table, was a chair for the chart-man. On the table lay a large outline map of North America and the adjacent waters, a tiny circle representing each weather station. As yet only the local report had been entered; the wind-arrow and little cluster of figures at San Francisco stood lonely and conspicuous against the vast area of continent and ocean.

By now more than one teletype was sounding. Whitey

came in with the first batch of reports, settled into his seat, and with a fine-pointed fountain pen began entering the data. An arrow graphically indicated wind-direction, and the number of barbs the wind-force. The amount and design of the shading within the tiny circle showed cloud conditions. Figures and other symbols served to record pressure, temperature, humidity, and other conditions as needed. North Platte, Concordia, Omaha, Sioux City. The map no longer looked so empty in the region of the Missouri Valley. Knoxville, Charlotte, Atlanta, Charleston. Whitey was working with the speed and accuracy of a machine. Pittsburgh, Cleveland, Washington.

Until the map was nearly finished, the Chief could not really begin his work. He walked into the teletype room. As he entered, its activity seemed to rise in crescendo. The machines clicked like maddened typists; their bells rang; conveyors from the vacuum tubes plunked into their baskets.

To an outsider, everything might have seemed insane confusion; to the Chief, it was the ordered rhythm of life. That machine which kept clicking out messages with scarcely a break—he knew that its impulses came from an office in Chicago which served as clearing-house for the weather reports of half the continent. Another machine clicked continuously and in addition, as if in mere exuberant good spirits, loudly rang a bell every few seconds. This was the Weather Bureau's own wire linking together the stations along air-lines. The other four machines, serving local telegraph and radio stations, were sometimes silent, but by contrast their bursts of activity seemed even more feverish. To add to the confusion one of his own men was cutting a teletype ribbon; for at the proper moment San Francisco must become a sending station and report the local conditions to the rest of the world.

In spite of years of routine the Chief felt a deep smoldering excitement; the moment drew nearer. Will the good priest ever fail to stir as the ritual of the mass rises to the climax? Will the true actor, even after a thousand nights, take as a matter of course the cue which yields him the stage for his great scene? And for the Chief this was no mere ritual or drama, passing inevitably toward a fixed end. It was a contest, a battle, in which the mighty forces of the air were preparing against him unknown attacks and ambushes. He hurried back to see how the map was shaping up.

Whitey was still working like a high-speed machine. Winnipeg, The Pas, Qu'Appelle, Swift Current. Most of the United States and Canada was now filled in. Between California and Hawaii a dozen ships had reported. Taking up a new batch of radio messages, Whitey dropped some thousands of miles southward and began with ships along the Mexican west coast; this work was a little slower, for he had to locate latitude and longitude. *Nansu, Olaf Maersk, San Roque, City of Brownleigh.* A moment later he was back above the Arctic Circle in the Canadian Northwest where stations lonelier than ships sent out the readings of their instruments by radio through the polar night. Coppermine, Aklavik, Fort Norman, Chesterfield Inlet.

The teletype room sent out less noise. The bells rang only now and then. The Chicago line was quiet. Occasionally some machine broke suddenly into action with a belated report, or something gone astray, or a correction. Whitey relaxed enough to make his first mistake. He cursed softly, and reached for his ink eradicator. Mr. Ragan and the Junior Meteorologist worked steadily at their table, plotting changes of temperature and pressure since the previous reports.

Although the Chief had not noted any passing of time since the reports had begun, he saw now that the clock stood at a quarter past five. The electric lights still blazed in the office; the blank windows showed only darkness outside.

"How's she stand, Whitey?"

"Pretty well filled up, sir. I think you can start."

The Chief slipped into his chair. In this position he was opposite Whitey, and saw the map upside down. But he had long since adjusted himself to this position so as to avoid joggling the chart-man's elbow and having to peer over his shoulders. After all, as he liked to demonstrate with pencil and paper– 9 is just as easy to read as 5 once you get used to it.

From whatever direction observed, the map as yet represented nothing but confusion. For each of several hundred stations and ships Whitey had recorded a half dozen or more separate notations. Over the United States the map was nearly filled with numbers and seemingly cabalistic symbols. Even to the Chief such a map was only a recording of data which he must reduce to order.

First of all, he set himself to locate the present position of the storm which had been advancing toward the south Alaskan coast. Heavy rain and a sharply falling barometer at Sitka indicated that the front had not yet passed but was probably close. With his purple pencil the

Chief drew a line lying just west of Sitka and curving slightly away until it ended two hundred miles west of the Washington coast.

Since no other storms of importance for his district seemed indicated, he began with his isobars. Through the maze of figures he worked confidently. With Denver reporting pressure at 1016 and North Platte 1012, he started his 1014 isobar about half way between the two. He drew it slowly in a curve northwesterly. As the reported pressures indicated, he left Rapid City, Miles City and Havre on one side of the line with North Platte. Cheyenne, Billings, and Helena rested on the other side with Denver. He drew the line onward, bent it around Kamloops in British Columbia, and then brought it sharply toward the southwest just including Vancouver and Victoria within its curve. Off the coast it met the purple line which he had drawn south from Alaska. Although no ship had reported from near this point of junction, the Chief took his isobar across the other line with a sharp angle to indicate the sudden drop of pressure associated with a passing front. Then he paused; a vast region of ocean devoid of notations stretched out before his pencil.

"How about the *Byzantion*? She's out here somewhere."

"No report from her, sir."

"Hn-n?— Must be a poor ship! Any report yesterday?"

"Yes, yesterday. But not the day before."

"She'll probably come in late, and spoil my map. Well . . ." With a further grunt of disapproval, the Chief drew his line on, southwestward, across the empty Pacific spaces. It might easily be a few hundred miles mis-

placed, but lacking information he had no remedy. Skillfully he looped the isobar around the Hawaiian Islands,
and ran it back toward the continent. He drew it across
the northern end of Lower California, kept Tucson just
within the curve, and finally joined it to its beginning,
east of Denver.

Starting with another line, he followed the same pro-
cedure. In ten minutes the map had taken form.

As he worked, the Chief felt a touch of sadness. He
remembered Tom saying: "Sure could use a rain." Well,
there was no rain in sight. That storm along the Alaskan
coast might bring a drizzle as far south as Oregon. The
Chief wished that he could repay Tom's confidence and
conjure up a storm somewhere from nothing. But for
three thousand miles to the west stretched off the great
high-pressure area. Every ship on the Honolulu run reported light winds and clear skies. On the great-circle
route from San Francisco to Japan there was a lack of
vessels, but the liner *Eureka,* sixteen hours out of San
Francisco, reported a pressure of almost 1020, discour-
agingly high. Just as he was contemplating the *Eureka,*
Whitey came in.

"Well, here she is, Chief—the *Byzantion.* We'll see if
she spoils your map."

The Chief shrugged his shoulders, and looked at
Whitey locating the position—forty north, one hundred
forty-three west. Whatever her nationality and business
might be, she was a little south of the Japan lane; the
Chief imagined that she was heading for Shanghai; but
he knew very little about the various ships and the commerce they represented. He judged them by the regular-
ity and completeness of their reports. By the set of

Whitey's shoulders, he knew that the *Byzantion* had turned the trick against him.

Whitey finished and straightened up. Yes, the ship reported 1015. With the resigned air of a man who deals in actualities, he erased a long section of one isobar, and redrew it in the indicated position two hundred miles farther north. Whitey grinned, not unsympathetically; still, the joke such as it might be, was on the Chief.

The shift of a single isobar meant little in the general situation. The Chief looked at the finished map, and felt a let-down. The excitement of the day was over, and as often, its end was anti-climax. From today's map even a fairly intelligent monkey could not go wrong. He turned to his typewriter; "Might as well have had a rubber-stamp," he thought, "for all this last month." Without hesitation he wrote:

SAN FRANCISCO BAY REGION: FAIR TODAY AND THURSDAY; NO CHANGE IN TEMPERATURE; WEST TO NORTHWEST WINDS.

He continued typing off the forecasts for his other areas. Much miscellaneous work remained to be done. But as far as the Chief was concerned, the best part of the day was past. The hour hand of the office clock was approaching six. Outside, a faint light had begun to transfuse the darkness.

3

Around the curve of the earth, the day-old storm moved eastward, leaving Asia behind. Upon the opposite face of the sphere the sun now shone, but the storm swirled over darkened waters. Although among its kind it must

be counted immature and small, nevertheless it had
grown so rapidly that it already dominated an area which
was a thousand miles across.

Around its center the winds blew in a great circuit—
counterclockwise. In the whole half of the storm-area
northward from the center there was little cloud or rain;
dry, cold winds were blowing from the east and north.
Most of the weather-activity lay to the south along the
two fronts, the boundary lines between cooler and
warmer air. Extending from the storm-center, like the two
legs of a wide-spread compass—warm front and cold front
—they moved rapidly eastward, and the storm center
moved with them. As a wave moves through the water
without carrying the water along with it, so the storm-
center and the two fronts moved through the air, yet
themselves remained a single unit.

The southwest breeze which, thirty hours before, had
first sprung up near that rocky island south of Japan, had
now grown to a great river of air five miles deep, five
hundred wide. From over the tropical ocean it poured
forth its warm and moist air. Then, as it might have
blown against a gently-rising range of mountains, it met
the slope of the retreating northern air, and spiraling upward, swerved in toward the center. Ascending, it cooled;
its moisture first became cloud, and then quickly rain.
Thus, like a great elongated comma—head at the center
of the storm, tail reaching five hundred miles to the
southeast—the continuous rain-belt of the warm front
swept across the ocean-surface.

Not all of the southern air ascended that slope; some
of it lagged behind and was overtaken by the advancing
line of cooler northern air which formed the other com-

pass-leg, the cold front. Here the northern air forcibly thrust itself beneath the southern air. And since the slope was much steeper, the warm air ascended with a rush, and the reaction was almost explosive. (Old navigators of sailing ships knew its like as the "line-squall"; most of all they feared its sudden treacherous wind-shift, which dismasted many a good vessel despite all seamanship.) Above a five-hundred-mile line of white-caps, the cold front swept forward. Dark thunder-clouds towered high above it. In contrast to the gentle rain-bringing warm front, its passage brought the terrors of the tempest—squalls, drumming rain-bursts, hail, thunder and lightning, the fearful wind-shift. The passage, however, was quick as it was violent. In a few minutes the front had rolled on eastward; behind it, here and there, heavy showers poured down, but before a cold steady wind from the north the clouds were breaking, and ever-widening patches of blue showed clear and clean.

4

The great clipper, one would have said, hung motionless between sky and ocean. Though the unloosed power of the four engines hurled the plane onward at close to two hundred miles an hour, still the surrounding vastness of featureless space offered no fixed point by which to observe its speed. Far below, too far for individual waves to be apparent, the blue ocean stretched off, unbroken to the sight by ship or island. The whole arch of the sky was cloudless blue. Only the sun gave a point of reference, but its movement was more rapid than the plane's; to judge by the sun, one could only conclude that the plane was speeding backward.

Though the Navigator was sometimes conscious of illusions, they never confused his sense of actuality. At any given moment he knew to a nicety his position on the predetermined route from San Francisco to Honolulu. Although his theoretical range of vision extended about a hundred miles in every direction and covered an area as large as Ireland, he did not rely on sight. Within this circle, to be sure, were at least three ships, but they were at distances which would probably make them invisible to the unaided eye; to hunt for them with a telescope might be as tedious as looking for a penny dropped on a landing-field; and when spotted, they could yield him no new information. Without the direct aid of sight, by instruments and by radio, he nevertheless plotted his course confidently.

The Navigator's face, however, was worried. A passenger seeing him might have thought that he feared some impending disaster. Actually, like many another mortal, he was worrying about the monthly bills. Last evening, instead of thinking epic thoughts about the morrow's flight through space, he had sat down at the dining-room table with his wife, and spent several hours going over the family budget. Three small children with contradictory tendencies toward too large tonsils and too small sinus openings kept a man guessing. Yet this month there had been no doctor's bills; the water bill, however, was high.

Then he suddenly smiled, realizing a series of connections which on the previous evening had escaped him. It should have been simple to a man in his profession. While the Pacific High stood firm, California had dry weather. The garden would require water, but the children would not need the doctor to drain their sinuses. And of even more importance to the family, as long as these conditions held, his own flight of fourteen hundred miles across the open ocean was hardly more dangerous than a street-car ride.

He did not look at the weather-map—he saw it plain in his mind. From San Francisco the great concentric ovals of the High pointed off southwestward. Around those ovals, clockwise, the wind blew steadily. Today, with the course charted south of the High, he was sure of a favoring tail-wind which would bring the plane to Honolulu with gas-tanks still comfortably full. On the return voyage, if the luck held, he might have a course along the north side of the High with the same steady tail-winds.

That nest of ovals upon the weather-map looked dull and uninspiring enough. He himself, not primarily a meteorologist, had no clear idea of what the High meant in the whole cosmic scheme. But he had a vivid sense of how those ovals affected his own air-route. They shunted off the storms toward British Columbia, and so gave generally fair weather for the Honolulu run; and also they formed a great benign swirl of air which with ingenuity might be made, paradoxically, to serve both going and coming. When the High broke up, there was a different story.

Looking ahead, the Navigator now saw a ship. By the rate at which it seemed to come dashing toward him, he again became conscious of the plane's own rapid motion.

5

Since the glacier-ice began to melt from the mountains and the crags to show their shapes, the quiet lake has lain at the foot of the gorge. No one knows who first crossed the Pass.

While the ice still lingered, mountain-sheep must have worn the first trails—faint dull traces across the granite. After some centuries the black-tailed deer followed; by then the ice would have been gone. Next come Pai-ute or Washoe, gathering seeds and pine-nuts. So recently as if it might have been yesterday, some trapper may have watered his horses at the lake, and leaning on his long rifle squinted into the westering sun as he worked out in his mind a route upward from ledge to ledge.

For certain, we know, the covered wagons came in '44. Old Caleb Greenwood and hawk-nosed Elisha Stevens guided those emigrants down the Humboldt River. At the sink they found a Pai-ute chief whom they called Truckee. Squatting, he drew them a map in the sand. So they crossed the desert, and went up along the swift river which they called Truckee for the map-drawer. They met the snow at the lake, and with the snow they fought panic. Some went to the south, but others forced their way onward through the snow and over the Pass above the lake.

Next year, following the wheel marks, came William Ide, and rigged a windlass at the granite crest to pull up his wagons. In '46 came a great wave of emigrants—five hundred wagons. Last of all that autumn came the Donners; the snow caught them; they starved through the winter; the horror of their story imprinted their name upon both lake and pass, and broods still over peak and canyon like a legend of Greek tragedy.

In '49 the wagons swung round a little to the south through an easier gap. So it went through the fifties, and one might have said that the great days of the Pass were over, that it would lie in the future like a thousand other Sierran gaps—untrodden snow or wind-clean granite. In the sixties the main road followed the double-summited route by Lake Tahoe. There in fiction Hank Monk drove Horace Greeley to Placerville on time, and there in reality passed the stages and the great freighting-wagons to and from the Nevada mines. There galloped the pony-express riders, and there stood the poles of the first transcontinental telegraph.

But railroad-crazy Theodore Judah craftily shunned the double summit, and changed everything. For after Judah's surveyors came Charlie Crocker and his coolie gangs digging like ants. The railroad reached Auburn and Illinoistown; it rounded "Cape Horn" and came to Dutch Flat. There it paused, but a wagon-road was laid out ahead. Once more Donner Pass woke to life, and echoed back the sound of cracking whips and teamsters' bawling. But the rails came on again. In '67 the coolies were camping at the summit where Ide had set up his windlass. (There, even yet, you can dig up fragments of cheap Chinese bowls.) Then in '69 the Gold Spike was driven, and the trains went through.

With routes as with people, success breeds success. The new wagon-road preceded the railroad; the telegraph came with it. In their due time, each supporting the other, came the transcontinental telephone, the all-year automobile highway, the electric transmission-line, and the air-lane. Because Judah chose that crossing for his railroad, the pass of the ill-omened name is now a main channel of world communication.

So we come, in less than a century, from the death-dogged snow-shoers of the Donner Party to the carefree week-end skiers dotting the mountain-sides with bright costumes. Above the place where little Stanton sat to smoke his last pipe, Cisco beacon flashes out to Donner beacon. Where John Denton, plucky Yorkshireman, waited in the snow for death, the streamlined trains slide by. And over that camp where the poor emigrants ate the forbidden meat, the pilots of the wide-winged planes follow the whining Reno beam to Blue Canyon, where—turning—they set their last course for the airports of the Bay.

6

Like Casey Jones, the Road Superintendent kissed his wife and started out for the day's work. He was not a rail-road man, and the hour was not half-past four. Nevertheless, the comparison is sound; for about the Superintendent and his job gathered something of that matter-of-fact heroism which makes the song of Casey Jones the epic of the American working-man.

He drove slowly along the Highway; he was inspecting, not traveling. CALIFORNIA—U. S. 40 stared at him from the neat shield-shaped markers. He passed between the slender bright-orange snow-stakes standing at hundred-foot intervals on both sides of the Highway. He saw a stake leaning over, and got out to straighten it. A car with a Minnesota license slowed down beside him.

"What those stakes for, brother?" called an abrupt voice.

"Snow-stakes," said the Superintendent, but the face into which he looked was blank. "You see, when there's snow—deep—the snow-plows have to steer by these stakes."

"Say—you kidding us, brother. It's January—where's your snow? Why *we* had fifteen inches in one storm the other day. You telling *us* about snow?"

The car started forward suddenly, but the Superintendent heard a woman's voice trail back from it.

"Those things must be eight feet high. Just like California!"

He drove on, a little disgruntled. People from northern states always made trouble—thought they knew everything about driving in snow. He'd like to see that crowd now, getting around Windy Point on a bad day. Fifteen *inches* of snow—why, man, on Donner Pass you figure snow by feet, not inches!

Well, that was MINNESOTA anyway. CALIFORNIA and NEVADA didn't count. He got NEW YORK, and ILLINOIS before reaching the Lake Tahoe turn-off. Noting "foreign" licenses was an unbreakable habit of no practical importance; it was perhaps a sign of his pride in the great Highway which he served. UTAH, OREGON. A big gasoline truck thundered by; its trailing chain struck sparks. Then went a towering van with a trailer; half a dozen special licenses spattered its rear-end. A streamlined transcontinental bus speeded toward him. A big truck passed, laden with bulging sacks; "Idaho potatoes, or onions," he thought. PENNSYLVANIA, NEBRASKA. Yessir, he'd bet, considering how high it went, U. S. 40 carried more traffic than any other road in the world. And he was the one who saw that it got through, summer or winter. ALBERTA, MISSOURI.

He passed the Donner monument; the refreshment stand was boarded up for the winter. Dirty remnants of snowdrifts lay here and there. Now the road skirted along the Lake; it was unfrozen; glittering in the sun, it did not seem even very wintry. At the western end of the Lake he came to the gates which at his word would be closed across the Highway. Beside the road the big sign read: *Snow conditions over Donner Summit—U.S. 40,* and then below in large letters ROAD OPEN TO ALL TRAFFIC.

By now he was in the shadow of the Pass. The ground was thinly snow-covered; little windrows of snow thrown aside by the plows (remnants of the November storm) lay at each edge of the pavement. Beyond the gates, the grade began. He passed the six-thousand-foot marker and Turn-out. The road clung to the side of the gorge, curve after curve. A heavy truck came down, back-firing. Too fast, that fellow. He passed a jalopy—ARKANSAS. It was steaming hard from the radiator. Migrant-laborers they looked like, not many on this road, in winter anyway.

He went by Big Shot where the road had been blasted out of a great granite cliff—a bad place here for snow-slides. The snow was getting deeper as he ascended, but still the ridiculous-looking orange stakes stood up high, even where the plows had piled snow against them.

Rocky Point brought a puff of wind, and then he swung back into the quiet of the little hollow around which the road swung in the Horseshoe. He was right beneath the crags now; high above, he saw the Bridge. He heard the mutter of a plane overhead; a locomotive whistled from somewhere. ILLINOIS (had that one already) ; COLORADO; MICHIGAN.

Windy Point always lived up to its name—some trick of the slopes around it probably. From the Point he saw the snowsheds of the railroad, and the line of many-wired telephone poles which plunged right down the face of the Pass without needing to twist and turn like the road. He was almost above timber-line now; trees were stunted and grew only in sheltered spots.

Between Windy Point and the Bridge he passed men working along the road. He tooted his horn gently, and waved at them as he went by. In the rear-view mirror he noted that they did not hurry to return to work, but stood talking and lighting cigarettes. No matter. They knew as well as he that shovels would never keep Donner Pass open. Still, you couldn't just let men sit around the bunk-house all day, playing poker—had to make a gesture of keeping them at work. Let them loaf a little while they could. They'd work hard when they needed to.

He came to the Bridge. Two cars had halted at the turn-out, and some women were oh-ing and ah-ing at the view of the lake and of the road twisting down the face of the Pass. UTAH again, and TENNESSEE.

He swung around the last loop, drove through a cut deep-blasted in granite, and came to the big garage of the Maintenance Station. The building was chiefly an immense, high-pitched roof of corrugated iron designed to resist snow. It looked ridiculous now, like the snow-stakes. Not more than three feet of dirty-looking old snow was piled up under the eaves.

Inside, he walked down along the row of four great rotary plows, giving them a quick inspection which he knew was useless. They fairly glistened with readiness. Tire-chains were already on, and spare chains hung in place. The great truck-like bodies were piled with gravel for weight to give traction. But in the blunt noses, the cutting edges of the great augers were dim with the rust of disuse. On the opposite side of the garage were the push plows with their big, twelve-foot shares, and the single V-plow. Ready to roll!

In the work-shop too many men were standing around with little to do. The whole set-up made the Superintendent think of a military post with the garrison built up to war strength and waiting for the oubreak of hostilities.

"Hello," he greeted the Day Foreman. "Everything O. K.?"

"The machines are O. K. all right, but the men not so good—goin' stale. Can't keep 'em busy." He dropped his voice. "Swenson and Peters started a fight last night, but we pulled 'em apart."

The Superintendent's jaw thrust suddenly forward. "Can't have any of that stuff," he said, and started for the bunk-house.

The bunk-house was only a hundred feet from the garage, but connecting them was a tunnel-like passage-way for protection against the snow.

Peters was out working, but the Superintendent took Swenson into the wash-room. He was six inches shorter than the big Swede and forty pounds lighter, but he was boss and he laid down the law. Swenson was properly apologetic, and the Superintendent said to forget about it but not to do it again. You couldn't be too hard on the men; they needed their jobs; Peters had a wife and three kids down in the Valley.

Driving on westward along the Highway, the Superintendent was still thinking about it. Come a good snowstorm, and Swenson would be swamping and Peters operating in the same rotary, thick as thieves. Funny—the machines could stand lying around idle, but the men couldn't. Well, machines meant more than men on this job. MICHIGAN again. He could fire a couple of men and get others. But if he smashed a rotary in a storm, he might lose the road.

West of the Summit the road descended much less rapidly, and was less spectacular; but it was just as hard to keep clear. The Superintendent let his car glide along more swiftly. At Norden and Soda Springs and Fox Farm there were respectable depths of snow; but on south slopes in the bright sun the snow was melting and trickles of water ran across the Highway. Near Rainbow Tavern the Superintendent took off his coat. As he drove, he noted the condition of the pavement and the shoulders, making sure that nothing would interfere with the work of the plows.

Finally he pulled up at the little corrugated-iron garage which the road-men had dubbed Tin Barn. He got out of the car to stretch. The sun was brilliant overhead; the air was spring-like. The longer the storms held off, some people said, the harder they hit. But the Superintendent cared little for weather-lore—or for official forecasts either. When snow fell, you just turned out your plows and started throwing it off the Highway. He cast an unnecessarily defiant look at the harmless, clear blue sky. *Let 'er come!*

7

The Junior Meteorologist began to map the Pacific area with a feeling of almost paternal interest as to whether Maria had survived the perils of babyhood. As he filled in the map, he saw a small storm in about the expected position, but he reserved judgment.

Sylvia had moved out over the Atlantic beyond range of his map. Reports from Port Nelson, God's Lake, and Fort Hope vaguely indicated that Felicia was centering over Hudson Bay. Cornelia was beating in fury against the south Alaskan coast. Antonia was not developing as he had expected; she had suddenly matured, and moving off sharply to the north was entering Bering Sea. And certainly—yes—that small storm well to the east of Japan could be nothing else than Maria.

Already, the J.M. noted, Maria was showing personality. She was fast-moving, having traveled a thousand miles in twenty-four hours. This meant an average rate of over forty miles an hour, and yet none of the reporting ships indicated a wind of more than twenty-five miles; Maria, therefore, must be moving as a wave. As another individual quality, Maria was keeping a little to the south of the previous storm-track. He attributed this immediately to the influence of Antonia, which from her position in Bering Sea partly blocked the more northerly route. But he shook his head. Such reasoning got nowhere; it only raised the next question: what caused Antonia to behave as she did? He thought of his old professor's saying: "A Chinaman sneezing in Shen-si may set men to shoveling snow in New York City."

He decided that in general Maria might be called a normal child. She had certainly grown in healthy fashion. Along with this growth had come a sharp lowering of pressure, brisker winds, and heavier rainfall. Nevertheless Maria was still young and undistinguished. Along her cold front she might be kicking up some respectable local squalls, but elsewhere ship-captains would log nothing more than Fresh Breeze and Moderate Sea. And as for size, a storm only a thousand miles in diameter rated in the Pacific as a half-grown child. Nevertheless, the J.M. still felt his paternal discoverer's partiality: "A darn good little storm," he felt himself wanting to say to someone.

His map was finished, and he called the Chief over.

"Hn-n? Anything special?" said the Chief.

Then the words popped out before they could be suppressed: "Fine little storm developing there east of Japan!"

The Chief looked, and the J.M. was embarrassed at his own enthusiasm, almost an emotional partisanship, certainly not scientific.

"Where'd she come from?" said the Chief in his matter-of-fact voice.

"Incipient yesterday, north of Titijima." The words were professional, but hardly concealed the tone of pride.

The Chief glanced back at the map of the preceding day. "Hn-n? Yes. I should say you're right. A fast mover!"

But the Chief naturally showed no special interest in Maria. His eyes swept back and forth. Then they rested upon the Canadian Northwest. He turned to the map of the preceding day, again studied the same region, and then came back to it on the current map. Beginning to be curious, the Junior Meteorologist watched the glance shift to Cornelia in the Gulf of Alaska, then pass on to Antonia and again to Maria, come back through the vast Pacific High to California, sweep over the United States, move north to Felicia over Hudson Bay, and finally return to the point of departure. But after this rapid circuit of nearly half the northern hemisphere, the only comment was the usual, non-committal, "Hn-n?"

For a few seconds the Chief still bent over the map, and the lines on his forehead creased as if he tried to solve the problem. Then seeming to feel an explanation in order, he remarked shortly. "Too many unknowns."

He straightened up. "That's a very neat map you've drawn. Pressure rising a little at Coppermine—did you notice?" And retreating to his own office, the Chief shot behind him a final arrow: "About time, too!"

8

A proud City, set upon hills, pearl-gray in the winter sun, swept clean of smoke and dust by the steady wind from the sea. Last warder of the West, a City looking forth upon that vast water where West in the end became East, space so wide as if to defeat Time the ancient, and cause the calendar to lose a day. A City bearing the Phoenix for its symbol, proud that like the Phoenix it had more than once sprung to life from its own ashes. A City of towers and banners.

From those towers the great banners stood out stiff in the northwest wind. These were not the national flag; *that* emblem you might see floating modestly from the squat Customs House, the very wind stolen from it by the tall surrounding towers. (One might think of some medieval city where feudal strongholds rose defiant, one against another, commanding the King's own palace.) Highest of all, as if it ruled the City, flew the blue banner of Telephone. Across a narrow street the two lords of oil flouted each other—red and yellow against blue and white. Maroon of Grand Hotel, crimson and black of the Bank, blue of Power-Light, blue and gold of the Railroad. One might have said that these and their like were the rulers of the City and the World.

Yet one might well look again. Was it perhaps by some inter-company agreement that all the banners streamed off to the southeast? No, not the Board of Directors, not even the stockholders voting as one man, could make their flag fly to the north. The Chief Engineer himself could not contrive that miracle.

From sources too mighty and too far removed for even the great companies to manipulate, that wind drew its power and assumed its direction—from the contrast of ocean and continent, from the whirling of the earth, from the sun itself. That air had come on a long journey. Northeastward from the doldrums of the equator it had moved, miles high above the ocean in the great upper current of the anti-trades. Upon a spiral two thousand miles long it had flowed back to earth around the gentle swirl of the Pacific High. Now it was swinging southward until it would doubtless join the wide sweep of the trades, reach again the doldrums, and exploding into thunderstorms rise to the upper atmosphere and start north once more.

Upon this very day the directors of Power-Light meeting in their room on the sixteenth floor had just heard a

discouraging report about the depleted water-reserves in
their hundred and more artificial lakes. The directors
would gladly have paid many thousands of dollars to any
man who could alter the direction of that flag by ninety
degrees and bring in a southwester. But they did not even
consider such a solution. Instead, with long faces, they
approved the expenditure of certain huge sums for the
operation of auxiliary steam power-houses.

Upon the sidewalks of the City, people on the shady
side drew their coats around them, but on the sunny side
they felt cosily warm. The cool clean air filled the lungs;
there was vigor in it. Shrewd merchants put forward their
best displays, and quoted the proverb: "Do business with
men when the wind is in the northwest." At street-corners the eddies of air set men clutching at their hats,
women at their skirts. "Fine day . . . Fine weather . . .
Bracing . . . Good for golf . . . Puts life in a fellow."

High upon the towers, in the sweep of the far-traveled
wind, the great banners streamed out steadily southeastward.

IN AN AGE all too familiar with war the yearly cycle of
the weather is well imagined in terms of combat. It is a
war in which a stronghold or citadel sometimes beats off
assault after assault. More often the battle-line shifts
quickly back and forth across thousands of miles—a war
of sudden raids and swift counterattacks, of stern pitched
battles, of deep forays and confused struggles high in the
air. In the Northern Hemisphere the opponents are the
Arctic and the Tropics, North against South. Uncertain
ally to the South—now bringing, now withdrawing aid—
the sun shifts among the signs of the zodiac. And the chief
battle-line is known as the Polar Front.

There is no discharge in that war, nor shall be until
the earth grows cold. Yet every spring as the sun swings
north through Taurus, it renews the forces of the South,
and they sweep forward as if to final victory. Night van-
ishes from the Pole, and in unbroken day Keewatin and
Siberia grow warm. The northern forces shrink back into
their last stronghold over the ice-cap. The sun moves from

Cancer to Leo. The Polar Front is no longer a well-marked battle-line; few and weak storms, mere guerrilla skirmishes, move along it close to the pole.

Then, as if thinking the victory won or as if wishing to preserve some balance of power, the sun withdraws into Virgo and Libra. Again night falls over the Arctic. The northern ranks re-form and advance. But the forces of the South still feel the sun at their backs and will not be routed. The line of the Polar Front becomes sharply marked—cold polar air to the north, warm tropical air to the south. And along the Front, like savage champions struggling in the death grapple, the storms move in unbroken succession.

In January the sun rides deep in Capricorn far from the northern Pole. Unbroken darkness lies over the Arctic, and from the ever-deepening chill of that night the cold air sweeps southward. Now it battles fiercely along the Polar Front, and now at some favorable point a lightning column breaks through and pierces clear to the Tropic. But still the forces of the South fight stiffly, and their ally never wholly deserts them. For even in midwinter the broad equatorial belt lies hot in the sun, and high in the air through the great current of the anti-trades its reserves move northward toward the battle-line.

So in mid-winter the combat is fiercest, for then the forces of heat and of cold both are strong, and have drawn most closely together. At that time, as in many another war, the citadels of the combatants are quiet and peaceful. In the South the trade winds blow gently, week in, week out. Far to the North the stars shine in the calm polar night. Only in that No Man's Land which is the Temperate Zone the storms raid and harry.

STORM 50

Then the sun moves from Aries into Taurus, and the southern forces drive northward once again.

In meteorology the use of such a military term as "front" may be a chronological accident—that the theory was developed in the years following 1914, a time when such military expressions were on everyone's tongue. The theory has become much complicated, but men still talk of the Polar Front, and may even yet talk of it when the Western Front has happily become a dim memory.

Had the discovery been made in more peaceful years, men (who involuntarily try to humanize nature) would perhaps have derived a term from marriage rather than war. This comparison also is apt—love, as well as hate, arises between unlikes, and love like hate breeds violent encounters. Best of all would be to use words unrelated to human feelings. Those great storms know neither love nor hate.

2

Through the darkness after moon-set the big owl flitted, ghostlike, upon noiseless wings. The forested mountain-side held out thousands of convenient branches, and he circled first around a small pine tree, seeming just ready to alight. Then, driven by whatever force controls the destiny of owls, he spiraled down to a pole of the electric transmission line which ran straight along the side of the ridge.

The owl sat in contentment upon the wooden cross-arm. In due time he neatly regorged, owl-fashion, some skins and bones of mice, and felt ready for further flight. He stretched out a wing comfortably, and with a feather-tip happened to touch one of the copper wires.

A crackling flash of blue-white light illumined the mountainside. Then came darkness again. In the darkness the scorched body of the owl tumbled to the ground; a few feathers drifted off in the breeze; from the wire a faint emanation, as of smoke, rose momentarily.

Later a wild-cat picked up the owl's body; he carried it away from the smell of man which clung to the pole and made a meal of it at his ease.

3

Huddling in overcoat and muffler against the winter chill, leaning heavily upon a cane, the old man moved along the sidewalk. With dimly seeing eyes he peered uncertainly through the yellow half-light of the street-lamps. He was very old; once he might have been fairly tall, but now he was bent and shrunken; the hair which showed at his temples was snow-white. As he came to the steps of the Federal Building, he paused and then tapped with his cane to be sure that he had seen aright.

He rang the night-bell. The watchman recognized him, and let him in without question. Going up in the elevator, he was silent. Yes, he could remember the situation well. The low had moved in across Tennessee; the pressure at the center was 29.5 or close to that; and the year was '98, April. But there was something else he couldn't remember, something about Maine. Pressure had been high over Maine, he was sure of that all right; but there was something else and it bothered him—Maine, rain, Spain. And a senseless rhyme kept bobbing up in his head: "He drove the span-yards, back to their tan-yards."

The elevator-man spoke to him.

"Think we're goin' to have some rain soon?"

"Yes, it will rain soon."

"Feel it in your joints, eh!"

"I do not feel it in my joints," said the old man formally. "But—but—but I *know*."

"Well, I guess if the boys upstairs can't figure us a rain with all them maps, we'd better not try."

"I—I *know*," said the old man, and drew himself up stiffly.

Feeling ahead with his cane, he came into the chartroom.

"Good morning, sir," he heard a voice say.

"I should like to see the observations taken. I trust I am not too late."

"He's just gone up, sir. . . . Here, I'll help you."

"Thank you, sir; I see better sometimes than others."

With his right hand gripping the steel rail of the circular staircase the old man moved more confidently. He ascended carefully step by step, went through a door, and came out upon the roof. A row of electric lights showed him the way through a maze of skylights and ventilators. He came to the little louvered instrument-shelter, at which a man was reading a thermometer.

"Good morning, sir," said the old man.

"Good morning," said the other, and as he noted something upon his pad, the light falling on his face showed him to be very young.

With professional courtesy the old man said nothing more during the taking of observations. But he watched carefully. The young man read temperatures on the maximum and minimum thermometers, and gave the former a spin for resetting. Then he dipped the wet-bulb thermometer in a can of water, spun the handle vigorously, read the result, spun again, then once more, and recorded wet and dry temperatures. Next he observed the star-covered sky for clouds, "None," and visibility, "Unlimited." He made his notations and turned to go.

"Have you taken wind direction and velocity, sir?" said the old man.

"They're recorded automatically downstairs."

"Oh, yes. I had forgotten." Then the old man made a little snorting noise. "You youngsters—pretty soon you'll make up a forecast without even going outdoors! In *my* day a weather-man had to be good. Now, with all your instruments and reports coming in by wireless, anybody can do it. In *my* day, we used to say, you read the barometer, and stuck your head out the window, and then made a forecast. You had to be *good,* sir, to do that."

"You think so, eh!"

They moved back toward the stairway. The old man was ahead; the young man was impatient, but he could not shove past among the skylights and ventilators.

"We are going to have rain," said the old man.

"Well, Grandpa, I'm sorry to disappoint you, but that's impossible with the present air-mass situation—for several days anyway."

"Air-mass poppycock! I don't need any square-head Scandihoovian telling me about my own weather. Why, in those days we didn't get reports from west of the Mississippi half the time. We had some stations—Fort Benton, and Corinne, and so forth—but the Sioux were still on the warpath, and I guess they cut the wires. Yes, you had to be *good,* then. We were quite a crowd in the old Signal Service days. 'The duties of this office,' our Chief used to say—'permit little rest'—yes—'little rest and less hesitation.' "

Both were silent a moment, and the old man's next remark was startling for lack of connection.

"The New York papers had editorials."

"What!"

"Yes, I remember the *Herald* distinctly; the editor commended our work. Of course it really was a good deal colder than we expected. Some of the West Point cadets were frost-bitten quite badly."

"Oh, you mean the forecast for Grant's inauguration? I've heard that one before, thanks."

As they came to the stairway, the young man moved ahead and went rapidly down.

The old man descended slowly. He went on through the chart-room and along the corridor. He was almost sure that he had forgotten something. Also he felt a little hurt and confused. The young man had seemed almost disrespectful to him. Sometime he must take up this air-mass matter; he wasn't sure that he really understood it, and these strange three-dimensional storms.

Then his mind turned in sudden flight from the present, and he was in the winter of 1881. That was the year he had been in Chicago; he remembered things very clearly, even a red-haired girl. Yet the memory of her was not half so vivid as the memory of a storm which had moved down from Minnesota. He saw the whole map clear in his mind. Then he entered the elevator, and went down.

On the ground floor as he walked toward the door, someone greeted him:

"Good morning, sir."

"Good morning, sir," he replied, blinking to clear away the little haze before his eyes. "I remember the face, but I'm afraid I don't know who you are."

"I'm the Chief Forecaster, sir."

"Oh, of course. You look older."

"Not since day before yesterday, I hope!"

(But the old man was thinking of 1902, and the bright youngster he had hired that year to sweep out the office and such things, over in the old building.)

"It is going to rain," he said.

"Well, in that case you'll want to stay, won't you, and see the map made up."

Then he remembered—that was what he had forgotten. He should have stayed, but now there was his pride.

"No, thank you, sir. No, thank you. I have some appointments." And he walked out as stiffly as he could, into the morning darkness.

As he went along, he tapped now and then with his cane to be sure where he was. "It is going to rain," he said to himself sometimes. "I know, I know."

4

The Load-Dispatcher entered the Power-Light Building promptly a little before eight. His entry caused no flurry among the dozens of employees who were moving toward the elevators. Only, in one corner of the lobby two burly men were standing; there was a certain country-jake look about them, and they stood ill at ease—strangers to the city. As the Load-Dispatcher passed by, one of them nudged the other.

"That's him!"

"Gosh, you mean the L.D.!"

Those two—down to see the white lights on a vacation —were from Johnny Martley's maintenance gang which worked out from French Bar Power-House. In their lives the President of Power-Light was only a vague "big-shot," but the L.D. spoke with the voice of God. In this opinion they did not differ from some thousands of other employees in the far-reaching system—linemen, oper-ators, ditch-tenders, switchboardmen, foremen, even su-perintendents of sub-stations and power-houses. Many hundreds of them had never seen him, but he was as close as the telephone-bell. Generally some subordinate was on the line: "The L.D. says . . ."; occasionally it was even more like a thunderbolt: "The L.D. speaking . . ." In Plumas County a ditch-tender's wife kept her children quiet by threatening to "tell the L.D." During the fire at North Fork Power-House a Mexican laborer in immi-nent danger of being cooked had spontaneously called for help to the L.D. instead of the Virgin.

Nevertheless the actual Load-Dispatcher who entered his office at 7:59 was not god-like in appearance. His of-fice too was ordinary; since the public did not penetrate to it, the company saw no reason to replace a shabby desk which had stood there out of memory.

The L.D. pressed a buzzer. A man in shirt-sleeves en-tered; he wore a green eye-shade, and had a portable tele-phone-transmitter on his chest.

"Hello, Terry," said the L.D. "What news?"

"French Bar reported a momentary short—just after midnight—on their sixty k-v line."

"Has Martley reported what caused it?"

"No, not yet."

The L.D. was silent for the space of six seconds.

Through his mind were rushing figures which represented time and space modified by conditions of topography, season of year, and efficiency of men. From long skill the calculation was so rapid that it resembled intuition; thus by being so highly rational the L.D. had gained the reputation of playing hunches.

"If Martley doesn't call before eight-seventeen, get in touch with him."

"Yes, sir."

The L.D. noted, not without satisfaction, the slightly awed air with which Terry departed. Well, he hoped eight-seventeen would be all right; Martley was as good as any of them, but the open winter tended to make men get slack. Nevertheless, to ask for a report too soon merely made men think the L.D. was nervous or petulant or demanding the impossible. To let them report before you asked encouraged them to be slow. But if by keen calculation you hit close to the exact minute, word of it would run along the company lines from Shasta to Tehachapi, and every man in the system would get on his toes, feeling that the L.D. was watching.

He turned to the papers on his desk. The weather forecast—fair, no change in temperature. He looked at his own forecast of power requirements for the present day, shown as a red line plotted on graph paper. In the early morning hours the curve was lowest, for then the only demands were from the twenty-four-hour industries and an occasional night-hawk. The red line mounted as (from long experience) he had made allowance for early risers snapping on their lights. It jumped suddenly around seven-thirty as daytime industries took over, and thousands of housewives plugged in percolators and toasters. It stayed high until noon, dropped suddenly for the midday lull, rose at one o'clock, and mounted to its peak at five-thirty when in the winter twilight millions of lights came on. Beneath the forecast curve, plottings in colored pencil showed the distribution of load among the many power-houses, allowance made for repair work in progress, depleted water reserves, and a hundred other factors.

This was the forecast, but any unforeseen happening would disturb it. If a sudden cloud appeared, twenty thousand office-workers might casually turn on the lights, and the L.D. was responsible that those unexpected lights should neither flicker nor be dim. If the evening was warmer than usual, five thousand old ladies might decide not to plug in the electric heater, and the L.D. was responsible that this unused energy did not flood the system and disarrange the delicate continuous process in operation at the Consolidated Paper Mill.

Nevertheless, the L.D., sitting at his desk, was not busy that morning. Like all first-class executives he arranged that assistants handled the routine, and he held himself for emergencies and long-time planning. And this year had been easy. As often, he thought of the paradox in which he was involved. In the long run, not only Power-Light but also the whole state depended upon the water furnished by the great winter storms; yet these indispensable storms were his chief problem, and sometimes he caught himself, against all rationality, wishing for a dry year.

Yes, this was an easy season, so far. The November rains had caused little trouble; in fact they had been a help rather than otherwise, for they had shown up a few weak places which had since been made strong. But eventually something would happen. No need to say that he had a hunch or felt it in his bones. Sooner or later, it was a mere matter of record, the storm struck.

He thought of his thousands of miles of power-line. In their great spans the 220,000-volt wires hung from the high steel towers—dipping and rising in their perfect curves, mile after mile. In never-varying sets of three the graceful waves of copper crossed hill and valley, spanned river and canyon, formed the sky-line along foothill ridges—165,000-volt, 110,000-volt. Less majestic, the 60,-000-volt wires hung from sturdy cross-arms upon wooden poles. And below the high-voltage system came the low-voltage distribution lines, a mileage of them that was dizzying to contemplate.

Yet the wires were not all. They headed up at the power-houses, but above the power-houses were penstocks and canals and dams and lakes like inland seas. Then, mixed in with the power-lines were sub-stations with maze-like bus-structures and myriads of switches.

It was all his responsibility, and it all lay open—open as the face of the town clock—to every storm. You could hardly blame him if now and then he inconsistently wished for a dry year.

To be sure, he was neither single-handed, nor defense-less, nor unprepared. Except in occasional nightmares, he felt himself master of the situation. First of all, his ally, the age-long experience of man against the weather, stood behind him. Next came the half-century of trial and error which his predecessors had undergone—and paid for. Brains long since moldered had discovered for him the proper length of span and height of tower, the strength of wire, and toughness of wood and steel. He was wise with the knowledge gained as men died in blinding flashes, or lay crushed beneath broken poles.

Every wire in that system, every tower and pole, every dam, yes—he thought—the strength and courage of every maintenance-man was figured to balance the power of that old storm-bringer, the southeast wind. The lines were strong enough to stand average bad weather; beyond that they had a margin of safety for any bad weather of record. Moreover, during the autumn all lines had been patrolled. Men had inspected every doubtful point with field-glasses, and had replaced worn wire, spotted insulators, and uncertain cross-arms.

In spite of it all, the L.D. did not scoff at storms. The system was so large that concealed in it here and there must lie countless flaws—faulty material, slips of workmanship, totally unpredictable injuries. All those flaws now lay quiescent; or cropping up one by one, they could be repaired in good weather by routine maintenance-gangs. In rain, wind, snow, and clinging ice, many might let go all at once and under conditions which would make their repair a tenfold problem.

It was a condition of his life. To build equipment so strong that it never broke down was not economically feasible, even if it were practically possible. The system had gone through '16 and '38; it could keep on going.

The door opened and Terry stood there again, telephone on chest.

"French Bar reporting," he said; "their men couldn't find anything that caused the short."

Terry hesitated, and so the L.D. restrained the question he wanted to ask.

"Say," Terry went on, "I called him at eight-seventeen —you know—like you said. Martley said he didn't know yet, and then the men came in while I was on the wire." A touch of awe came into Terry's voice, as he faded again through the door. "You sure hit it on the nose that time."

Even when left alone, the L.D. maintained his poker-face. No one could have been sure that he smiled when, for further assurance as to the weather, he glanced through his window and saw, two blocks away, the blue banner of Telephone still streaming out before a northwest wind.

5

Among the many thousand employees of the great companies, only three equaled the L.D. in their concern over the winter storms. One of them was the General Manager of the Railroad. He was an old-timer, and his hair was gray. Also he had stories from his father who had bossed a coolie gang and heard the strokes that drove home the Gold Spike.

"In those days," he would say, when he had a chance to talk, "in those days, they had a lot of trouble with slides in the storms. Now, the cuts are so old that they've weathered back, and sometimes all grown up with brush and trees, so they look like natural hillsides.

"Yes," he would explain, if anyone seemed interested, "even in my time we used to have our trouble with sinks during the rainy season—plenty of bad spots in the Valley. But we kept piling in rock ballast year after year, and eventually we got down to bottom. And surface water too. To begin with, they put the road through against time. Ditches and culverts were skimpy—kept us worried for years. First thing you knew, something would plug—you'd have running water across the track and a wash-out on the lower side. We put in bigger culverts, and dug the ditches deeper.

"Snow too. I guess we have the heaviest snowfall of any main line in the world. In those days, they just had push-plows; they'd gang up locomotives behind them and run in till they stalled, and then back out and run at it again. Pretty soon the snow would be piled up so deep there was no place to push it to. I was only a kid in '89, but I remember. You know how much snowfall we had at Summit that season—sixty-four feet! Not inches—*feet!* (And that's not the record either.) We were blocked for two weeks—had hundreds of men with shovels digging out the plows. But now we don't even bother with snow-sheds except over switches and sidings. We shove the snow back with flangers, and then the rotaries go through and throw it all over the country."

"Well," the listener might reply, "I guess you've licked the weather." And he would wonder why the Manager smiled wryly, as if belying his own words.

The Chief Service Officer at Bay Airport was another man whose greatest concern was weather.

Like most men in the flying business he was young, and so people usually accepted his statement that he was second generation in the business. "Sure," he would go on to say, "my dad was a sky-pilot—Methodist."

The sermons and Bible-readings of his youth had left only a few perceptible and curious tokens upon him. For one thing, he was fond of the expression "act of God," but since he confined it to disasters he must apparently imagine God as practicing sabotage.

This conception was borne out by the few biblical verses which he liked to quote. "Get this!" he would say to some youngster who was in training. "This is the one business you can't take any chances in. Why?—because the Lord's working against you. It says so in the Bible. 'Praise the Lord from the earth, ye dragons, and all deeps —Fire, and hail; snow and vapors, stormy wind fulfilling his word.' 'Fulfilling his word,' that means they work for him. Dragons and deeps you can maybe forget about. But fire. That's lightning, and all kinds of electrical disturbances that go with it—static that mixes up the radio beams and gets a pilot lost. Hail and snow—that's icing conditions. Vapor means fog and low ceilings. Stormy wind means turbulence. Remember that verse and you've got all the inside of what a storm means to the air lines."

He would pause a moment for effect, and then go on:

"What's more, who is it that the Bible calls the prince of the power of the air? Why, the Devil! And, believe *me*, when you got the Devil and God workin' against you, you got to watch your step."

No one was ever sure whether this diatribe was serious or whether it was a pedagogical and mnemonic device to impress his subordinates with the fundamentals of good flight-dispatching.

As for his own practice the CSO played safe by employing every good principle of meteorology and aerodynamics. Beams, beacons, and constant radio communication kept his pilots on their courses. No plane went out with an overused engine, and he was ruthless against pilots of doubtful skill or intelligence.

"For this is the way," he would express it. "You can't foresee the weather all the time. Eventually you get caught. Then, if you have a good plane and a good pilot, he can most likely come through anyway."

Upon the expanse of the vast switch-board, repeated before each of the dozens of operators, appeared the names not of mere local exchanges, but of cities. NEW YORK, LOS ANGELES, SEATTLE, CHICAGO, DENVER, VANCOUVER, HONOLULU, and dozens more. Beneath the names were small round holes, each the opening of an electrical connection known as a jack. Let an operator push the plug into one of the ten jacks labeled NEW YORK, and she talked across three thousand miles as easily as someone talks across a room.

Sometimes, walking through that operating-room, the District Traffic Superintendent of the telephone long-distance lines thought of a football game. Like linesmen, shoulder to shoulder, the scores of operators faced the great switch-board. Close behind them, like backs supporting the line, the supervisors shifted here and there, caring for anything which might disturb the operators' steady routine. In the rear, like a safety-man, the chief operator sat at her desk ready for trouble which might prove too much for a supervisor. The DTS himself, the coach, remained generally in his office, far on the side-lines, planning and directing.

The analogy, he told himself, was far from exact. In fact, one of his chief efforts was to remove from his workers the sense of strain and constant emergency which was the essence of any athletic contest. And yet in the same way, he imagined, every coach must plan his defense. His hope must always be that the line would stop each play as a mere matter of routine. The other defenses were for greater or less emergencies.

Sometimes during long periods of calm he welcomed those walks; they seemed his only touch with concrete reality. Of his company's three operating departments, Plant cared for wires, cables, and poles, and Commercial kept and collected the bills. But in his own department—Traffic—he was seldom immediately concerned with anything so material as wires or money. Instead, he dealt with such abstractions as voice-channels. His traffic consisted not of freight-cars or motor-trucks, but of minute and invisible electric pulsations by which ideas crudely and conventionally interpreted in voice-sounds moved from place to place. Thus like a magician of telepathy he supervised over a vast area the miracle of thought-transference. For him space had lost its power.

Yet he realized always that his work was not magical, just as in the end it was not abstract. His voice-channels passed through real wires and cables which hung from poles or lay buried beneath the ground. In his imagination, partly picturing maps, partly remembering actual landscapes, he saw the three great long-distance leads running out from the City—north, south, and east. Eastward, the Central Transcontinental, its stout poles carrying forty wires, surmounted Donner Pass; across the Nevada deserts its insulators glittered in the sun; it reached Great Salt Lake, and passed on toward the Atlantic. Northward the Seattle lead skirted the base of Mt. Shasta, and twisted among the labyrinthine gorges of the Siskiyous. Southward, the Los Angeles lead followed the valley highway and mounted over the treeless slopes of the

Tehachapis. Close at hand, the leads were vivid in his mind; farther away, they dimmed; at last, passing beyond his jurisdiction, they disappeared also across the horizon of his mind.

At every point those thin strands of copper were subject to failure, and most of all they suffered before the assault of the winter storms. The underground conduits were safest, but even they could be washed out by floods. As for the overhead cables and open wires, they could resist rain, but were vulnerable to every unusual attack of clinging snow, ice, and wind.

When the storms came and the lines lay broken, the men of the Plant Department must go out to replace wire and set poles. But the Traffic Superintendent, dry in his office, also fought the storm—patching together new circuits, rerouting calls, keeping the traffic going through.

6

San Francisco calling Colusa. Hello, hello. . . . Oh, hello, Jim. This is Pete, Consolidated Flour Company, you know. . . . Sure, you big horse-thief, hope you're the same. . . . But look here, I'm comin' up through your one-horse town Sunday afternoon—can I see you? . . . Okey, okey. I'll see you there; maybe I can sell you a coupla pounds of flour even on the Sabbath. Good-bye— Oh, no, say—you still there? . . . Good. Say, you were tellin' me about that cut-off last time. Where do I hit it? . . . Okey, I'll remember—turn left at Tom and George's Service Station. I can maybe use that five minutes it'll save me. Well, good-bye. . . . Good-bye. See you Sunday, Good-bye.

7

"Public service—" said the Chief with a little gesture of his hand toward the door. He did not blink, but the Junior Meteorologist wondered if there wasn't the little flicker of a wicked smile. The J.M. went into the other room, and greeted the two nuns and the dozen gawky girls in ugly uniforms with black stockings—the physics class from a local convent school. Sister Mary Rose was plump and youngish; she taught the class, and was obviously trying to be progressive. Sister Mary Dolores was thin and oldish; she apparently came along to chaperon Sister Mary Rose, and her attitude seemed to be that if God had wanted us to know about the weather he would have informed St. Thomas Aquinas.

The J.M. showed them some instruments first, and when he pointed out the barometer, Sister Mary Rose said, "Torricelli!" as if she had that one located properly.

Then the J.M. showed them his map. The wind-arrows were easy to explain, because all you had to say was that they pointed the direction of the wind and the number of barbs was proportional to the strength of the wind. Isobars were harder, but the J.M. made a shift at explanation by saying that if a ship could voyage at that particular time all the way around one of the isobars the barometer would show the same pressure all the way. After that success, he warmed with enthusiasm, and discoursed five minutes about some elementary matters like air-masses, fronts, and extra-tropical cyclones, before he realized that nobody had the slightest idea what he was talking about. Then he talked in simpler and simpler terms un-

til finally he broke out into a sweat and got down to words
of one syllable.

"You see," he said, gesturing to help himself out, "a
high is more or less like a deep pool in a stream. Everything is quiet there. Or it's like a dome in the air, and the
air keeps kind of sliding down the sides, in a spiral. And
since the air is coming down, it gets warmer and can
hold always more water, and so there isn't rain from that
air, or even cloud."

"You remember," said Sister Mary Rose to the class,
"Boyle's Law—about pressure."

The J.M. took a long breath to cool off, and saw Whitey
grinning from across the table.

"And a low," the J.M. went on manfully, "is like a shallow whirlpool where everything is going fast. There's less
air at the center and so the outside air tries to flow in and
fill up the center but that makes lots of wind and kind of
spins round so fast that another force—centrifugal force
. . ." He paused doubtfully again.

"Yes," said Sister Mary Rose brightly, "Newton."

"Well, centrifugal force throws it—helps throw it—out
toward the edges, and—and—well, anyway, in a low there
are places where the air is rising. And where it's rising,
it's getting colder and the water-vapor it has in it has to
come out as rain, and that's why—well, more or less—why
we get rain when a low comes along. And we know a low
is coming when the pressure falls."

The J.M. did not look, but he could feel Whitey's grin.

"And what, children," Sister Mary Rose was saying,
"indicates the rise and fall of pressure?"

"The-barometer-sister," said the class in unison, having obviously been well coached on that point.

"And always remember," the J.M. went on in polite desperation, "that warm air is lighter, and so tends to rise over cold air."

"Just like in a hot-air heating system," said Sister Mary Rose.

"Yes, that's right," said the J.M. cordially, being glad of any assistance, "and our rain falls out of warm rising air that's getting cooler."

"Does the class have any questions?" asked Sister Mary Rose.

"What," said a determined young voice, "is a typhoon?"

At this sign of interest and intelligence Sister Mary Rose beamed. Even the J.M. was encouraged.

"A typhoon," he said, and then was suddenly overwhelmed by the impossibility of decently explaining a typhoon without the aid of integral calculus.

"A typhoon," he repeated, "oh, that's a big storm at sea they have over near the Philippine Islands." To his amazement this answer satisfied everybody.

The class went out, each bobbing and thanking the J.M.

"That sure was a fine, *scientific* lecture—" said Whitey, "in terms of 1902. I thought *you* were trained in air-mass."

But the J.M. had done his duty, and was not going to be badgered. "Public service," he said, feeling that he was learning some of the answers. But he thought to himself that the Chief ought to put someone like Whitey on jobs like that, not someone with a real scientific attitude. Then he settled to his desk and forgot all about it.

The storm now dominated a region which was as large as the United States westward from the Mississippi.

The Junior Meteorologist again looked at Maria with interest as for the third day she appeared on his map. At the time of observations she had centered, as closely as he could determine, at the one-hundred-eightieth meridian, almost in mid-ocean. Since this meridian was also the international Date Line, Maria had thus been in the anomalous position of having her warm front still in Thursday while her cold front stretched off through Friday for a while, until its trailing end was again in Thursday. In spite of her size Maria nowhere touched land. She centered exactly between Midway Island and the southernmost Aleutians, almost filling the broad space between.

The J.M. decided that on the whole Maria had changed but little since yesterday. She remained a fast mover, having again traveled more than a thousand miles in the twenty-four hours. She would still have to be called a vigorous and growing young storm. Already the horsepower developed by her winds was enough to equal that of a dozen tropical hurricanes combined, but this huge energy was spread over such a wide area that nowhere, except perhaps in a few squalls along the cold front, did her winds reach gale force.

Now that Maria was well advanced into girlhood she was no longer the youngest of the family. Two new storms had already developed along the Asiatic coast, and were moving out to sea. But the J.M. regarded them with no special interest; he did not even find names for them, but since they had appeared at the same time he called them The Twins and let it pass at that.

The rest of the map also had little to offer. Antonia, continuing her erratic and suicidal course, had moved close to Bering Strait and come into a region of polar high pressure; she was rapidly disappearing. Cornelia was still beating against the south Alaskan coast. She too was losing energy, but a bulge of isobars eastward showed that some of her Pacific air had crossed the mountains. This eastward elongation, the J.M. decided, would bear watching.

As his eyes wandered north toward the stations along the Arctic Ocean, he realized even more surely that something might be about to happen. The Chief, as he remembered to his chagrin, had commented upon Coppermine the day before. Quickly now he checked back over his previous maps. On Tuesday, Coppermine had reported 1020; on Wednesday, 1022; now on Thursday, 1023. During the same time the wind had been blowing from the east or northeast and growing stronger; the temperature had fallen slowly.

Tantalized, he looked at the broad blank spaces over Beaufort Sea, and beyond. How could anyone know what was happening when there were holes like that in the map? And here in California he did not have reports from the Atlantic or from Europe and western Siberia. That little rise of pressure over Coppermine seemed slight, and might be some local development. Or it might be the bulging snout of some great mass of cold air from over the polar ice-cap. Even if it were, without round-the-world reports you could not be sure how it would move.

The Chief came, and looked at the map, particularly at the Arctic stations. He said nothing, but two or three times he emitted his doubting little nasal grunt. The

J.M. wanted to ask a question, and felt his scientific curiosity urging him to gather information in all humility wherever it might be found. But his pride as a recent distinguished graduate of the Meteorological Institute suddenly objected to asking a question of the Chief whom he often felt to be nothing but a weather-guesser. He compromised with an affirmation which was really a question:

"That polar air-mass is about ready to let go, I should say."

"Hn-n? Well—yes, and no."

The tone of voice was so level that not until after several seconds did the J.M. begin to wonder whether the non-committal reply had been a snub. At the idea he grew angry—these Weather Bureau old-timers! He remembered his experience of the early morning.

"That old fellow was around again when I was taking observations. He gets in the way quite a bit. He says it's going to rain—he *knows*. Maybe we'd better take him back on the staff."

It was funny the way when you started talking about personalities, other people gathered round. Now Whitey and Mr. Ragan were standing right there.

"Hn-n?" said the Chief. "The Old Master! That's what Whitey calls him. Well, he was a good forecaster, one of the best, for his time."

"Good forecasting demands good data and good theory," said the J.M., quoting a professor's lecture. "They didn't have either, fifty years ago; but they may have been good guessers, and their wording was always vague."

"I met him down below," said the Chief. "He told me about the rain too. Of course, he's right—as long as he doesn't mention any time-limit. It's always *going* to rain. What they say about the barometer—the only time you can believe a barometer is when it reads CHANGE; the weather is always sure to change."

He moved off, but Whitey and Mr. Ragan remained.

"The Old Master is all right," said Whitey belligerently.

"He's nuts!" said the J.M., not mincing words now that the Chief was gone. "He's got a light in his eye. Why, this morning on that little rickety platform on the roof I watched out. He might push somebody off!"

"Nuts yourself! He's past ninety, and you're a good strong kid. You sure must be easy to scare."

"He's a bore too. He told me about Grant's inauguration again."

"All right, we've all heard that story pretty often too. But when I get to be as old as the Old Master I'll probably tell how we predicted forty days and forty nights of rain for Noah's flood—right here in this office."

As Whitey talked, Mr. Ragan stood nodding his head solemnly. But the J.M. turned back to his map, pointedly, dismissing them and the controversy.

Nevertheless, even as he put the final touches upon the unquestioning lines of his isobars, Whitey and the others seemed to stare at him from the map. They were jealous of him, he reasoned—of his training. Even the Chief must be; the Chief hardly knew enough mathematics to figure *theta-e*. And Whitey would never rise higher than Observer; he had tried the Civil Service examination three times and always failed the mathematical part. Mr. Ragan had been a promising youngster once—had even published an article on cyclone tracks; but he had died above the ears about 1915, and been a routine worker ever since.

Yet the J.M. was not too well pleased with himself either. He knew that he was a good meteorologist, but he wanted also to have companionship. He was in a strange city, and lonely. But he always seemed to be giving the cold shoulder to the boys in the office. He knew their nickname for him—the Baby Chief. The Chief part he liked; but the other word gave the whole nickname too ironic a tinge.

The phone rang. He answered it, and listened to the question put by a raucous female voice. He almost winced, and he grimaced as he answered. "Yes, madam," he said, trying to maintain professional courtesy in his voice and yet make it vibrate with deepest irony. "The forecast is for fair weather; I'm sure that you will be quite safe in hanging your washing outside."

He turned back to his map in irritation. Even if you put in an automatic telephone system to answer anyone who dialed Weather-1212, still people called up with petty questions. He wished suddenly that he had taken the airline job when he had the chance.

Between earth and stratosphere the storms moved eastward, and he was trained to plot their courses. But he had to answer questions about hanging out the diapers— he was sure it was diapers!

He pulled open his drawer, and saw the well-worn leather case containing his slide-rule. Reflectively rubbing a finger-tip across it, he noticed that he left a track in a faint film of dust.

8

Over a large region of the ocean near the Hawaiian Islands a long calm had rested. Through a cloudless atmosphere the tropical sun beat down upon the water. The air grew warmer and warmer, and day after day absorbed moisture from the surface of the ocean. This water-vapor, even without becoming visible as cloud, was able to intercept much energy from the sun's rays, and thus the humid air grew warm even at high levels.

The passengers of a liner traversing the region declared themselves on the verge of heat-prostration. They lay in deck-chairs, and sipped constantly at tall glasses of iced drinks. On the outsides of these glasses water at once formed in a film, and then quickly in large drops which trickled down until the glasses stood in puddles on the table. The passengers frequently expressed surprise that such weather did not relieve itself in a shower, not realizing that the upper air also was sufficiently warm to prevent the sudden up-burst of heated surface air which would make possible a thunderstorm.

In an area a thousand miles long and five hundred miles broad, above an ocean which was smooth to the suggestion of oiliness, the air nowhere offered any zone of quick transition in temperature and moisture. Warm and languid, soppy with tepid water as a wet sponge, far and wide the air lay quiescent.

9

After half-past eight the rush-hour in the restaurant was over. Jen got away from her cashier's booth to put the call through to San Francisco.

"Hello, Dot, hello. This is Jen, *Jen*—your sister Jen."

Dot expressed surprise, pleasure, and anxiety, as one may when receiving an unexpected long-distance call. Jen cut her short, because the tolls would be running up.

"Sure, I'm in Reno—as usual; and I'm fine. And say, I got it fixed up to come down and stay with you Saturday night and Sunday, if it suits. I got a boy-friend driving me down—get to your house maybe around midnight —leave late on Sunday. All right?"

Dot expressed delight at the proposed visit, and then the usual married-sister's doubt about such runnings-around with a boy-friend. What if the car broke down? And who was he? She got the usual answers:

"But I'm often out till after midnight around here, and you wouldn't think anything of that. He's just a fellow I know—name's Max Arnim. But, say, the time on this call is running up. Thanks, and I'll see you then. 'Member me to Ed and the kids."

Jen went back to her place at the cashier's booth, and the proprietress eyed her approvingly. Jen kept her accounts straight, and as to looks she was just about right. She had a rounded little figure, and her light-brown hair had a touch of red in it. Otherwise she was just nice-looking, pretty maybe, not beautiful. Older men liked to pass a word with her, but the younger fellows didn't hang around too much trying to date her up. In a wide-open town like Reno you had to watch things like that if you were running a respectable place.

10

Over all the top of the world rested unbroken darkness like a cap. Through that polar night the flow of heat off into outer space was like the steady drain of blood from an open wound. As the air thus grew colder and colder, it shrank toward the surface of the earth, and to fill its place more air flowed in at the upper levels. Upon every square mile of snow-covered land and frozen sea thus rested hourly a heavier weight of air.

Until two days previous this accumulation had been relieved by a great flow of cold air southward from Siberia into China. But since that time a series of storms had developed, and by their interlocked winds had blocked off this flow. All China now had mild temperature.

If the earth had not been revolving, if it had presented no contrast of sea and land, or even if there had been no mountains, the frigid air might merely have moved out in all directions from the pole, pushing beneath the warmer air in somewhat orderly fashion, as ink spilled upon a blotter seeps out to form an ever larger circle. But actually the cordon of storms surrounded the polar air, holding it back by the force of their winds as a line of police, now jostled back a little, now pushing forward, restrains an angry crowd. In Greenland, in Alaska, and in Scandinavia, high mountains also were barriers. But elsewhere, here and there, the line of the polar front bulged southward, as the crowd pushes forward against the police-line, not everywhere, but at spots where those who are boldest or angriest, most wronged or most desperate, whisper to one another and make ready for the sudden push.

Or, as a momentarily defeated army driven within a fortress daily restoring its morale and knowing itself too strong for the besiegers begins to renew the battle, so the polar air pushed out southward, now here, now there, feeling for weaknesses. Blocked in China, it thrust down the open ocean-corridor between Norway and Greenland; but a wide-spreading storm moving swiftly out from New England across the Gulf of St. Lawrence brought rain and snow to the mid-Atlantic and checked that sally. So the polar air pushed elsewhere, at every point where the mountain barrier was broken or the storms seemed weaker—into the broad arctic plain of Canada, at Bering Strait, under the lee of the Ural Mountains.

A fur-trader upon Victoria Island in the Arctic Archipelago, stepping from his cabin into the shadowless daylong twilight, felt a change of weather. He had long ago stopped bothering with the thermometer, but from experience he knew that the customary twenty or thirty below zero had yielded to something far colder. He spat experimentally, and the spittle crackled as it struck the ice-covered ground; that meant about fifty below. It was much too cold for snowflakes to form, but a few tiny spicules and ice-needles settled upon the fur of his sleeve, as the falling temperature squeezed from the already dry air some last vestiges of moisture. A steady breeze moved from the northeast. Along the lines of his cheek-bones above his thick beard, already he felt a numbness. The dog which had followed him from the cabin whimpered a little. "Softy!" said the trader; but he recognized the warning, and went back into the cabin. He brushed from his beard the frost which had formed from his breathing. Then he filled the tea-kettle, knowing that the dry air, when warmed inside the cabin, would suck the moisture from his throat and eye-balls. He decided to stay inside.

Undimmed by day the circling constellations glittered over polar ice and snow; the North Star stood at the zenith. Now and again, above the frozen ocean, the aurora flared bright. Hour by hour the heat radiated off. The temperature fell; the weight of air grew heavier; the pressure rose. And inevitably the hour of the break grew closer.

WEATHER-WISE after their kind, men say, the frogs from their puddles croak before rain, and the mountain goats move to the sheltered face of the peak before the blizzard strikes. Such also may have been the wisdom of man's ancestors before man was. In nerve-endings now decadent, they felt the moisture in the air; in the liquids of their joints they sensed the falling pressure.

The ages passed; brow and chin moved forward; man walked two-legged upon the earth. Hunter lying in wait, seed-gatherer wandering afield—they came to know vaguely the warnings of wind and cloud. And as fire (the new-found ally) flickered upon the cave-wall, they entrusted their knowledge to language (that great preserver of knowledge), fashioning rhymes and saws and proverbs. But language, which always said too much or too little, was also a great corrupter of knowledge. He who handled words most cunningly was seldom the wisest, but the catchiest proverbs, not the truest, survived. (So even yet those who speak English say:

80

> *Rain before seven,*
> *Clear before eleven.*

But those who speak other languages do not say that particular foolishness, not because they are wiser, but because in their speech the two numerals fail to rhyme.)

Then, when many generations had passed, came high-priests and shamans and medicine-men. Self-deceived, stupid followers of tradition, or mere cynics, they beat drums for rain, and cried that the gods were wroth. They sacrificed bullocks, and gashed themselves with knives and lancets before the altars of Baal.

Next, too briefly, came the clean Hellenic mind searching rational truth. "The storm lasted three days," wrote Herodotus. "At last, by offering victims to the Winds, and charming them with the help of conjurers, while they sacrificed to Thetis and the Nereids, the Magians succeeded in laying the storm." And then he added dryly, "Or perhaps it ceased of itself." Plato first used the word *meteorology,* meaning talk of high, celestial things, beyond the realm of air. Aristotle, canny north-country man, shunning such poetic flim-flam, took over the word for the study of all actions of wind, rain, and vapor in the air itself.

Ptolemy recorded his observations systematically, and Hippocrates studied the effect of weather upon his patients. But the Hellenic spirit withered, and the Roman mind was incurious and superstitious. Even the great Virgil commended the heifers and the rooks as divinely inspired weather-prophets, and the keen-witted Horace (more in jest than in earnest, we hope) saw the warning of Jove in an unexpected clap of thunder. Augur, astrologer, and wind-selling witch held sway through long centuries.

At last Galileo questioned nature's abhorrence of a vacuum, and recommended the problem to one of his students for investigation. From this beginning sprang modern meteorology. Temperature, wind, even humidity, man could feel through his own senses and roughly estimate. But pressure, most valuable guide of all, was too subtle for him, until he achieved the barometer. Then at last he came to know the waves and whirlpools, the swirling shallows and stagnant deeps, of that ever-changing ocean of air on the bottom of which the civilizations flourish and decay.

And since the storm knows no boundary of race or continent, men of all nations perforce have labored together to learn the ways of weather. Torricelli, the Italian, invented the barometer. Halley, the Englishman, mapped the winds. Franklin, the American, audaciously grasped the idea of a revolving and traveling storm. Coriolis, the Frenchman, discovered how the earth's own rotation shifts the wind. Buys Ballots's Law derives from a curiously named Dutchman; Dove, the German, stated the laws of storms; Bjerknes, the Norwegian, probed their nature and explained their life-history.

To these and many others man owes it that he no longer babbles a charm, or tears his flesh in supplication to a storm-demon. Ahead, if man can but conquer himself, lies every hope of greater victory. Still farther off, beyond limits of rational prophecy, lies the time when by arts as yet unimagined man may attain that dream of Magian, witch, and druid—not to predict weather, but to control it.

2

A medium-weight truck, unloaded, was being driven northward along one of the secondary highways in the Sacramento Valley. On its floor was lying a piece of two-by-four lumber about two feet long, recently used to block a wheel. The pavement on the secondary highway was not very smooth, and the truck bounced considerably. The two-by-four worked back a little at every jolt until it balanced at the edge. The truck then crossed a badly designed culvert. The two-by-four toppled off, rolled over and slid by the force of its own momentum, and then lay near the edge of the pavement.

In the year 1579 Sir Francis Drake landed on the California coast, and in the same year a cedar tree was sprouting on the lip of a ravine far up in the Sierra Nevada. Where thousands of contemporary seedlings succumbed to the pitiless competition of the mature forest, this particular sprout survived; it grew for more than two centuries under moderately favorable conditions, and attained a thickness of nearly three feet. It was, however, rooted somewhat insecurely, and in the year 1789 a windstorm overthrew it. The long trunk toppled across the ravine and downhill; with a shattering crash it struck a ledge of rock, and broke into three pieces.

Decay is slow in the Sierra; nevertheless, the base and top of the tree, having fallen into somewhat moist spots, disappeared before the first emigrant train passed close by, letting their wagons down the canyon-side with ropes. The central section of the tree, a jagged-ended bole about twenty feet long and two feet in diameter, lay upon the rocky ledge, as if upon a prepared foundation, almost insulated from contact with moist earth.

The railroad was put through not a hundred yards uphill from where the bole was lying. Below, along the river, men constructed the highway and the pole lines for telephone and telegraph and electric power. The planes hummed high overhead, and upon winter week-ends an up-ski operated nearby.

The bole had lost its bark, but otherwise still seemed sound timber. Inevitably, however, the slow fire of decay burned within it, and chiefly in the lower parts, which were in contact with the rock. Since even partially rotted wood is lighter than sound wood, this process of decay caused the gradual rise of that theoretical point called the center of gravity, until the log was in unstable equilibrium. During the last autumn, as decay weakened the fibers along its lower side, the bole had begun to settle downhill, sometimes as much as a hundredth of an inch a day. Every movement in this direction, however small, brought closer by a month or two the moment at which the bole would have to readjust its position.

Moreover, during the past summer, a chipmunk had burrowed beneath, and now lay hibernating comfortably. By removing a pound or two of gravel he had lessened the capacity of the foundation to resist the slowly shifting weight.

"Dirty Ed" was sixteen and a holy terror. He took his .22 rifle, and with a friend called Lefty went down along the marshes of the Bay shore. The two were bad shots, and managed only to splash water in the vicinity of several mud-hens. They thought their ammunition was all used up, and started home; then Ed found one more cartridge at the bottom of his pocket. They looked for a bird, cat, or dog, and then Lefty dared Ed to shoot at a switch-box which loomed up plainly on a pole some fifty yards away. The pole was on the highway along which was passing a continuous stream of traffic. At this particular point, however, the highway dipped into an underpass beneath the railroad tracks. Shooting right across the highway was thus not really very dangerous, and it was a swell thing to say you had done.

Ed sighted, and fired. For once his aim was good, but the sound of the shot obscured the *pang* with which the bullet pierced the thin steel. The boys scrouged down in a gully, in sudden fear that a passing motorcycle-policeman might have seen them. After a minute they went on, not enough interested to investigate the unlikely possibility of whether or not Ed had hit the switch box.

On this day, Tony Airolo went out to see how Blue-Boy was getting on. Blue-Boy was not blue, but he was named after the boar in the old Will Rogers movie. Tony was letting him take care of himself for a while just now; it was good weather, and there were plenty of acorns. About half of Tony's ranch was rolling foothill country, and the rest was this steep hillside pitching down into the canyon and bounded at the base by the railroad right of way. It was too steep and rocky to be really a pasture; sheep could manage it well enough, but quite possibly the boar could not. As Tony worked along the hillside a freight train went by, up-grade—a three bagger. Tony felt he was looking down right into the top of each of the belching smoke-stacks, just as if he were standing on an over-pass.

Several natural gullies ran down the hillside, and as Tony came to one of these he saw the boar. Blue-Boy looked in good condition. Just now he was busy grubbing for acorns under an oak tree which hung on precariously to the slope. Watching for a minute, Tony decided that a boar was more sure-footed than you would think. Blue-Boy was getting along all right.

3

The storm centered now between the Hawaiian Islands and Alaska, somewhat nearer the latter. The dry east winds upon the northern fringe of its circuit swept Kodiak and Dutch Harbor, but the rest of its vast expanse lay over the ocean, and all its rain returned to mingle again with the salt water from which it had been drawn.

The storm had grown still in size, and might now be called mature. If it had centered at Chicago, ships a hundred miles at sea off Hatteras would have tossed before its south winds, and Denver would have been at its opposite edge. From Hudson Bay to the Gulf of Mexico it would have controlled the air, with its rain belt sweeping from Lake Superior to the Gulf. If it had centered over Paris, it would have extended from the Shetland Islands to Algiers. But as an elephant may be large but not among other elephants, so the storm was far from record-breaking among its kind.

Moreover, it was not likely to grow bigger. As most obvious symbol of its maturity, the cold front had overtaken the warm front along a line five hundred miles long, and was rapidly overtaking it along the remaining half. The elimination of the advancing front of warm air meant that no more moist tropical air could enter the storm system, and that, unless some new phase developed, the storm could only exhaust the energy which it already contained, and then die.

But to speak of a healthy man of twenty-five as dying, although in some ways justified, would be counted an over-statement. The man is no longer growing, and his physical condition probably shows a decline. Nevertheless, most of his life and his best years of power lie still ahead. So also the storm actually contained within itself an amount of energy which in human terms was the equivalent of many millions of kilowatt hours. To expend this energy, even if no trick of air movements served to augment it, might take a longer time than the storm had as yet been in existence.

In fact the activity of the storm was still rapidly increasing. Its recent maturity meant that it could no longer glide swiftly and easily as a wave; now, for every foot it advanced eastward, it bodily carried its air along. The pressure was falling at the center, the rainfall was heavier, the frontal winds had risen to the intensity of strong gales.

4

Above the City the banners still rippled out south-eastward in the steady breeze. In the mountains, looking at the long lakes which stretched off behind the dams, you would have said it was October, for around the receded water-lines lay broad belts of mud, dried hard and cracked in the winter sun.

Oscar Carlson owned, under a mortgage, five hundred acres in Tehama County, half pasture, half grain land. On this day he received a letter from the bank; it was worded in polite and impersonal terms, but the upshot of it was that he must pay his overdue interest. Carlson was a kindly man, but seldom gay like his Italian and Portuguese neighbors. Sometimes he was moody; a vague brooding sorrow which was his northern heritage welled up within him from bottomless inexhaustible deeps. He cursed God, and in the same minute said there was no God. After receiving the letter Carlson fell into one of his moods. He went out around the ranch to the pasture and looked at the grass which was being eaten off faster than it grew. "Should buy some feed," he thought, "if I had credit." In the wheat field he pulled up a few stalks; they showed no sign of recent growth, but were curled, conserving moisture; he inspected the condition of the soil. "It's too much," was all he said. An hour later, in the barn, they found his body hanging.

The Secretary of the Trade Association was preparing his weekly confidential report for members. He was a university-trained statistician and proud of his scientific detachment. "The market," he wrote, "for cotton-seed meal and other prepared feeds is encouraging and definitely bullish. . . . Valley merchants report marked retail sales resistance, especially in automotive lines. This must be overcome, and several retail centers are planning a Mid-Winter Buying Week. . . . The adverse psychology is attributed in some quarters to augmented taxes and the relief situation. Noted by other reporting agencies is a deficiency of precipitation. Improvement is expected after Congress adjourns."

5

The J.M. was working as chartman that morning. He lacked Whitey's machine-like speed and precision, but he did not let that worry him—just mechanical skill, he thought to himself. Ordinarily he would have looked at the twelve-hour map made up the preceding afternoon, but this morning he wanted to see the situation develop from the actual reports instead of getting a premonition from some other person's map. He was sure something was going to happen.

Recording station after station, he could sense the set-up. There was no need to wait for the Pacific chart, to find out about Maria. She was close enough now to show, and she was a roarer! The *Byzantion* reported today, after skipping yesterday. A slack ship, if there ever was one! She was plowing head on into Maria, taking the wind right abeam. She reported a strong gale (nine-point intensity) from the south, overcast with rain, and pressure at the even thousand. She would be taking it even worse for the next few hours. Three hundred miles northeast, farther from the center, the liner *Eureka* had 1006, and a five-point southeasterly. Five hundred miles northwest the *Kanaga* reported 993; she was closest of all three to the center, but being to the north and far away from the fronts had only a seven-point gale, north-northeasterly.

After all, Maria was doing just about as expected. But there were some queer things beginning to show up elsewhere on the map—little matters which might not be important. Not even the best meteorologist could tell till he worked out his fronts and isobars. There were definite changes just the same, more than usual. Low pressure at Edmonton, rain, and rising temperature. Light drizzle at Galveston. Fog at Dallas, enough probably to button up the airport. And, wonder of wonders, clear sky on the Alaskan coast—at Sitka and Anchorage and Cordova where it had been raining for weeks—clear sky, and temperatures below freezing. It all pointed him on farther north, and he waited for the Arctic stations; they were late as usual. What about Coppermine? He remembered its 1023 of yesterday.

The Canadian Northwest must be on this page. There was nothing much else left. He let his eye run down the column, and found the Coppermine number. He almost started as he read the pressure—1032. She'd cut loose all right; there'd be plenty happening now.

He filled in the rest of the stations, not surprised now to find that Fort Norman was 1035. He sat back, and with some reluctant admiration watched as the Chief's pencil moved rapidly and deftly among the clutter of notations. Watching the map take shape, the J.M. felt his excitement grow. With every isobar the drama of the situation was clearer.

The Pacific High still stood firm, and also the eastern United States lay beneath another high-pressure area centering at Pittsburgh. But between the two the 1014 isobar showed a tongue of low pressure thrust up sharply from the tropics, covering Texas and reaching north through Oklahoma into Kansas. Following counterclockwise around the curve of the isobar, warm and moist breezes were blowing inland from the Gulf—thus the drizzle at Galveston and the fog at Dallas.

Farther north the drama was more obvious. Trapped and dying, Felicia lay over Hudson Bay and Ungava. She was not strong enough to break over the high mountains of Greenland; north and south, areas of high pressure blocked her off. But Cornelia had made the crossing of the Rockies, and now, rejuvenated on the Alberta plain, was ready to sweep south, moving again with the speed of a young storm. And beyond, dominating all the north, was the piled-up menace of the polar air. Behind Cornelia's cold front this mass could rush south across the plains, with no mountain range anywhere to check it. What sort of conflict might arise between Maria and the polar air?

He studied the map intently a moment, and decided what was likeliest. The great outflow from the north would deflect Maria from the usual course into the Gulf of Alaska; she would come on due east, smash the Pacific High, and let go her rain along the whole length of California.

"Golly, Chief," he burst out. "It's rain in forty-eight hours, plenty of it."

"Hn-n?" said the Chief, looking up.

The J.M was embarrassed, interrupting with such childishness: "I'm sorry, Chief. I guess I'm excited."

"Well, why not? You haven't seen as many storms come across that map as I have." Then there was a miracle, for the Chief relaxed a moment from his work. "But don't go throwing out any forty-eight-hour guesses. Storms are hussies, in this part of the world anyway. I've known a lot of them—storms, I mean. You can't trust 'em twelve hours out of your sight." And he went on with his work.

The J.M., the Chief was thinking privately, was something of a whippersnapper, but might have the makings of a good weather-man. Enthusiasm was proper in a youngster, and a forecaster needed imagination—not too much, but some. Rain in forty-eight hours would be his forecast too, if he had to make one that far ahead. Just the same, there were two possibilities which would prevent rain. The Alberta storm might not go south, but go east following that other storm which was hanging around over Hudson Bay; the polar air would follow, and the advancing Pacific storm move against the Alaskan coast as usual. Or the polar air, on the other hand, might sweep southward so violently that it joined with the Pacific High; then the advancing storm would be blocked a thousand miles to the west, and California would have only dry cold winds from the northeast.

In any case the next twenty-four hours offered no problem, and with confidence he began typing off a no-change forecast. Then Whitey shoved a telephone at him.

"You better take this, Chief—sounds bad!"

"Hn-n?" said the Chief, and then he heard someone plenty excited talking over the line.

"Weather Bureau, hello! Hello there! Weather Bureau, Weather—"

"Chief Forecaster speaking."

"Say, we got—This is Brownington Steamship Company. We got a ship in trouble. She just let loose an SOS. The *Eureka* relayed it to us. She's making for her but she'll take six hours. What's the weather like out there?"

"Can you give me the position?"

"Not exactly—the *Eureka* didn't give it. But we'll get it."

"What ship is it?"

"*Byzantion.*"

"Don't bother then. We have her position when she reported two hours ago. She must have been all right then. Just a minute—"

But the man on the other end was almost wailing: "For God's sake, hurry. It's mostly a local crew; they got wives and families. The *Register* has an extra getting ready now."

Turning toward the map the Chief bumped into the J.M., dividers and slide-rule in hand.

"I'll have the gradient wind calculated in about—"

"Put that damn thing away!" snapped the Chief. "No, figure it. But get out of my road!"

The *Byzantion* was a slow ship, and once disabled would not move at all. He could figure her still being just about where she was before. But the storm had been tearing down toward her at a rate which would be around forty miles an hour. So the ship would be that much nearer the front. He looked at the close-spaced isobars. The ship's barometer, if anyone bothered to look, would be down around 997 by now; the wind might have risen a full point, maybe more.

"Hello—when she reported, the *Byzantion* had a nine-point wind—about, well, say fifty miles an hour. Now look here—don't tell all this to the reporters or to the families either. But you better know. It's going to get worse. In an hour it'll be blowing a whole gale, sixty miles an hour anyway. Then for another hour it'll be worst of all—gusts running over seventy. After that it'll fall off, but there'll be lots of wind for twelve hours, and a heavy sea after that. The storm out there is plenty big."

"Thank you—" the voice still had a wailing tone. "There isn't anything you can do about it?"

The Chief did not smile, for he recognized the appeal of despair.

"Not a thing. I'm sorry." And then Whitey was holding out another telephone to him. It was the *Register*.

For the next hour the Chief spent most of his time trying to tone down the language of editors. "No, it's not a typhoon. . . . No, it can't be called a hurricane." Since it could do no good, he dodged a public statement as to whether the storm was growing worse.

All the time, as the early sun flooded in at the east windows and the City basked in the calm of a cloudless morning, it was hard to realize that at a distance of a few inches on the map, even in reality only a small fraction of the earth's circumference, some of your fellow-townsmen were battling for their lives on a broken ship, and the front rushing down upon them.

6

"O.K., Jerry, change oil, lubricate, tires, battery. Give 'er the works!"

"O.K., Mr. Goslin. Off from San Francisco again, are you?"

"Sure thing. Starting Sunday, cover all north end of state—first stop, Colusa."

"Fella was tellin' me the drought's getting pretty bad up there."

"It sure is, and the luxury trade's not so hot. But still they gotta buy flour—you know—the stuff they keep weevils in. I'm doin' as good as I gotta right t' expect."

"The new tires look swell."

"*Are* swell too. A guy that drives like I do, gotta have safe tires. Have 'er ready at two."

7

It was hell on the *Byzantion*. The rudder-controls were jammed or smashed, and everything gone haywire, and she was taking them green. The First, best officer they had, had gone overboard, and Johnny the Greek lay white-faced and groaning from a dislocated shoulder, and the cook was burned all over the face. The Old Man wasn't much good, and most likely was hitting the bottle again. And the boats gone or smashed—but then you couldn't have launched them anyway.

But they still kept steam up, and followed orders when there were any, and the radio was working. Sparks said the *Eureka* was coming full-steam. It made you laugh anyway, to think how full-steam in this gale would shake up the goddam first-class passengers; they'd be puking their guts.

So, weary and wet and bruised, they hung on minute by minute, waiting for the big ones to hit, and wondering whether she'd start breaking up.

8

Max Arnim turned off the ignition, slipped the clutch, and let the car roll to the gasoline pumps.

"Fill 'er up, Bob—ethyl."

"Oh, hello, Max. I hear you're having a week-end off from Reno—going below—taking Jen down to Frisco."

"You sure hear a lot on this job."

"Sure do. Sounds like a swell party."

"She's stayin' with her sister."

"Oh, sure, sure. Jen's a nice kid, I know. When you leaving Reno?"

"Tomorrow—after work."

"Pretty late—be dark all the way."

"Couldn't get off earlier. Anyway I know old U.S. 40 like a book. We'll pull in to the City around midnight."

9

The J.M. bought a paper and stood at the street-corner, reading. All the Chief's cautious language had been of no use, for the headline stood out:

SHIP IN TYPHOON

His first thought was that the *Byzantion* had it coming— sending in weather reports so irregularly, a slack ship. He read the details.

But more than of the ship, the J.M. thought of the storm. Only four mornings ago he had drawn on the map that tiny closed isobar in the shape of a football. Now, already, Maria was a killer. The papers called her a typhoon; actually (though less violent) she was far greater than any typhoon.

Other people stood at the sunny street-corner reading the same paper. The J.M. felt distant from them. They must be thinking of the battered ship, of the drowned First Officer, of the man with the dislocated shoulder. If they considered the storm at all, they thought only of a sudden and unrelated cataclysm, arisen in a particular part of the ocean to the misfortune of a particular ship. They did not know of Maria's birth and growth, of which way she was moving, or even of what she was. They did not know that now in her massed power, from Alaska to Hawaii, she swept the ocean and ruled the air.

10

There was a dance at Blue Canyon that Friday night. Usually you wouldn't be having a dance at Blue Canyon in mid-winter; the road would be snowed over, and the only way you could get in or out would be by the railroad. But for this dance (maybe because it was so unusual) a lot of people turned out. From high up on the Pass they came, and from all the way down to Dutch Flat. There were railroad people and Power-Light people and telephone people, and highway people. There were young fellows and girls who worked at the resorts up in the snow-country. There were a few people from little mountain-ranches. And there were some men—pretty well broke— who were just hanging around out of work, knowing that as soon as the storms came the big companies would need extra men for emergencies.

It was a big party, and Rick the lineman went to it. He met a girl, and as soon as he met her he knew there was something about her. He saw that she was not as pretty as lots of girls, but she had good blue eyes that looked just a little strange along with her dark hair and skin.

She was with her sister and her sister's husband, and Rick made her his girl for the evening. They danced, and got along well. And in some way when he talked to her Rick found that he wasn't kidding along or trying to get fresh, the way he usually did. He found himself telling her about how it felt climbing poles and mending wire up on the Transcontinental Lead—serious things like that

—and what kind of man was good on the job, and just what some of the tricks were to it.

Once she said, "Isn't it dangerous?" But the way she looked at him and the way she spoke made him feel that really she meant, "Isn't it dangerous for *you?*" When he thought that maybe she meant it that way he felt funny—and not from the whiskeys he'd had.

He didn't really even get her name straight until well along in the evening, and when he was dancing with her sister he felt himself thinking of her just as "the girl."

When it was time to go, she was wearing a hat that covered up the dark hair, but he could see the good blue eyes and the dark-tanned face. Then he wanted to say something free and easy, like "So long, sister, see you in church!" But all he found himself saying was just, "Good-by."

"Good-by" was all she said, too.

Rick wanted to call something after her as she went away, but he felt funny again, and couldn't remember anything that was important enough to say, and all he could think of was "blue eyes in a dark-tanned face" as if it were a song.

11

Before the melting ice disclosed the Pass, there was the River. Once it flowed into the ocean through a canyon. But the land sank and the sea-water flooded in through the hills, drowning that canyon so that it became a strait leading to a land-locked bay. But still the River, drawing its strength from the mountains, running in a hundred loops and reaches, flowed southward through the Valley.

This was the nature of the River during the long dry

season. It was lean and dark, and idled from sand-bar to sand-bar. The banks were high and thickly grown with willows; farther back, lay long reaches of marsh with massed growth of tall reeds: next came grassland, and then park-like stretches where grass grew beneath great oak trees. Elk with branching antlers browsed the willows; huge bears dug among the roots for food. And after several ages came a dark-skinned people, building poor huts, snaring fish, and gathering seeds.

But in the wet season the River changed its nature. The clouds hung heavy upon the mountains; the rain fell; and—with a gentle *swish* in the night—the River stirred into life. Where sand-bars had shown yesterday, brown water flowed today. A tree, uprooted somewhere far in the foothills, slid noiselessly by. The bears moved off toward the higher lands, where acorns now lay beneath the oaks. The long-legged elk, good waders and swimmers, were in less hurry, but they too began to move. The dark-skinned people looked out and saw muddy water knee-deep among the willows; then they followed bear and elk. Waist-deep they floundered and splashed through creek and swale and slough toward the oak groves.

Then, like Father Nile himself, the River swelled and rose. Gently, in a thousand places, it overflowed into the tule-swamps. Mile by mile the shallow waters crept across the grassland; water lapped at the oak-roots. From high above, the flying wild duck saw a paradise of wide-stretching, quiet, inland lake, with here and there a grassy island. In long looping parallel lines, the bare willow-tops showing above water forlornly marked the summer channel.

At last, more deadly than flood-waters, the gold-seeking

white men came to the lands along the River. After a few seasons, the tall elk, the bears, and the dark-skinned people vanished, and were as if they had never been. Even of the River itself, the white men were contemptuous. First of all, they cast into it the debris of gold-mining, so that even the summer channel clogged. After some years, came men called farmers. In disdain and ignorance they plowed the rich valley lands, and then cursed when the river rose and destroyed the new crops.

But these white men were not like the dark-skinned people who in the old days bowed before the River's will. They were not even like the pliant Egyptians who made use of the Nile's flood for their own ends. Instead, these white men made no truce with nature. For, in those days, it might happen that a man rode horseback around the boundaries of his land, and noticed that nowhere was the water more than a foot or two deep. Then he thought craftily that if he scraped up a little berm of dirt three feet high around his land, he might raise crops and market them at high prices when his neighbors' lands were flooded. So he did, and grew rich. But his neighbors also wished to grow rich; so singly or banding together in companies, they too built dikes.

Then something unforeseen happened. The waters of the River, shut out from much land, rose higher upon the lands that were left, and so broke over many dikes and again flooded the farms. The white men cursed, thinking that the rains must have been heavier than before; they decided to build levees a little higher, and be safe forever. In those years that followed, a confusion as of a nightmare fell upon the Valley. More and more levees were built, and each one made the water rise so that men had to build up the old ones higher still. The white men would not withdraw from the lands, and neither in their peculiar madness would they all work together against the River. Instead, in the dark rainy nights a man might break his neighbor's levee to lower the water-level against his own; so, not with shovels, but with loaded guns, men patrolled the levees, like savages brandishing spears against the river-god.

At last, although the white men hated the very sound of the words, they began to talk more and more of "the government" and "regulation." Then finally came engineers who looked shrewdly not at one part of the River, but at the whole. They measured snow and rain, and the depth of streams. They surveyed; they calculated with many figures how high the levees must be and how wide the channels between. Gradually even the fiercest fighters among the white men came to see that the River (which was always the whole River) was too great for any man or any company of men. Only the Whole People could hope to match the Whole River. So, after many years of disaster, the white men began to live in a truce with the River.

The terms of the truce are these. Around the cities and around the best lands shall be the highest levees, and in times of flood men may even pile sand-bags to raise these levees higher. Around other lands shall be lower levees; these lands can be farmed in ordinary years, but in time of high flood they must be overflow-basins and their levees shall not be raised. Finally, broad stretches of land shall have no levees at all; into these great overflow basins the River can pour, exhausting its fury, and through them as by-passes it can reach the Bay. The land of these by-passes may serve as pasture of sheep and cattle which can be driven behind the levees in time of flood.

It is a truce, but no real peace. Year by year, the white men work upon their levees; also they build dams in the mountains to cut off the full burst of the River's power. Year by year, too, the River frets openly and in secret against the levees, and sometimes still it pours forth over its ancient flood-plain.

To THE CREW OF the *Byzantion,* clinging to their battered ship, feeling the wind take her and the waves strike like solid masses—to that crew, hour by hour, the storm had been an all-engulfing reality. The *Eureka* had come and stood by, and the very sight and company of her had cheered them, what with the wind and sea beginning to fall also. Things were patched up now. The old tub was sound and no leaks, the jury rudder-controls were working, the Greek's shoulder was back in place, and they were heading south for Honolulu and repairs. Best of all, the storm had blown itself out, and there was only a stiff cold breeze from the north and a choppy, tossing sea.

To the crew the storm had been simple and real, and now was gone. But actually, from hour to hour, what was that storm?

It cannot well be compared to a mountain or a machine or any physical thing, for they exist continuously of the same materials. But a storm constantly draws into itself new air and casts out the old.

103

In this a storm is like a wave or whirlpool which exists
in the water but never of the same water. But a storm is
vastly more complicated than any wave or whirlpool.

There is a closer analogy—with a living organism, even
with a human being. As a man is conceived in the fierce
onset of opposing natures, so also a storm begins in the
clash of the dry cold air from the north and the mild moist
air of the south. Like a person, a storm is a focus of activities, continuing and varying through a longer or shorter
period of time, having a birth, youth, maturity, old age,
and death. It moves; in a sense, it reproduces its kind, and
even takes in food, exhausts it of energy, and casts out the
waste. The storm, to be sure, develops only in a manner
determined by its antecedents and environment—but
many philosophers think little also of man's apparent
free will. As for sensation and consciousness of which we
talk much and know little—a storm seems to sheer off from
a high-pressure area much as the human hand shrinks
from the touched nettle.

But a community or a nation yields a still better
analogy. Rome or England may endure through centuries
although Romans and Englishmen die and are born
hourly. The new storms sprung of the old are more like
colonies than children; as with Rome and Constantinople
there may be doubt as to which maintains the continuity
of empire. The life-cycle of a storm is like that of a nation
which from apparent decadence is sometimes renewed
into full vigor. Finally a storm, like a nation, has an in-
definable abstract existence. Men speak of England when
they mean neither its land nor its government nor its
people, but merely some symbolic centuries-old ideal.
And more, when men think thus, tears come·to their eyes,

and they march with high hearts to battle. So also in every storm exists a something which meteorologists cumbersomely name "a center of low pressure." This is neither air, nor cloud, nor wind, nor rain—yet, as with a nation, this mere abstraction represents the continuing reality of a storm.

2

From the Arctic islands and the ice-floes of Beaufort Sea, from the tundras and pine-barrens and frozen lakes, the polar air swept southward across the plains. Its overwhelming front rushed onward at fifty miles an hour.

This was the manner of its coming. Before it, there was clear sky, and the sun shining upon new-fallen snow, a soft breeze from the west, moist and not cold. Then to the north was a line of high-banked, slate-gray cloud, and the mutter of thunder. Next, suddenly, the clouds darkened sun and sky, the north wind struck frigidly, and the air was thick with furious snow.

All day Friday the line of that front had swept southward across Alberta and Saskatchewan. At noon it engulfed Edmonton; just before the winter sunset, Saskatoon and Calgary. In the open, life lost all semblance of pleasure or dignity or even of safety. From the Rockies to Lake Winnipeg animals and men alike sought shelter. The blizzard held sway.

About midnight the front approached the international boundary just north of Havre, Montana. No immigration officers demanded passports; no customs officials searched for contraband. Although the Weather Bureau had given warning, not even a hastily mobilized regiment of the National Guard held the border. At the very least, the Department of State might have sent a sharp note to Ottawa, warning that the Dominion Government would be held strictly accountable for damage done by the Canadian air.

Reasonable expectation could only be that a hundred or more citizens of the United States would lose their lives in the cold wave, and that wreckage of property would reach millions. Indirectly, through pneumonia and other means, the loss of life would run into many hundreds and the sum of such items as increased consumption of fuel, snow-removal, and delays in transportation would total an appalling figure. Yet the United States of America (often called by its citizens the greatest nation of the earth) merely cowered before the Canadian invasion.

The northern air crossed the border just after midnight on Saturday morning; by daybreak it had occupied much of Montana and North Dakota, and was advancing upon Minnesota, South Dakota and Wyoming.

3

Beyond the window-panes was again the blank darkness of the winter morning. From the teletype-room seemed to come, minute by minute, a wilder confusion of staccato clicks and ringing bells.

Working on the chart, the J.M. felt his throat grow tight with excitement. Maria was driving in hard. He had no need to wait for the Chief's isobars. Along the southwesterly sea-lane, from San Francisco to Honolulu, the usual string of ships reported. This morning these ships close to either end had fair weather, but those near the middle had rain, and wind running up to forty-mile gales. That could only mean that the edge of the near-by circular storm moving in rrom the west had cut right across the ship-lane. He could even locate exactly Maria's single remaining front, for by luck two ships had reported from within a few miles of each other; one had had a northwest, the other a southwest wind, sure sign that the advancing front lay right between.

Low pressure (1001) at Winnipeg—that would be Cornelia rushing southeast. Low pressure (1009) at Corpus Christi—that meant a weak storm developing on the Texas coast; it had begun to show the day before. Towering high pressure (1044) at Fort Simpson in the Klondike. Clear skies and snappy cold along the usually drenched Alaskan coast. And most startling of all, the sudden fall of temperatures behind Cornelia's cold front—over all the Canadian plains and south into Montana and North Dakota. Williston reported twenty-five below, Calgary thirty-seven, Edmonton thirty-nine, Dawson fifty-eight.

Yes, Maria would come driving in hard; even the temperature over the Yukon was an indication.

Then the J.M. started suddenly, for at his elbow was the Old Master. Wraith-like he had slipped in, and now was looking at the maze of figures which covered the map.

"Good morning, sir," he said.

"Good morning," said the J.M. Then thinking he had been too abrupt, he added awkwardly: "You're out early."

"I cannot sleep much. I am getting old. I like to see the map."

He stood there blinking his old eyes, and the Chief moved in and began to draw fronts.

Only now and then was the old man's sight clear enough for him to see the figures. The red, blue, and purple lines which they put on maps nowadays were, he thought, very confusing. Still, he could make out a well-developed storm over Winnipeg.

"Well, sir, how does it look this morning?" said the Chief.

"You have not finished the map," said the old man, and his shaky voice sounded reproachful. Then he went on simply: "There will be rain. I have learned that even the longest droughts come to an end." He was not looking at the map, but seemed to be staring somewhere far off.

The Chief looked across the map at the J.M., and they smiled at the way the Old Master talked. The Chief's pencil was moving deftly; the map was shaping up.

"And what do *you* think of it?" said the Chief to the J.M. He was drawing the youngster out, not asking advice; but he saw immediately that the J.M. took the question seriously.

"I said yesterday it would rain inside forty-eight hours. I say now, rain inside twenty-four hours."

The Chief studied the map. As had happened often before, he wished for the moment that he were engaged in some simple line of work such as being a G-man or teaching literature. All very well for the others to predict rain—the one had his inner light, and the other his textbooks. And neither of them was responsible. But the Chief knew what would happen if he went to the typewriter and tapped off RAIN on the forecast blank.

That single word would be about as big a news-story as could break in California. Thousands of people would change their plans; hundreds of industries, big and little, would make adjustments. Money would be spent, wisely and foolishly. The very process of adjustment to that single word would mean damaged property and jeopardized lives. Then, if the rain did not come, everything would be ridiculous anti-climax, with people blaming the weather-man.

Say that he wrote FAIR or even UNSETTLED, and the rain came. Then people would go on with their fair-weather plans, and would be caught wide open. His error might mean millions of dollars loss of property and the snuffing out of more lives than a man liked to think about.

There was another point too. In the old days the Weather Bureau made the only forecasts, and people were charitable. But now the air-lines and even some other big corporations had their own meteorologists—bright young fellows trained in technical schools, fresh with all the latest theories, like his own J.M., but with more experience. They talked a jargon about isallobaric ascendents and austausch coefficients; it made the Chief nervous. They referred to a three-day-old polar air-mass as if it were a chick they had seen hatch from an egg. There were even some private agencies selling weather information, persuading their clients that it was better than what the Weather Bureau gave away free. Those fellows, it seemed to the Chief, stuck together. When he made a mistake, they pounced on it; when they made mistakes, they argued themselves out. They called him, the Chief knew, "that old fuddy-duddy." As he looked at the map, he grew hot thinking of it. "Salesmen," he thought, "not meteorologists!" Then he stopped himself, for he knew that they were meteorologists, and good ones too. He must be a better one, not call them names. He must work to match them in theory, and in the meantime must pit against their equations and diagrams the experience of thirty-five years, which had imprinted upon his memory the pictures of hundreds of weather situations against their dozens. "I can't maybe remember Grant's inauguration," thought the Chief, "but those babies can't remember Coolidge's."

So today he doubly checked all the possibilities. He quickly studied the chart of upper-air winds and temperatures, and the maps showing rise and fall of pressure and temperature. Then he returned to his own map.

The telephone rang. "It's the *Register* for the forecast," said Mr. Ragan.

"Hn-n? Tell 'em to wait ten minutes."

The Chief sighed, and thought of the Old Master's favorite quotation: "The duties of this office permit little rest and less hesitation." Well, ten minutes was enough.

From his point of view on the California coast, the Chief saw himself on neutral ground at the center of four great forces. What happened would depend upon their relative strength and the resulting way in which they shoved one another around. Just to his south, the Pacific High still stood; it was probably the weakest of the four and was retreating, but it still possessed much capacity for passive resistance. Far to the north the great mass of polar air was rushing southeasterly across the prairies. Its most southerly isobar, however, bent around Seattle, and formed a disturbing southwesterly point. If it spread farther, this bulge might block the storm away from the coast. The third force was the storm over Winnipeg; its indications were definitely favorable. The fourth force was the storm which was approaching the coast; it too seemed to have plenty of energy and to be moving in the right direction.

With a slight exception, all the immediate forces thus seemed to be working for rain. But the Chief knew that more distant forces could have their influence—the new storm on the Texas coast, for instance. It too happened to be a favorable indication. There must be many forces even beyond the range of his map. Something happening anywhere in the temperate zone, in the northern hemisphere, or for that matter anywhere in the world, might falsify his forecast. But that was only a possibility, and a man must forecast probable, not possible, weather.

He made his decisions, and his actions suddenly came to have a continental, almost a god-like, sweep.

"Hey, Whitey," he called, "get on the telephone, and order up storm-warnings on the coast—Point Arena to North Head." He turned to his typewriter.

But the nearest telephone rang before Whitey could get to it. "It's the *Register* again," he said. The Chief committed himself to the inevitable.

"Complete forecast in five minutes. But tell 'em to set the headlines and get ready—it's RAIN."

4

In the engraving-room Whitey worked rapidly at the chalk-plate for the daily weather map. The room was sticky and acrid with the smell of the type-metal already melted for the casting. But the map would not reach many of the subscribers until the afternoon delivery, and already its news would be old.

"Sure—radio says there's a rain comin'. I better be gettin' the sheep sheltered. There's quite a few young lambs."

(From the *Register*. Page one.)

RAIN PREDICTED. *Large Storm Nears Coast.* The U. S. Weather Bureau this morning forecast that rain would fall generally throughout the central and northern parts of the state beginning late Sunday afternoon. A storm of large proportions is now centered a thousand miles west of Cape Mendocino and is advancing rapidly. Officials of the Weather Bureau declined to state what would be the duration of the storm and the amount of precipitation, other than to say that it would be considerable.

Valley farmers in those regions which have been suffering heavily from drought are jubilant. Snow-sports enthusiasts were today preparing to return to their favorite haunts.

In the meantime, while California enjoyed its accustomed sun, reports from Montana indicated widespread suffering in the wake of a cold wave. Thermometers were tumbling, with lowest temperature in the United States reported from Havre at twenty-nine below zero. Three people were lost and feared dead in a blizzard near Wolf Point, Montana. (For details, see Page A-4, Col. 3.)

EXTRY! EXTRY! EXTRY! ! ! Well, folks, this is Ye Old-Time Newsy calling you the headlines over KTEY.

And the first big news this morning for all you folks in California is that there's goin' to be rain. Yessir, rain. I'll spell it—R-A-I-N. Those little drops of water coming down—"little" maybe, but plenty of 'em. That's what the old Weatherman says. So get out the umbrella and the old gum shoes. But you people in the South, don't get too excited—just showers down your way. Now, of course, Your Old Time Newsy doesn't guarantee this rain; he's just bringing you the report. But what I say is any re*port* in a *storm!* Ha, ha, folks! Don't mind me; it's just a way I have.

"O.K., oil's O.K. Say, how about lettin' me make you a deal on some new front tires; those old ones are pretty smooth. There's a rain comin'."

"Sure, so is Fourth of July."

"Naw, I mean it. Just got the news on the radio."

"Say, is that right? Well, in that case I better be movin'. Got a roofin' job on my hands. Thanks."

"Gimme a beer. Say, what's this about it goin' to rain?"

"No, Billy, you can*not* plan to go with Bob tomorrow. They say it's going to rain."

"It's going to rain."

"Going to rain."

"RAIN!"

5

There was a story, the L.D. remembered, about a chief-of-staff so well prepared in advance that when awakened with news of war he merely said, "Look in Drawer B," and went back to sleep. The L.D. felt much the same that morning, after he had read the forecasts from both the Weather Bureau and the company's own meteorologist. Somewhere in his maze of high-voltage wires, his power-houses, and his dams there would be trouble, but everything was ready.

Just to be doing something he called up French Bar. Johnny Martley's slow-spoken voice, transmitted along two hundred miles of wire, assured the L.D. that in that region machines and equipment were ready, and men mobilized.

"A couple of the boys was down to the City, but they just got back. We may need 'em too. Say, they said they saw you down there, goin' into the building."

"Yeh?—You talk as if I were the two-headed man or something. Why didn't they speak to me? I like to see the boys. Come to think of it, I've never even seen you, Johnny."

"Hell, this system is so big you couldn't meet everybody in it if that was your full-time job."

"Well, O.K., Johnny. Just wanted to see how things were."

But the L.D. was thinking he would really like to meet Johnny. It was crazy knowing so many people by telephone only. Johnny's record was good, and the L.D. liked his slow-spoken manner, suggestive of reserve power.

Air-Lines depended principally upon its own meteorologists, and their forecast too was for rain. The Chief Service Officer called up the Commercial Department and told them that cancellation must be considered likely for all flights scheduled after two P.M. on Sunday, and purchasers of tickets should be so informed.

The Railroad considered its schedules inviolable, no matter what the weather. "There comes a time," the

white-haired General Manager liked to say, "when the
buses are blocked and the planes can't fly—but we go
through just the same." The railroad had weathered so
many storms that one more meant nothing further in
the way of preparation. But as staff officers move to
their posts before a battle, so the Assistant Divisional
Engineer and the Chief Trainmaster went up by Number
77 out of Sacramento that morning and dropped off at
Emigrant Gap and Norden to take charge of track-
clearance.

The District Traffic Superintendent always got a little
nervous when a big storm was coming and he thought
of all his long-distance wires out there exposed to whatever hit. This morning he called Chicago, but Chicago
had the news already of course, and there was nothing to
talk about. Then, mostly out of nervousness, he called
the Plant office. Plant said that they were sending some
extra men up along U.S. 40 to be ready in case things
went bad on the Pass.

6

The little green truck with the telephone insignia on its
side hummed merrily up U.S. 40, past the two-thousand-
foot elevation marker, and on. Inside, it gave a paradox-
ical impression of cluttered neatness, everywhere all
kinds of diverse things lay ready at hand in a little space
—coils of wire jostled spare insulators, and tools touched
skis and snow-shoes.

Rick, driving the truck, was happy. He was going up
to play what he knew was a man's game, and in the next
few days he would play it lone-handed. He liked the deep-

snow country on the Pass, and working on the Transcontinental Lead meant more than just mending local wires in some foothill town.

And also Rick was happy because he had fallen in love, or dangerously close to it. He kept thinking of the girl he had danced with the night before. Sometimes he felt almost as if he had a few drinks in him, and he swung the curves a little absent-mindedly so that the outside tires went off the pavement and he could hear the gravel fly.

It was good to be a man, and to work on a job that called on you to do things that were a little dangerous, and to have "blue eyes in a dark-tanned face" to think about, and to breathe the clean mountain air sweeping in from the pine woods, feeling cooler and snappier the closer you got to the Pass.

7

The General was not exactly making a tour of inspection, but in his capacity as Flood-Control Co-ordinator he found himself unable to drive anywhere in the Sacramento Valley without observing river-channels and levees. So he stopped his car at the Landing, and went out on the bridge. He walked a little stiff-jointedly, and he limped with his right leg. He stopped at the middle of the bridge and looked out up-stream. The water stood at nine-point-seven on the gauge. None of the gauge-readings had varied much in the last three weeks; a certain amount of snow-melting in the mountains was compensating for the lack of rain. The General let his eyes follow along the bridge to the other side of the river where from the slope of the levee in big black letters

CABLE CROSSING stared back at him. In its shrunken stage the river was only about sixty yards wide, and the levees sloped up like high natural ridges. Their crests, as the Colonel well knew were at the thirty-two-foot level, more than twenty-two feet above the present water surface. Penned in between the levees the river seemed puny, as if flowing in a canyon. But the General wasted no pity on the river—not when the forecast was RAIN.

8

The manager of the Palace Department Store read the forecast in the morning paper and immediately went into action. For the coming week he had planned an emphasis upon hats, baby-carriages, and bed-sheeting. He shifted it to ski-clothing, rain-equipment, and blankets.

The Director of the Observatory gave up his plans for some lunar photography.

The proprietor of the Gaiety Amusement Park shrugged his shoulders. He had gambled his last dollar on a fair week-end. Rain would break him. He called up his lawyer, and said he would probably have to make an assignment on Monday.

In the Eagle Lumber Yard the owner kept his men working over-time on Saturday afternoon, and picked up two extra helpers. He had a lot of finished lumber in the yard, and to save it from getting wet and warping was hundreds of dollars in his pocket.

When the advertising manager of the *Register* checked up the results he decided that the paper had broken about even as far as the rain was concerned. The real-estate companies had called off most of the advertising because they knew how cold and gloomy empty houses seemed in the rain, even if you could get people out to look at them. But he had five new ads from resorts in the snow-country, and a tire company had broken out with a half-page announcing a new non-skid tread.

The effects of the forecast tended to spread out link by link until they formed long chains. The shrewd proprietors of several restaurants called up the factory, and reduced their orders for ice-cream. The manager of the factory found his needs for milk and cream lessened, and passed on his word to the dairy. Since the cows could not be forced to co-operate, the dairy company diverted the surplus to its subsidiary corporation which manufactured butter and cheese. The manager then hired two extra men, whose wives on the strength of the prospective jobs spent more freely than usual at one of the smaller retail stores. The retailer optimistically imagined an up-swing of business, and said he would take the new car over which he had been hesitating. At this point, however, the chain of effects turned back upon itself and ended. For the store-keeper, later in the day, read the forecast, and believing that his retail business always suffered in rainy weather, he called up the automobile salesman and cancelled the order.

9

The great banners above the City hung at their poles, or flapped languidly, now this way, now that way. No longer did they ripple out bravely before the northwest wind, for in the night that wind, dominant through many weeks, had faltered and then died. Blue and white, red and yellow, maroon, crimson and black, they no longer flaunted proudly above the pearl-gray city against the clean blue of the sky. Now from west and south and southeast in uncertain puffs the shifting airs served only to wrap the banners around the poles and tangle them with the halyards. Caught at the calm center among far-off mighty actions, the banners flapped and fell, symbols of interregnum and coming change.

10

If there had been a moderately high range of mountains running east and west along the Canadian border the cold wave would largely have spent itself at that barrier or been diverted; the existence of such a mountain wall would have been a more potent factor in American history than the institution of slavery. But the isolated Black Hills only impeded the advance slightly; the polar air swept around them, reunited its front, and went on.

By noon of Saturday temperatures had fallen far below zero over all the northern plains. Five persons, foolish or unlucky, had been caught in the open and frozen to death; more than fifty others had been killed or injured in accidents attributable to the blizzard.

Rushing toward the south and southeast, along a front of a thousand miles, all through Saturday afternoon the polar air swept onward. About one o'clock Duluth went under, along with Pierre, and Casper; within an hour, Minneapolis, St. Paul, and Cheyenne. As the sun grew low, the blizzard hurtled upon Sioux City, North Platte, and Denver. In the winter twilight the lights came on in Milwaukee, Des Moines, and Omaha; they shone for a few minutes and then in the flying snow were blotted out. Next in line before the fury of the North lay Chicago, Kansas City, and Pueblo.

Throughout the day the polar air had advanced more than eight hundred miles southeastward. It had warmed slightly, and because of mixing with the more southerly air its line of demarcation was not quite so sharp. But still its temperature was below zero, and its northwest winds at forty miles an hour whirled before them a blinding and cutting blast of snow.

Of old time, that broad country of the plains knew raiders, but none more furious than this. Swifter than Sioux, more terrible than Assiniboine, more pitiless than Arapaho, it swept upon town and farmstead.

MAN IS OF THE AIR, but through dim ages that-which-was-to-be-man lived not in the ocean of the air but in the ocean of the water. And even yet the saltness of blood is as the saltness of the sea.

Natural man, living in the air, is unconscious of the air, as the fish of the water. But man having left the ocean behind grows conscious of water, and acknowledges his dependence. Also, perhaps, in racial memory he strains backward through mythology and religion toward that time when water, as in the womb, was his all-surrounding element.

In the Christian Bible the theme of water runs from the second verse of *Genesis* to the last chapter of *Revelation*. As symbol it is multiform—water of purification, water of separation, water of baptism, water of life.

Even more is water the theme of that ancient religion of nature which pervades so many lands—of Tammuz pierced and dying, of Adonis lamented, of the Freeing of the Waters, of the Waste Land and the wounded Fisher

King. For if Adonis come not again or if King Pelles be not healed of his wound in the thighs, then the rains fall not and the waters flow not, neither do the tamarisks blossom nor the heads form on the barley, nor the cattle bow themselves and bring forth. Nay, if the waters be not freed, no man has power to beget the child within the womb. Then man is afraid of his own weakness, and the land of the Dolorous Stroke lies waste; there is no rain, and only far off the crackle of dry thunder.

But if the waters are freed, then the land shall flourish. That which was withered and laid low shall again stand on high; the seed is shed in fertile ground, and the earth no longer lies parched and dry; and children play by the door-steps.

The land lies tense, awaiting water and release. If only the rain come, then shall all be whole.

2

"Well, Jen, *Jen!* I *thought* I heard a car, and I came right out."

The sisters fell into each other's arms, and kissed.

"And this is Max Arnim, I guess. (Jen never *thinks* of introducing anyone.) Was it a nice drive down from Reno?"

"Yes, fine, thanks. Where'll I put Jen's suitcase?"

"Right here in the hall. Won't you come in for a while?"

"Oh, no, thanks. It's after midnight. I've got to get to my friend's."

When he had gone, Jen had to tell her married sister everything about him; only, as she said, there wasn't anything to tell—that is, anything. Dot watched her; the little sister, she decided, was mostly chubby and whole-some-looking, but rather pretty too, especially with the copper glint in her light brown hair.

3

Standing on some miraculous point of lookout, possessing more than human vision, the Chief saw clearly the far reach of the Bay. Blue and quiet it lay in the sunshine. On its surface, with breeze just enough to fill their sails, moved hundreds of pleasure craft—yawls and ketches, starboats, and snipe-boats, little home-made pumpkin-seeds. Then suddenly a great black cloud arose, covering all the southeastern sky, and the little boats turned for shore. But the storm struck, and they were overwhelmed. The bodies washed ashore where women stood screaming. Then upon the Chief fell a sense of unutterable shame and guilt, for he remembered that he had seen that great storm dominating all the map, and yet in some moment of incredible blindness he had forecast fair weather and on his word all those pretty craft had sailed out upon the Bay. And always, he knew—as he felt himself sinking into the pit of madness—that he would carry with him the horror of that sight and of the screaming.

He awoke writhing, the pulse drumming in his ears. "Same old nightmare," he thought, and wondered whether other forecasters had the same dream. He lay tense and shaken; his heart still raced. At such moments he always decided that he must resign, that he could no longer carry such responsibility of life and death. He felt bitter—at ships which failed to report, at ships with faulty barometers, at the vast spaces of ocean with no ships at all, at scanty appropriations, at the public which failed to realize the difficulties under which the Weather Bureau worked.

To calm himself, he got up and turned on the light. His alarm clock pointed to three-ten, and ticked stolidly on. But the worry about the forecast which had formed his dream did not leave him. Like any rustic, he leaned from the window and looked at the sky. There was not a star in sight. "She's coming all right," he said to himself, for he felt the southerly wind, and knew that during the night the far-flung cloud-deck of the storm must have moved in. First of all would have come the little banners of cirrus, scattered wisps of ice-crystals, miles high; after them the high, wide-spreading cirrus haze; and then the thicker and lower clouds of the middle air, water-droplets held suspended as in fog, dense enough to obscure the moon and let even the dullest person know that the storm was nearing. From the intensity of the night he judged that this dark layer of altostratus now covered the sky.

He began dressing. Too late to go back to bed, he said to himself; but he knew that really he wanted to get to the office and see what was happening.

The barometer had started to fall, and most of northern California reported cloud. But there was as yet no rain at any of the land stations. By the time the Chief had got the map drawn, he was back to normal.

Yesterday he had felt himself at the central calm of four great atmospheric forces. Today there were only three. The Pacific High, dominant for so many weeks, had taken a knock-out blow from the in-driving storm. The other great storm which had moved down from Alberta centered now over Indiana, and held in the swirl of its winds all the United States east of the Rockies. Behind its cold front the blizzard was engulfing Oklahoma and the Texas Panhandle. But this cold wave covering all the interior of the Continent was only one discharge from the vast high-pressure area which dominated the Canadian Northwest and the interior of Alaska. For so immense was the accumulation of cold air that it was forcing a way across and around the high mountains of Alaska and reaching southward in a long tongue across the Pacific behind the storm which was just approaching California. As for that storm, the Chief decided, it was growing old, but still had plenty of fight left in it, and was in a situation where it might well be rejuvenated.

Today's decision was easy; it really did nothing but confirm yesterday's; and that forecast had already been confirmed once in the afternoon bulletin issued by the Associate Forecaster. Rain, the Chief decided, would begin during the afternoon and continue throughout the next day; snow in the mountains, unsettled in southern California. Fly storm warnings, Cape Flattery to Point Conception; small-craft warnings south of Conception. He checked off the rest of his district—snow flurries in Nevada, rain in southern Oregon, clear and cold over the northern plateau and in western Washington. This was going to be one of those rare times when California had rain and Seattle had sun.

"Well, Whitey," he said to his chart-man, "There'll be plenty happening in California today and tomorrow."

4

The two-by-four which had fallen from the truck still lay at the edge of the pavement. No highway patrolman passed that way, and no driver thought the piece of wood worth stopping to remove. Catching sight of it as their cars came over the hump of the culvert, some quickly reacting drivers swerved to the left. Others, slower witted or more careless, drove right across it. One of these was a truck-driver with a load of cow-manure, and as he bumped over it, a few pounds of manure sloughed off, and spilled beside the two-by-four.

5

Far at sea the rain-belt moved steadily shoreward, but already the forerunning wave of pain had reached the land. Old lumberjack joints grown stiff in the dripping of the redwood forests twinged and throbbed. From Cape Disappointment to Point Arguello overworked mothers winced with headaches. Nerve-ends of leg-stumps tingled. Old wounds of the Argonne ached again. In a moving belt a hundred and fifty miles before the rain, renewed tortures prevailed in the hurt and maimed limbs of men.

6

The congregation was poor and the church was bare; but the warm imagery of the preacher's words illumined it. Yet he prayed simply, only using for his prayer the words rich in ancient memories. For he too was of the land; he knew that the grass was withering, and that his people suffered and were afraid.

"And if it be Thy will, O Lord, on this Thy day, send

us the rain. Even now Thy clouds pass over us, speak the
word and let fall the water that is above the earth. Let
Thy clouds also drop water as when Thou wentest out
of Seir. Send rain for the wheat and for the barley, that
the tender ears may form. Send rain for the beasts of
the field. As of old when Thy people thirsted in the
desert Thou didst command Thy servant Moses to smite
the rock in Horeb and the waters did flow forth, so
raise Thy hand, O Lord, we beseech Thee."

7

Over Alberta and Saskatchewan and Montana now rested
a vast calm. In a steel-blue sky the low sun of the short
winter day shone without seeming warmth, not compensating for the heat lost during the long clear night.
Havre reported forty-nine below zero. The northern
plain was temporarily a cold pole from which new out-
bursts of frigid air might be relayed on.

Southeastward the cold front speeded along. It burst
upon Cincinnati and Louisville, plastering hard-driven
snow against poles and buildings; it swept on toward
Huntington and Nashville. But in this country of wood-
land and tangled hills the front lost its knife-like edge;
the flying snow no longer cut with blizzard-force. Even
west of the Mississippi the Ozarks broke the sweep of
the wind, before it reached Little Rock and Shreveport.
Only as the front bore southward across the vast plains
of Texas could the storm maintain something of its full
fury.

That morning in Abilene and Fort Worth and Dallas
men looked up and saw the high blue wall of cloud sweeping down upon them. In its long journey the polar air

had grown warmer, so that the Texans called the storm a norther more often than a blizzard. Even so, the temperatures dropped from well above freezing to close to zero, and with the whistling wind and the driving snow mid-Texas became suddenly a province of the Arctic. People battling their way along gale-swept streets quoted the grim proverb: *Between Texas and the North Pole there's only a barbed-wire fence for a windbreak.* In San Antonio and Houston men made ready; at the wharves of Galveston and Corpus Christi seamen looked to their mooring-ropes; in the orange-groves of Brownsville there was setting-out of smudge-pots and laying of fires. And radio cast the warning on to shipmasters far out upon the Gulf.

8

All day, from Cape Mendocino to Point Conception, the south wind blew steadily and grew stronger. The slow Pacific groundswell rolled in heavily, wave by wave, breaking white over ledge and reef, tossing spray high on the rocky points, crashing solidly on the long beaches. Hour by hour the cloud-deck grew lower and thicker and darker; swift-blown scud sped beneath the low stratus, seeming to skim the wave-crests. In the early afternoon the wind grew stronger. The mild air was dank with moisture.

There was neither thunder nor lightning, nor any gale. Such petulant displays might be left to smaller storms, just as a small man wins attention by showing off, but a great man keeps his dignity. This, indeed, was no local thunderstorm, no tornado spitefully leveling a town here and yet so petty and evanescent that it dissipates before reaching the next county.

Far around the great circle, a third of the world away, this storm had taken shape. It was a part—and not a small part—of a vast and complex system of atmospheric forces covering the hemisphere. No longer was it a young storm racing its thousand miles a day. Now, powerful and sedate in maturity, it moved with the steady, sure pace of majesty. Along a line of hundreds of miles, its rain belt pressed upon the coast. What need to announce such a coming by showy fireworks? Only, along the beaches, the vast unhurried pounding of the groundswell made known that far off some great force moved upon the waters.

The clouds were lower still; mist veiled the tips of the headlands; and there was rain. No tropical downpour, no sudden burst of heavy drops. First, so fine was the rain, it was as if the low-lying mist had merely swooped a little lower. Then for a moment it was gone. But it came again. A wind gust took the falling drops and swirled them out like a wisp of fog. Minute by minute, unhurrying, the rain grew thicker and more steady.

Along all that straight mountainous coast, five hundred miles from Mendocino to Conception, there was rain. Rain on the rocks and the headlands, rain on the beaches and lagoons, rain on the high grass-slopes. Rain sweeping inland, stippling the surface of the shrunken rivers, swirling mistily up the canyons among the redwood trees, cresting the ridges.

Broken into mile-deep turbulent eddies, impeded a little, nevertheless across the mountains as across the ocean the rain-bearing air moved irresistibly ahead, controlled by cosmic forces far too powerful to be blocked even by the high ridges of the western shore.

Driving in parallel with the coast, the rain had struck along five hundred miles almost at the same moment. But now the rain-belt lost all its simplicity. The ridges and canyons here of themselves impeded and there aided, and still elsewhere caused great waves within the air. Here, around some rocky shoulder the wind howled at gale-force; a mile away in a sheltered corner the leaves hung limp on the bay-trees. On the windward slopes of steep ridges the rain was a thick torrent, but in long leeward valleys where the air-currents swooped downward, it slacked off to a drizzle. Following open valleys, long arms of rain ran miles ahead, and once two of these curved together and, meeting, momentarily surrounded by rain a narrow island of dryness.

So, on a scale small enough for men to see, a wave rushes into a rocky cove. Here it pours through the gaps, there it beats against a larger stone, elsewhere it rushes ahead and then turns for a moment back upon itself. Yet always the wave rises and pushes on, until suddenly the whole cove lies beneath the weltering surface of the water, and the rocks are covered and impotent. Thus too the rain-belt drove onward, overwhelming the hills.

Mile by mile the rain moved swiftly inland, toward the broad valleys where the clods were dry and the earth lay cracked and men waited for the freeing of the waters.

9

All day the Chief Service Officer at Bay Airport had bent over the weather charts and asked advice of the meteorologist, waited for the latest reports and talked with every pilot who landed. What about cloud conditions over the coastal stations? What about velocities and windshifts at ten thousand feet? Any icing yet?

The 12:45 from Seattle came in ten minutes late. The pilot had fought headwinds all the way, and reported rough air and bad conditions generally over the Siskiyous.

The CSO cancelled the seven o'clock and one A.M. flights for Seattle, and felt easier. It was going to be no night to have planes out feeling their way around Mt. Shasta and fighting turbulence over the Siskiyous with probably every airport south of Seattle reporting low ceiling.

The rain commenced at the airport about two o'clock, but there was a high enough ceiling, and the two-thirty plane from Los Angeles landed a few minutes early. The pilot had had tail-winds, good visibility even over the Tehachapis, and nothing to worry about. Fresno and Bakersfield reported good enough ceilings and only moderate winds. Without qualms, the CSO sent the three-o'clock off to Los Angeles.

But conditions were going to get worse, not better. Minute. by minute as he looked from his windows he seemed to see the clouds settling lower and the veil of rain growing thicker. Already under the thick overcast the winter daylight was dim; the night would make no difference to the storm in the upper air, but it would mean lower ceilings over the airports. Word came that the seven-forty-five from Seattle was ordered grounded at Medford. The pilot of the four-fifteen transcontinental reported by radio that he was flying by instrument, over the Sierras at twelve-thousand feet through clear air with cloud strata above and below him.

The CSO called the Ticket Office. "Tell them we expect the five-o'clock for Los Angeles to be O.K. I'm going to let the five-thirty transcontinental start, if nothing happens between now and then, and I don't think it will. Don't promise anything on six-thirty and eight for Los Angeles. I still expect to get the nine o'clock transcontinental off all right, but we may have to skip Reno and make it non-stop to Salt Lake. And that finishes off tonight." The CSO looked over the field. The lights had come on already. The great transcontinental plane from Salt Lake City was coming in for a landing.

"She's here all right anyway," he thought. "I'll have to talk to the pilot." The drifting rain seemed thicker and harder blown in the gathering darkness. He wished suddenly that all his planes were safely tucked in for the night. "Act of God!" he thought ironically. " 'Fire, and hail; snow and vapors, stormy wind fulfilling his word!' " Over thousands of square miles the rain was falling, and wind was swirling, and clouds were creeping closer and closer to earth. Over the hump at Donner Pass snow was falling thickly, and perhaps in the air over the treacherous Tehachapis there were icing conditions. He checked off his four enemies—turbulence, icing, radio disturbance, low ceilings. Also he had his allies—cunningly built planes, powerful engines, de-icing devices, radio-beams, trained pilots. But most of all he counted upon telephone which let him know the weather any minute at any of his stations, and radio which let him order his pilots to land at some mid-way point, or even to turn back and seek safety at the airport from which they had started.

10

"Well, good-by, Jen; good-by, Mr. Arnim. Drive carefully. How you youngsters tear around—get in after midnight and start back that evening. It's a shame this rain had to come up and spoil your trip. It'll make you pretty late getting home. Remember me to my friends in Reno. Good-by."

"Good-by, Dot!"

"Good-by."

The car moved off down the street, and Dot waved from the doorway. That Max Arnim's a nice boy, she thought; Jen could do a lot worse. Maybe they really were interested. Through the drifting rain she saw the moving car and the momentary dull marks it left on the shining wet asphalt. It turned the corner and was gone.

11

If he was too late in getting to Colusa, he would not be able to see his man, and might miss the sale of flour he was expecting. He had been delayed in leaving San Francisco, and also the rain had slowed him down. Now it was growing dark; he pushed on as fast as he could, driving the limit on the wet road. But he had confidence in his own skill, and he knew that his car was in perfect condition.

He was on the look-out for Tom and George's Service Station where he was to leave the main highway and take the cutoff. He did not want to miss it, for he could save five minutes at least. Nevertheless, he was right there before he noticed, and not daring to throw on his brakes too hard because of the wet road, he ran by. For a moment he thought that he might as well go through on the main road; then, being a man of set purpose, he backed up to the service station and turned north into the secondary highway.

Keeping at fifty an hour he drove a mile northward. Then, just as he passed over a rather high culvert, he saw sharply in the glare of his headlights some little obstruction at the edge of the pavement—a stick of wood with some dirt beside it. By quick automatic reaction he swerved to the left, felt his wheels skid, and straightened out.

But the film of sodden manure which had spread across the wet pavement was so slippery that the tires could get no grip. The car skidded off the road, rolled over twice, and landed on its top with a terrific crash. With a shudder as of a dying animal, the car—its four wheels in the air—vibrated for a moment, and then was still.

12

Snow had been falling for an hour or so, and two or three inches lay upon the upper reaches of Highway 40. Already the yellow tow-car from Truckee had had to pull out a coupé, stuck in the ditch at Windy Point. Right now, in front of the Maintenance Station, a car had stopped, and its driver was fumbling with jack and chains; he looked very uncomfortable, half-blinded by the swirling snow, with the white powder sifting in around the collar of his overcoat.

From the broad doorway of the Maintenance Station the Superintendent looked out upon the storm. He could estimate the rate of snowfall pretty accurately from the visibility; just now he could see a certain tamarack tree which was about a hundred yards away, and so he knew the storm to be of only ordinary winter intensity. About time, he decided, to order out the push plows. The sound of a locomotive whistle came shrilly from the mountainside, and as if it had been a signal the beacon began flashing from the rocky crag just above the pass.

Two men of the night shift were standing in the doorway, and the Superintendent heard them laugh shortly as the beacon came on. "A lot of good that'll do tonight," said one of them. "No plane'll dare fly low enough to spot it." Then they argued whether the transcontinentals had stopped flying or whether they were merely flying so high that you didn't hear the engines.

For luck the Superintendent himself took out the first plow. It trundled awkwardly from the Maintenance Station, its big chains chunking on the concrete floor. He swung it to the left down the westward slope, set the level of the plow-share, and was off.

At ten miles an hour the snow merely tumbled from the end of the mould-board. But at twenty miles an hour the snow rose in a white curve like the curve of water rising from the prow of a fast motorboat. He pushed up the speed to twenty-five. The great plow with its tons of gravel for ballast held the road firmly, and the snow flew madly. The curve of white stretched out and flattened; in an arc the snow cleared the ditch and deluged little pine trees ten feet back from the pavement. Now and then dirty streaks of yellow and dark brown flashed across the clean white as the plow scooped up gravel from the shoulder.

There was more to running a plow than to running a truck. The share must be kept at just the right height.

The speed must be fast enough to throw the snow well off the road, but not so fast as to cause vibration and leave the road-surface washboarded. And always the wheels must be held just at the edge of the road. Since the end of the mould-board extended two feet beyond the wheels, this meant that when crossing fills the outer front wheel seemed to hang clear out into space, and even the experienced Superintendent had to stifle a sudden fright that he had left the road and was about to plunge down the mountain-side.

The powerful windshield wipers clunked rhythmically. The lights shone with a yellow glare, but in the last of the twilight he could see that the visibility was still fair. It would be a wild night, but nothing which they could not handle as routine.

13

The CSO went to bed at ten-thirty, the day had been hard and the next day might be harder. But the rain spattered against his window, and he kept thinking of the big transcontinental plane flying east. At eleven he got up and called the airport. Yes, she was fine; reported from over Buffalo Valley, flying at three thousand under a high ceiling, good visibility. Had some icing over the hump and bad turbulence, but kept at twelve thousand and flew right through it in a few minutes. Just as well, though, we didn't try Reno—snow squalls there, keep blanketing everything out. Elko reports ceiling at twelve thousand. No trouble ahead. Better get some sleep.

The CSO wanted to ask how things were shaping up for tomorrow, but at the news that the transcontinental was out of the woods he felt suddenly and beautifully relaxed. "O.K., thanks," he said, and, tumbling back into bed, went to sleep.

14

The sentinels of the coast did not sleep. In the darkness, through the night, the lighthouses stood, flashing out their beams against the storm. Beneath their foundations the pounding waves jarred the cliffs. Wind and rain beat upon their towers. Low-flying scud veiled them in mist. Salt spray spattered windows that were two hundred feet above high tide. But still—flash, flash, darkness, flash—they sent the message through the night, and even when mist veiled the lights, the horns blared forth, and the subtle radio-beacons reached out to sea.

(This is the roll-call of the sentinels, whose names are partly English, and partly Spanish, as hard-pressed Viscaíno named them, sighting point beyond point through the fog and rain as he sailed north, that long-ago winter when the old queen lay dying and *Hamlet* was a new play at the *Globe*.)

Far to the north, St. George from its wave-swept reef flashed the warning seaward. Then Crescent City, Trinidad Head, and Table Bluff. High-placed and lonely, sending its beam twenty-eight miles to sea, Cape Mendocino stabbed the darkness. Blunt-nosed Punta Gorda. Then from the pure white tower Point Arena of the Sand flashed on toward where Point Reyes of the Kings stood firm on that long seaward-reaching finger of high rock above the seal-rookeries. Far at sea on the Isle of Cliffs the Farallon beam flared out; on the bar the light-ship rolled and pitched; Mile Rocks guarded the Golden Gate. Montara, Pigeon Point, Año Nuevo of the New Year.

Santa Cruz of the Holy Cross, Point Pinos of the Pine Trees, Point Sur of the South, Piedras Blancas of the White Rocks, its tapering white tower wreathed in rain. San Luis Obispo of the Bishop-Saint. Then from its long point, across twelve miles of foaming sea, Arguello cast its light on to Conception. And beyond Conception was only here and there a shower, with the clouds resting low on the mountains and in the long channel the waves heaving.

WHILE AS YET he scarce walked upright steadily, man fashioned for himself many gods—of earth and of sea, of the nether world, but (most of all) gods of the sky. Of these, sometimes he imagined gods of the farther air, high and serene, celestial in the empyrean. Sometimes they were of the middle air, rulers of the four winds, of thunder and lightning, of rain. Still again, they were demons of the lower air, malignant, haunting headland and cliff and rim-rock, pouncing in squall or sand-storm. But most often, each god had many aspects, being now the far master of the sky, now the rain-bringer, and again the spiteful demon crushing the corn-field with hail.

Of all lands and peoples is the roll-call of the storm-gods. Zeus the cloud-gatherer, lord of lightning. Adad-Ramman, the duplex, sender to the Babylonian plain alike of nourishing rain and devastating tempest. Jupiter of the rain; Thor, the thunderer; Indra, freer of the waters. Pulugu of the Bengal sea, before whose wrath the pigmy Andamanese cower low. Kilima, Mahu, Dzakuta.

139

Pase-Kamui of the Ainus; Asiak who rules the air above the far-off northern ice. Tlaloc of Mexico, thundering from his mountain-top.

Man walks the earth, but is of the air. Everywhere he pays homage, not to the air itself of which he is unconscious, but to the powers which move within the air. He bows his head before wind and rain.

And what of Jehovah? Jehovah who poured the Deluge forty days and forty nights, and then sent the rainbow, his sign and pledge! Jehovah who came as a thick cloud upon the mountain and spoke to his servant Moses through thunders and lightnings!

2

In that part of the western United States which the storm now dominated, a highly civilized race of men had hung so many wires upon so many poles that hardly a landscape was devoid of them. These wires served many purposes. The larger ones supported bridges, and served for trolleys and conveyors. A very great number carried electric current for power, light, telegraph, and telephone. Others served as guys, fences, aerials, and clothes-lines.

A common quality of almost all these wires was that they were erected in the open air, wholly exposed to the atmospheric forces. Yet such was the ingenuity of these men, and the tenacity of steel and copper that even a great Pacific storm could discommode only a few of the wires.

In the heaviest winds the wires swayed easily back and forth. Rain served only to increase their weight a little, and then dripped off harmlessly. Snow was scarcely more effective. In the higher mountains the snow clung to the wires, and frequently built up to a diameter of several inches. The wires sagged somewhat beneath this load, but sooner or later the very weight of the snow overcame its cohesive power. At that moment a small amount of snow dropped off; this sudden change caused the wire to vibrate sharply and to dislodge most of the remaining snow. Thus relieved, the wire swung back and forth for a few seconds, and then settled down to receive its next load.

In one zone, however, the attack of the storm upon the wires was more serious. Between the snow of the higher mountains and the rain of the foothills lay necessarily a region of transition in which the precipitation was neither rain nor snow but something about half way between and much more clinging and tenacious than either. This half-frozen rain and half-melted snow often built up a solid sheathing, not to be shaken off of its own weight, and steadily growing heavier as the storm lasted. A catastrophic snapping of wires was prevented only by the saving circumstance that the zone was seldom more than a few miles broad and frequently shifted location as colder or warmer air blew in from the Pacific. With each shift of position the wires of any particular region had a respite and might manage to relieve themselves of their loads.

So, although no storm passed without damage, the actual damage could usually be attributed to some pyramiding of accidents which managed to overcome the margin of safety which man's ingenuity had established.

During the early hours of Monday morning such a critical condition existed at a point where the transmission line from French Bar Power-House ran along the side of a foothill ridge at an elevation of about three thousand feet. The line was of a kind which may be seen almost anywhere in the United States. The sturdy spruce poles were sixty feet high; each bore two well braced cross-arms, and eight wires. The three topmost wires were the heaviest and served as the three-phase high-voltage transmission line. These wires were carried upon large insulators, one at the very top of the pole, and the others at the ends of the upper cross-arm. Upon one side of the lower cross-arm, smaller insulators supported the three service wires, operating at a lower voltage and supplying current to the near-by district; the other side of this cross-arm carried the two wires of the company's telephone.

The conditions of the storm were such that a strong south wind, funneling through a gap, was blowing up-hill and across the wires. Several miles farther south snow was falling from the clouds. As it fell, the snow half melted; then, as it was about to reach the ground, the strongly blowing wind swept it along and carried a large part of it actually up-hill. Since rising air grows cooler, the half-melted snow was quickly chilled below freezing, and in that condition was blown across the wires. Every particle which lodged upon them froze into solid ice at the moment of coming to rest. The lower wires were somewhat protected by the pine trees growing along the edge of the right-of-way, but the upper wires took the full attack of the storm.

Under these conditions the sheathing of ice built up rapidly. By the time it was a half foot in diameter each span of the three upper wires was supporting a ton of ice. The wires, however, were constructed about a steel core, and each was normally capable of supporting several times the weight which had as yet accumulated.

Some days previous, however, an owl had happened to alight on one of the cross-arms. The ensuing electrocution had caused a shower of electric sparks, and had burned and weakened one of the wires.

3

In the orange groves of Brownsville the norther lashed the branches, and the temperature at dawn was two degrees above freezing. Men made ready their fires for the bitter, still cold which follows the ceasing of the wind, and women prayed to God and to his Son. Across the Rio Grande in the orange groves of Montemorelos wind and temperature were the same; the brown-faced men shrugged their shoulders in resignation, and women prayed to the dark Virgin of Guadelupe.

Across the broad reach of the Gulf the storm drove on. It tossed the ships in its path—tankers of the oil ports, cotton- and banana- and coffee-boats. Over the warm waters the air grew less chill; and its lower levels, sucking up the spray from every white-cap, grew thick with moisture.

Beyond the Gulf, in the wind's path, lay the long crescent of the Mexican coast. *"El Norte!"* said the brown-faced people, and drew their serapes closer. In early morning the storm struck Vera Cruz; waves lashed the quays; spray wreathed the ancient castle of San Juan. Upon the mountain slopes by Jalapa the storm broke in torrents of rain; it tore the great leaves of the banana trees; it whipped the coffee-bushes and the gardenias. In their wattled tropical huts the people huddled shivering. Higher up, there was snow on the peaks—Orizaba, and Perote, and Malinche.

Through the passes—fiercer than Aztec or Spaniard—the storm poured down upon the Valley of Mexico. The wind stirred the lakes to foam; the cypresses of Chapultepec tossed wet branches; the flowers of Xochimilco were wet and sodden. Clouds covered Iztaccihuatl and Popocatepetl; snow was white upon Ajusco.

But farther that way the storm could not go, for the great mountains blocked its passage. And by the swimming-pools of Cuernavaca the fair-skinned tourists lay in the hot sun, and wondered why that morning the little cloud-banners streamed off from the peaks to the north.

Blocking the norther's path, to the southwest lay the wall of the Mexican Cordillera; to the southeast, the highlands of Chiapas and Guatemala. But between were only the low hills of the Isthmus of Tehuantepec, and into that gap the wind poured as into a funnel. It spent the last of its rain upon the northern slope; dry and cool it started down toward the Pacific. Descending, it warmed; it ceased to be a chilling blast from the Arctic and became almost mild. But because of the funnel, the wind was stronger. On the Pacific it met the steamers from Panama, and buried them bows-under. "Tehuantepecker!" explained the stewards. "Have to expect them this time of year." The captains logged a ten-point gale.

Grown moist again from the tropical ocean, the wind skirted the coast of bananas and coffee. Striking the mountains the air exploded in thunderstorms. *"Chubasco!"* said the Salvadoreans. Like the men farther north, the soft Nicaraguans shivered in a cold wave, although the temperature did not fall below fifty-six. "*Papagayo!*" said the Costa Ricans.

At last, having penetrated to within ten degrees of the Equator, grown warm in the tropical sun, the far-sent invasion from the north felt the drag of that great current of air which belts the earth's central zone, and turning westward mingled with the steadily blowing trade wind.

4

Theoretically, the J.M. knew that such things could happen. At the Institute he had even heard a visiting specialist in dynamic meteorology read a paper on the synoptic preliminaries of a polar outbreak and demonstrate mathematically the sources of energy involved. Nevertheless, when he saw the map that morning, the J.M. almost gasped. To know that all this was in the actual process of happening was very different from thinking of it as equations—and at the same time to realize that as part of the Weather Bureau he carried his share of responsibility for charting it and forecasting its progress. He felt as if the government of the air had suddenly been overwhelmed by revolution.

In the orderly hemisphere of the text-books there was a high-pressure area over the Pole and another near the Tropic of Cancer in what were known as the "horse latitudes." Between the two, in the temperate zone, a succession of storms moved steadily from west to east. South of the sub-tropical high pressure was low pressure again, and the trade winds blowing from northeast to southwest.

But now, in two great tongues of cold air, the polar high pressure had broken clear through the chain of storms. It had joined with the high pressure of the horse latitudes, and even broken into the region of the trade winds.

He kept telling himself that such an outbreak was fully in accord with meteorological theory. The regular circulation of air was (like most things on the earth) imperfect; it resulted in too much air being carried northward, so that cataclysmic polar outbreaks such as this were necessary to restore the balance. But still, to be actually in its presence was fearful.

With pressure risen to 1050 the polar air mass centered over Fort Yukon. From it one tongue of cold air reached far south across the Pacific, and then in a long curve to the eastward joined the remnants of the old Pacific High off the Lower California coast. But the greater discharge of cold air poured southward across the plains of North America and even over the Gulf of Mexico. There also it had joined the remnants of the sub-tropical high, and that air (set in motion by the northern incursion) was now blowing a gale along the Pacific coast of Central America.

Surrounded almost entirely within the two arms of this polar outbreak, Maria was brought to a standstill off the coast. The J.M. looked at her with a fatherly feeling. First she had been an active little storm running her thousand miles a day, slipping through the air as a wave. She had matured, and with heightened winds had bodily carried the air along with her; she had broken a ship, and swept a man overboard. Then she had shrunk, and seemed to be declining. Now, caught between the two polar arms, she had become stationary, and again vast and vigorous, and in her nature more complicated than ever before.

In fact, she was so complicated that the J.M. had to

admit he did not wholly understand her. She was no longer a baby; a baby ate and slept, and was a fairly simple affair. By now, Maria was more like a middle-aged person who has grown too individualized, not to say crotchety, to fit any rules. At first, she had been a storm right out of a text-book. She had had two fronts, and then only one front—just as you expected. But now, because of the complex mixing of her air and because of the mountains along the coast, she might have a dozen fronts and be developing new ones all the time. That would be the reason why the rain sometimes fell in torrents, and sometimes quit altogether for a half hour or so.

Yes, he had a fatherly feeling, but he was no longer in a position to say "Father knows best." The very fact that she had traveled across the Pacific and arrived off the coast in such vigorous state showed that she was not following the rules. Usually the storms which reached California were secondary developments from the storms which had formed off Asia.

Like a father whose child has suddenly become a powerful and famous person, the J.M. began to feel his affection mingled with awe. From Sitka to San Diego was now Maria's domain. She was a gigantic creature of the atmosphere, drawing moisture from the great Pacific and expending it as rain and snow upon a thousand miles of coast.

The Chief, that morning, moved about with a smile on his face. His forecast could have been no better if he had made the weather himself. And there was plenty of rain still to come.

5

The weakened wire on the transmission line was becoming so heavily loaded with ice that it could no longer withstand the strain. At eighteen seconds after 9:02 A.M., it broke. In the next fraction of a second the following results took place.

The wire began to fall toward the ground. Thirty-six thousand horse-power ceased to flow into the general P-L system. The immediate region (an unimportant foothill district) suffered a complete failure of electric energy. In towns within a radius of thirty miles the few lights still burning grew dim. In the operation-room at French Bar Power-House a bell rang loudly, the automatic oil switches broke the circuit, the ammeters hit the bumper, and the dynamos changed tone sharply. At Ringgold Sub-station, a hundred miles to the south, voltmeters and ammeters reacted and a bell rang. The frequency of the whole P-L system fell from 60.02 to 59.88. In the L.D.'s office, still another hundred miles away, a vibrating red line upon a recording-drum indicated this fall. At Elk Power-House, which was controlling the system, the same change was indicated on a dial. In the reserve steam power-house at Holladay the large turbine valves opened. Every electric clock from Shasta to Tehachapi was threatened with losing time, and many delicate automatic processes were endangered.

During the next fraction of a second the wire continued to fall. The operator at French Bar Power-House reacted to the signals and began to reach for a switch. The operator at Ringgold Sub-station moved his hand toward the desk-telephone. The controlling operator at

Elk Power-House turned clockwise the valve upon which his hand was resting. In the Holladay steam power-house the steam pressure released by the opening of the automatic valve set a dynamo in motion.

Since the ice-laden wire had been at its lowest point about twenty-five feet above the surface of the snow-covered ground, the time of its fall was somewhat more than one second. Almost as the wire struck the snow, the Holladay operator was closing his hand around the telephone, and the French Bar operator was just touching the switch control. Because the Elk operator had already opened his valve, more water was flowing against his turbines and the frequency of the whole system was rising toward sixty; the Elk operator was watching the record of this rise upon the dial. The same rise was indicated by the red line in the L.D.'s office. In the near-by towns lights were growing brighter after a lapse so brief that to human eyes it had been merely a flicker. The functioning of electric clocks and automatic processes was no longer threatened.

By the time the Ringgold operator had drawn the telephone toward him and removed the receiver, the P-L system had adjusted itself to the loss of the French Bar line and had supplied the 36,000 horse-power from other sources.

The Ringgold operator got the telephone receiver to his ear, and heard a man's voice in the middle of a vigorous conversation. The Ringgold operator spoke into the transmitter: "I need the line for operation," and the voice stopped talking between two syllables as if someone had suddenly closed fingers around the speaker's throat.

The L.D. was reading a letter when the telephone rang.

"Ringgold operator speaking," said the voice. "The French Bar sixty k-v line just went out."

"Don't say 'just,' " said the L.D. "When did it go?"

"Nine-two," said the operator, abashed.

The L.D. saw that the minute hand of his electric clock was a little past nine-three. "O.K.," he said, and called French Bar.

Meanwhile the broken wire had continued to sway and vibrate; it had set the other wires into motion; great chunks of ice were cracking off and falling. The operator at French Bar had reached the switch-control, and thrown in the switch, which had immediately tripped out again. At this indication that the break was permanent, he had telephoned Johnny Martley, the power-house superintendent, at his house a hundred yards away. Since Martley was in another room and had to be called to the phone, he got the news of the break later than the L.D. had. He had scarcely hung up when the bell rang again, and the L.D. was on the line.

"The switch went out again; so she looks bad," he informed the L.D.

"That's the same line that went out temporarily three days ago. Whatever it was, the storm made it worse."

"We patrolled every inch of that line the next day— couldn't find a thing."

"I'm not blaming you," snapped the L.D. "But get your men out now, while we sectionalize the line. Wait a minute though—how's the storm up there?"

"Plenty bad. She started at sundown, and she's been blowin' and rainin' and snowin' and sleetin' ever since

—ain't even stopped long enough to spit on her hands. You can't see a hundred feet."

"O.K. Get your men ready."

The L.D. slapped down the receiver, and looked up to see his assistant standing in the doorway, telephone on chest.

"What power-house do you want to take over for French Bar?"

The L.D. was piqued that he had given a chance for the question to be asked, for at a time like this when water would be going to waste it was sheer extravagance to use an emergency steam-plant for a minute longer than was necessary. The L.D. considered a moment; in his brain he saw clearly a diagram of the company's fifty-one hydro-electric plants scattered over a territory as large as Great Britain. Some of them were already carrying a full load; others were more or less out for overhauling; others had reservoirs depleted by the drought. But there was still plenty of reserve. Two Rivers Power-House, three hundred miles north, had plenty of water and had been operating at half-load that morning.

"Tell Two Rivers to take over," he said. With these words, the L.D. had made the last adjustment necessary until (as was likely enough) the storm developed some new emergency elsewhere. He estimated an hour at least before Martley would report, but the time might be more, depending upon snow conditions and other difficulties. The L.D. then began to devote himself to his regular routine—bizarre enough at best, since it involved electricity, a product which cannot be stored but must be manufactured, transported, and consumed, all in the same instant.

Two hundred miles away Johnny Martley got busy on the telephone, but since even maintenance-men are human beings, their mustering consumed minutes in place of the fractions of seconds which had been all that was needed for the automatic electrical devices. One man off duty except for emergency, was still in his slippers and had to climb into his boots and "tin pants." Another had just retired to privacy with the current issue of *Ranch Tales*. Nevertheless, within ten minutes they were fighting their way through the storm and assembling around the truck in the garage.

In the interval the French Bar operator under Martley's direction and in co-operation with Ringgold had ordered switches closed at various points along the line, and by a series of tests had established that the break must be within five miles of the power-house. Ringgold informed the L.D., and the L.D. called French Bar again.

"Is your gang started?" said the L.D.

"Ready to roll. I'm talkin' from the garage now."

"O.K. Roll! In a storm like this we've got to get French Bar going before something goes out somewhere else." The L.D. hung up, and noted the time as 9:21.

In the garage Martley turned to the four men of the gang. Three of them were making jokes at the last comer about his late arrival and (imagined) bleary-eyed appearance—jokes about marital activities which must have been current before Agamemnon. Muffled and gauntleted, the men were almost as well sealed against the weather as if they had been deep-sea divers. They were heavy and burly, for on transmission lines the work demanded more than a mere pole-monkey.

At Martley's word two of them mounted to the truck-seat, and the two others crawled in at the rear among the tools, coils of wire, grounds, insulators, jugs of drinking water, and skis.

"Why don't lines ever fall in nice weather?" said one of them, joking by ancient formula.

The engine roared. The windshield-wipers started. Martley rolled up the door, and a blast of snow-laden wind whirled blindingly into the garage. With chains slapping on the concrete floor, the truck moved out.

The truck had heavy going to get away from the power-house. Twice it stalled in drifts, and had to be backed up for another try. But on the highway the snow-plows had already cleared the way. For a mile the transmission line was close to the road; then the gang had to leave the truck and take to the snow. They parked by one of the U.S. 40 signs. They were close to the three-thousand foot level, and the snow was much too wet for webs; it would be bad going even for skis. In the lee of the truck, still joking, they got their skis on and loaded themselves.

They worked along the hillside in single file. Although each of them used skis constantly all winter, they plodded heavily and awkwardly. A man weighted down with fifty or sixty pounds of miscellaneous, hastily packed material cannot dash down hills and execute perfect Christianas. Already snow coated them; it clung to their eye-brows; it built up weight upon the tools and coils of wire which they carried. Each man bent himself to meet the wind's force, and plugged steadily on. They followed the pole line, and each pole—as they won up even and then passed it—marked a definite progress. Once they stopped to breathe themselves. They shook off some of the weight of snow, and puffed luxuriously. In the sweep of the storm no one tried to light a cigarette.

"Let's go, boys," said the foreman. "The L.D. will be callin' in a few minutes, wantin' to know where the hell we are."

They went on. Each man could see for himself that the wires above them were weighted with accumulated snow and ice. They had no doubt what they would find the trouble to be. When they came to the fallen wire, they gratefully threw off the weight which they were carrying, and rested a minute.

Then one man went on a half mile to the nearest telephone to report, and the rest set about repairing the break. First they grounded the line on both sides, for there must be no chance that a fool somewhere could throw the wrong switch, and kill a man while he worked. Then one man climbed the ice-coated pole; every time he struck his spikes in, the ice scaled off in chunks.

It was heavy work, and dangerous too, in the storm. But the men, shut in by the flying snow, had no chance for either sympathy or applause. A wrench slipped, and blood spurted from where the skin was stripped from three knuckles; the man flexed his fingers to see whether they still would work, and picked up the wrench again. The man on the pole reached too far; something gave way, and only the lucky grip of two finger-tips saved him from a fifty-foot fall. He did not even stop to curse.

They restrung the wire, but for all their heaving it still hung a foot lower than the others.

"Let 'er rest, boys," said the foreman. "She don't look so pretty, but if she lasts out the winter, we'll fix 'er up next summer."

They took the grounds off, and telephoned in that the
line was ready. They stood by while the operators at
French Bar and Ringgold tested the line. Then they
loaded up, and plugged back. The truck was plastered all
over with snow, and they had to scrape snow and ice
from the windshield before the wipers would work.

They stopped in at a highway lunch-counter for some
coffee. The waitress bawled them out for coming in that
way, looking like a bunch of gorillas and making the
place look like a tough joint. She was a local girl, and
they told her to go to hell. But they had to admit they
looked pretty bad, and Larry's hand with the blood on
it was messy. So they hurried with their coffee. The foreman called up the power-house. When he came back from
the phone-booth, he was already buttoning his jacket.
"Come on, you," he said. "There's a lady up to Gold
Creek, and her electric iron won't work." So they went
on there to see if any of the local lines needed fixing.

"O.K.," said the L.D., "French Bar is patched up. Cut
Two Rivers out, and put French Bar back in again. Anything else?"

"Just a lot of little stuff on distribution lines. Nothing
important."

The assistant faded into the outer office, and the L.D.
sat back for a moment relaxing. That had been a nice
little skirmish with the storm that morning, but now it
was eleven-five, and everything fixed up and back to
work. Tough spruce, copper, steel—they were hard even
for a great storm to beat. And the men too. Finally it
came back to the men. For a moment he thought of calling up, and telling Martley to thank the boys for the good

job they did in the storm. He shaped the words. But he never made the call.

After all, he decided, that was only routine for the boys. Granted, they gave more than the company paid for. But still, thanking them, you made them soft. Amateurs should be patted on the back, but it cheapened professionals. A man shouldn't be congratulated for his daily work, even though that work was hard and dangerous.

6

As yet only a trickle of water ran in the gullies. The river still showed its sand-bars; it had scarcely deepened half a foot by the gauges; its surface was dark, not brown, beneath the ruffling of the south wind and the rain-drops. In these first hours of the storm, the shrunken, long-dry earth drew to itself all the moisture.

He would have been a brave mathematician to calculate how many billions of dry clods had lain in the fields of California. The clods must first grow dark and heavy and soft; they must swell, and then losing their identity sink back into the earth itself. Only then could the water flow freely. Every crack in the parched soil was a canyon into which poured thousands of rain-drops.

By deep affinity, every grain of dust drew water to itself. The punky dryness of rotting logs grew slowly sodden. In the thickets of blackberry, and toyon, and poison oak, the dead leaves lay deep; beneath these rested the half rotted leaves and twigs of older years, and still deeper the mould of generations. This porous mass sucked moisture like a stiff sponge, and paradoxically the life-giving water even woke to new vigor the very processes of decay.

Still more, the living vegetation sucked in and held the

rain. How many bucketfuls to change from black to green all the moss upon all the rocks? How many tank-cars to wet all the pine-needles and all the oak-leaves? How many trains of tank-cars to uncurl all the blades of grass upon all the hills? Leaves shrunken to conserve moisture expanded and grew heavy; drooping shoots stood up stiff and vigorous. The very cells expanded, and the protoplasm for its subtle chemistry absorbed to itself countless tons of water.

Even animal life drew in the water. Cattle and horses grew dark beneath the downpour. The fleeces of the sheep were heavy. Deer in the forest glades changed from dun to brown. Through the tunnels of ants and beetles the moisture seeped downward. The channels of earthworms were as millions of conduits. The myriad far-ranging burrows of gophers and ground-squirrels took the trickles deeper still. Then at last following the fissures of the earth itself the seeping moisture from the surface reached ground which was no longer dry, and began to join that great fluctuating reservoir of the waters which are beneath the earth.

Until all this should be fully achieved, the river was low. As well expect water to stand in a sieve as streams to run high before the land itself was satisfied.

7

In the Valley the rain slacked off sometimes; now and then even a scrap of blue sky showed through. But the long, canyon-gouged slope of the foothills forced the moist winds upward, and there the downpour never ceased. From three thousand feet up to four thousand was the shifting zone of rain and snow. But where the long crest of the Sierra thrust its peaks skyward like a great wave upon the continent, the wind-driven snow flew so steadily and thickly that a man might remember that ancient tale of a northern land where the air was full of feathers.

At noon the Superintendent looked out from the Maintenance Station at the top of the Pass. He had never read the story, but the thought came to him that the air looked much as if someone had emptied a pillowcase in front of an electric fan. He could still see the snow-crusted tamarack tree which was his gauge, and so he knew that the storm was as yet only of average power for the Sierra crest, although in most places it would have been a blizzard of unparalleled intensity.

So far he had held the road with the push-plows. But now as one of them drew near, he saw that much of the snow which it pushed aside tumbled back from the high bank already built up. "Time for the rotaries," he said to himself.

Peters took out the first rotary; big Swede Swenson was his swamper. The Superintendent crawled in beside Swenson to ride for a few minutes; he remembered that the two had been fighting a few days before, and he wanted to step on any trouble. Peters steered the great machine, and angled it into the snow-bank until the right-hand cutter-bar bit deeply. Then they stood still for a minute while Swenson worked the controls to set the level of the augers.

"A little lower," ordered Peters.

"O.K., Chief," said Swenson the swamper.

The Superintendent smiled comfortably; now with work to be done they were good-natured as fat puppies.

With a sudden whir which rose at once to an all-enveloping roar, the big machine was off. It vibrated and shook and pounded. The heavy windshield wipers seemed to labor frantically. Driver and swamper leaned anxiously forward.

Crowded into one corner the Superintendent could see only snow-encrusted glass and the inside of the cab. For a moment in spite of long experience he felt panic; the ponderous plow seemed with all its shaking and bouncing to be tearing down the highway at death-dealing speed although its driver could obviously not see more than a few feet ahead. But the Superintendent knew that this was mere illusion, that the working of the plow itself caused the vibration, and that its actual speed forward was much slower than a man could walk.

Now and then one of the men spoke to the other—some word of direction about steering or about the working of the plow. In a few minutes the sense of tension grew less, and as the nerves grew accustomed, even the motion of the plow seemed to become steadier. But still the two leaned forward, peering; for some of the snow which the rotary threw aside blew back across the windshield, and their vision was cut down almost to nothing.

From the corners of his eyes the Superintendent watched Peters. Running a rotary wasn't as easy as it looked, and Peters was an artist. Now and then the muscles of his big, powerful hands sprang out into sharp lines as he fought the wheel, holding the plow steady or working it a little this way or that. His boot-sole was thick and hob-nailed, but still his foot rode the throttle-pedal with a curious delicacy of touch. It was like a good mouth-organ player, thought the Superintendent. Those

fellows didn't read notes and think of their harmonicas
as something separate; they just thought of a sound and
out it came—like whistling. Peters was the same—just as
if the snow-plow had a brain and he was it. He didn't
need to think: "The engine is laboring; I'll give it more
gas." He just gave it more gas. From long-practiced skill
the snow-plow had become part of him like arms and
legs.

The Superintendent opened the side-window a few
inches. The gusts blew streams of snow into his face, but
he could see out a little. A few feet ahead of him he could
make out the orange cutter-bar rising high above the
piled-up snow, slicing it off to a sharp four-foot wall as
the plow ate its way forward, inch by inch. Below the
cutter-bar he could not see, but he envisioned the great
augers working from both sides toward the middle, carrying snow to the swiftly rotating "blower." Now and then,
as some gust cleared the snow away momentarily, he saw
the high fountain of snow which the blower was throwing out among the pine trees. Peters had ordered the
angle set high, and the spout of whiteness rose at more
than forty-five degrees. At intervals an orange-painted
snow-stake seemed to move slowly nearer, come even,
and then fall behind out of view. Never did the cutter-
bar miss the snow-stake by as much as four inches; sometimes it almost scraped the paint. To come as close as
possible and yet not hit the stake meant a good rotary
operator.

"*Clank!*"—without warning. Peters cut off the power,
and the sudden quiet was almost as startling as a thunder-
clap.

"Shear-bolts gone!" said Swenson, but the other two knew it as well as he.

The three of them piled out into the storm. Some passing car had cast a tire-chain; the augers had picked it up and jammed. It was a veritable monkey-wrench in the machinery, but the machinery was designed for just such emergency. The only damage was that two little bolts had sheared off neatly; Swenson had a pocketful of such bolts and could replace them in a few minutes.

8

From the San Francisco *Register:*
MILLION DOLLAR RAIN

The headline in the *Register* was three inches high; *Storm to Continue,* ran the smaller lead. The news account waxed lyrical: "From the Oregon line to the summits of Tehachapi agriculturists and businessmen rejoiced as a soaking rain from the Pacific swept across pasture and plowed field."

From the Los Angeles *Day:*
STORM FLAILS NORTH

"As Angelenos basked in the warm sun, San Franciscans huddled beneath waterproofs and umbrellas; heavy seas pounded the coast and devastating rain drenched the valleys. Damage reported from several points was considerable. A continuation of tempestuous conditions is forecast for tomorrow."

From the Seattle *Press-Inquirer* [Editorial]:
OUR WEATHER. The past twenty-four hours have refuted the ancient and honorable myth that "it always

rains in Seattle." We have enjoyed fine sunny weather with just that tingle of frost in the air which puts the natural roses in our girls' cheeks. During the same period (to point the moral better) California has been deluged.

From the Winnipeg *Royal Manitoban:*
MERCURY AT 34 BELOW
PROVINCE IN GRIP OF COLD WAVE

From the Minneapolis *Gazetteer:*
TWENTY-SIX BELOW
THREE FREEZE

From the Kansas City *Planet:*
NINE BELOW; FIFTY-MILE GALE

From the Dallas *Lone Star:*
NORTHER SWEEPS STATE
ZERO IN MID-TEXAS

From the San Antonio *Texas Sentinel:*
FREEZING WEATHER; HUGE
DAMAGE TO CROPS FEARED

From the Mexico *Gaceta:*
TEMPESTAD FURIOSA
MUCHOS DAÑOS; DESGRACIAS DIVERSAS

From the San José (Costa Rica) *Prensa:*
TIEMPO FRÍO É INOPORTUNO

On this day news about the weather was more important over the length of the continent than news of murders, strikes, politics, or international affairs. Although the individual man went on stolidly about his usual tasks, he in most cases resented this sudden change in his environment and considered it essentially local. His attitude of mind was primitive, as if he felt that some angry storm god had overwhelmed his own city and district for no better reason than a spiteful whim. He did not realize that the wind which blew upon his cheek was part of a planetary system. Rain in San Francisco, sun in Sitka, sub-zero weather in Calgary, a norther in Tampico, an east wind in Boston—their conjunction was as reasonable as that when one spoke of a wheel rotates all the others should rotate at the same time.

9

EXTRY! EXTRY!! EXTRY!!! This is Ye Old-Time Newsy calling you the headlines over KTEY. And the first big news is that it's a grand million-dollar rain. I've got the reports right here, and it's just raining around everywhere you can think of. And another nice thing is that it's been a big rain, but not too much in one place— not any big winds or cloudbursts, and so, not much damage. But—uh-*uhh*—this isn't so good. "Peter Goslin, salesman for a flour company, was killed today when his automobile skidded on a wet pavement and overturned ten miles south of Colusa. State-patrolman Hardy who investigated the accident declared that death must have been instantaneous." That's the first casualty of the storm, folks, and maybe we'd better all make a note just to drive a little slower the next day or so.

10

When he sighted the broken wire through the flying snow, Rick edged the little green truck to the side of the highway, and parked it carefully.

Just getting started at all was something of a job. The rotaries had cut a four-foot sheer wall of snow along the road, and farther back the snow was heaped up still higher. Rick first laid his skis and ski-poles up on the snow-surface. Next he loaded himself with his wire and climbers and tools. Then, using the fender for a starting-place, he scrambled and floundered up; he ended by being more or less on top of the wall, but hip-deep in soft snow. After more floundering he strapped his skis on, climbed out of the hole, and got going. By this time the parts of him that had not actually been buried in the snow were well covered by the hard-driven flakes which the storm was blowing in.

Between him and the broken wire lay a fifty-yard space of treacherous-looking hummocks. It must be full of gullies and big boulders, and the snow was not yet quite deep enough to have drifted in and leveled the surface. As a shrewd storm-fighter he took his time, for in the storm and the soft snow broken skis and a sprained ankle could mean serious trouble for a man working alone, even though he was close to the highway.

The wires were heavy with clinging snow, and every pole had four or five inches caked on its windward side. Rick maneuvered so that he came first to one of the ends of the fallen wire. Several feet of it were buried, but he pulled it up and knocked the snow off. He saw that it had broken close to the insulator. The end was tapered neatly to half its diameter as the heavy copper wire under the pull of its snow-load had first stretched out like warm taffy, and then snapped.

Rick snipped off the damaged end; the fresh red of the cut contrasted sharply with the dark weathering of the outside surface. He took a little hollow sleeve of copper from his pocket, fitted one end of it over the wire, and squeezed it with his pliers to make it hold temporarily. From the coil of shiny, new wire on his back he cut off six feet, inserted one end into the sleeve, and squeezed it also. He unhooked from his belt his sleeve-rolling tool. Fastening this over the copper sleeve, he turned its crank, and by this mechanical aid squeezed the sleeve and the wires into a permanent joint stronger than the wires themselves. Then, moving over the soft snow on his skis, he found the other end of the broken wire. It easily reached the new copper wire by which he had extended the other broken end; he twisted the two together loosely and laid them at the foot of the pole.

He stopped for a moment, slapped his hands to warm them, and shook the snow from his stocking-cap and wind-breaker coat. The thick-falling flakes shut him in like fog; he could not see the line of the road, though he heard the rumble of a passing truck. He made his preparations to climb the pole. Every move was meticulous; a man working by himself in the storm does not dare make mistakes. He stuck the ski-poles upright in the snow within reach of the base of the pole. Close to the windward side of the pole he took off one ski and strapped on his climbing-iron. He detached the other ski, but still standing on it he put on the other iron. He faced the pole, picked up the loosely joined wire, laid it across his arms, and clasped his hands around the pole on the bare, lee side.

He went up suddenly with the effortless, rhythmical movement of a skilled lineman. As he climbed, his body scraped off the snow from the pole, and at the shaking of the pole loose snow cascaded from the wires. It deluged him in its passing, but almost before it had hit the ground he was at the lowest cross-arm.

There were four cross-arms, and the broken wire belonged on the highest one. Rick snapped on his safety-belt. To get the broken wire upward he unfastened its loosely twisted ends, raised it above the lowest arm, and rejoined it. Then he unsnapped his safety-belt, raised it also above the cross-arm, climbed up through the wires, and re-snapped the belt. Methodically he repeated the process until he arrived at the highest cross-arm.

Detaching from his belt a little block-and-tackle, he fastened its ropes to the two parts of the broken wire, and tugged with all his strength. By means of this added mechanical power he was able to pull the wire almost to the tautness of the others. He snipped off the excess length, and by the aid of another copper sleeve joined the two ends permanently. Then he unfastened the block-and-tackle, and again attached it to his belt. With some of the extra wire he fastened the mended wire to the insulator. The short length which remained he dropped carefully to the ground, taking care that it did not tangle with the other wires. The work was done.

He shook off the accumulated snow, and rested for a moment. From its position he judged that the broken wire had been one of those leased by the radio companies for their transcontinental programs. Well, he thought to himself, I guess some girl can start squawking over that one again. For to Rick the wires were all-important, and to keep them working he would labor through any storm that blew, but for the messages which the wires carried he had a curious contempt.

But the thought of a girl who might be singing over the radio brought to mind the other girl, and for a moment still he rested in contemplation. Then he worked down through the wires and the cross-arms, and rapidly descended the pole.

11

"Sure, Bob, check the oil too. Say—you seen Max Arnim today?"

"No. No reason why I should, though. Why?"

"He wasn't at the office this morning. Didn't get back from Frisco, I guess. I tried to smooth things over, but I think the old man is sore."

"Oh, yes. I filled Max up with ethyl—Friday, I guess it was. He said Jen was ridin' down with him."

"*Say!* I didn't know *that*. Is Jen back?"

"Come to think of it, I know the answer to that one. Jen's roommate, Marge, was in here, and she said Jen hadn't got back yet."

"Well—"

"Well, it's not my business. I fill the tanks, and I don't ask 'em where they're goin'."

"Well, it's a nice storm; there'll be ski-ing at Mt. Rose after it's over. I don't see anyway why Max didn't get back in time for work."

12

The Assistant Divisional Engineer at Emigrant Gap and
the Chief Trainmaster at Norden kept the trains going
through on schedule. On this day they had no great
trouble; the snow was falling thickly, but had not yet
had time to pile up. First, the little plow on the front of
each locomotive threw aside the newly fallen snow. When
the ridges by the side of the tracks were a foot or so high,
a flanger went through. Pulled by a locomotive and looking much like an ordinary caboose, the flanger carried a
cleverly designed plow-share. When lowered, the plow-
share had two projecting knives which scooped out the
snow from the inside of each rail. Pulled along at thirty
miles an hour it threw the snow well back from the tracks
and piled up a long ridge. Every flanger had to have orders
just like a fast through train or a heavy freight. Sometimes, when traffic was heavy, there was difficulty in finding a space to send one through between trains, or (the
other way round) to get the flanger off the track in time
for the other trains to get through on schedule. But the
snow was not yet deep, and on the whole the day was an
easy one.

13

The planes were going through. There were delays and
a few cancellations of flights, but service was never really
interrupted. The storm seemed to have settled down into
a good steady rain—no severe turbulence, and ceilings
sufficiently high everywhere. There was some icing over
the Hump, but by keeping above twelve thousand feet

the pilots could either avoid it altogether or fly through before it got serious.

14

The General had not gone to the office that morning, but had kept in touch by telephone. He gazed at the rain through his windows, and it looked very wet. He was sixty-four, and dampness was likely to arouse tinges of rheumatism. He himself saw the humor of his present situation. Retired from the Army, he had taken his present job, which had to do chiefly with rain; and yet the state of his joints was such that he must shun actual contact with rain.

The General was of that older generation which kept Collected Works in its libraries and looked upon Bret Harte as an important writer. After lunch, before going to the office, he pulled out the proper volume and again read what was to him, partly for professional reasons, a favorite passage:

It had been raining in the valley of the Sacramento. The North Fork had overflowed its banks, and Rattlesnake Creek was impassable. The few boulders that had marked the summer ford at Simpson's Crossing were obliterated by a vast sheet of water stretching to the foothills. The up-stage was stopped at Granger's; the last mail had been abandoned on the *tules,* the rider swimming for his life. "An area," remarked the "Sierra Avalanche," with pensive local pride, "as large as the State of Massachusetts is now under water."

Harte, as the General had decided, was thinking of the great floods of '61, which had transformed the whole valley into a lake. Since Massachusetts contains over eight thousand square miles and the plains area of the Sacramento Valley not much in excess of five thousand, the General had sometimes suggested that the local editor was exaggerating, but remembering that much of the adjoining San Joaquin Valley must have been flooded at the same time, he always admitted in the end that the editor may have been within the limits of accuracy.

The General was professionally interested because, roughly speaking, he was responsible that it did not happen again, at least not without warning.

When he got to his office that afternoon, he found that his secretary had received and codified the rainfall reports from all the stations in the Sacramento drainage system. The General glanced at the record—moderately heavy everywhere, nothing startling, heaviest in the Feather River basin with Pulga reporting ninety-eight hundredths in twelve hours. He had no great interest in the immediate situation; this first rain would mostly sink into the ground, and yield little run-off.

Sitting at his desk, he looked with satisfaction at the map on the wall in front of him. It represented the Valley. Ramifying pairs of parallel black lines indicated levees. Blue coloring between the black lines showed the regular river channels. But paralleling these blue channels were even broader spaces of red; these were the by-passes into which the flood water spilled—great auxiliary rivers. There were also green-colored areas, representing regions which must be allowed to flood in times of very high water in order to lower the level and prevent a more serious break elsewhere.

The General liked to explain matters in military terms.

"The blue is enemy country. If he attacks strongly enough, we give ground and he takes over the red territory; if that doesn't hold him, we yield the green, and then put up our last fight along the levees to hold the white."

Upon the General's map each blue and red channel bore a figure for its capacity in thousands of cubic feet *per* second. Above Colusa the river could carry 155 and the by-pass 120. But at Colusa Weir the river, if it was necessary, spilled 87 into the by-pass, for its own capacity was reduced to 66 and that of the by-pass rose proportionately. Lower down, the dimensions of the whole system grew larger. Below Sacramento the river carried 110 and the by-pass, miles wide between its levees, carried 490.

If the discharge rose above this maximum of 600,000 cubic feet per second, theoretically the condition of '61 would be repeated and an area the size of Massachusetts would be under water. In actuality a flooding of one part of the valley would probably save the rest, unless the conditions should be too long continued. Time, as the General knew well, was often a deciding factor. It might even be possible, in a sense, for the maximum to be exceeded without any general break, because the crest from each branch of the river might pass at different times. Thus high water from the American usually went by before the crest arrived from the Feather and its tributaries, and that in turn was out of the way before the flood from the upper Sacramento rose to full height. But if time under some conditions was a help it could also cause disaster. A sudden cloudburst in one drainage basin might bring down a crest which would top the levees locally while elsewhere in the system the channels were far below capacity.

Sometimes the newspapers referred to the General as "The Czar of the River." As a military man, the General loved command well enough not to resent the title, but he knew that his authority was not very effective. The planning and construction of the vast levee-system had to be done months and years in advance, and once the rain started falling, even a Czar was little more than a spectator.

In his office during each storm he collected data upon actual rainfall; he co-ordinated this with the Weather Bureau forecasts; he estimated the advance of the crests of various streams by reports of the readings of numerous river-gauges. From all these data he predicted the hour at which water would begin to spill over the various weirs, and the area which this water would cover. Then he sent out warnings. The broad lands of the by-passes pastured thousands of sheep and cattle; in some places certain crops could even be grown. At the General's word the sheep and cattle were hurriedly collected and driven to safe places; the roads across the by-pass lands were closed; men began to patrol the levees to guard against breaks and seepage; and all the river towns passed into what was almost a state of siege.

There was, moreover, one prerogative which the General jealously guarded. The city of Sacramento, state capital, population a hundred thousand, was—as the General often said—by far the most valuable piece of property in the whole Valley. It stood in the narrow angle between the American and Sacramento rivers, a ticklish place. And of all the tributaries, the American was quickest to rise, and most treacherous. Besides its levees, the chief protection to the city was Sacramento Weir, four miles up-stream. It was more than a third of a mile long, and of all the weirs it alone had gates. Only at the General's order could those gates be opened.

15

In the City, as if symbolic of a new regime, the great banners no longer flew from the high towers. Here and there some smaller flag rode out the storm—tossed and whipped in the south wind, its colors dulled and sodden.

Wisps of fast-driven scud swirled around the bare flag-poles, and lower—until the tops of the towers were dim in the cloud. By the clocks it was day, but lights shone from the windows. Stone-work was dark with wetness. Under the high archways of the portals people huddled, peering out for street-cars, signaling cabs.

Water spattered upon the sidewalks in rain-drops. Water ran in the gutters; it gurgled through the gratings of the storm drains; it dropped from awnings and cornices; it cascaded from broken drain-pipes.

Sleek wet asphalt reflected the glow of neon lights in long unreal lines of pink and blue. Drivers of cars leaned forward nervously, peering through the windshield-wipers. The professionals—truck- and taximen—sped along as nonchalantly as ever; their impudent wheels threw water from the puddles; pedestrians drew back, fearful or angry. Street-cars came along stolidly; from beneath their wheels little sprays of water flew sideways.

The flower-stands no longer glowed with sun-bright colors; the vendors did little business; they covered the blooms with water-proofs, and hoped for a better day.

Newsboys no longer pre-empted the best corners; now they withdrew toward sheltered spots and guarded their papers against the wet; when they made a sale, they quickly drew the folded paper out and handed it to the customer.

On the sidewalks fewer people moved along. They no longer strode boldly, heads up and confident faces, as they had a few days before, when the Pacific High ruled the air and the northwest wind swirled through the sun-lit city. Now in an environment suddenly grown half-aquatic, they scurried along, uncomfortable, in costumes only partly adapted to the rain. Men's hats, dripping water, lost symmetry and spruceness; below overcoats, trouser legs collapsed damply; shoes lost all trace of shine, or disappeared beneath clumsy rubbers. Pink, green, and blue, women's raincoats put up a brave front, but the color was infirm and chalky with no touch of gayety. And below the raincoats, shoes and clammy silk stockings were spattered and muddy. The very faces of men and women were hidden beneath umbrellas; as people passed at the corners, the umbrellas clicked and tangled.

And all the while, sprung of the forces of sun and earth, part of a vast system which covered the hemisphere, the south wind blew steadily. High above the wet sidewalks and the streaming gutters and the scurrying people, the hard-blown scud swirled about the towers and bare flag-poles; still higher was only the thick cloud-deck, and clean rain falling.

THE PLACE of man's birth is unknown; but in poetic dreams (as if dimly remembering) man yearns back toward some land benign and equable, far from the path of storms. Such was the Earthly Paradise. Such was Lotus-Land, and that far country of Those-beyond-the-North-Wind. Such was the Isle of Apples, Avalon:

> *Where falls not hail or rain or any snow,*
> *Nor ever wind blows loudly.*

Still, near the Tropics, such regions may be found; in milder epochs they spread far toward the Poles.

Even yet, man seems to carry with him mementoes of some idyllic past. In his mind a grasshopper, each summer he assumes that the ever-blooming tropics still surround him. Only by hard-won wisdom, not by racial aptitude, does he lay up for the future. The birds fly south without waiting for frost; the bear stores up fat to hibernate; the bee and the beaver hoard food. If such creatures had grave and reverend philosophers, they might teach more concern with the present, and less with

175

the future. But the average man always has difficulty in getting round to mend the roof in dry weather.

From the tropics also may stem man's dislike of the violent changes of the temperate zones. For (as the saying goes) the tropics have climate but no weather; they display a set diurnal or seasonal rhythm. In his deepest instincts man seems to expect such sameness, to resent sudden shifts. He has never learned that in mid-latitudes unusual weather is all he can expect. He always grumbles.

One belief of man's growth is that when as a proto-human he faced a more severe climate, he was forced to work harder and so survived and started on the road to civilization. But this negative theory fails to explain why man did not retreat to the tropics or else like other species merely die off after a few uncomfortable lingering generations.

Another theory of survival stresses weather instead of climate. When the gentle epoch ended and storms became many and violent, then those very storms—the shock of constant adjustment—stimulated man out of his tropical languor, and gave him power and will to outface a harsher world. With each storm and passing front, blood pressure rises and falls, nerves react, secretions alter. So physicians have learned, and they quote from Hippocrates, father of medicine: "Air is lord."

Some theorists say even that civilization can flourish only in the lands along the storm-track, where man most often feels the bracing shift from warm and moist to cold and dry, back and forth. For evidence, they point to Ptolemy's records, which seem to show that in their times of greatness the Mediterranean lands knew more turns of weather than now in these decadent days.

This marriage of civilization and storms has not been proved, or yet refuted. If it is true, then those atmospheric powers which seem to overwhelm men in the temperate zone, also stimulate the energy to live and conquer. Civilized men are like Napoleon's grenadiers—they always grumble, but they always march.

2

At Brownsville men weary from tending fires fell into bed, and slept the peaceful sleep of those released from fear; at Montemorelos the brown-skinned people no longer shivered upon their straw-mats. The still cold of the night was broken. The oranges were safe, and the fires might burn low. On this side the Río Grande and on the other, a softer air was moving from the Gulf. Whether women had prayed to the Son or called upon the dark Virgin, whether men had cursed or been silent, upon all the orange groves the gentler wind was blowing. On the coast of Texas and the coast of Tamaulipas, no matter the flags, it blew.

No longer did the stars glitter coldly in the cloudless sky and the heat drain off to outer space. Now, in the darkness before dawn, from Galveston Bay to Río Pánuco the overcast hung low; as the moist air blew across the cold land, long arms of fog moved up every valley.

Mile by mile the southern breeze pushed inland. Monterrey felt it, and Saltillo; it moved in the streets of Laredo. It came to San Antonio and Houston, to Austin and Waco. Reaching far to the north along Trinity River a finger of mist touched Dallas. And even farther, along the Red River and the Cimarron, men waking in the night knew that the power of the cold was breaking.

The teletype machines were clicking in wild confusion; Whitey was entering data. The Chief, sitting in his chair, was looking at the map upside down. Reading a notation here and there he already sensed the continued power of the storm.

As usual, it gave him a feeling of his own futility and insignificance. Even his forecast made little difference today; anybody could see the rain was going to keep up for a while. Usually he had a keen sense of interest in the men with whom he worked; he felt the importance of whether the J.M. was just a whippersnapper with a lot of crazy ideas out of books, or whether he had the makings of a good weather-man. But today the Chief did not even inquire about Whitey's sick wife. Personalities were important in fair weather; when a storm stretched from Sitka to San Diego, what happened to individuals seemed of little moment. The storm was so great that it monopolized his mind.

After he had drawn the map, he saw that the situation had changed remarkably little as far as the Pacific Coast was involved. The storm still centered off Cape Blanco. There was room for argument, the Chief knew, about how a storm could stay in one place, and even about whether it actually did. Some maintained that what looked like the same storm was in some way really a succession of storms, continually dying and being born. Others talked of waves along a stationary front. But as the Chief liked to say, if you're crossing a tropical river and something grabs your leg, you're not much concerned whether it's an alligator or a crocodile. From the practical point of view the storm was all one, although quite possibly it had as many parts as a centipede.

But what really interested the Chief that morning was a bulge eastward of the 1011 isobar, looping around Salt Lake City. It was not a prominent feature of the map, but to the Chief it was the indication that things were getting back to normal, that the ordinary movement of air from west to east was being re-established. It meant that some of the air from the Pacific storm had got across the mountains, and was about to form a secondary storm-center over Nevada or Utah. From there it would go east. Already air was moving up from the Gulf and warming Texas and Oklahoma.

In this plains region and farther east had come the greatest weather-shift of the last twenty-four hours. Over most of the Mississippi Valley the north wind had ceased blowing, and had left the weather cold, clear, and still. The center of the High forming the calm area had drifted slowly eastward from Kansas City to Terre Haute. Peoria reported eleven below zero. Farther east the temperatures were not so low, but the air was still pouring down from the Arctic. Crossing the Lakes this air picked up some moisture, enough to let loose snow flurries upon Buffalo, Cleveland and Detroit, and even as far south as Pittsburgh.

As the Chief decided finally, the restoration of more normal conditions would not proceed very rapidly. The storm off the coast still looked good for forty-eight hours of rain in California. But the bulging out eastward had already caused a breaking of the cold wave on the plains.

Then he checked himself, and shrugged his shoulders. "Hn-n?" He had merely yielded to that incurable human tendency to see things from your own point of view. Weather-men in the plains states would be saying that the flow of air from the south across the plains had caused the storm to bulge out eastward. Did one side of the scale go down because it was heavier, or did the other side go up because it was lighter? It all depended upon how you looked at the matter. The whole atmosphere was in exact balance; this particular problem had no solution. The more you thought about which caused what, the more you felt cause and effect to be nothing except words—convenient to use at times, but not really meaning much. The Chief wondered whether he would know more about it if he had taken courses in philosophy.

The same problem was involved in what was happening concurrently in South America, where an intensely heated tropical air-mass had moved down from the Amazon Valley. Superficially, one might have said that the great incursion of polar air, reaching clear to Panama, had disturbed the equilibrium and pushed the equatorial air southward. Equally well, one could say that the movement of the equatorial air had permitted the unusual southern push of the polar air. Both statements would have ignored the existence of an intensified circumpolar whirl over Antarctica, a willy-willy in Western Australia, and the weather elsewhere in the world.

But even a perfect solution of the problem would unfortunately have brought no comfort to the sweltering people of Uruguay and Argentina. While Chicago newsboys were crying, "Six die of cold!" twenty-two persons were treated for heat-prostration in Buenos Aires, and a man dropped dead in the Plaza Belgrano.

3

Upon the Sierra each tree after its kind withstood the storm. The aspens that bordered the high meadows, the alders and the willows along the streams—these had flared with autumnal yellow, and now raised against the winter storm only bare branches, skeletons upon which the snow found small lodgment.

The fir trees rose in tapering pointed cones. Their broad thick-set needles held the flakes, until the trees grew solid white. So perfect was their cover that around each trunk, beneath the shelter of down-sloping branches, was a cup in the snow, a refuge for the hard-pressed grouse and rabbits where sometimes even bare ground was showing. Beneath their loads the fir trees stood stiffly—like Puritans, prim and uncompromising—saying between tight-drawn lips, "We shall not bend, though we break." And often they broke; the over-strained trunk, brittle in the cold, snapped like a match, and the tree lay in ruin.

Not so were the cedars. They bent easily and pliantly beneath the weight, until at last they sloughed off the snow and again stood upright.

Still different were the yellow pines. Their slender, thinly set needles let the snow slip through. On the wind-ward side a sheathing built up on the scaly-barked trunks; white ridges lay upon the big horizontal branches of the crown. Otherwise, the trees looked almost as dark and green as in summer.

More like the cedars were the lodge-pole pines, which the people of the Sierra call tamaracks. These flourished only at the highest levels and must survive the full force of every storm. Each smaller tree caught the snow as thickly as a fir; then just as the weight was about to become crushing, the whole tree seemed to shake itself violently, and after a moment it emerged from the cloud of falling snow, again upright with only a powdering of crystals upon its needles. The mature lodge-poles cleared themselves branch by branch, loosing a few bushels of snow to drop upon the drifts beneath; in heavy stands one heard constantly the long *shu-u-sh* of falling snow.

Most curious of all were the lodge-poles which stood twenty or thirty feet in height. As the snow-load built up, these formed the curious shapes like the sheeted dead and known as snow-ghosts. Inch by inch the white columns bent over until they leaned one against another in weird confusion. And those growing alone arched farther and farther. They did not break, but to some of them the weight clung too tightly, and they never straightened. Spring and the melting snow found these stretched along the ground in wild contortions, still growing strongly. But most of the snow-ghosts, though they arched clear over and touched the ground, in the end shook off the snow and stood again upright. For upon the Sierra the lodge-pole grows highest of trees; to live at all it must live vigorously; timber-line is only the frontier which the lodge-pole, ever yielding and ever up-springing, holds against the power of the storms sweeping in from the far Pacific.

4

Neither Max nor Jen had turned up for work at nine o'clock. Through the hours of that morning an undercurrent of speculation eddied back and forth. In the office where Max worked, two typists exchanged ideas hurriedly.

"I tell you, they got married."

"Yeh, don't you know they got a three-day law in California?"

"But maybe they got married in Carson or Verdi—'fore they ever left Nevada."

"I'll bet they picked up a couple of swell jobs somewhere, and are just givin' us the ha-ha."

In the restaurant where Jen worked, the proprietress was in the cashier's booth.

"Where's Jen?" said a regular customer.

"Oh, she's off for a few days," bluffed the proprietress.

Jen's roommate who worked at the candy counter was worried, and sniveled secretly into her handkerchief. She was glad she remembered the name of Jen's sister in San Francisco. At nine o'clock not twenty-five people had known anything. By noon the knowledge had spread to a hundred. Through the lunch hour, as people mingled and relaxed and fell into talk, the story radiated out until possibly a thousand people knew some vague version, and the diverging chains of gossip began to meet.

"You know a guy named Arnim? Well, anyway, he's disappeared—him and a girl."

"Oh, him? Sure, I heard about him. Only, what I heard was . . ."

Neither Max nor Jen had any family in Reno. People liked to talk, but nobody wanted to stick his finger into what might be after all just some other person's very private business—live and let live. In the restaurant the waitresses began to whisper together, and Jen's roommate felt they were looking at her. She broke down openly into a sudden fit of crying, and the proprietress just about snapped the heads off a couple of the girls.

But when hundreds of people know something, the story must by the law of averages soon reach a person who will act instead of talk. This happened when someone passed the time of day with a policeman named McNenery.

"D'ya hear about this Arnim fellow?"

The citizen who passed on this information leaned to the prevalent romantic theory that the missing pair (like Tristram and Iseult having drunken of the potion) had suddenly looked into each other's eyes, and counted the world well lost for love. But fifteen years on the force had destroyed McNenery's illusions, and left him correspondingly clear-headed. In his world people did not endanger good jobs to go to bed, not when they could keep the jobs and go to bed anyway.

McNenery looked at the sky, which was thickly overcast. There were several inches of snow on the streets, and snow was falling thinly. McNenery suddenly talked about the weather.

"She's raining a lot harder than this on the other side, and snowing plenty on the Hump. The mountains squeeze all the juice out of a storm before it ever gets to Nevada. It's a long road back from Frisco."

Then he called headquarters to find out whether anything had come in from the California Highway Patrol. There was nothing. He made no report to Headquarters, but went around to the restaurant and dropped in, as if about nothing of importance. But the entrance of his uniform seemed to make electrical connections all over the establishment; even the dish-washers came peering out.

McNenery talked with the proprietress, who called over Jen's roommate, who again went into tears.

"I think you ought to call that sister in San Francisco," said McNenery gently. "Tell her something—you and Jen had a date, and you wanted to check up when she'd be back."

The roommate hesitated.

"I'll pay the tolls," snapped the proprietress, who saw the restaurant demoralized until the matter was settled.

The roommate went to the booth, and called long distance.

A light glowed on the Reno long-distance board. The operator plugged one of the San Francisco lines. More quickly than the mind of man conceives, the impulses ran along two hundred miles of circuit—through wires over the pass loaded to the breaking point with snow, through wires in the Valley dripping with rain, through the cables beneath the Bay. A light glowed on the great San Francisco board; an operator plugged the local exchange, and at that board another operator plugged the proper number. A bell rang in the house of Jen's sister.

Dot was washing the lunch dishes. "Drat it!" she said mildly, and went to the phone.

Jen's roommate came from the telephone booth weeping hysterically. Everybody crowded around—patrons who were still eating their lunches, even the dishwashers.

"They left her house Sunday night, and were going to drive right straight here. . . . She just went right off the handle because I hadn't called her sooner. . . . She's calling the police right now."

5

The old coyote who ranged the summit of Donner Pass found the storm scarcely even an inconvenience. At the first warnings he had withdrawn to a rocky ledge on the lee side of Donner Peak. In a deep crevice he was comfortably protected from wind and snow; his winter coat was thick and warm; from the innermost recesses of the rocks a little ground water dripped continually and he could lick up what he wanted before it froze. He spent forty-eight hours, mostly in sleeping. Then he was hungry.

He floundered heavily in the deep snow, but had little difficulty in working down the steep face of the mountain-side. When he came to the railroad track, he smelled the wind cautiously. But he was used to the works of man, and like a trout inhabiting an irrigation ditch, he made use of them for his own ends. He trotted along the cleared track until he came to a point near a thick stand of fir. He hunted patiently and methodically, and soon was crunching the bones of a big rabbit. His meal finished, he needed water.

Though it was broad daylight, the thickly flying snow gave him cover, and he moved boldly. He came to the highway, trotted along it easily for a short distance, and then scrambled rapidly over the snow-wall as he heard a car approaching.

Close under the cliffs below the point at which the highway crossed the summit, he paused and sniffed suspiciously. The air was carrying a smell which he did not expect at this place. The smell was a mingled one. Some of the suggestions were alarming. Others were pleasant, as of meat and eating. He sniffed about in the snow for a few moments, and then went on. The association of the odors and the place was recorded in his excellent memory for possible future investigation.

6

During ten years of work for the telephone company Rick had climbed more poles than anybody could count in a blue moon. He had climbed them by day and by night, in rain, in snow, in sleet, in fog so thick that from the ground you could hardly see the cross-arms; he had climbed them in blazing summer suns which made your head swim, in September northers which filled your eyes with dust, in the smoke of forest fires which half-strangled you. He felt that he knew about climbing poles, anywhere, any time. Climbing a pole was no more to him than going upstairs was to other people.

On this day he kept at it, working alone. Where the wires were farther from the highway, linemen had to work in pairs for safety, but in this section the lead was everywhere close to the highway, usually within sight of it. Rick was glad today that he could work alone; it gave him more chance to think of the girl.

Lower down in the foothills the snow was sticky, and several crews were busy on the local lines. But on the transcontinental there had been only sniping trouble—here a wire, there a wire.

When he saw this particular break, Rick halted the truck and parked it as usual. The snow-wall was high and clean-cut, for recently a rotary plow had passed by. Down around the first curve he could see it throwing its curve of snow out among the pine trees.

There was a hundred-yard stretch of rough going to the pole. When he got there, he saw that the broken wire was from the lowest cross-arm, and would be an easy job. He was glad, for he was thinking of that girl—maybe the next time he got a chance he would telephone her for a date, and the sooner he fixed this wire the sooner he could do it.

The pole stood in a rather open spot in the forest, but near it was a young lodge-pole pine about thirty feet tall and bending over heavily with snow. If it had been bigger, the maintenance-men would have felled it; but they had not bothered with this tree, for even though it should be blown down or bend clear over because of the snow-load, it would be too short to touch the wires and too small to damage a pole.

Rick finished his work on the ground, and made ready to ascend. He stuck his ski-poles into the snow. As he did so, a thought of the girl came to his mind; he did not thrust one of the poles quite hard enough; it leaned over so that its top touched against the top of the other.

In a sudden flurry the snow came more thickly in great flakes. The near-by tree loaded more heavily and bent over still farther. The wind blew it back and forth a little, but from some trick of its own growth it leaned into the wind and in the direction of the telephone pole.

Rick climbed up to the cross-arm, snapped on his safety-belt, and started working.

The tree, weighted beyond its strength, leaned farther and farther.

Rick worked on. Above him passed the forty wires of the Central Transcontinental Lead—a miracle of engineering. Each of those pairs of wires could carry many voices at the same time, and yet unscramble them perfectly at the end. Booming voices put through deals and shouted orders. Anxious voices inquired about the operation or the accident. Triumphant voices called for congratulations, and sorrowful voices passed into sobs.

To Rick upon the pole, the wire was only something to be mended. He attached his little block-and-tackle. The tree leaned still lower, almost brushing the pole.

Voices coursed along the wires in English of a half dozen different intonations, in Dutch, Japanese, German, Spanish, and Greek. An Assistant Secretary of State was talking to the Minister to Thailand. Teletype circuits were being operated; cable messages were going through in code; a symphony orchestra was playing for a radio network.

Rick was just attaching the wire to the insulator. Below him, the tip of the tree settled noiselessly against the pole.

The Minister to Thailand was taken with a fit of coughing, and two faithful wires just above Rick's head transmitted half way around the world the senseless spasms of his mid-riff equally as well as they had his keenest comments upon the international situation.

Rick finished his work, and rested a moment. He shook the snow off his coat, and brushed it from his eyebrows. He was warm from his work, and unbuttoned his coat. He did not glance down the pole, and see that the tip of the tree rested lightly against it a few feet below him. The thought of the girl with blue eyes and dark-tanned face was in his mind; he felt in some way touched with nobility; for the moment he was again absent-minded. Upon the pole on the mountain-side with the falling snow thick about him in all directions, beneath the wires which reached to all corners of the world, he was wholly alone.

He unsnapped his safety-belt and started down, his coat blowing loosely about him. At its second stroke the climbing-iron on his right foot pierced deceptively the top twig of the leaning tree, and through it barely nicked the pole itself. As Rick shifted his weight to that leg, the climbing-iron cut loose; and he fell sprawling through the air.

He whirled round as he fell, his coat flew open; with no protection but his shirt and underwear he lit squarely with the middle of his body upon the tops of his two ski-poles. One pole might have given way, or been pushed into the soft snow, but the two poles together thrust stiffly against his diaphragm, just below his heart.

The tree, jarred by his fall, released its load, and sprang upright. Snow scattered upon Rick where he lay.

In a moment he came to, without realizing that he had been unconscious. "Must have knocked the wind out of me," he thought, afraid to admit anything worse. The great numbness around the base of his chest frightened him.

Rick was mountain-bred, a fighter. He managed to get himself from the hole which he had made when he fell; he wormed along inch by inch to his skis, but when he reached them, he could not get to his feet and put them on. He decided to lie upon them and use them as a sled. Before he could get himself placed, he was growing numb; he thought that he should have eaten more heavily before coming out on this job.

Overhead were passing the strains of the orchestra playing Beethoven's *Third Symphony*. "This connection is rotten," said a man in Pocatello angrily to a man in Fresno. A teletype circuit was recording an unsettled market in Chicago caused by nervousness as to the crop-effect of the cold wave which was sweeping the wheat belt.

Rick slid down the first little slope. "It's easy!" he thought for one joyous moment. Then he plunged head-on into the tangle of a cedar tree. He found himself so stiff that he could not possibly turn himself around and crawl out. He began doggedly to back himself out feet first, squirming, inch by inch. Then he realized that his circulation was not working as it should; he thought fearfully that there must be a great bruise close to his heart; he was cold. The pain of the squirming motion was intense. Nevertheless he worked himself back until his head was free, and then he felt himself growing dizzy and faint. He realized that he must rest for a minute. It was an extreme pleasure to stop struggling and lie still.

Down on the highway the little green truck was already so plastered with snow that a man driving along the highway could hardly distinguish it from a drift.

7

On the rocky ledge the rotting bole of the cedar tree was settling by minute gradations, but steadily. The direction of the storm was such that snow piled up on top of the bole, and was swept out from beneath it. This distribution increased the tendency toward rotation instead of mere settling, as the rotten fibers yielded under increasing weight. By infinitesmal fractions of an inch the center of gravity moved forward.

Blue Boy, the big boar, did not mind the rain. His fat kept him warm, and as a natural wallower in swamps and marshes he was adjusted to water. As the ground softened, he rooted after what he could find. This occupation was chiefly a pastime, for there were still plenty of acorns lying about. As he worked back and forth along the steep hillside, he saw with incurious eyes the trains passing along the double-tracked railroad below him—heavy freights, swiftly moving expresses, the shiny streamliner. When the downpour became uncomfortably heavy and the wind was high, Blue Boy withdrew for shelter to the thick covert of a low-growing live-oak.

The bullet which "Dirty Ed" had shot at the switch-box had pierced a little hole in the metal, pinged against the other wall, and then fallen to rest on the bottom of the box. The electrical connections had suffered no damage.

The switch-box controlled the power for Underpass 342-2 by which U. S. Highway 101 went beneath a railroad. The underpass was in flat country close to the Bay, and could not drain by natural flow. During heavy rains much water ran down the slope of the highway on either side, and collected in a sump at the bottom of the underpass. In the sump was a float; when the rising water had lifted this float to the proper point, switches were automatically tripped, a motor started with a whir, and a pump began to work. If the water-level rose still higher,

a second pump started. One pump could keep the underpass clear of water in any ordinary rain; the second supplied an ample reserve of capacity for even the heaviest
cloudburst.

The construction was similar to that used in hundreds
of underpasses so situated that they could not drain by
gravity. Accident, of course, was possible, as with all works
of man. But the maintenance gangs inspected the working
of the underpass when a storm was expected, and frequently during the storm. The results were so nearly perfect that every day thousands of drivers dipped into the
slope of the underpass and steered around its curve without ever thinking that this stretch of the road was at all
different from any other.

8

Station KPDS calling all cars of the State Highway Patrol.
Car, driver, and passenger reported missing. License—
Nevada, seven, seven, one, two, four. *Repeat:* License—
Nevada, seven, seven, one, two, four. Details of description
will be broadcast later. That is all. . . .

(From the *Register*)
RENO PAIR MISSING
Left Here Sunday
Evening: Fail
to Arrive.

EXTRY! EXTRY!! EXTRY!!! This is Ye Old Time
Newsy, folks. . . . And now here's an item that's not so
good. "Max Arnim, 30, and Jane Stongliff, 24, both of
Reno, left San Francisco on. . . ."

A million people read it in the headlines. A million heard it by news broadcasts. Amateur detectives and boys playing G-man picked up the police broadcasts.

"Say, y'see the headline there! I used to know that guy Arnim, went to high school with him. What you know about that!"

"Maybe it was that nice young couple I served coffee and doughnuts to Sunday night. I remember thinking about them at the time—had a kind of funny feeling. I didn't see the car, but maybe it was Nevada."

"Wish to hell I could remember the number of that Nevada car I serviced. It was Nevada all right, and it had some sevens. I always notice sevens."

9

The airport lights came on, and the Chief Service Officer saw the sudden long lines of reflection cast from wet asphalt and shallow puddles. He had worked through a hard day, and it was time to be laying off. The planes had been kept going, except when low ceilings and turbulence over the Siskiyous grew too bad about midday and he cancelled the 12:30 for Seattle; the situation looked better now, and probably the seven o'clock could go north; that would be up to the dispatcher on the night shift. The planes did not have to stop for much weather, these days. Staunch and powerful, they could bore through any except the very worst fronts.

He watched the big transcontinental leave for Salt Lake City. He himself had worked out the course of the flight.

The pilot would climb steadily until, when he turned to the path of the Reno beam above Blue Canyon, he would be at thirteen thousand feet and above the level at which icing was likely. He would keep at that level until he crossed the summit, and then he could drop down to Reno. Reno reported ceiling at two thousand. If by any chance Reno should be buttoned up before the pilot got there, he had plenty of reserve fuel to take him on to Elko, which reported only scattered clouds and a northeast wind. There was no guess-work involved. Most likely, however, this flight would be held up at Salt Lake City. All through the day fog had been creeping northward across the plains. Dallas had been buttoned up tight since early morning. Amarillo, Oklahoma City, Wichita, Denver, North Platte—one by one they had gone under. Cheyenne and Omaha would be next. But as far as Salt Lake City everything was safe, and beyond that point was out of his own territory and responsibility.

10

Red and green, half obscured by flying snow, the blocklights gleamed above the railroad tracks. A rotary was just starting out of the Norden sheds. When it had gained a sufficient head-start, a faster-moving flanger would follow it. The rotary would pull into a siding at Emigrant Gap, and a few minutes later the flanger would pull in behind it. This would leave the track clear of equipment and freshly plowed so that the Limited from Chicago would go through without a stop. Everything was closely timed. The Limited would have passed Norden and be halfway to the Gap before the flanger was switched off the main track.

Compared with the compact little rotaries which cleared the highway, the steam rotary was ponderous. Instead of merely an operator and a swamper, it carried a crew of nine. In the compartment just behind the rotating blades were the conductor, the operator, a brakeman, and an oiler. In the boiler-room were an engineer and a fireman. Behind the plow to push it forward was a locomotive, and in it an engineer, a fireman, and a brakeman.

The four men in the front compartment really operated the plow, and no one envied them their jobs. The conductor spent most of his time leaning out the side-door into the storm, trying to see what was happening. The operator and the brakeman crouched uncomfortably upon a raised seat trying to see through little windows usually obscured by the snow which the plow itself cast into the air; they strained to see even whether the lights were green or red. The oiler moved about with his rags and cans, inspecting the bearings.

From the heat of the boiler just behind, the compartment was steamy and hot; oil fumes made the air heavy and sickening. But occasionally an icy jet of outside air swept through the compartment, and fine powdered snow covered the beads of sweat which stood on the men's faces. As it cut into the drifts the plow bucked and vibrated. The great wheel bearing the cutting-blades revolved at high speed; it roared and pounded. Every man in the compartment knew that he was engaged in about as dangerous work as railroading affords. With so much ice and snow on the tracks derailment was always likely. And in the event of any collision, they would be caught behind the fan and rammed back into the steam of the boiler just behind them. All in all, the compartment was about as uncomfortable a place as could be found—heat and cold, bad air, racking vibration, dinning noise, and the threat of sudden death.

Clumsy as it was, the rotary made a good job of throwing snow. On one side a vane scooped in the wall of snow which the flangers had left standing between the two tracks. On the other side a vane bit deeply into the high ridge which the flangers had built up. After the rotary had passed, there was four feet clear along the outside of the track. But the rotary did not clean the snow from between the rails, and so a flanger had to follow before the Limited could speed through safely.

In a great parabola the spout of snow rose from the rotary, cleared the ridge of snow, and fell far across the mountain-side. Striking the telegraph wires it knocked the snow from them, and set them wildly vibrating. Striking the small pine trees it threw them into a sudden agonized tossing of branches. It tore off dead limbs and sent them flying through the air.

In the compartment the operator and the brakeman leaned forward, looking for the light which they knew must be close at hand.

"Green," said the operator.

"Green," said the brakeman, confirming.

The plow moved on.

11

The long process of soaking up was completed; the earth was satisfied. Streams ran in the gullies; the rivers were rising.

Before leaving his office at six o'clock the General checked over the situation. Snow was falling at the twenty-five-hundred-foot level and above; accordingly there would be a negligible run-off from the higher mountains. On his desk, neatly codified, were hourly reports of river depths at the gauging stations on the Sacramento and its tributaries. All of them recorded the rivers rising, but slowly. The prospect, as reported by the Weather Bureau, was for more rain.

The General walked the length of his office twice, and then dictated a brief forecast:

A general rise is developing in all streams, and with continued rain higher stages will result in the Sacramento River and its tributaries. Within the next twelve to twenty-four hours water will begin to flow over Moulton, Colusa, Tisdale, and Fremont Weirs and to pass through the lower parts of Sutter and Yolo By-passes.

12

On the east slope by the gates at Donner Lake, on the west slope just below Emigrant Gap, the chain warnings were posted. In front of them were burning the flares, smoky oil-flames, hard-whipped by the wind, flickering from the top of squat iron balls, like witches' fires. The wording of the sign was educational rather then mandatory:

STOP
MOTORISTS PUT ON YOUR CHAINS.
WITHOUT CHAINS YOU ENDANGER
YOUR OWN LIFE AS WELL AS OTHERS.

In spite of the signs numerous motorists drove on without heeding. "Ah, y'don't need chains," some argued. "The Highway Commission is in cahoots with the garages; they want you to stop and pay four bits to get your chains put on, and maybe have to buy the chains too." Egotists went ahead, trusting to their own presumed skill as drivers. Optimists assumed that the other fellow would get into trouble. Gamblers enjoyed taking a chance. Plain fools considered that man and his works were superior to the storm. About one car in five on this particular evening went ahead without chains.

At the Maintenance Station the day-shift was finishing dinner. Food came to the table on heaped platters—steaks, boiled potatoes, canned corn, tomatoes, and spinach, hot biscuits, coffee in gallon pots, stewed apricots and cake. After a hard day the men were tired. Their arms and body muscles were dull from long wrestling with the steering-wheels; their eyes were blood-shot and their eyelids snappy from the long effort to see through the snow-storm.

The Superintendent ate with them. He was tired too, and ready to drop into bed at the first chance. He had driven back and forth along the road that day more times than he could remember; he had jumped from the car, waded through snow, shouted orders. But most of all what wore him was the sense of a pressing-down responsibility; even as he ate, he could feel the traffic going through his own mind. Cars, trucks, and buses—hundreds of them—converged from dozens of valley roads toward the snow-clogged bottleneck which was the Pass. Just as the roads converged so did the responsibility; first upon his plows and his men, then upon the foremen, then upon the Superintendent himself. As long as he could hold the road, throwing the snow off as fast as it fell, then he was master of the situation. But if ever the road was blocked and the traffic snarled up and the work of the plows impeded, then the drifts would build up, he might lose the road, and the process of getting it opened again might take hours or even days.

A mark of the difference between the Superintendent and his men was that the men had thrown off their heavy working-outfits and had settled in for the night; their wet clothes already steamed in the drying-room. But the Superintendent still wore his boots; while the storm lasted, he was never really off-shift.

When he finished eating, he went wearily down through the covered passage-way into the garage, wondering what would happen next. The garage was warm, and water was dripping from a snow-covered rotary which had pulled in for minor adjustments. But at the wide doorway, the wind whistled, and the Superintendent buttoned up his short coat as he stood looking out.

Darkness had fallen and the storm was thick. It looked like a bad night. A heavily pounding truck came up-grade from the west; a car with yellow lights followed it at an interval—then another car, and after some minutes another. Smoking his cigarette, the Superintendent was vaguely conscious of something not just right, but he could not yet analyze his feeling. Another car came up the grade from the west, then another—and the Superintendent's vague feeling crystallized in thought. No cars had come from the *east!*

He looked at his cigarette. It was down to the butt, and he threw it from him into the storm. Moreover, he had been standing there a little while before lighting the cigarette. In that time no car had passed from the east. But in the same time a half dozen had passed from the west and here came two more. It might be a coincidence, and also it might be a traffic-block on the eastern slope of the Pass. He called to the garage-foreman where he was going, jumped into his car, and drove out from the calm of the garage into the blinding confusion of the storm.

In spite of the constant work of the plows, little drifts of snow lay across the road; the tire-tracks of the cars which had just passed were half obliterated. Even an expert like the Superintendent could not make speed on a night like this, no matter how great the emergency. He swung around the curve of the bridge, still meeting no car from the east. Then just as he was nearing Windy Point, he came to the first of the parked cars.

They were all on the right-hand side of the road, but farther ahead there must be a block. The Superintendent pulled up behind the last car, and jumped out. If anyone, he thought, ever needed to be three or four people at once, he at that moment was it. He ran down beside the line of cars, clicking off in his mind the things to be done and the order of their doing. Save life; see what's the matter; keep it from getting worse; straighten it out; get the road open.

As he ran, he mapped out the situation. Windy Point— the road swung around a steep out-jutting of granite. On the outside of the curve a cliff fell away. And the Point was named because from some trick of topography a re-doubled wind swirled about it. Elsewhere the storm might ease off, but at Windy Point there was always a blizzard; if no snow was falling, the wind picked it off the ground and blew it through the air.

Ahead on the curve the Superintendent saw the moving beam of a flashlight. "There's where the block is!" he thought. Then, just as he most wanted to rush forward, he dug his hob-nails into the snow, and turned to a car he was just passing. He pounded vigorously on the closed window-glass; he could feel the throb of the engine.

The window-glass lowered two inches and a blankly wondering pair of eyes stared out.

"Open your windows or shut off your engine," shouted the Superintendent without ceremony. "Want to suffocate to death with gas-fumes?"

He saw the look of sudden consternation come into the eyes, and then he ran on. "Idiots!" he thought, "Closing all the windows and then running the engine to keep warm!"

Now both lanes were full of halted cars pointed down hill. The reckless and over-confident drivers had tried to pass the cars ahead, and now the road was blocked solidly. The Superintendent raged within himself at the stupidity of man.

The flashlight was in the hands of a truck-driver whose big truck had slewed around, blocking both lanes. The Superintendent knew that no professional truck-driver would have got into such a jam by himself; so without pausing he climbed around the truck's bumper, and saw two cars stalled just beyond it. They were at crazy angles to the road, and one of them had a half-crushed fender. A man in a long city overcoat and a soft felt hat covered with snow was scraping away ineffectively with a jack-handle behind one of the cars, trying to put on chains.

The Superintendent grabbed him by the shoulder. "Anybody hurt here?"

The man, frightened and shaken, yielded to the voice of authority without questioning.

"Nobody hurt. That truck—"

"Never mind the truck. You ran past tire-chain warnings yourself."

But it was no time to argue. Knowing now that nobody needed first-aid, the Superintendent scrambled back across the truck, and grabbed the truck-driver.

"Hey, Jack," he said, "I'm road-superintendent here. Take that flashlight and go back and flag all the cars coming down grade. Don't let 'em block the left-hand lane any more than it is already."

"O.K., boss."

The Superintendent was thankful again for truck-drivers; they knew there was more to driving a car than just sitting behind the wheel. Just then a big deep voice spoke out at the Superintendent's ear.

"Anything I can do, officer?"

The Superintendent overlooked being mistaken for a snow-covered highway patrolman. The man who spoke was in a city overcoat and a felt hat, much like the man who was trying to dig his car out with the jack-handle. But he was different. The Superintendent recognized his type at once. Most drivers of private cars were idiots in an emergency, but now and then one kept his head. Sometimes a man like that, wearing good clothes, would straighten out a jam on his own initiative; people would take advice from him when they wouldn't from a truck-driver.

"Sure you can help," said the Superintendent. "See if those cars in the left-hand lane can back up. If they can, help 'em do it, and we'll get one lane clear above the block."

The Superintendent climbed back across the truck

again, and went past the man who was still digging in the snow with the jack-handle. Below the block, things looked the same as on the upper side—cars jammed thick into both lanes—big cars and little, old and new, a jalopy with a broken window plugged with a quilt. Already wind-shields were plastered over, and snow was drifting be-tween the cars. Enough headlights were still burning to throw a yellow glare over everything.

On a half-run, as fast as he could go, the Superintendent hurried along between the two files of cars. He glanced right and left as he ran. From windows lowered just a few inches he saw one pair of eyes after another staring out stupidly, looking a little perturbed but just waiting for somebody else to straighten things out. Yet as he hurried on, he met two men bending forward into the gale, plug-ging through the storm, ahead. The Superintendent felt a quick warmth within him; those snow-covered figures let him know that Americans weren't all soft with civili-zation; some of them still piled out into the gale and the snow, and marched to the front, to see if anything could be done—and do it. The blood of the frontiersmen hadn't yet gone altogether thin.

Again he had to stop to warn people about closed win-dows. But the next time he stopped, it was because the door of a car was standing open. He looked in—nobody there. He thought of the two men he had met, but they would have shut their doors to keep the snow out. And there—of all things—were some gloves lying on the front seat, a woman's gloves!

He hurried to the next car, and beat on the window-glass. Another pair of stupidly wondering eyes looked out at him.

"What happened to that woman in the car ahead?" shouted the Superintendent.

"Her?" came the word from an invisible mouth below the level of the glass. "She and the old man was with her —they started t'walk down the road. She yelled in—said we was all goin' t' get buried in by the snow and froze. Just like somebody named Donner, she said. Think we'd better start walkin' out like she said?"

"God's sake, no! When did they leave?"

"Oh, maybe five minutes."

The Superintendent really ran now. Five minutes! But a hysterical woman and an old man could not move very fast. Crazy! There ought to be a law against books about the Donner Party; but he had known it to happen even when people had never heard of the Donners.

At the end of the line another car was pulling in. The Superintendent yelled through at the driver: "See a man and woman down this road, walking?"

"Yes. We wondered—"

The Superintendent opened the door without asking leave.

"Slide over," he said, "and give me the wheel. You got chains on?"

"Yes."

"Don't argue then."

The Superintendent flipped the wheels to the left, and drove the front bumper into the snow-wall. He reversed, spinning the steering-wheel. He felt the back tires slip, but the chains bit and held her. He flung her into low again, steered left, just grazed the snow-wall with the bumper and was off—downgrade.

"How far away did you pass those people?"

"Gee, I don't know," said the man. "Quite a way."

"Just the other side of the big bend," said the woman who was sitting crowded against the other door.

"Thanks." It was funny; sometimes a woman had better sense about such things than a man did.

It was a fine big car; he put it into second and went down around the Horseshoe as fast as he dared; and that was about twice as fast as any ordinary driver would dare. Out of his eye-corner he saw that the man beside him was scared, pea-green.

He met a car going up; it was a knife in his ribs to think that another car was going up there to add to the clutter, but he had to see to this other matter first, even if it lost him the road. In theory the Highway Patrol handled traffic and people, while he took care of the snow. But there might not be an officer within ten miles, and so he had to look after everything, all at once.

He slowed down. "Keep a look-out on the other side for those two people, will you, please?" he said to the woman. She lowered the window a little. The snow came with a blast in her face, but she kept looking. She was a good one.

The Superintendent was thinking fast. There must be a rotary working close to here. He would stop and see if the operator had seen these people walking, and they could set their radio working to bring up help. Perhaps, he kept hoping, one of the men who had enough courage to get out into the storm would also have the sense to start flagging cars and keep them from piling into the jam on the lower side.

Then he saw them—two figures scurrying awkwardly to the side of the road as the car-lights hit them. He threw on the brakes.

"I'll have to bring them into your car."

He was afraid that the woman might be hysterical, but ten minutes in the storm had taken the fight out of her. She was middle-aged, and the man must be close to sixty. They were a miserable-looking pair, plastered with snow, not too warmly dressed. The woman's gloveless hands were blue with cold already. And it was five miles down the Pass before the first house.

He bundled them into the back seat of the big car. The woman in front gave them a steamer-rug. The Superintendent climbed in again behind the wheel, and started again downgrade toward where the rotary must be working. He had saved life; now he must get his road open. He spoke quickly and quietly to the man beside him.

"Look here. Confidentially, that jam up there won't be cleared for a little while. Why don't you go down and wait at the bottom of the Pass? There's a joint there where you can keep warm and get some coffee, and our friends," he jerked his head toward the back-seat, "need some. Might save a case of pneumonia. I'll have their car brought up to the Maintenance Station, and you can drop them there."

"Sure, we'll do that," said the woman next the window.

Then he saw the lights of the rotary, and stopped.

"Thanks, folks," he said to the people who owned the car, and jumped out without ever explaining who he was.

He crawled into the cab of the rotary, and gave orders fast. "Raise the plow, boys, and take me up the road as fast as you can. We're all needed."

Then he pulled the handle that elevated the aerial, and turned the current on, to warm up the tubes. The forty-five seconds they took seemed a long time tonight.

Usually it was a little like playing house, to have a rotary fully equipped as a radio sending-station, registered and everything, with its own call-number. But tonight it was all serious. Twenty seconds. Half a minute.

The swamper was working his levers hard, getting augers raised; the operator was backing the plow away from the snow-wall. Forty-five seconds—and there was life in the tubes.

"KRDM-4 calling KRDO-1; KRDM-4 calling KRDO-1."

Already the operator was taking the plow upgrade as fast as he could push it. Then the Maintenance Station answered back through the storm. The Superintendent gave orders to the night-foreman.

"Halt all east-bound cars at the summit—quick! Telephone to halt all west-bound cars at the gates. Contact the Highway Patrol and tell them there's a block at Windy Point. Send two of our men down there right away to handle traffic—pull them off the day-shift if you have to. And send down a push-plow besides."

They were back at the parked cars. The Superintendent set another truck-driver with a flashlight to flag up-coming traffic. He put the operator of the rotary to work going along the line of cars assuring people that there was no danger and making certain nobody was killing himself with carbon-monoxide fumes. The swamper began clearing the left-hand lane below the block; that was comparatively easy, because you can usually back a car down-hill even in snow, but you may have a hard time backing it up-hill.

At the actual block the situation was better. The left-hand lane on the upper side had been cleared. Then the truck-drivers had got together—the way they always did —to help the truck that was in trouble. They had brought forward another truck and got a chain from it to the one which was slewed across the road. There was not much room to maneuver, and the darkness and flying snow impeded the work and slowed it down. Still, they were moving the stalled truck a foot at a time, and would have it out of the jam and back on the road in a few minutes. Working with the truck-drivers and really directing the show was the man with the city overcoat who had volunteered to help; but he was so covered with snow that now you couldn't have told what he was wearing.

The Superintendent took charge, but there was nothing much more for him to do. Thank God for truck-drivers! It's the professionals that keep going in time of trouble. But the man in the city overcoat and the others who had come up to help were all right too.

As soon as the left-hand lane was cleared below the block, the truck-drivers and some others got their shoulders at one of the stalled cars and pushed it out of the snow-bank. It was without chains, of course, and its driver had lost his nerve; the man in the city overcoat backed it down-hill a few yards, out of the way.

The other stalled car belonged to the man who had been digging in the snow with his jack-handle; he had not managed to get even one chain on. But the trouble was that he had been trying to go forward up-grade, and all the while he could have eased his car, crumpled fender and all, down-grade without much difficulty, and got it to some easy spot where he could have got started forward again without chains. With a few directions that was exactly what he did, and once he got going he went right on.

without even a thank-you, up the cleared lane above the block, and around the curve out of sight, right on for wherever he was going. He even left his jack-handle lying in the snow. The truck-drivers were so mad they could have lynched him, but the Superintendent thought it was good riddance. You could hear the car-horns from above tooting in triumph because one car had gone through, and the people knew the block must be breaking.

Next the Superintendent got rid of the east-bound cars. They were all pointed down-grade, and so had no trouble to get going. The man with the city overcoat drove away in one of them, but before he got into his car, he asked the Superintendent if there was anything more he could do.

The west-bound cars were harder. The snow had blown in around them, and they had to get started against a heavy grade. It meant a good deal of backing and wallowing and unscrambling, and the drivers were nervous because they couldn't see much. Those with chains had no real difficulty, but the others slipped about and spun their tires. All of these drivers were liable for tickets, because they had ignored the sign to put on their chains. The Superintendent told them so for a warning, but he was more interested in getting them off the road than in holding them until the Highway Patrol got there to give tickets. One by one the chainless cars were backed up until they got to a place where the snow was hard enough for them to get started up-grade. Once they got up a little speed they could keep moving, and the summit was only a mile farther. One of the highway gang drove the car which the woman and the old man had abandoned. Finally there were only two cars left, and the

Superintendent radioed the Station to telephone Truckee for a tow-car; being towed out would cost more than a ticket, and would be an equally good warning. The people in the two cars looked cold and scared, but the Superintendent wasted no sympathy on them. People like that might make him lose the road, and besides it was just luck that nobody was killed.

He ordered the push-plow and the rotary to get to work cleaning up the mess. From the look of things there had probably been a little snow-slide to begin with, and that might have blocked the first car and started all the trouble. The push-plow began shoving the snow to the outer side of the road, and scraping off the crust, which had built up into a low hummock. The plow had to rush, and when it hit the hummock it bucked and pitched; the driver gunned the motor, and then in spite of chains the big double-tired rear wheels spun and skidded. Then the driver had to back up and rush again. Sometimes the plow accomplished little, and other times the cutting edge bit in close to the top of the pavement and broke off great chunks of consolidated snow eight inches thick.

In every rush the slanting stroke of the great plow-share flung the plow off to the left, and once it "did a wind-ding" by skidding all the way round in a circle. And all the while the gale whistled around Windy Point, and the air was thick with flying snow like feathers.

In ten minutes the push-plow had got the blocked place opened up to two-lane width again; the rotary moved in and started throwing all the piled-up snow over the side.

Let down after the emergency, the Superintendent

stood by his car. He was wet and cold, heavy-legged and heavy-eyed; he thought only of tumbling onto his cot. Then he noticed that one of the men who had been sent down from the Station was standing there wanting to speak to him. The fellow's name was Mart; he was a fair enough swamper, but maybe not too good in the head.

"Well, what is it, Mart? Spill it!"

"Say, Supe, I got uh idea. I just been a-figurin'. It's these here damn cars causes all the trouble. Why don't you get 'em to keep all the cars off the road? Then we can keep it nice and clean as anything all winter."

13

The District Traffic Superintendent slept in a bed which had a telephone-set screwed into the panel at its head. That night he got under the blankets fairly early. When he was all settled and ready to go to sleep—just as a man might say his prayers—he reached for the telephone and talked with the office.

"How are things?" he asked.

"About the same," said the assistant. "No trouble on the Los Angeles lines—nothing but rain down that way. A few failures on the Seattle lead, mostly around Shasta. But there's been quite a bit of trouble on the Central—up on the Hump."

"What's been the matter?"

"Just a good big storm, I guess. There's a lineman lost up there too—"

"Lost?"

"Well, hurt, I guess. But just disappeared so far. They're out now looking for his truck."

"That's too bad! Yes, that's bad. Hard on service too.

Men get jittery—don't work well when that sort of thing's in the air. You'll get through tonight all right; traffic will be light."

"Oh, we'll get through—barring accident."

"Well, call me if you need me."

The DTS settled himself to go to sleep. He could hear the steady spatter of rain outside; somewhere water was dropping and splashing loudly from a clogged roof-gutter. He knew that he would go to sleep immediately, and wake up at four to call the office again. His was a twenty-four-hour shift during storms. Then he was asleep.

14

Against all the long rampart of the Coast Range the storm was beating. Northward, and here and there upon the higher peaks, there was snow. Elsewhere was only the slanting rain, and low cloud above the ridges. Upon the Trinity Mountains (most orthodoxly christened) the storm beat; equally it beat upon those other mountains (un-Christianly named in half-altered pagan tongue) Bully Choop and Yolla Bolly.

This is the roll-call of those chief summits rising against the first in-sweep of the storm from the ocean. Mt. Sanhedrin. Mt. Kinocti that watches above the lake. Sulphur Peak on whose slopes the geysers fume and spout. Then flat-topped St. Helena, named for a Russian princess, transmuted in romance to Spy-Glass Hill. Tamalpais of the long ridge, overlooking the Golden Gate. Grizzly Peak, high above the tall white tower, facing toward the Bay. Twin-peaked Diablo, where the beacon flashes into the night. Black Mountain over against Loma Prieta, the Dark Hill. Mt. Hamilton of the star-watchers.

Fremont Peak where the moldering intrenchments sink yearly closer to the ground. Southward, stretching far off, the ridges which bound the long Valley of the Salt Pools. Out of the pounding surf the Santa Lucias, rearing up their cliffs. Blanco Peak, Mt. Mars, Saddle Mountain by the Bishop's Town. St. Joseph and St. John. Upon them all was rain.

At last came the turn of the coast and the long trend eastward. There the Coast Ranges lost themselves among those higher mountains which bear the name of Gabriel, the Archangel. And on those peaks which shadow the Town of Our Lady Queen of the Angels—there too was rain.

FOUR TIMES in the known history of the earth have the mountains risen like a tide. Three times have the forces of air and water made head against those mountains, eating away the towering granite peaks into little rounded hills. Two hundred and fifty million years is the period of that cycle—majestic among earthly rhythms.

When, as now, the mountains have risen and stand high, then the storms rage most often and most fiercely. When the mountains again are low and the ice-caps melted and the seas grown shallow with wastage of granite, the air grows calm, and the languorous mood of the tropics reaches far toward north and south.

In this great struggle the chief allies of the hills are the plants. They bind the soil with their roots as with fine tough threads. With grass and fallen leaves they mat the earth against the rain-drops.

Dubious partners in the struggle are the animals. A few, like the beavers, work to hold back the water. Some, like the flyers and light-footed climbers, scarcely enter

215

the conflict. The burrowers—rodents, insects, and worms —ease the rush of the water and give it entrance to the earth, but their castings of loose dirt wash away quickly. Worst of all, enemies against the hills, are the grazers and browsers. Like the stag in the fable, they eat away the cover of leaves and grass; with their sharp and hard hoofs they wear trails into the raw earth, and along the trails the running water cuts gullies.

Man, whose ancestors crawled out from the salt water, remains still a creature of the sea-margin, his habitat the low plains. A thousand feet is a small fraction of the ocean's depth; yet, if the ocean were suddenly to rise a thousand feet, man would be largely destroyed. Of Europe would remain only some mountainous islands; the United States would fare not much better. Mexico City, cupped among its mountains, would survive as the largest center of habitation in the world.

Living thus upon the plains, man is upon neutral ground between the mountains and the ocean. The torrents from the hills grow quiet, and let fall their silt. The great slow rivers here and there cut into the banks, and elsewhere build up the flood-plains or thrust forward the long fingers of their deltas into the sea.

Man allies himself now with the mountains, now with air and water. Like the beaver, he builds dams and retaining walls. Like the sheep, he strips the earth and cuts trailways. He protects his habitations against the water, so that through the centuries the level of a city rises foot by foot. In the main, swayed by immediate need and convenience, he remains through the long course of time careless of the struggle, planless.

A father was out walking with his son, and they came to a small stream.

"Why is the water so muddy?" asked the little boy.

"It means the soil is washing away," said the father. "The government is sending a lot of men out to build dams and stop it."

But the brown stream was sign and symbol of a great conflict. Its present cycle would not be completed within a hundred million years, before which time man would very likely have run his course and vanished. By then the sky-towering crags would be reduced to gnawed stumps of granite, and a stormless climate, as in the Eocene, would cover most of the earth.

2

On the higher mountains snow was falling. Far beneath the surface the shrunken streams flowed in dim tunnels arched by snow; deep ground-waters fed them. The summer-darting trout were sunk in lassitude, half-hibernating. While the drifts covered the high country, it could suffer little erosion; that was for the time of thaw, when melting snow loosed the torrents.

On the foothills rain was falling. Brown water flowed in the gullies; it ate at the cut-banks; it foamed in the narrows.

For a certain section of canyon-rim above the South Fork of the Yuba River the hour approached. Neither accident nor the work of man was involved. The area was uninhabited. It offered foothold to few trees, and had never been lumbered. Its quartz yielded no gold. On the bare outcroppings, forest fires died for lack of fuel. But through centuries the river had worn at the base of the canyon-wall, and the side-gulches had grown deeper. At last the flowing water in one of the gulches finished washing away a little sand, and a tall rock shifted a quarter of an inch. The earth was already heavy with soaked-up rain. This small movement of the foundation unloosed the whole mass. With a long roar four million tons of the canyon-rim—rock, soil, chaparral—slid down five hundred feet before again coming to rest. Through trees and undergrowth masses of rock crashed a thousand feet farther until they reached the river-bed, and clogged the flow of the stream. Halfway down the canyon-side a tall cedar rooted in the slide stood leaning drunkenly.

In the valleys rain was falling. As it soaked through the earth, it leached away salts; rapaciously, the gnaw of its acidity ate even at solid limestone. By its buoyancy it floated away fallen leaves and seeds, pods and bark-scalings; as the water rose, logs and up-rooted trees yielded to the strange upward pull; they lifted from the mud where gravity had held them, and began the journey toward the sea-bottom.

Now swiftly, now more slowly, the water flowed always onward and downward at the pull of the earth's center. In the torrents of the stream beds, it moved boulders before it. The same force worked subtly in every turbid trickle which held some clay in suspension or rolled a little fine sand along with it.

Whether the cut or gully was man-made or "natural" was no concern of the rain. Here and there occurred a land-slip. Of much greater importance was the continual unheeded fall of loosened gravel and small stones. Blue clay soaked up until it grew soft, and flowed by its own weight, oozing slowly forward like hot candy poured upon a platter. On hillsides the adobe soil grew heavy until great sections settled and slid, leaving behind them wide crescent-shaped scars of raw earth. And always the movement was downward, from the hill-tops toward the sea.

3

Along by Fox Farm was a stretch of highway that was in pretty bad shape that night. A rotary was working on it. The men in the rotary could see next to nothing; the flying snow reflected the lights right back in their faces. They were feeling their way along from snowstake to snowstake. Then came a bang, and a jolt, and the shearbolts went.

"That's no pebble," said the swamper, and they both piled out into the snow, expecting to find that a boulder or tree-trunk had fallen down on the highway.

"God, it's a car!" said the operator, for he could see the end of the rear bumper where the rotary's augers had chewed into it; everything else was drifted over with snow, or plastered. The two men looked at each other, and each saw that the other was scared.

The operator knocked the snow off the handle and opened the door. "One of those little telephone trucks," he said.

The swamper rolled up the tarpaulin at the back. The headlights of the rotary glared into the truck. The swamper took a good look. "Skis gone," he said. Then he looked at his watch—just after midnight.

"One man or two in these outfits?" asked the operator; he really knew, but he spoke to be saying something.

"One, along the highway," said the swamper, "two, when the wires are farther away."

They stood a moment staring at each other. Around their ankles the snow was moving; the force of the wind held it tight along the surface; it drifted heavily, like dry sand creeping on a dune.

Facing toward the forest on the side where the telephone-lines ran, the operator let out a mighty "Hal-*loo!*"

They waited, and in the hush of expectancy could hear the engine of the rotary throbbing steadily. A faint call came back from the forest. "Hear that?" cried the swamper, starting forward impulsively.

But the operator called again: "Hal-*loo*-oo, hal-*loo*-oo!"

"*Loo*-oo," came back.

"Echo," said the operator. "Hardly think there would be one in this wind."

While the swamper replaced the shear-bolts, the operator got into touch with the Station by radio, and talked with the night-foreman.

"I guess that's the fellow the telephone people were calling up about," said the night-foreman. "He hadn't reported in for quite a while. I'll call them."

"Do you want us to go look for him?"

"You can't without skis, and anyway if he's been in there that long—"

4

During the course of the storm more and more water leaked through the bullet-hole into the switch-box at Underpass 342-2. The wires and insulation became wet. At 1:12 A.M. the white flash of a short-circuit lighted the interior of the box; a fuse blew out; the pumps stopped.

Rain was falling heavily, and draining from the long slopes of the underpass into the sump. The two lanes of the underpass were separated by a concrete wall, and all the water drained into the northbound lane, whence it was pumped out. The northbound lane was therefore much more quickly affected.

Because of the storm and the lateness of the hour, only eight cars were approaching the underpass from the south within a distance which would involve them. They were in order:

1) A pick-up truck.

2) A small sedan.

3) A coupé containing three college youths.

4) Another coupé containing Miss Miller, a school-teacher. She was unused to driving in the rain or to being out alone on the highway so late at night; she was in what is known as "a mild state of nerves."

5) A jalopy containing a migrant worker, his wife, and their two children. The children were asleep in the back, on top of a clutter of household goods.

6) A car of the Highway Patrol containing Sergeant Daly and Officer O'Regan.

7) A truck-and-trailer laden with crates of carrots.

8) A large sedan containing a uniformed chauffeur, Mr. Andrew F. Magnusson (the mining magnate, no less), Mrs. Magnusson, and their twin daughters Deborah (Debby) and May (Mebby). They were returning from a formal dinner, and were dressed accordingly. Mr. Magnusson was asleep; Mrs. Magnusson was having digestive troubles; the girls were bored.

The patrol-car was going slowly; its presence and example stabilized the traffic. Drivers who passed it slowed down. The cars were therefore to arrive at the underpass with only a few changes in position.

The pick-up truck dipped into the underpass. Coming around the curve, the driver saw a sheet of water upon the pavement. He threw on his brake, and managed to check his car a little. The water sprayed out on both sides, but he was through almost before he knew what was happening. "Not more than three or four inches," he said to himself.

The water, rising rapidly, was six inches deep by the time the small sedan came along. It hit the water hard and skidded round a little, but the driver skillfully shifted into second and went through.

The college youth who was driving the coupé gave out a whoop when he saw the water, and stepped on the gas. The car slewed to the right, and water flew in all directions. "Yip-pee!" they all three yelled. Then, without even a cough, the engine died. The driver whirled it with the starter for a little, and then remembered that this particular model was likely to stall in high water. They all did a little perfunctory cursing, and then lighted cigarettes. Their momentum had almost carried them through the flooded part. They discussed making a jump for it, but decided they would have more fun just sitting and seeing what happened.

The next thing that happened was Miss Miller and her mild state of nerves. When she saw water ahead and then a stalled car, she flipped her steering-wheel much too suddenly to the left and stepped hard on the throttle-pedal instead of dropping into second. Her back wheels spun and skidded; the car went half-way round; in confusion she threw on the brake before releasing the clutch, and killed her engine. Underpasses were terrifying to her at best; now she looked out, saw the good-natured grins of the college youths, and misinterpreted them as lascivious gloatings. Her confusions becoming panic, she snapped her ignition-switch, and tried madly to start her engine. It did not respond; having first killed the engine, she had turned the ignition off, not on, by snapping the switch; but this was a mistake to which she was prone even in her less excited moments. With a sideways glance at the grinning youths she abandoned herself to kidnaping, murder, and worse.

The truck-driver was skillful, but even a professional cannot do much when he rounds a curve into eight inches of water and sees two cars at crazy angles blocking three-quarters of the passage-way. At best a high-loaded truck with an equally high-loaded trailer is not a handy combination to maneuver. The driver did all he could; he dodged Miss Miller's car. But his outfit jack-knifed on him, and the trailer almost tipped over. All that saved it was the spilling off of some dozen crates of carrots. The truck-driver's cursing was not perfunctory.

But just as he was getting warmed up, the Magnussons arrived in their big sedan. The curve of the underpass was now so completely filled that the chauffeur saw the trailer in time to stop the car without hitting anything. Mrs. Magnusson and the twins squealed, and Mr. Magnusson came out of his sleep with a jump. The chauffeur sized up the situation quickly; he was just about to back out of the water when the jalopy arrived behind him.

The jalopy had only dim lights, and scarcely any brakes. The water, however, checked it a little, and it hit the rear of the big sedan with only a moderate bump. The Magnusson females squealed again; the migrant's two children awoke and bawled; the migrant mingled some barnyard epithets with the truck-driver's South-of-Market profanity.

Just at that moment a freight-train started to go over the rails above.

Jammed in an underpass, surrounded by water, with cars front and rear and a freight-train overhead—all this was too much for Mrs. Magnusson's well-established claustrophobia. With a determined "Gotta get out of here!" she reached for the door-handle. Mr. Magnusson made a gesture to stop her and then (knowing his wife) gave it up. Ermine cloak, gold snood, and diamonds—Mrs. Magnusson stepped out into the muddy water. The twins, no longer bored, followed her with delighted yaps; it was the greatest lark.

"Go after her," ordered Mr. Magnusson to the chauffeur. "See they don't get into trouble."

As with a homing instinct, Mrs. Magnusson continued northward, although this direction brought her into deeper water. Followed by the chauffeur, she plodded on through the floating carrots, passed around Miss Miller's car, and reached the farther shore where she stood, magnificently draggled, and called back for her young.

But the college youths had sighted the girls, and piled out of their coupé to be of assistance. Mebby (having the time of her life) threw a carrot at the boys; then both twins, hoisting their long dinner gowns well above four very attractive identical knees, dodged around the truck.

Just then the two officers arrived in the patrol-car.

They stopped successfully, and surveyed the scene within the glare of their lights.

"Kee-riced!" said Officer O'Regan. Then he stepped out manfully into the water, well-shined puttees and all. He disliked accidents, especially gathering up fragments of people, and he was much relieved to find that nobody was hurt. On his way back, Debby got him under the chin with a well-hurled carrot. She was unbelievable enough to look at, and when he looked around he saw another one of the same. He relieved himself by bawling out the truck-driver, and asking him if he didn't know better than to go jack-knifing his outfit in an underpass.

In the meantime Sergeant Daly had set a flare back on the Highway to halt other drivers. Also the migrant had managed to back his jalopy out of the water.

Officer O'Regan reported to the Sergeant that nobody was hurt. The Sergeant then went back down the highway in the car to the nearest telephone to call headquarters and the highway-station and a tow-car. Officer O'Regan went sloshing back into the mess, wishing he were a sergeant.

He found Mr. Magnusson comfortably puffing a cigar. "I can't drive," said Mr. Magnusson. "Somewhere around here you'll find a chauffeur and three crazy women. They all belong to me." Officer O'Regan climbed in, and backed the car out.

Since everybody assumed that Miss Miller's car was stalled on account of the water, there was nothing more to be done at present. At this point the twins felt that the water was getting definitely cold, and so did the college youths; one of them remembered about having a full pint in the coupé. The truck-driver could not accomplish anything until the car in front of him was moved, and so they invited him along. The appearance of the policeman had reassured Miss Miller; she thawed out and invited the twins into her car. Everybody, including Miss Miller, had a drink, and began to feel warm and chummy.

"I wish we could get out of here before the tow-car comes," said one of the youths. "Those guys sure soak you."

"Why don't you try to start your car again, lady?" said the truck-driver.

"Surely," said Miss Miller. And since this time she looked to be certain that the ignition was on, the engine started perfectly. Miss Miller drove right out of the water.

Someone got a tow-rope, and Miss Miller pulled the other coupé out of the underpass and parked it. Then she said good-by and drove on. The boys knew they could get their engine going, once they were out of the standing water.

With the coupés out of the way the truck-driver managed to get straightened out and going again.

Shortly afterwards the Sergeant got back. He walked over the railroad tracks to the other end of the south-bound lane. He flagged at that end, and Officer O'Regan at the other, and in that way they moved two-way traffic through the upper side of the underpass. Even yet the water in it was not above six inches deep, and a driver who was forewarned and going slowly would have no trouble.

The tow-car got there next. Officer O'Regan told the garage-men that there was a whole mess of cars in the underpass, but when the garage-men drove in there, all they could see was a lot of carrots floating around in the water. They said some things about a dumb cop, and then backed out and told him so.

"Kee-riced!" said Officer O'Regan.

The highway gang got there next, and just behind their truck a fire-engine to pump the underpass. But before the fire-engine could get started, one of the highway gang located the trouble in the switch-box. He pulled the switch, dried things out a bit, plugged the bullet-hole with a wad of paper, put in a spare fuse, and threw the switch back in. The pumps started with a whir. The highway gang collected the carrots, so that they would not plug the drains.

An hour after it all began, the drivers who were going through the underpass did not know that anything had been happening.

5

At ten minutes after four, through the workings of a well-adjusted sub-conscious mind, the District Traffic Superintendent woke up. Automatically he reached for the telephone on the head of the bed, and talked with the office.

"She's not so good," said his assistant. "Up on the Hump, I mean—the Central."

"What's the trouble?"

"Oh, just a line here and a line there—too much soft snow, I guess."

"Isn't Plant fixing them up for you?"

"Oh, yes. We keep getting them back, but we're losing them faster than we get them back. They're just sending in another crew from Sacramento, and a Modesto crew is going north to back up at Sacramento. We're all right now—hardly any calls to go through. But we'll have to start delaying calls when the nine o'clock rush comes, if things don't get better."

"No big breaks?"

"Not yet."

"Well, I don't like it. Just a moment while I figure it out. . . . All right. Get me Chicago, will you, please?"

A minute later he was talking with the Chicago office, which co-ordinated the telephone routings of the continent. He explained his needs briefly, and asked that some of the lines from San Francisco to the East be connected *via* Los Angeles so as to relieve the hard-pressed Central Transcontinental. Chicago agreed, and the DTS again made himself comfortable beneath the blankets.

Even before he could settle fully into slumber, Chicago had talked with Los Angeles and Denver. But Denver demurred. A new storm was reported over Utah, moving easterly into Colorado. Because of this threat, Denver was nervous, and was loath to assume any additional load. Chicago granted the difficulty. Chicago then talked elsewhere, here and there, over the continent.

As the result of these far-flung conversations, certain switches were flipped. The operators in San Francisco were ignorant of these changes; every girl still continued to see before her, for example, ten jacks beneath the name NEW YORK. For six of the jacks the voice-channels still followed the route over Donner Pass and through Salt Lake City and Denver. For the other four the voice-channels passed by way of Los Angeles, Oklahoma City, and St. Louis.

The DTS, knowing that he had prepared as well as possible against the power of the storm, sank deeper into sleep.

6

The great mass of polar air centering over the valley of the Yukon was discharging itself in two far-reaching rivers of wind. In their life-histories these two great wind-torrents may be compared to identical twins parted soon after birth and reared in different environments. The first, which passed over the land, altered but slowly; it remained cold and dry, and penetrated far toward the tropics as a frigid blast. But the second, which passed over the water, became rapidly moist and temperate.

This second polar discharge, as one of its functions in the current scheme of weather, fed new supplies of moisture into the storm which was still centered off the coast of Oregon. The process was grandiose. The cold and dry air was blowing as a northeast wind when it descended from the mountains. A little south of the Alaskan coast, it came definitely within the orbit of the storm, and thereafter followed around a roughly semi-circular course from two to three thousand miles in circuit depending upon the distance from the center. During the long transit the wind shifted from north to northwest, to west, to southwest; finally, as it approached the California coast, the current of air was moving directly from the south.

Nearing the coast this now temperate and moist air was forced upward, partly by overrunning colder, heavier air near the coast, partly by ascending the barrier of the mountains. Rising, it was cooled and discharged its moisture. The raindrops and snowflakes falling upon California could therefore in the main be traced back to a great arc of northerly ocean-surface beginning in the Gulf of Alaska.

Even before this polar air had begun to pour out from the Arctic, a mass of tropical air had been lying quiescent between Hawaii and the North American coast. During the days of the polar outbreak this tropical air continued on the whole intact and unchanged. The unusual atmospheric activities to the northward had jostled it to the south, but had not sucked it in toward the storm-center. It remained warm and saturated with moisture—the atmospheric opposite of the polar air.

If these bodies of polar and tropical air had been brought suddenly into contact, the resulting weather disturbance would have been catastrophic, beyond the experience or even the imagination of men. Any such unprecedented, world-shaking disaster, however, was rendered impossible by the intervening temperate zone, three thousand miles in width. What actually happened was that the polar air which reached southward across the Pacific became temperate, and only then, as it began to turn eastward toward the coast, came into contact with the tropical air. The contrast between the two was still sufficient to produce thunderstorms and heavy rain-squalls. But the easterly-moving current just grazed the more southerly air-mass, and during the first days of storm only a negligible amount of tropical air was carried along to expend its rain on the coast.

During one of the earlier days, however, a divergent

tongue of northern air actually thrust itself some few hundred miles southward into the tropical area. This advance was accompanied by the usual thunderstorms and torrential showers which may be expected when cold air thus protrudes itself beneath warmer, moist air. The advance, if long continued, would perhaps have resulted in the formation of a wholly new storm center. But the complex of air-currents around the whole world shifted slightly at that time so that the main stream of the polar outbreak continued its easterly course, leaving the intrusion of northern air within the tropical air.

For a day or two thunder continued to grumble and rainstorms to form and dissipate. But in the absence of any general wind-current to force them one against the other the northern and the southern air accommodated their differences. Lying over the surface of the tropical ocean the northern air rapidly became so warm and moist in its lower levels as to be indistinguishable from its neighbor. Higher up, however, a cloud deck still remained to mark the boundary between the still frigid upper levels of the northern air, and the much warmer tropical air of the same altitude.

The passengers of a liner crossing that part of the ocean watched the beads of water continue to form on their tall glasses of iced drinks, but did not know that they were passing from one air-mass to another of very different history. They were conscious of no change in the weather conditions except that some clouds for a while cut off the sun. But if they could have ascended, they would have found that in one place the air grew cooler much more rapidly than in another.

Because of this difference, the two bodies of air, so alike

at the surface, were vastly different in their potentialities. The tropical air could produce extremely heavy and long-continued, but steady, rainfall. The old polar air would be likely to let loose its smaller amount of moisture with almost explosive violence and full accompaniments of thunder and lightning, towering formations of massed cloud, high winds, and violent turbulence.

During the morning of the ninth day since the storm had formed off the coast of Japan, as part of a readjustment of atmospheric forces around the world the storm-area extended to more southerly latitudes. A large portion of the tropical air-mass began to move northeasterly toward the California coast and behind it followed the old polar air.

7

The J.M. could feel the letter in his pocket. That air-line job was open to him again. It paid more than he was getting, and the chances for the future might be better too. He admitted that he had been unhappy in the Weather Bureau; his mathematical training did not seem to help him, and sometimes he thought that it even was a handicap. Sometimes it seemed as if the Chief were using only the same methods that any shepherd might have used back in the time of the Patriarchs; he just looked at the sky, and decided from the appearance of things what weather would probably be coming along after a while. The shepherd, of course, never saw farther than the actual horizon. By the weather-map the Chief extended his view for several thousands of miles. There was a tremendous pyramiding of information, but not much change in method.

The J.M. broke off his musings about the personal problem, and turned to the map.

Maria had had a baby! The event was no more unusual than in organic life, and had not been unexpected; in fact, during the last twenty-four hours, the eastward bulge of the isobars had given a distinct suggestion of mammalian pregnancy. Now, however, the appearance of the map suggested rather the process of cell-division known as mitosis; the new storm centering over Utah was already an independent entity, but had not yet wholly separated itself from the mother storm off the coast. Already the J.M. was thinking of the newcomer as Little Maria, and his attitude was that of an old friend of the family. "Why, I've known your mother," he found himself thinking, "since she was a little ripple on a cold front north of Titijima!"

But to know the mother, he realized, did not allow anyone to predict much about the daughter. The daughter would develop her own personality, and follow her own career. Little Maria would probably make herself well known to the world. Three-quarters of the United States lay ahead of her, and over that area there were many contrasts of atmospheric conditions as the result of the recent north-and-south movements. All this region was a reservoir of energy for Little Maria to tap. And beyond the United States lay the Atlantic and Europe. Given opportunity and a little time, the J.M. thought that he could work out mathematically the route which the storm would follow and the characteristics which it would display at given points.

The Chief came to take a look at the map. "That new

storm," he said, "she's not so much now, but she'll be headlines when she gets to New York."

The J.M. jumped mentally; he had been about to say almost the same thing. "What?" he blurted in his surprise, "you mean Little Maria?" Then he shut his lips quickly, realizing that he had exposed his childishness; perhaps the Chief would miss the point.

But the Chief smiled with a little quizzical expression. "Hn-n?" he said. "You name them too? It must be nice to be new at the game. I used to do it, but I ran out of names years ago. I called them mostly after heroes that I read about in history—Hannibal, and so forth. I remember Marshal Ney developed into a terror; but Genghis Khan fizzled out."

Suddenly the J.M. felt at home in the Weather Bureau. Never before had the Chief and he had anything between them in confidence. He had never suspected the Chief of any hidden imagination.

"That's Maria off the coast there," he volunteered.

The Chief let his eyes move out across the Pacific. In mid-ocean were three little storms; the J.M. had never named them individually. First there had been two and he had called them the Twins; now he thought of them as the Triplets; for several days they had been blocked behind the great sweep of the polar incursion, and now they were dying. But the Chief let his eyes pass beyond the Triplets to where a new vigorous storm was just leaving the Sea of Okhotsk.

"Named this one yet?"

"No. I've been using girls' names in -ia, but I've nearly run out."

"How about Victoria?"

"Fine."

"All right—Victoria she is, but Victoria won't concern us much for several days, if ever."

The Chief brought his glance back along the more southerly ocean clear to California.

"Hn-n?" he said finally. "There's just one thing I don't like."

"You mean that belt of cloud?"

"Yes. There's a big lot of tropical air moving in toward the coast, but that cloud belt means something is happening in the upper air. It may be some little local eddy, and it may be something a lot more."

"If one of those ships could send up a radiosonde, it would be fine."

"Hn-n? Yes, the radiosonde—" The Chief's voice rang with irony. "A whole radio sending-station weighing next to nothing; you send her up with a cute little balloon, clear into the stratosphere; and as she goes, she sends you back messages about temperature and humidity—just the kind of gadget Americans all love. It's the best publicity that meteorology ever had, but it seems to me I never have one of those upper-air reports when and where I need it."

He stared again at the location of the two ships reporting cloud.

"Well," he went on, "today we're in a little ridge of higher pressure between the two Marias, and we'll have something of a lull. Tomorrow the tropical air will move in, and there'll be rain a-plenty. And about the next day we ought to know whether that cloudbank out there means anything."

Half an hour earlier the J.M. had been telling himself

that at the first chance he would show the letter to the Chief and say he was leaving. But now, for the first time, he felt warm toward the Chief. Paradoxically, he realized, this sudden friendship came not because the Chief had been scientific, but just the reverse. And he himself had been equally unscientific. Then he had a sudden new thought. Perhaps there was something about the human mind itself which made it feel comfortable to think of a storm as a person, not an equation.

At the same time a new little glow of pride came to him about the Weather Bureau. Why, the Bureau recorded and distributed the very observations which the air-line meteorologists depended on! The Bureau made the only public forecasts, and then stood by for the blame —usually not much praise—that was coming. In the end, a private meteorologist was only another fellow working for a company. And the professors were only theorists. But ever since he was a kid, he'd wanted to be a weather-man, and there was only one place he could be that. When you came right down to it, the air-line people dealt in air-lines; only the Weather Bureau dealt in weather.

8

Mr. Reynoldhurst was a very great man in the domain of petroleum; from Maracaibo to Bahrein his lightest opinion was quoted, and his official pronouncement was as the *yea* or *nay* of a tribal patriarch.

From Mr. Reynoldhurst's hotel suite in San Francisco his private secretary had just put through a call to New York. "Good morning, Davy," said Mr. Reynoldhurst, casually and informally; transcontinental calls were for him no novelty.

The impulses conveying the sound traveled in about one-tenth of a second the three thousand miles from ocean to ocean, by way of Salt Lake City, Denver, and Chicago. Every modulation of Mr. Reynoldhurst's resonant and authoritative voice was vibrating in the ear-drum of his chief legal adviser.

Just then the decaying bole of the tree which since the year 1789 had lain on a rocky ledge in the Sierra Nevada became weighted with snow past its point of equilibrium, and began to roll. For a moment it hung on the last projection of the ledge; then it slid sideways, up-ended, dropped thirty feet, struck on a rock, catapulted through the air, spun end-over-end, and crashed through the tops of three small spruce trees; gathering speed—now rolling, now hurtling through the air—it began the descent of a long, snow-covered canyon-side.

"The matter will bear watching," said Mr. Reynoldhurst into the telephone transmitter. "In view of the present international situation we can scarcely—"

At that moment the tree-bole, finishing a last hundred-foot leap, struck squarely among the cross-arms of Pole 1-243-76 of the Central Transcontinental Lead. That pole was fifteen inches thick at the base and thirty feet tall; it was of selected, flawless Douglas fir from the Olympic Peninsula; it was firmly set in rocky soil. The four heavy cross-arms were reinforced with steel braces; each cross-arm carried ten glass insulators each bearing a heavy copper wire. The strength of the pole was calculated to withstand any attack of wind, ice, or snow.

As the tree-bole struck, the pole snapped like a dry twig; every cross-arm broke; the steel braces bent and twisted; most of the insulators were shattered; nearly all the wires broke and the curling loose ends crossed and short-circuited the few which remained unbroken.

At one moment the Central Transcontinental Lead had been an important link in world-communications. One moment later it was nothing.

"Hello, hello!" said Mr. Reynoldhurst sharply; inefficiency always irritated him. He had certainly been cut off. He pressed his buzzer.

"Put that call through again," he said to his secretary. "Some fool telephone girl cut me off. And register a complaint with the Telephone Company."

"Yes, Mr. Reynoldhurst."

Some ends of the broken wires were still swinging back and forth; the tree-bole was settling into the snow bank where it had landed.

The secretary jiggled the telephone. "Operator," said a voice from the other end. "Mr. Reynoldhurst's call to New York has been broken off," said the secretary. "Will you kindly restore it at once?" Her voice was honey-sweet; but, underneath, it was resonant (as was fitting in Mr. Reynoldhurst's secretary) with authority and the suggestion of threat. "God—" thought the operator. "What have I done?"

"One moment, please," was all the operator said. Even while she was saying it, she split the connection and listened to the New York wire. It was dead. Of the nine other direct lines to New York, she saw that five were busy. She plugged in on one of the others; it was dead. She plugged in on another and another—both dead. She plugged in on the last, and in sudden relief heard the clear hum of an open line and then the voice of the New York operator.

Mr. Reynoldhurst, as the seconds ticked away, drew circles on his desk, and then crossed out each circle with an X. There was no use beginning anything else; this call would be re-established in a moment. His glance sought the window, and he saw that it was still raining. Thirty years earlier when he was sleeping under a boiler during the Tampico boom, rain used to mean a great deal to young Tom Reynoldhurst; but since he had entered his epoch of limousines and covered entrance-ways with doormen holding umbrellas, Mr. Reynoldhurst had lost his personal feeling for rain.

"Your call, Mr. Reynoldhurst."

Lifting the receiver he noticed that twenty-five seconds had elapsed; "Inexcusable!" he thought.

"That you, Reynoldhurst?" said the voice from New York.

"Oh, yes. Irritating to be broken off! You'd think a big outfit like Telephone would get things organized better —well, anyway, here we are talking just as before. Now, as I was saying—"

But Mr. Reynoldhurst was incorrect. He was no longer talking as before—by way of Salt Lake City, Denver and Chicago. Instead, the impulses now passed through Los Angeles, Oklahoma City, and St. Louis, over one of the alternate circuits which through the foresight of the District Traffic Superintendent had been established some hours earlier.

Except for two hikers who had sat upon the bole for a few minutes in 1923, no human being had ever known anything about it. During the half hour following its fall down the mountain-side, nobody knew that it had fallen.

But the fall affected the lives of many people over a hemisphere.

A man in Boise was delayed fifteen minutes in getting a call through to Sacramento and lost a prospective job.

A girl in Omaha was prevented from talking to her mother in Honolulu before she went into the operating-room, not to return alive.

A woman about to enter a Reno courtroom for divorce proceedings had grown panicky and put in a call for her still hopeful husband in San Francisco; when the call was delayed, she cancelled it.

Almost before the echoes of the crash had ceased reverberating among the mountain solitudes, the toll testboardmen at Sacramento knew that the Central Transcontinental had suffered a total failure. A few minutes later, merely by using their instruments, without even stepping outside, they had located the break within a quarter of a mile. By telephone the word went to the repair crew closest to the break, and in five minutes more the green trucks were moving on U. S. 40. Since the break was a total failure and might be extensive, the Modesto crew was ordered up from Sacramento toward the Pass, and crews in Stockton and Marysville (like reserves mustered for a counter-attack) were told to stand by.

To every important long-distance office in the West the fall of the tree brought sudden emergency. Lines were dead, calls could not go through, tickets piled up as calls were delayed. Operators felt the sudden tenseness. Supervisors talked to irate or worried or importunate customers. The rule was "First come, first served," but there had to be exceptions. Police and hospitals had precedence; there were other real emergencies. But also there were the egotists who thought their own business was always most important. Big small-town business-men foh-ed and fummed; reporters bluffed about the exigencies of getting to press; rich women threatened to report supervisors for impertinence.

Most of all the San Francisco office felt the stress. All eastern calls must be routed to the south. The change was accomplished chiefly by the testboardmen; by flipping a few switches in co-ordination with the Los Angeles office they soon established new direct circuits over which San Francisco might talk to Chicago, Denver, and the other chief centers. The sudden increase of traffic overcrowded the southern wires, and tickets started to pile up. And even Los Angeles was affected; ordinarily Los Angeles calls reached Reno *via* Sacramento, but now the connection could be made only *via* Salt Lake City.

The congestion and delay of traffic was the result of the decrease in the number of wires, and also of the destruction of the carefully planned direct routings. To increase the number of wires the Plant Department "warmed up" all the extra circuits which were generally not in use except during disasters and the Christmas holidays. To patch up new direct routings without creating new confusion was a work demanding both knowledge and skill. Since the eastern calls were going through Los Angeles, the need for more circuits in that direction was imperative. The Chief Testboardman took over the San Francisco-Merced wire, and re-routed Merced calls through Modesto. From Merced he patched on with a Fresno line; then he took a Fresno-Bakersfield and a Bakersfield-Los Angeles circuit. The adjustments at the various offices took only a few minutes, and the result was another direct circuit to relieve the congestion between San Francisco and Los Angeles. When this circuit had been connected with one between Los Angeles and Omaha, the San Francisco operators could again get Omaha directly.

Shortly after the fall of the tree a man in a town on the west slope of the Sierra Nevada had occasion to call a friend and business-partner in a town on the east slope; the two places were by air-line about fifty miles apart. "There will be a slight delay; I will call you," said the local operator. The man making the call was surprised, for he usually got his friend without delay. The local operator had orders to route all eastern calls through Sacramento, fifty miles to the west. From Sacramento the circuit was next established to Los Angeles four hundred miles to the south; next it passed on to Salt Lake City six hundred miles to the northeast; another jump of four hundred miles westward brought it to Reno, and from Reno thirty miles more took it to the final destination.

The man making the call completed his business and since the toll-rates between the two towns were inconsiderable, he spent an extra period in conversation. During this time he was holding up the use of fifteen hundred miles of badly needed circuit, but was paying on the rate adjusted to a distance of fifty miles.

Directed with exactitude to the point of failure the nearest repair crew halted at the closest spot on the highway, strapped on their skis, and reached the broken pole within half an hour. They began to restore service, in temporary fashion, by laying across the gap some heavy insulated duplex wires which could lie in the snow and yet carry messages.

As each circuit was re-established, the testboardmen in

Sacramento discovered the hum of life, and then San Francisco put the circuit back into use where it was most needed. The situation became easier. Time also aided, for after mid-morning the number of new calls began to fall off toward the noon lull. By ten-fifty the worst of the emergency was over.

In the mountains the repair men were still laboring. Their foreman had a portable telephone attached to the wires, and through it he kept in touch with Sacramento. Once he came back looking not so comfortable.

"Well, they found him," he said.

Everybody knew what he meant. They paused.

"He was under the snow, but some fellows from Truckee brought in a collie dog that was trained to work in the mountains, and the dog found him."

Still they waited.

"For Christ's sake, who do you think you're workin' for—the Old People's Home? Sure, he was dead. Why don't you get on with the job?"

They worked hard after that, and nobody talked much.

9

For the newspapers Max and Jen were not very useful. Their being unmarried lent a touch of piquancy, and her hair could be played up as blonde. The reporters got a photograph from Jen's sister, and after the art department of the *Register* had put in some work the picture was not very valuable for identification, but it had some suggestions of the *femme fatale*. From the newspaperman's point of view, however, the trouble with the story was that it had no follow-up; the pair just went out of the picture as Dot saw them drive away into the rain.

A rumor cropped up about a Nevada couple who had been married in Yuma. But when a reporter located an embarrassed young couple in a tourist-court, the girl turned out to be a Mexican-type brunette, and the story was a flop.

The officers of the Highway Patrol kept working, especially between San Francisco and Sacramento, and from there by U. S. 40 over the pass to the state line. In the thorough and unhurrying way of good professionals they asked a lot of questions at garages and service-stations; conscientiously plying their trade, they ran down a few unlikely rumors. But they discovered absolutely nothing.

10

On the University campus the sea-gulls stood about by ones and twos on the green lawn—refugees from the storm. (Now, over their homes on reef and ledge the furious invading waves pounded and swept and foamed; high upon the cliffs the salt-spume filled the air.) Misplaced-looking, they stood, or flew here and there in restless, purposeless flights, or walked a few steps this way or that, raising feet awkwardly as if at the foreign feeling of grass tickling on their webs.

A professor preparing a lecture on modern literature looked out and saw them. "Sea-gulls on the grass," he thought. *"Sea-gulls on the grass, alas!* Perhaps that was what she meant. That would make sense—means a big storm at sea. They look the part too—moping! *Sea-gulls on the grass, alas!"*

11

Keeping U. S. 40 open over the Pass, thought the Superintendent, was just one crisis after another. Yesterday
it had been the jam at Windy Point, and tomorrow it
would be something else, but today it was wind. Not so
much snow was falling; the clouds were thinner; little
scraps of blue sky showed through. The Superintendent
could feel some shift in the weather, although he could
not figure out just what was happening. But the end of
the storm would come with a sharply rising barometer
and a wind-shift into the north, or northwest at least. And
now his barometer stayed low, and the wind had veered
only from south to west.

This wind had been growing stronger all morning. By
noon it was a gale. The rotaries had been throwing snow
over the windrows since Sunday, and now the wind
seemed to pick up all this snow on the windward side,
and blow it back. The snow-walls on both sides of the
roadway were six, or eight, or ten feet high by now. Across
the top the wind swept unhindered, but within the shelter
of the walls it swirled and eddied and dropped the snow
which it was blowing along. From the crest of the windward side the snow blew out sometimes until it looked
like a snow-banner from a mountain peak, and at the foot
of this wall the drifts built out so fast that you could
stand and watch them grow. A rotary would go through
leaving a clean track behind it, and before the rotary was
out of sight, six inches of snow might have drifted across
the road.

So far during the storm the plows had kept a two-lane
highway open, but now the snow blew in faster than the

rotaries could move along to throw it out, and after each push-plow the cleared passageway was narrower than it had been the time before. By eleven in the morning the Superintendent realized that he was going to have a real struggle to keep the road open at all. He mapped out his campaign.

He gave orders. At the Lake and at Baxter his men swung the long steel gates across the highway, and neither truck nor car went through without chains on. At Baxter the drivers protested in plenty; Baxter was sheltered in a thick pine forest, and the wind did not seem strong; not much snow was falling. People never realized that conditions higher up might be different, and might have grown worse while conditions lower down were growing better. But all their protesting made no difference; they went ahead with chains, or not at all.

Next, the Superintendent checked over mentally the location of all his plows. For the last forty-eight hours they had worked continuously; many of them had not been under shelter in that time; they took gasoline and oil from the service truck. There were six rotaries and nine push-plows for about thirty miles of highway, and from long experience the Superintendent, even without the aid of radio, knew very nearly where each one was at a given moment. The location of the push-plows was not so important, for they moved at twenty or thirty miles an hour, and could soon get anywhere they were needed. But a working rotary moved at only a half mile an hour, and to shift it to some other spot meant that it would be out of action for a while, at a time when it was most needed.

From the wind-direction the Superintendent knew

that the problem in the next few hours would be the five miles just west of the summit. One rotary was on the east face of the pass and would have to stay there; two others were similarly pinned to the lower fifteen miles of the west slope; that left him only three for the real fight, and two of those were not well placed. By radio he ordered one of them to turn around and start working back on the opposite side of the road; the other one was coming the right direction already.

Closing his eyes a moment, the Superintendent figured the future positions of all the plows—at twelve, one, and two o'clock, which stretches of road would then be freshly cleared, which ones would be drifted beyond the power of the push-plows. He knew that by one o'clock three miles of the road near Fox Farm would be next to impassable. He mentally tried various rearrangements of his plows, but there was always a bottle-neck somewhere or other. And all his figurings assumed that the wind got neither worse nor better, that his operators made no bad errors, that his machines did not break down, and that no accident blocked the road and hindered the work of the plows.

The Superintendent sighed. To lose his road was to lose his honor. Already he realized that the road was half-lost, but by taking the cars through in convoys he might prevent its actual closing. At such a moment he felt like jumping into his car and dashing through the storm to exhort his men to greater efforts. But that course would have been foolish; the machines, not the men, were doing the work, and the rotaries had already been driven as hard as they could be forced. Instead, he went into the radio room.

It was a quiet warm little place where a man was not even conscious of the storm outside. The lights glowed on the instrument-panel. In a calm voice he talked with the gate-keeper at Baxter—stop all trucks with trailers, tell people they'll have to go through in convoy probably. He gave the same orders to the gate-keeper at the Lake. He organized the convoy. With the present wind the east face of the Pass was a leeward exposure and could probably be kept two lanes wide; so the one end of the convoy could be at the summit. He placed the other end a little below Fox Farm.

He grabbed some dinner, and then it was one o'clock. Over the radio he talked to two of his rotaries. Things were pretty bad, they said. Except just behind a plow the passageway was scarcely more than one-car width, and cars meeting had a hard time to pass.

The Superintendent went down to the garage. "Get ready to start convoying," he ordered. Then he jumped into his own car, and drove out down the road into the storm. He had to have a look at things for himself.

He came to the first rotary. It was faced downhill, on the windward side of the road. To throw into the wind would mean that much of the snow blew back immediately and so the great parabola of snow was arched right over the highway. But the angle was too low, and some of the snow was not clearing the wall on the leeward side. The Superintendent jumped out and yelled orders; the operator raised the angle.

Beyond the rotary the road was drifted. Even in the narrow center lane the snow was here and there eight inches deep. The Superintendent pulled aside to let an approaching car pass him. The car stalled and stopped.

"He's stuck!" thought the Superintendent, half in panic. But the car had an Idaho license, and the driver must have been experienced in the mountains. He backed out, shoved in again as far as he could, backed out again, without even stalling his engine, and then pushed through the drift and went on. The Superintendent waved enthusiastically out the window; most drivers would have stuck right there and jammed the road. But the incident settled his mind about the need of convoying.

About one-thirty the first convoy started through. The orange-colored highway truck led it down from the summit. Following in its tire-tracks came a dozen cars, three trucks and a bus. Another highway car followed to be sure everyone got through safely. By no stretch of imagination could anyone say there was a two-lane passageway; in places the question was whether there was a passageway at all. As usual, some of the drivers were nervous and frightened; the Superintendent always wondered why such people ever tried the Pass in winter; perhaps they didn't try it more than once. But actually everyone was safer than in fine weather, for in the convoy even the reckless drivers had to go slowly and the high snow-walls on either side made it impossible for anyone to drive off the road. All you could do was merely to follow the car ahead of you, and after a while you came through and the convoy was broken up. Beyond the ends of the convoy the road was still bad, but it was two lanes wide in most places.

About three o'clock the situation began to improve. The wind fell off a little, and besides, by this time the wind had already blown into the road most of the loose snow which lay readily at hand to windward. Also at this time the Superintendent was able to have three rotaries converge on the worst stretch of road.

First he ordered the convoy cut down to three miles, and then to two. Finally, at four-thirty he stopped convoying altogether, and gave orders to the gate-keepers to let the trucks with trailers start coming through. There was still a chance that one of these might jack-knife and block the road, but the Superintendent liked to feel that the road was entirely open.

By five o'clock he was sure that things were in hand. More snow was falling again, but the wind had eased off considerably and was shifting back into the south. It had been a close call, but he hadn't exactly lost the road, even though convoying was the next thing to it. If he had to close the gates for a while after midnight to get a chance to clean the road up, that hardly counted either, for during those hours there was scarcely any traffic. And tomorrow would be another day, most likely with an entirely different problem.

12

From every river and creek in the great horseshoe of mountains about the Sacramento Valley the water was pouring out. Foot by foot the level rose at the gauges.

From the lowest parts of the by-pass lands men herded out the cattle and the sheep, and drove them to pastures a little higher, close to the levees which formed the boundaries of the by-passes. The steers sloshed through the soppy ground, bawling now and then. The ewes were draggled and heavy with rain. The lambs trotted uncertainly, stopping and starting; they bleated nervously.

In every river town came a stirring of excitement;

people went out on the bridges and stood there in the rain, watching the brown water flow and the bits of driftwood slide by. "Nineteen-point-three," someone would read, looking at the gauge. "She's risen more'n a foot since noon."

That afternoon the water at Colusa bridge rose to an even twenty on the gauge, and then quietly began to spill over the long crest of Colusa Weir into Butte Basin, and thence flow into Sutter By-Pass. The water topped Tisdale Weir next, and then Moulton. On the other side of the Valley, gauge-readings were rising rapidly on the Feather River and its tributaries, the Yuba and the Bear. At Vernon where the Feather flowed into the Sacramento, the great stretch of Fremont Weir—nearly two miles long —offered passageway for the combined rivers into Yolo By-Pass. In the early darkness the brown water rose to the concrete lip of the weir and flowed across into the wide plain between the levees.

At Sacramento the gauge-reading was as yet just under twenty. There the American was pouring its flood into the main stream. As yet its outflow had moved down the channel of the Sacramento between the levees without preventing the waters of the upper rivers from following the same course. As a result, water had not yet begun to flow over the wicket-tops of Sacramento Weir, four miles up-stream from the city. But the level at the gauge was steadily rising.

The General had stayed in the office later than previously. He only sighed when the phone rang again, and his secretary said, "Long-distance." It was one of the big asparagus growers in the delta country; his thousands of rich acres lay behind low levees which he was legally restrained from raising.

"Well, I don't know," said the General. "Up to this morning I would have said you were safe, but the Weather Bureau thinks we may get a lot of rain tomorrow. We have some leeway left even so, and a good deal depends on just how the rain hits."

"You won't open those gates any sooner than you need to, will you?"

The General had been a military man for many years, and he bridled at the implication of the question.

"Look here," he snapped. "I'll order those wickets opened exactly when I think is the *right* time, and no down-stream rancher and no up-stream Chamber of Commerce will tell me when *is* the right time either."

The General accepted an apology and hung up.

13

"We've been having a pretty easy time of it," said the L.D. to his assistant. "No break on any big line except that one up by French Bar. Of course we aren't through with it yet. Anyway, we're going to have something to fill the reservoirs with, next summer. The company ought to be able to pay its dividends."

"There's a big lot of tropical air moving in some time tomorrow," said the Chief Service Officer of Air-Lines. "That means heavy rains, but pretty quiet conditions generally. We ought to have a fairly good day."

14

Before midnight the Transcontinental Streamliner began
to pull out of the station at Chicago. Its departure, like
the sailing of an ocean-liner, mingled festivity and
solemnity. On the platform a woman dabbed at her eyes
with a handkerchief, and near her an after-theater party
muffled in evening wraps waved gayly at a corsaged
debutante who waved back through the window of her
drawing-room. Even inside the shelter of the train-shed
the cold was bitter.

The streamliner clicked along over the switches of
the yard at a leisurely pace. Two young men were sitting
in the lounge-car. One of them was reading a pamphlet
which described the train, and was commenting upon it.

"The mildest thing the publicity-men can say about
this train is 'a miracle of modern engineering and art.'
From there they work up. 'And truly the train may stand
for a symbol of what is best in modern civilization—tough
steel, aluminum alloys, resplendent chromium, satiny
copper, crimson leather, shining glass—all shaped into a
creation for safety and speed, power and comfort—a thing
of beauty!' Whoever wrote that passage didn't think re-
straint a virtue."

Across half a continent the tracks stretched out ahead.
Through the cold sheen of the winter moonlight the
streamliner would cross the snow-covered plains of
Illinois and Iowa. It would speed through the long reaches
of Nebraska during the forenoon, and give afternoon and
early evening to Wyoming. Less than twenty-four hours
upon the way it would click down Echo Canyon, fifteen
hundred miles from Chicago. Before the second night was

ended it would cross Utah and Nevada. Daybreak would find it climbing the Sierra wall into California; at noon it was scheduled to end its run, and halt at the shore of San Francisco Bay—twenty-two hundred miles in forty hours.

Over all those miles of track the streamliner had privilege and right of way. Freights, locals, and working-equipment took the sidings. The green lights glowed; the semaphores signaled open track. Dispatchers sent the streamliner through; trackwalkers patroled ahead of it; snowplows cleared the way. The premier train of the run must not be halted.

Already the city was behind. The train had gathered speed. Now it whistled for a crossing.

The deep note sounded far through the moonlight— like the sudden mysterious bay of some great hound, unearthly and night-running. Here and there some villager lying awake in bed heard it and turned to look at his clock. "The streamliner," he thought. "On time!" The train rushed onward through the night.

15

Over all the Valley rain was falling—on plowed land and stubble, on pasture and fallow and orchard. It fell on the black soil and the red soil, on the loam, the clay, the adobe, on the silt of the bottom-lands and the peat-earth of the delta.

It poured upon the mile-wide fields of new wheat and barley. It turned the alfalfa a brighter green. It glistened upon the gray leaves of the olive-trees, and made darker the dark green of the orange-trees. It wet the up-turned, delicate branches of the leafless peaches and plums and almonds, and the stiff rods of the cherries and the pears; it wet the myriad stubby branches of the figs—rigid, like gnarled fingers. It wet alike the wide-spreading walnut-trees and the close-pruned grape-vines.

Against all the cities of the plain the storm was beating—Oroville of the olives, Marysville of the peaches, and Colusa of the rice and barley; river-girt, high-domed Sacramento; Stockton, where the ocean-steamers dock far within the wide-reaching plain; Lodi of the grapes; Corcoran of the wheat; Fresno of the figs and raisins; Porterville of the oranges; Tulare of the cotton. Over them all was rain.

(That the shoots of wheat and barley might stand upright, and the rice and cotton sprout in their season. That in long rows the asparagus might thrust its stalks through the peat of the delta. That the almond-blossoms might soon be like a shining white cloud on the slopes, and in the summer sun the trays of drying prunes and apricots be bright rectangles of purple and orange.)

Five hundred miles from Red Bluff to the Grapevine, all the rich, flat land—over it all was rain.

WHILE MEN built Westminster Abbey and King Louis the Saint rode to his crusades, the cliff-cities of Mesa Verde —first civilization within the area of the United States— knew their last prosperity. For seven centuries they have lain empty, shunned by Ute and Navajo as spirit-haunted ruins of the Old People. But those centuries have meant little to earth and sun; as today, the winter storms swept down when Balcony House was new and fat babies rolled on its terrace.

Most likely a storm made little difference in the life of those diminutive, nimble-footed people whose ancient toe-holds still pit the face of the cliffs. In the winter their corn-fields on the mesa-top needed no care; the season held off the nomad raiders who came harrying in summer. While the storm raged and ice-glaze made the cliff-paths impassable, the dwellers in Balcony House may have settled down to their quietest and happiest days. The granaries were deep with corn and beans; the spring at the back of the rock-shelter flowed (as it still flows) with pure, cool water. Their dogs lived with them, and their turkeys were penned at the back of the houses. A fire of a few sticks sufficed in the thick-walled houses and the underground club-rooms of the men. For clothing there were deer-skins and blankets of turkey feathers. The great over-hang of arched rock was a shelter from snow and wind.

An interval for talk and laughter, for weaving, for fashioning of arrow-heads, for discussion about next year's corn-planting, for long rituals of religion—when the storm had passed by and the ice-glaze was shattered beneath the unveiled sun, then was time enough to climb the cliffs, and go visiting to the other villages.

But modern man cannot withdraw. He expects much more of his civilization; he has spread it far and wide until it sprawls; he has given hostages. Therefore, he must sally forth about his flocks and herds; he must look to his roads and ditches, his levees and culverts, his wires and rails. To protect his machines he must invent other machines and with them labor against the storm. The honor of the battle is now not so much to skill and courage as to flawless steel and cool bearings.

At the end, our cities will stand like those others. In the year when Edward of England made war on Llewellyn the Welshman and Ser Marco Polo was new in the court of Kublai Khan, the rains failed; year after year, drought lay upon the mesa-land. As some think, the people began to raise a great temple to placate the gods of storm; that temple still stands unfinished. Before the twenty-four years of drought had passed, the people were gone; dry winds swirled ashes in empty courtyards.

Whether the civilization of a land withdraws before

the storm or fights against it, the end will be the same. Man is of the air, and the air must rule him. Drought or flood, cold winds and ice, heat, blown dust, shift of the storm track—in the end they overcome even the imperturbable machines.

2

During a lull in the storm the old coyote went hunting again. He saw the airplane-beacon flashing into the darkness; he crossed the railroad; he leaped into the highway just after a push-plow had gone by.

He came to the remembered place where he had scented something strange beneath the snow. High above him at the top of the cliffs a rotary was working; some of the thrown snow, falling a hundred feet, settled as fine powder upon his fur. He nuzzled about. The depth of snow was greater than it had been before, and so the scent was fainter. As yet that night he had not killed, and now the saliva began to drool at the corners of his mouth. But mingled with the pleasant smell were others which made him suspicious and wary. He went prudently on his way, remembering the spot for future nights.

3

In San Francisco the rain was a steady downpour, heavier than ever. In Los Angeles the rain had stopped; there was a bright blue sky between broken clouds, and a brilliant sunrise. Portland had rain and Spokane snow, but in Seattle men pulled their overcoats closer to shut out a chilling dry easterly.

El Paso was having a sudden cold snap with snow-squalls. Abilene reported trees blown down in a fifty-mile gale. Galveston and Corpus Christi were being deluged with warm rain drifting in upon a steady southerly wind.

Tampa, half way between Miami and Pensacola, was ten degrees colder than either, but had a clear sky. Jacksonville and Savannah were dank and chilly beneath thick low-lying fog.

Washington had calm air and a brilliant sun which seemed to shed no warmth; the temperature was eight above zero. New York lacked two degrees of being as cold as Washington, and Philadelphia was a little warmer than either of them. In Boston the temperature was even higher, but a steady north wind made people feel chillier.

Buffalo was the cold pole of the country. As at Washington the air was still and the sun brilliant. But the temperature was sixteen below zero, and the newspapers reported four deaths from cold.

Detroit and Cleveland were below zero, but were warmer than they had been on the preceding day. Chicago was growing much warmer. Memphis had fog; Kansas City reported a thaw. Havre and Bismarck were almost as cold as Buffalo.

All these reports suddenly presented to the average common-sense citizen would certainly have led him to conclude that the weather in the United States upon this particular day was a mere crazy-quilt, wholly lacking in scheme.

To the J.M., looking at the ordered isobars of the finished map, the weather displayed a pattern which was precise, comparatively simple, and in a sense even purposive. The weather of any place in the eastern United States, for instance, could be readily explained by reference to its location within the high-pressure area which centered over Lake Ontario. In addition, the usual circulation of air from west to east was re-establishing itself.

The most obvious sign was Little Maria. She centered over Abilene, and was giving Texas almost every variety of weather. But there were other signs. The high-pressure area was slowly drifting eastward. He checked back upon the maps of the last three days and traced its movement—Kansas City, Terre Haute, Cleveland; and this morning its center was east of Buffalo. Maria still stood firm, and the Triplets were dead; but Victoria, growing in power, had already reached the western Aleutians. Over the Pacific the long arm of the northern invasion was shrinking back, and over the Yukon valley the pressure was falling. Again he looked at the preceding maps. On Tuesday that pressure had stood at 1050; on Wednesday it had dropped to 1042; today it was 1035. Once this pressure should have fallen a little farther, the outflow of northern air would cease, and Maria either would pass into some new phase, or else—cut off from fresh supplies of air—must die.

The Chief came in, and the J.M. felt himself suddenly grow warm with the new sense of comradeship.

"How's Maria?" said the Chief, quietly, so that no one else could overhear him.

"She's fine," said the J.M.

"I want to check again on that line of cloud."

It was still there—no doubt of that. One of the ships reporting cloud today had reported cloud yesterday. She was a fast liner from Honolulu heading for San Francisco, and the cloud bank was moving at just about the same rate.

"Hn-n?" said the Chief. "You know, those passengers on that liner will think there's been cloud all over the ocean all this time. Not so bad though, as when a ship gets in slow-moving storm-center, and keeps in it maybe half way across the ocean. Well, have you figured out anything more?"

The J.M. felt a new uplift at being asked a question as though he were an equal.

"No," he said, regretfully but honestly. "We've got a whole line of ships reporting between here and Honolulu, but they don't show enough wind- or temperature-shift anywhere to indicate a front. Whatever it is, it's only in the upper air."

"When would you say it'll get here, whatever it is?"

"Two or three tomorrow morning," said the J. M., but he did not say that he had used his slide-rule.

"Hn-n? worst time possible. In the afternoon it'll still be too far away for any good forecast, and it'll be on top of us before the morning forecast goes out. Maybe it's nothing, of course; and then again it may be a matter of a million dollars' damage and twenty lives. A plane with a good observer could fly out there in a few hours and find out what it's all about. Yet—" His voice was suddenly bitter. "If I asked the Navy for a plane, all the gold-braiders would laugh their heads off. But we have to take the responsibility of a forecast."

He bent over the map again, and studied it for any clue which might have so far escaped discovery.

The J.M. heard the door open and glanced around. He started with surprise. The Old Master was standing there, dripping wet. He looked pitifully small, draggled, and cold. His white hair straggled damply from beneath the sodden black felt hat. The light overcoat with the velvet collar clung to him, soaked. He was shivering.

The Chief looked up. "Lord!" he said sharply. And then both of them sprang to their feet. But the Old Master carefully shut the door behind him, and spoke in his outdated, formal way.

"Good morning, gentlemen. I thought that I should like to look at the map. My barometer has risen this morning, and I judged that the storm is over. I did not think it worth-while to carry an umbrella when I started out, and I am afraid I have been somewhat dampened by an unexpected shower."

The other two glanced at each other, and the Chief shook his head quickly.

"Here," he said. "Let me take your wet coat off. Sit by the radiator awhile, and dry your feet."

"Oh, no. I thank you, no. I shall just take a look at the map, and be on my way." He took his hat off out of politeness, but he only pulled his coat tighter about him as they started to take it. He walked toward the map, but a shiver took him, and he tottered.

"I'm afraid, sir," said the Chief, "you shouldn't trust a barometer too far. It's a wonderful instrument. But still—"

"Oh, yes, of course. Sometimes you get heavy rain with a rising barometer. I remember two such cases in eighty—eighty—eighty-seven. Yes. I know, I know. But still, other signs confirming, you can go with the barometer."

The Chief steadied him by the right arm; the J.M. held him by the left; he leaned over and peered hard at the map. A drop of water fell from him right upon a 1008 isobar. The J.M. mopped it up with his handkerchief; the Old Master did not even notice. Probably he was seeing next to nothing. The Chief was trying to explain the map.

"You see," he said, "there's a lot more rain to come in." The Old Master shivered violently; he did not seem to notice what was being said. Then he pulled himself together and seemed to come out of the fog; he spoke clearly and stiffly.

"I thought that I should like to see the map again. I shall be going along now. I know—*I know.*"

The Chief spoke hurriedly to the J.M. in a tense low voice: "Call the Navy Recruiting Office downstairs. *Somewhere*—get a doctor!"

4

Bright yellow in the winter sunshine, agleam with resplendent metal, the streamliner was making eighty miles an hour along the Platte River. Thin snow covered the land; in the channel the swift water ran black between the ice-fringes.

In the lounge-car two young men had joined with two older ones and were playing cards, listlessly. "One heart . . . two diamonds." Though it meant rubber, no one cared enough to put up a fight. When the points were added up, there was no suggestion of continuing.

"Are we on time?" asked one of the young men, just to be saying something.

"Were the last time I checked," said the second young man. "God, what a bore this trip is, even on the streamliner."

"Looks cold out there," said the first, gazing idly out the window at the bleak landscape.

"Plenty cold when we left Chicago—haven't stuck my nose out since, to tell the truth."

"Well, neither have I. Be good to get to California, and have a little decent weather."

"I hear they're having rain out there too."

"If there's one thing that bores me more than riding on a train," put in one of the older men, "it's discussing the weather. Riding on a train *and* discussing the weather is too much."

Between Norden and Emigrant Gap snow was falling at the rate of six inches an hour. A fast freight had to be side-tracked for twenty minutes until a rotary could punch through and clear the track, and then the freight had to follow a flanger, keeping one block behind.

The men piled out of the rotary, and fought their way to the station-house. They were shaky in the legs from the unceasing vibration; they walked uncertainly. Their clothes were soaked with perspiration from the heat and steam, and they shivered in the cold, snow-driving wind. They grabbed themselves sandwiches and coffee; and standing with coats opened they tried to dry their clothing around the roaring, red-bellied coal stove.

Then orders came through. They plugged back to the rotary through the snow, and started out again. In this kind of storm the snow-equipment had to be kept moving. A fast train with mail was due through in a little while, and stopping a train like that was more serious than holding up a freight.

In the foothills rain was falling instead of snow. In ground well softened by the long downpour Blue Boy, the big boar, rooted in contentment. From his precipitous pasture above the railroad he looked down incuriously with his little eyes at a train passing below him. It had come down from the higher altitudes so fast that in spite of the heavy rain a little snow still clung to the tops of the cars. For a moment there was the roar of the locomotive and from the circular orifice of the smoke-stack thick blackness belched upward at the boar. Then came the click-click of passing mail-coaches and Pullmans. The noise faded off around a curve, and only the sound of a whistle came back faintly. The boar rooted on, undisturbed.

5

In the early hours of morning the tropical air had arrived at the coast; by noon it covered all central California. While passing over the surface of the ocean it had produced only moderate rains along its advancing front where it overrode the cooler air ahead of it. But at the coast line the mountains forced it upward. Rising and cooling, the air released its stores of moisture. There were no displays of violence—no thunderstorms or wind-blasts. In fine drops the rain fell almost quietly, but the downfall was unceasing, and intense.

Mile by mile, swiftly, the tropical air moved inland. It crossed the Coast Ranges, and the air upon the long ridge-tops grew strangely mild. It moved over the Great Valley, but the air in that long trough was cool and heavy so that the tropical air moved across its top and nowhere touched the surface; but the rain which fell was not cold. Reaching the long westward slope of the Sierra the tropical air again rode upward, and the downfall was most intense of all. The snow-line lay about the three-thousand-foot level, but as the warmer air moved in, thick rain began to fall clear up to five thousand feet.

Some few days before, the Arctic had swept down across Texas; now as if in compensating reflux California became an outpost of the tropics. That air which swept the peaks and ridges had lain for weeks over the warm ocean. It had sucked its rain from the creamy foaming of lazy blue waves, from the spouting of whales, from the splashing of porpoises, sporting in the sea-trough. Its air had smoothed the plumage of gull and gony; it had laved the sides of leaping swordfish, and the backs of sleeping turtles awash in the long swells.

Over all of central California the tropical air was moving, but most intense was the precipitation in the foothills northeast of Sacramento, the basin of the American River. Five days of rainfall had saturated the earth, and now for every drop that fell another drop must somewhere pass into a stream and move rapidly downward toward the valley. Into the North Fork and the South Fork and the Middle Fork the water poured out from every side-canyon and gulch and gully. The North Fork of the North Fork came surging down. High up, the melting rain fell upon the snow which arched the East Fork and the Rubicon, and a thousand little streams which lay dormant in their snow-tunnels; beneath the insistent rain the snow grew soft and heavy; the arches fell and the water went foaming downward.

The streams poured out from all those creeks and

canyons named by the Forty-Niners—in hope and despair
and ridicule, now in flat matter-of-factness, now in flamboyant fancy. From Deer Creek and Otter Creek, from
Bear Creek and Grizzly Creek, from Jaybird Creek and
Redbird Creek. From Alder Creek and Willow Creek,
and Lichen Creek, and Brush Creek; from Granite Creek
and Slab Creek and Slate Creek. From Indian Creek and
Dutch Creek and Irish Creek. From Pilot Creek and
Whaler Creek, and Soldier Creek and Sailor Creek. From
Iowa Creek and Missouri Creek. From New York Creek
and Manhattan Creek, and Knickerbocker Creek and
Hoboken Creek. From Dry Creek, no longer dry. From
Lady Creek, and Widow Creek, and Secret Creek, which
mask (men say) far ruder names. From Devil's Creek and
Humbug Creek and Shirt-tail Creek; from Hangtown
Creek and Robbers' Creek and One-eye Creek. Out of
them all and a hundred more the water came foaming.

6

In the late afternoon the Superintendent stood again at
the wide entry-way of the Maintenance Station, and
looked out. Even here at the crest of the Pass there was
only a steady, moderate wind, but the snowfall was
thicker than it had yet been. It was more than ever like
feather-down spilled from a pillow, and the flakes descended in what seemed an impenetrable mass which the
eye strove in vain to pierce. The Superintendent could
not see the tamarack which he used as a gauge of snowfall; he could not even see the other side of the road.

A truck was coming up from the west. It was laboring
heavily, and he heard the engine pounding long before
he made out the headlights, dim and yellow. The truck

was plastered with snow, and even as it passed along the road thirty feet away, its outlines were indistinct and obscure. He could see, however, that it was a big van; the snow was piled high on its flat roof. No wonder she's laboring, thought the Superintendent; she's got maybe a ton of snow there on top.

The day-foreman was just behind the truck, and drove into the Station. His car looked like a moving snow-bank. The wipers were barely keeping two little sectors clear on the windshield; the chains were so clogged with snow that they hardly clicked on the concrete floor. One of the garage-men pulled up a hot-water hose, and began to wash the snow off in preparation for the next trip out.

The foreman walked across toward the Superintendent, his hob-nails scratching on the concrete. He had been out in the drifts wading around at the dozens of little matters which a foreman had to look to, and he was almost as snowy as his car. He took off his fur cap, and knocked the snow from it.

"Heavy today," he said. "Soda Springs says we've had over five feet of snow during the storm up to this morning, and there must have been a good foot since then anyway."

"Yes, it's a pretty bad storm," said the Superintendent.

The foreman grinned. "About the first time I ever heard you admit that much!"

"I've seen a lot of storms," said the Superintendent shortly. "Much traffic?"

"Just the ones that have to go through, and a few fools who don't know what they're gettin' into. Tomorrow afternoon the skiers will start comin', and then we'll have traffic troubles again."

From overhead came the sound of a plane.

"You wouldn't think those things would be running today," said the foreman. "But they've been going over regular as clockwork."

"Maybe they're above it all. It may be calmer up there than it is here."

"I hope it is—for those planes!"

The foreman stood a moment, scratching on the concrete with the hob-nails of his left boot.

"Well," he said, "I've got to see about takin' out some extra snow-stakes. There's gettin' to be a lot of places where the old ones are hardly showin' above the snow any more, and we'll have to splice new ones on their tops."

The foreman went off for the snow-stakes. The Superintendent got into his car, and drove down the east slope of the Pass to see how things looked.

The east face was to leeward, but around Windy Point was the usual swirling blizzard. Just below the Point he met a rotary. It was working up-grade on the inside of the road against the rock-wall, and was throwing its arc of snow across the highway and down the steep slope beyond. As he drew near, the rotary stopped throwing to let him drive by; he tooted lightly in salutation. He noted that the rotary was working heavily in very deep snow, over the top of the cutter-bar. A snow-nose must have just fallen off.

Around the Horse-shoe it was like a quiet nook, and the snow fell almost perpendicularly. At Rocky Point there was more wind again. Peering out through the windshield, the Superintendent could scarcely see anything, but by signs more than actual sight he knew that the snow-noses were many and were building far out. He could never exactly figure any logic to the ways of drifting snow. Against a telephone pole the snow always built out on the windward side. But at the crest of a cliff and along a cut in the road, it built out on the lee side. Farther and farther it would reach into space until the big blunt nose hung six or eight feet in the clear over the highway. Then eventually it grew too heavy and dropped, not doing any harm except to make a lot of mess for the plows to clean up. Some time, he supposed, a snow-nose would light on top of a car. Even so, it would probably not hurt anything, but it would certainly surprise the people in the car, and half scare them to death.

Below Rocky Point he met another rotary, also working up-grade on the inside. It seemed too close to the first one, but probably the operator was following orders from the foreman. Passing, the Superintendent leaned out, and caught a glimpse of big Peters in the rotary's cab.

He drove to the gates at the lake. Even at this slight distance to the east of the Sierra the snowfall was noticeably lighter. Beyond this point the rotaries were only needed occasionally, and a few miles farther was the open sage-brush country of Nevada which got hardly any snow at all.

As usual some drivers had come to this point without chains. A tow-car from a Truckee garage was standing by, like a vulture, waiting for people to get into trouble. The garage-man was putting chains on one car, but around another car two men were working unskillfully in the snow while a woman now and then lowered the window-glass far enough to yell advice at them.

The Superintendent drove up the highway again. A

big snow-nose had fallen, but it had left one lane still open. He passed the rotary, and tooted to Peters and Swenson. Just then he saw a tire-chain lying in the road; he stopped the car, and got out to pick up the chain so that it wouldn't get tangled up with the rotary.

Then—as he was walking back to his car—he heard it! It was unmistakable. He started to run for his car. The strange low hissing noise rose with a crescendo in pitch and intensity. Through the falling snow he could see nothing. Then as he ran, the whole roadway shook with some sudden impact; the hissing changed to a thudding. Like an advancing wave of water, a wave of snow came running along the highway. It pinned him against the side of his car, half-knocking his breath out.

In the next instant he found himself standing in three feet of snow. There was sudden quiet.

Pinned against the car, the Superintendent looked quickly to his right up the road; some twenty feet farther on, the wave of snow had come to a halt; for a moment with all the pressure of the mass behind, it had flowed madly, like a torrent of water; now it was only inert snow. He glanced hurriedly to his left, down the road. Where Peters and Swenson had been working with the rotary was now only a long unbroken slope of snow. The Superintendent wormed himself about, and got free. He saw that the snow behind his car was piled up too high for him to wallow through.

"Hey!" he shouted, cupping his hands in front of his mouth. "Peters! Swenson!"

He waited but there was no answer. Well, there was probably no need to worry. Things were bad, but they were most likely not nearly as bad as they looked. The road was not carried away. The slide had merely filled the roadway with snow, and swept on. On the outside edge of the road, the snow would be only a few feet deep; on the inside the depth might reach forty feet. Somewhere within that mass of snow was the rotary.

But the tough steel would withstand much more pressure than forty feet of snow could exert. Peters and Swenson were this moment undoubtedly still sitting inside the cab—white-faced probably, considerably surprised at their sudden entombment, perhaps still a little scared, but safe. Peters would already have had presence of mind enough to turn off the engine and prevent them from being asphyxiated. In a moment they would collect themselves enough to begin discussing whether they would try to dig themselves out, or merely sit tight until they were rescued.

Thinking of how flabbergasted Peters and Swenson would be made the Superintendent realize that he himself was almost as much appalled. And yet these great slides from the heights could be expected a few times during every hard winter; he had just never happened previously to be present during the few seconds when one occurred; he had been within earshot often enough.

Collecting himself, he saw that his car was hopelessly buried in three feet of snow. He floundered ahead out of the deep snow, and then set out, half-running, up the road toward the next rotary. As he went, he already was planning. Lucky, he thought, this other rotary was so close; it could be working on that slide in ten minutes after he got to it. In three hours the road might be open again. He had other luck too. He met a car coming down, flagged it, told the driver of the snow-slide, turned him around, and saved ten minutes walking.

Right at Windy Point was the rotary. With a curt thank-you to the driver, the Superintendent jumped out, and then he realized that the rotary was not working. The operator and the swamper were peering beneath it from behind.

"Anything wrong?" shouted the Superintendent, with a sudden feeling of depression.

"We were gunning her hard into that big drift," said the operator in half-apology. "An axle went."

The Superintendent stopped in his tracks, figuring hard. One rotary buried, and another temporarily out. Three hours, six hours, eight hours. He would order out the whole night shift, and bring up another rotary. Eight hours. But if he threw all his remaining power against the snow-slide, the rest of the road would become impassable. Ten hours, then. Ten, or twelve.

His depression deepened to blackness. For three or four hours he could simply hold traffic at the gates; it would be merely a block, not a closed road. But twelve hours—that would even be in the papers. This rotary had been running for four days steadily; that was the chief difficulty. In the end, machines were like men; you could drive them just so hard and so long before they went to pieces.

But in this fight there was no surrender. He got the day-foreman on the radio and gave his orders. Rout out the night shift. Send down every man you can spare from the garage, even the mechanics. Order up another rotary. Stop traffic. Get into touch with the Highway Patrol. Call headquarters in Sacramento.

The operator and the swamper were already at work under the rotary. But they would not get far until the mechanics came down from the garage, and even then the process would be slow. At Windy Point the snow blew into your eyes faster than you could blink it out.

The Superintendent hurried down the road again toward the slide. He told himself that he ought to be on the spot, mapping the attack; really it was just that he wanted to be doing something.

He could hardly see his own car. The snow had almost drifted into a mound over it. The track he had made in floundering out was obscured. He waded in, and with some difficulty got the shovel which he always carried in the back of his car.

In his excitement and his desire to be doing something, he even threw a few shovelfuls. Then he stopped, feeling foolish and almost embarrassed. He got back into the car, and sat there.

The Superintendent was thinking back some years to the time when he had been in high-school. One teacher had made him read a lot of poetry, and he had always had a sneaking liking for the stuff, although he would never have confessed to it to the other boys. The trouble was that things people did in poems were so often silly, even though the words were fine.

There was one poem he remembered now, while he sat in his car waiting for a rotary to come up. It was about a man who went through a lot of terrifying experiences and finally came to some place where he saw a tower, and just then he was going to be overwhelmed by some great mysterious power, far too big to fight against. Then the man got out a little horn, and blew defiance against the great mysterious power. The teacher had called it a magnificent gesture, and said something about the dignity of man, but the Superintendent remembered that he had always thought it pretty undignified to go blasting into a horn in a situation like that.

Take the way it was now. If this was a poem, he probably should get out and start shoveling snow. Would that be a magnificent gesture, or just ridiculous—in the face of a storm that covered all California? Only machines could clear that road, and he might as well settle himself and keep calm and wait for them.

He leaned back comfortably. Stolidly he lighted a cigarette. He had a fleeting suspicion that perhaps the cigarette itself was a gesture. "Well, anyway," he said to himself, "it's time I was having a smoke."

But as he pulled in on the cigarette that feeling of deep depression came over him again. He had lost the road! The storm had been too much. It had worn down the men, and beaten even the machines.

7

Once the water had begun to spill over the weirs, the gauge-readings rose more slowly; but still they rose. People going out after breakfast to stand on Colusa Bridge saw the brown swirling water just a hair above twenty-one. At noon they looked, and said, "Twenty-one-point-six." By three o'clock the water was just below twenty-two. But the levees stood up high and firm on either side; the river would have to rise seven feet more, and touch twenty-nine to reach the danger-point, and even beyond that the levees, with luck, might stand a foot or two.

For every inch that the water rose at the gauge, another inch spilled over the weir. By mid-afternoon a depth of two feet was pouring over the quarter-mile length of Colusa Weir; that flow itself already equaled a large river. But from the other weirs also great streams poured out. Over Fremont the flow was twenty inches deep and nearly two miles wide. Peering out through rain-sluiced windows, the people in cars crossing the long viaduct on U.S. 40 looked out to see Yolo By-Pass a mighty river three miles wide of swiftly flowing flood water.

Sacramento gauge, close to the point where the American flowed into the main stream, stood in early afternoon at twenty-one-point-five. It was rising slowly, but as at Colusa the city would not be endangered until the water rose seven and a half feet more, and touched twenty-nine. Before *that* happened, the weir-gates could be opened.

In the General's outer office three assistants had been kept busy all day. Each had a telephone, and all three lines were busy most of the time.

One of the assistants flipped the switch for the General's private telephone.

"Yes?" said the General from the inner office.

"Folsom reports seven-point-eight, up nine-tenths in an hour. I thought you'd like to know it right away."

"Yes, thanks. We're in for some trouble with the American, I think."

"And, General, Oroville wants you—Mr. L. D. Jackson. He wants you personally."

"Put him on," said the General with resignation. He had never heard of L. D. Jackson, but felt that he had been talking to him under different names and in different towns all day.

"Yes, General," said the long-distance operator. "And when you're through talking to Oroville, would you mind not hanging up? I've three more long-distance calls waiting for you."

The General talked with Mr. Jackson, giving him information and reassurance. Then he talked to Red Bluff, Redding, and some ranch-house out of Marysville. It was the same story with slight variations; each man had his worries which in his own mind loomed larger than the possible flooding of all the rest of the valley.

Fortunately at this stage the General could usually quiet people's fears very quickly. The water was flowing over the weirs and flooding through the by-passes on a much greater scale but with the same simplicity that water spills from one basin of a fountain into the next. Everywhere the gauges stood several feet below the critical point. With the rain still continuing, there was no telling what height the flood crest would finally reach, but as yet the tremendous capacity of the by-passes was not even severely taxed.

So far, the damage reported had been only incidental and fortuitous. Two boys venturing out in a rowboat had lost their heads apparently, and overturned in the swirling channel; one of them had been drowned. A sudden outbreak of Stony Creek had swept away two hundred sheep. Seepage, caused probably by gophers working in the levee, was being fought near Meridian; local authorities reported the situation controlled. An incipient break in the Feather River levee had been discovered by a patrol before it had time to develop. The near-by ranchers had mobilized hastily. One of them donated some bales of hay, and these clogged the flow until a sand-bag defense could be built up.

"Hold up any more calls for me," said the General into his telephone. "Unless there's an emergency; I've got to do some figuring and get out a forecast."

The American was the immediate problem. Reports from the mountains indicated very heavy rain was falling everywhere in that basin. Even worse, it was a warm rain and was washing off the snow-cover up to the five-thousand-foot level. Every creek and gully flowing into each of the three forks must be a-boiling. And of all the rivers the American was the most flashy; because of its steeper gradient and shorter length, its waters crested quickly, and came out with a rush. With Folsom gauge rising so rapidly, the lower country would soon feel the effects; by latest report Sacramento gauge had risen to twenty-one-point-eight.

The General dictated: "The Feather, Yuba, and upper Sacramento Rivers are rising slowly, but gauge-readings are not excessive; flood levels are not to be expected within the next twenty-four hours. The amount of water flowing through the by-passes will increase moderately. The American River is rising rapidly, and will reach twenty-five feet at Sacramento about midnight. This will necessitate closing the main highway between Sacramento and North Sacramento, and re-routing the traffic *via* Jib-boom Street."

The General settled back in his chair and looked at his desk-clock. That statement would go out immediately, and in about twenty minutes he could expect the Committee.

The Committee consisted of three business-men, a type of humanity for which the General as a military man had no liking. Two of them were tall and thin, but the chairman and the most aggressive was short and fat.

"General," he stated emphatically, "this has got to stop. When that road is closed, business in North Sacramento falls off fifty to a hundred thousand dollars *each day*. Sacramento clearing-house receipts fall off *five hundred thousand dollars—each day!*"

The man's overemphasis made the General think of a dog's barking; he disliked it intensely. Also, as a former officer he disliked being shouted at by a civilian. But he kept his temper.

"Look here," the man barked on, "if you open those gates at the twenty-five-foot gauge reading, that *road won't flood*. We represent the State *Businessmen's* Association, and we pay a *lot* of taxes. We're *about* ready to turn on the *heat!*"

In the long years since he had ceased being a junior officer the General had got out of the habit of keeping himself tightly reined in, but he still held on.

"Gentlemen," he said, "what happens to the delta farmers when those gates are opened?"

"They get *flooded* of course, but they take that chance. And there's not *half*—not a *quarter*—the loss of crops that there is loss of *business here.*"

The General reflected a moment, wanting to argue. Damage to land and crops was real to him, but as a military man he could never quite figure out the meaning of loss of business. Someone didn't spend money today because he didn't like to go out in the wet, but he must do something with the money some time. But that was not the point.

He put his last thought into words. "Gentlemen, that's not the point. There is the matter of an agreement. Possibly conditions have changed, and flooding the highway is more costly than flooding the farmers. That's still not the point—I hold the gates until I consider that the safety of the city is endangered."

The three men of the Committee looked at one another, and then got up. Last to go was the fat chairman. He turned around in the doorway.

"All right, *General*—" he barked. "And *say,* you don't by any chance *own stock* in the Delta Asparagus Company?"

The General was on his feet. He did not bark, but he roared: *"Get out of my office!"*

The General strode back and forth the length of the room. By God, by God, but civilians were a poor lot of mammals, by God! Didn't they ever learn that you had to work together, even sacrifice yourself, for the whole? That very moment the General limped as he walked, and he had that limp from the day he took his regiment against a too strong German position. Everybody knew it was a hopeless attack. But it pegged some German reserves, and kept them off the neck of another American outfit somewhere. The men who died—and there were a lot of them—at least knew that they helped the whole army. In war you fought a common enemy. But these buyers and sellers—faugh!—they strangled each other. They squabbled even when the storm allied itself with the river, when hour by hour the readings of the gauges were higher and the rising water lapped searchingly

along the levees. Suddenly the General felt a great dis-
gust with man as a species. It might be a good thing if
the situation pictured in his favorite passage should happen again and on a larger scale—if the whole valley (or
the whole world perhaps) should become only a far-
stretching welter of brown waters with a few heads
bobbing about here and there for a little while.

Still, he would like to have an ark to save some of the
better ones—a few good soldiers, and some of the men
who were out there patrolling the levees right now in
the rain, fighting the river and the storm, not figuring
how to get a dollar and thirty-six cents out of some other
fellow.

8

At the airport it was an easy day. In spite of the intense
downpour, the planes came and went nearly on schedule.
The tropical air was stable, and almost as trustworthy
as high-pressure. The ceilings were ample; the wind was
steady and moderate; there were no electrical disturbances. Even over the mountains there was no icing. The
clouds lay in great, long strata, and between cloud-levels
the pilots found good enough visibility. As for the heavy
rain, that in itself was no hazard; it flew from the pro-
peller-blades and from the fuselage and wings—and no
harm done.

It was the best day that the Chief Service Officer had
experienced since the beginning of the storm. But toward evening he grew a little nervous. It was like a dead
calm; sooner or later it must break, and you began to
wonder *how* it would break. He looked at the afternoon
weather maps, and talked with the meteorologist.

"What's that isolated line of cloud doing out there off shore?" he asked.

"Can't make out exactly," said the meteorologist. "Some kind of upper-air front. It's been moving in closer for the last couple of days. We're watching it."

"You'd better!" said the CSO shortly. He checked the latest weather reports from the air-lanes. There was no important change.

He passed into the dispatching-room, and checked the reports of progress which had been radioed in from the various planes. There was nothing of note.

He went back to his office. There he snarled malignantly at a stenographer who came in with letters. He knew that he was merely relieving his own nerves, but he did not apologize. Being rude to the stenographer was only a way of keeping himself from settling down into complacency.

"Act of God!" he thought cynically to himself, returning to that early religious training, now long perverted. "Fire and hail, snow and vapors, stormy wind fulfilling his word!" He checked over his old enemies wondering which was getting ready to strike next. "The Prince of the power of the air!" Yes, he too was working somewhere at his subtle sabotage—making pilots overconfident and careless, crossing the wrong wires in men's minds, causing meteorologists to be unobservant, lulling dispatchers into negligence.

In a few minutes now his assistant would be coming on and taking charge for the night. He felt that he should pass on some warning, but there was really nothing which he could transmit except perhaps his own nervousness, and that in itself would be misleading.

9

The first outfit that got to the snow-slide was the V-plow
with eight men of the night shift hanging on to it. First
of all they took in a chain, and hooked it around the
front axle of the Superintendent's car. With the other
end attached to the plow they yanked the car out of
three feet of snow by main force. Then the V-plow drove
right on into the slide. It went ahead easily as far as
the snow had just run up the road, but when it hit the
main part of the slide, where the snow was many feet
deep, the plow shoved ahead and made a hole in the
snow, and the V-plow could do nothing more.

Next a push-plow came up. It widened the narrow
track of the V-plow, and then barged around, pushing
the shallower snow back in various places. While it was
working, some of the men got their webs on, and climbed
up on the slide; they had to move gingerly for fear their
weight might start the whole slide again and take them
down into the canyon. When the lights of a rotary
showed up around the turn, the push-plow went off to
work on the road somewhere else; it would be no more
use for a while at the slide.

The rotary headed in as far as the push-plow had
opened up the way, and then started work. The men
gave a little cheer as it began flinging snow; for now they
were really getting somewhere. The operator had set
the augers so that the rotary climbed up on the snow a
little as it advanced. But even so, as soon as the rotary
got to the main part of the slide, the snow was high over
the tops of the cutter-bars. The rotary ate its way ahead
until soon it had dug out a cave for itself and the blower

had no place to throw the snow. Then the operator backed it out, and began shaving up the edges, and the men with shovels on top of the slide tumbled down great masses of snow, especially from the mouth of the snow cave. As soon as there was enough to work on, the rotary waded in again and threw it all over the side. But the advance was slow.

The Superintendent's job was to direct the fight, and mostly he was busy, plunging around through the snow, telling the operator where to head the rotary in, directing the men on top of the slide and warning them to be careful. Once he went back a little way to get a look at the whole set-up, and it was something of a sight to see. Darkness had come on, and the snow was falling as fast as ever. The lights from all the plows and cars that were there were playing on the slide. The men on top looked small and black as ants by contrast with the great white heap. The rotary was throwing its great arc. And all around, the flying snow reflected back the lights, and shut off the little scene of activity from all the world outside.

He had time then to figure out just what had happened. High on the cliffs a big overhanging snow-nose had got too heavy and dropped off. It lit on the loose snow which had just fallen, and below that snow would be the surface of the old snow which had fallen in November and grown slick and hard and icy by melting a little in the sun each day and freezing up at night. The new snow had started moving, not rolling like a snow-ball, but sliding along the slick surface below. It picked up speed and grew as it went. Now it would override the snow ahead, and now it would shove beneath and carry it along. There was nothing to stop it, for this was an old track where the snow had been sliding for centuries. No trees could grow there long enough to get big, and all opposing rocks had long since been carried away. So the slide was probably nothing but snow—and that would be lucky for the two men inside the buried rotary.

Up at Windy Point the mechanics were working on the broken axle. It was a tough job. As darkness came on, they had to rig up extension lights from the battery. They staked down canvas all around the rotary. But twice the canvas blew loose, and all the time the wind whistled under and over it and through all the chinks until a man could hardly see or hear, and had to work mostly by feel. But in the end they pulled the pieces of the old axle, and fitted the new one into place.

The men on the slide gave the rotary with the new axle a cheer when it came down the road. The Superintendent lined it up behind and to the left of the other rotary. With two arcs of snow flying the rate of progress picked up, and the scene was wilder-looking than ever.

Then suddenly there was a lot of yelling, and some of the men from the top slid down. Peters was just heaving himself out of the snow. They beat him on the back in triumph, and then dug in and pulled out Swenson who was just behind. The two of them had got the shovels out of the back of the rotary, dug their way in to the rock wall along the inner edge of the highway, and then followed it, tunneling foot by foot, and using the rock wall as one side of their tunnel.

"I'll send you right up to the Station, and you can get something to eat and turn in," said the Superintendent.

"Ah, I'm all right," said Peters. "Give me some webs

and a shovel, and I'll get up there with the boys on the slide."

Swenson said nothing, but went along with Peters.

By this time it was eight o'clock, and the rotaries had not eaten ahead more than fifty feet into the two hun-dred feet of slide which lay upon the road.

At nine the cooks came down with coffee and sand-wiches. Everybody felt a little better.

The men gave all they had, but there was something grim about it. You wouldn't have called it a joyous fight. The men did a lot of swearing—at the job, and at each other. Superintendent and all, they knew they had lost the road. It would be in the papers: Donner Pass Closed. Just as if it might have been U.S. 50 over Echo Summit or the Sonora Pass road which nobody even tried to keep open.

It's a fine thing to go below (as the mountain people say) in the spring, and meet up with a fellow you know, in Sacramento maybe, or Marysville. And you go in for beers and he says, "Where you been all winter?"

"Oh," you say, "I was up on the Hump with the snow-plows."

"That so?" he says, and he's kind of impressed.

"Yessir," you say, "we kept ol' Donner Pass open all through the winter, even that bad storm in January."

But now you couldn't say that. You'd lost the road. "Crise-tamitey, quit jabbin' me with that shovel-handle."

10

That night no car went east or west. From Shasta on the north to the Tehachapis on the south, every pass was blocked with snow. Unbroken, the long Sierra thrust its peaks into the air; where the mountains rose highest and boldest against the sky-line, there the age-old battle of air and rock raged most fiercely. The snow swirled around the pinnacles; it settled deep in draw and chimney; it drifted across the ledges. From the peaks trailed off through the air the mile-long snow-banners.

Far to the north on Lassen the snow lay thick, white-blanketing the deep volcanic fires. Like black flames, the Sierra Buttes thrust skyward, too steep for snow to find lodgment. Castle Peak and Donner Peak guarded the Pass; Mt. Tallac looked down upon the tossing waters of the wide blue lake, too deep for freezing.

Southward, far southward, peak over against peak (named and nameless), ran that line of mountains. Higher and higher they rose to the south until Mt. Whitney topped them all. Peak, butte, and pinnacle; dome, ridge, and crest—over them all was snow. Snow upon the glaciers, upon the thick frozen tarns, snow over all the stunted junipers and lodge-poles that lay close along the granite at timber-line.

No longer was the air mild and gentle as when it had lain over the tropical water. Cast upward miles high, it seemed now more like some frigid influx from the Pole. Its tepid moisture had now become hard-frozen snowflakes. No longer did it move languorously; but, sucked in toward the maelstrom of the center, it swept the ledges with hurricane fury. From Lassen to Olancha, five hundred miles, against every peak and crag whirled the storm-driven snow.

ONCE UPON A TIME (to tell a fable) a primitive tribe lived beside a broad, brackish river near the ocean. This river had a disconcerting and inexplicable habit. Sometimes when the people wanted to dig clams, they found the water lapping high against the banks, and the clam-beds flooded. Sometimes when the people went to fish, they found wide mud-flats where they had expected to spear salmon.

At first the people attempted no explanation. After many generations they came to realize that a river-god, capricious and sometimes malignant, was responsible for this rise and fall. They placated the god by throwing flowers and food into the water, and now and then (when famine came) a baby.

After further generations a wise man arose among the people. He showed them how to outwit the river-god, who was really stupid, or else subordinate to the sun-god. For, observing the time of high water by the position of the sun, you could return next day when the

288

sun was in the same position, and find the water high again. The priests were horrified, and had the man stoned to death for impiety, but the people found his ideas useful.

Throughout further centuries the knowledge of the tides increased. It was learned that they followed the moon more than the sun, that they were greater toward the north, that even the vagaries of spring- and neap-tides accorded to rule. Finally the people, having developed mathematics and printing, published tables showing for a year in advance the height and time of every tide. Local influences such as wind and rain still produced a little variation, but the tide was no longer mysterious, and fearful; it was wholly understood.

As is the tide, so is the weather; the atmosphere, like the ocean, moves under physical laws. But the atmosphere is more mobile, so that the forces seriously affecting it are more numerous. All its motions arise from the heat of the sun, but this simplicity lies obscured beneath complications. Gravity, inertia, electricity, the spherical shape of the earth, its rotation, the ocean-currents, the contrasts between water and land and between desert and forest, the height of mountains, the compressibility of air, the almost explosive qualities of water-vapor—these and other forces combine to produce the weather.

Man is now able to make approximate short-range forecasts. He has reached about as far as the people who estimated tides by the sun. But many of the forces of weather-control have already been stated with mathematical exactitude. The way of progress lies ahead, wide and open. A century hence, Siberia and Patagonia alike,

Arctic and Antarctic, the islands of the sea and the ships that cross the sea, may all report to one great bureau. Then the published tables of next year's weather may be as accurate as the published tables of next year's tides.

Only man's quarrelsomeness seems likely to prevent this consummation. To master and apply the laws of the air without a world-wide co-operation is like trying to predict tides with an imperfect knowledge of the motions of sun and moon.

If the final success is attained, what will be the effect upon man? Will he at last have to stop talking and speculating about the weather? Will the foreknowledge that he must prepare against a tornado upon a given day be more strain than grasshopper-like ignorance and sudden disaster? Will the removal of the daily mystery only serve perhaps to make life at once safer and more boring?

2

"The brave west winds" again were blowing. Across the continent from the Gulf of Alaska to the Atlantic, the linked storms closed their front against the north. As yet the eastward-moving current was weak, and its course was sinuous. Here it ran far to the north; here swinging to the south, it even eddied back westward. But still the final movement was from west to east. No longer did the polar air reach out deep toward the tropic. The forces of the south had restored their line of battle.

During six days and nights the Canadian plains had been an extension of the Arctic—ever since the morning when the blizzard had swept down from the north.

The blizzard had ceased after a few hours; then the clouds vanished, and the air grew still. But that stillness lay like death upon the land. Day by day, a brassy sun swung in a long arc through the southern sky, but it gave little warmth; at noon the stretched-out shadows lay blue across the snow. Night by night, a waxing moon rode bright in the sky; not even a wisp of high cirrus blanketed the earth; the heat radiated off far toward the cold stars.

In the dawn, steam rose visibly from the stables where the blanketed horses huddled. From the chimneys of lonely ranch-houses smoke rose straight and high until at last it bulged out like some great unnatural mushroom. On the range, cattle pawed and nuzzled through the crusty snow to reach the dried grass; their legs were scraped and bleeding; bloody icicles hung at their nostrils. They must keep to their feet; for, if they lay down, they froze to the ground. As, moaning, they huddled together for warmth, mist from the moisture and warmth of their breathing hung over them in the still air as mist hangs over a pool. (But far over the Pacific the air was moving.)

By mid-week, people had only one thought and one salutation: "Will the chinook never come!"

Then, late Thursday afternoon, there was a change. The temperature rose somewhat, and the Weather Bureau at Edmonton reported only seventeen below zero. At sunset, men looking southwest saw a long, unbroken bank of cloud, low-hanging over the mountains. Its lower edge resting on the ridges was dark and heavy, and straight as a line drawn with a ruler; the upper edge was broken and wind-whipped, and cast up the sunset in red-gold. "She's coming!" men said, and were loosed from fear.

Just after midnight the mild, dry southwester—the chinook wind—swept across the plains. At the Weather Bureau the thermograph showed a rise of thirty-three degrees—from thirteen below zero to twenty above—in ten minutes. To people waking in the night the air was soft and warm like a breeze of springtime. "The chinook!" they said. "Thank God!"

Pious people were well within their rights to thank God for the chinook, although (to be consistent) they should also have rendered thanks every morning for the rising of the sun. For, equally, the chinook and the sunrise were the result of natural processes. A week earlier the cold wave in Alberta had been associated with an approaching storm in California, not as cause and effect, but merely as the two parts of a broken cup fit perfectly, being really one. Now, in the same way, the long continuance of the storm matched the coming of the chinook.

Nevertheless, the mild and dry air now melting the snow upon the plains had a history during the past week which even by atmospheric standards was an Odyssey. On the preceding Friday, as frigid and dry polar air, it had moved from the frozen Arctic Ocean over the region of tundra west of Coppermine. On Saturday, grown even colder, it was moving west along the Yukon Valley. On Sunday, maintaining its speed of nearly eight hundred miles in twenty-four hours, it crossed the mountains of southern Alaska, became warmer and drier because of its descent, and moved southward in the region of Kodiak Island. On Monday it thrust south far into the Pacific as part of the western discharge of the polar air; over the ocean it was growing rapidly warmer and more moist. On Tuesday it felt the pull of the storm-center off the California coast and swung toward the southwest. On Wednesday the same storm brought it northeast at about the latitude of San Francisco; flung upward by the mountains, it discharged its newly gained moisture as rain and snow. On Thursday, it was again dry and moderately cold; still within the orbit of the storm, it was being driven rapidly northward as a severe wind, dry and below freezing, across the high plateau of eastern Washington; by the late afternoon it was reaching through and over the mountains of British Columbia. At this point, because of the pressure systems which were being built up, the old storm center was no longer able to hold it, and the air moved northeastward in the control of another storm just developing farther north.

Even on the mountain tops the air had been dry and only moderately cold. Descending, it had grown much warmer and drier. By daybreak temperatures from Edmonton to Regina were well above freezing. The snow had almost vanished; wide pools of water stood in the fields. Yet the streams did not rise greatly; the warm dry air sucked up the water almost as rapidly as the snow melted, and in many places evaporated the snow even before it could change to liquid. Over all the wide prairie, the saving chinook had broken the deadly grip of the north.

3

As a minor detail of the vast complex of storm, the pocket of old polar air which had intruded itself into the tropical air had continued to move toward the California coast. It was only a few hundred miles in diameter; nevertheless, it possessed almost explosive potentialities. It was warm and moist below and extremely cold and dry above. If anything contrived to force the lower layer upward, this air would cool as it rose, but still would remain warmer than the air of any particular level at which it arrived. It would therefore continue to rise more and more rapidly.

The first of the old polar air to reach the coast was a narrow wedge which lay beneath the last of the warm tropical air and so was prevented from rising. About three hours before daybreak, however, the full depth of old polar air arrived, and mountains of the Coast Range cast the lower level upward; immediately, as if a match had been touched to shavings soaked in gasoline, the reaction within the air itself became spontaneous. Great towers of cumulus cloud, miles in circumference, ascended higher and higher, billowing outward. From this rising air the rain, hard-drumming in great drops, poured in cloudburst torrents. But here and there the upper current was so strong that it carried the falling rain aloft and swirled it about until the drops froze and at last fell as hail. Close to the ground the air was sucked in violently, as toward a vacuum, to fill in behind the rising air; the sudden wind-flaws drove the rain before them, and snapped branches from trees. The disturbed electrical balance readjusted itself in stabs of lightning; thunder boomed above the roar of wind and rain.

With the staccato rattle of drums sounding an alarm, the heavy drops beat upon thousands of windows. Shades

flapped, curtains bellied out, water spattered upon floors.
Thousands of people woke from the death-like sleep
which comes before the dawn. Still drugged with obliv-
ion, men staggered to close half-opened windows. Mothers hurried to look at their babies. Children screamed in
fright at the sudden uproar. (As thousands of lights were
snapped on, the operator at French Bar Power-House,
two hundred miles away, spun his handle and let more
water pass through the turbines to meet the sudden de-
mand for current.)

The General Manager awoke. He thought of his thousands of miles of rails gleaming wet in the night, of the
waters running in the ditches beside the tracks, of the culverts and the bridges. He remembered the streamliner,
somewhere out in Nevada, coming fast. He thought also
of the men and the safety devices, of the snow-plows at
work, of the red and green lights shining through falling
rain and snow. He had confidence, and went back to
sleep.

Jen's sister awoke, and went to look at her babies. As
she heard the beating rain, she shivered and caught her
breath in a sob. She felt her little sister out there somewhere lying in the rain, or wandering lost, calling to her.
For the hundredth hopeless time she called the office of
the Highway Patrol. No news. Shivering, she went to bed,
and did not sleep again.

The Chief Service Officer did not quite awake. (He
was worn out with a hard week, and all the responsibility
of when to let his planes go, when to keep them
grounded.) He tossed about as the drumming of the rain
beat its warning in through layer after layer of sleep.
But his subconscious mind rejected the call of duty

which, waking, he would have assumed. It tricked him, and in dream he seemed only to be watching a parade. The rattle of the hail became the *ta-ratta-ta-tat* of snare drums, and the distant thunder was only the sounding of the great horns. He did not leap to the telephone with a word of warning and advice to his less experienced assistant at the airport. Instead, half-awaking, he imagined comfortably that it was merely a dream, and fell into another sound sleep.

The L.D. awoke. "Sounds like trouble," he thought. He remembered his wires and his poles, his dams and his ditches. But he had confidence in his men, and went back to sleep.

The District Traffic Superintendent awoke. He took down the telephone from the head of his bed, and talked with the office. "Just a local cloudburst," said his assistant. "No trouble yet on the long lines." The DTS went back to sleep.

The Chief awoke. He looked at the clock. "Hn-n?" he thought. "*That* was it!" Then, since there would be no use in getting to the Bureau before the reports came in, he rolled over for another cat-nap before getting up.

As it approached land, the old polar air had had a breadth of several hundred miles, bulging forward near the center. This center touched the coast first near San Francisco, and the violence of the action at that point was such that it pulled the air in from the north and south. The moving front of heavy rain and piled-up clouds thus shrank in breadth and became correspondingly more intense. It swept across San Francisco Bay, deluged the hill country and sluiced down its rain upon the delta.

Rushing northeast across the Great Valley it struck Sacramento.

The General awoke to full consciousness all at once. The rain crashed against the closed window like something solid. He called his office, where one assistant worked through the night.

"When did this get here?" he demanded.

"Just now, sir. But I knew it was coming. It hit the delta half an hour ago, and I've had a dozen long-distance calls already."

"Any trouble?"

"Nothing—yet."

"I'll be right down."

Dressing, he looked at his watch; the hands pointed at four-twenty-six.

"Big Al" Bruntton, the pilot, was checking over the trip forecast with the dispatcher at the Salt Lake City airport. It was five-twenty-nine (Mountain Time), and he was taking out the big sleeper-plane, non-stop, to San Francisco, a four-hour flight, better than six hundred miles. Either Al or the dispatcher, not liking the weather conditions, could cancel the trip. But it was hard even to think of canceling when conditions at Salt Lake City were perfect for flying. The forecast indicated that the same conditions would hold almost to Reno. Farther on, the storm was continuing.

"The five A.M. reports," said the dispatcher, "don't show anything very bad over the Hump. It's tropical air—stable. Trip six-eight flew it, and just went through between cloud levels. The Bay has been having violent showers, but that's very local—as yet anyway."

"Let's get started," said Big Al.

"If we have to ground you at Reno, all right. But I think the chances are pretty good you can go all the way through."

Big Al walked out to the plane. The night was snappy cold, not much above zero. Only a slight drift of air was moving up from the south. The sky was a wide arch of stars, glittering bright through the desert air. Far to the west, ahead, a full moon was low in the sky. Back eastward, over the mountains, was just a hint of the coming dawn. On a night like this the idea of storm was unreal. Big Al could hardly bring himself to believe that within five hundred miles he might be ordered down.

He settled himself at the controls; trying not to bump his sleeping passengers more than was necessary, he took off. Gaining altitude he swung around and headed west; the beam was a dull steady buzz in his ears. He leveled off as soon as he had reached safe flying height, for if he went higher he would meet heavier headwinds. He settled to cruising speed. Ahead he saw the moon. As always he felt that he was racing the moon, even overtaking it. Actually, he knew, the plane was making about one-hundred-eighty miles an hour, the moon at this latitude roughly seven hundred. He could not even keep the moon in sight. And even faster, the sun was racing up behind him. Tonight the moon would not set, but would be caught in the open; and somewhere over Nevada he would watch it grow dim ingloriously before the rays of the sun.

As the plane rose higher and the never-freezing waters of Great Salt Lake lay beneath, the streamliner pulled out of Reno. After two thousand miles it was still on time to the second. In the sleeping-cars the corridors were dim. Most of the passengers were asleep; those who had awakened because of the stop at Reno were settling down again. The bar was closed; shining chromium and crimson leather, the lounge-car was empty except for a dozing trainman.

The wheel-clicks came faster as the train picked up speed. Like the bay of some huge unearthly hound, the horn sounded through the night. A swaying and creaking of the cars let even a man lying in his berth know that the train was pulling up-grade.

On the crests ahead, thick clouds hung low, but overhead broken clouds slid across the sky. The moon shone between, gleaming upon scanty desert snow. The clumps of sage-brush were snow-encrusted; in the moonlight they glittered like wedding-cake ornaments.

Ahead of the streamliner, red lights winked into the green. Fifty miles farther on, a rotary snow-plow pulled out of Norden yards to get the track clear; a flanger crew was making ready to follow. Track-walkers dragged themselves out of sleep, and set out to patrol their sections. The crack train of the run must go through on time.

The wheels ground on a curve; the streamliner, a few miles out of Reno, was entering Truckee Canyon. In San Francisco the Chief was drawing the last of his isobars.

Against the blank darkness of the windows the rain was a continuous crash, varying only as some gust raised it to a crescendo and then let it fall off a little. The Chief was working with a half-smile on his lips. With that beat of rain against the windows it seemed silly to think that the storm was over. Yet he had already in his mind worded his forecast: "Heavy showers, then clearing." By the time the average citizen sat down to breakfast and, picking up his paper, looked for the weather-report, the rain would already have ceased; very likely the sun would be shining.

Yet the Chief was not dabbling in astrology or staring at a crystal; the forecast lay all upon the map, clear for anyone to read. Off-shore about a hundred miles, sharply defined by ship-reports, he had drawn a blue line marking a cold front. Eastward of that boundary line as it advanced toward the coast was falling pressure, warm moist air, and a southwest gale; behind it was rising pressure and cooler air borne in on the northwest wind. That front with a sharp wind-shift line of more than ninety degrees, would cause plenty of disturbance as it passed over California, but it would be the storm's last kick.

He called the J.M. over for a look. "Well," said the Chief, "your friend Maria is about done for." East and west, like hostile forces, areas of high pressure had developed and were pressing in. To the south, the Pacific High showed again. Northward, Victoria had drawn close, taking to herself the northern air which had been feeding Maria. At the center, the pressure was rising rapidly.

"What about this?" asked the J.M., motioning with his head toward the windows where the storm still beat.

"Pretty local. Fresno, you see, reports only a drizzle."

"Well, Maria was a good one, while she lasted."

"Don't speak of her in the past, quite yet. Wait till that front goes by. Say, have you called the hospital?"

Racing on from Sacramento, northeastward, at forty-five miles an hour, the front of the advancing old polar air met the line of the foothills shortly before six o'clock. The steady rise of the slope forced the air still upward, and threw it into even wilder confusion.

Blue Boy, the boar, awoke and grunted in displeasure. His thick covert of oak was good against most rains, but not against this one. He stirred resentfully, bringing to life some vague boar-memories of a warm dry shed. Then he settled down, trying to make himself more comfortable.

Johnny Martley awoke. His house was near one end of French Bar dam, and close to the lip of the canyon. The house was of wood, solidly constructed, company-built. He could feel the tough timbers give before the wind-pressure; he heard the crash of the rain. "Cloudburst," he said to his wife. "Rain (hear it?)—not snow. There'll be a lot of water down the North Fork."

(Rick, the lineman, did not awake. In the little mountain town where he had been born, he lay quietly in his coffin.)

It was just after six when the J.M. talked to the nurse on the ward. He reported to the Chief.

"She says the Old Master is pretty bad—that chill, or something, got his heart."

"Hn-n?" said the Chief. "He's ninety if he's a day."

Just after six also the radio operator at Bay Airport talked with the plane over Elko. There was some crackling of static, but the words came through clearly. Big Al Bruntton was flying smoothly through the calm high-pressure area which stretched across most of Nevada. The radio-operator gave the information which the Night Service Officer had ordered. "Conditions over the summit, still flyable, but be ready for orders to land at Reno. Worse on this side of the summit—considerable turbulence. Cumulus cloud masses rising to an undetermined height, probably some icing conditions at certain levels as previously reported. Airports available: Reno open; Sacramento doubtful; Bay open, and conditions expected to improve after passage of a cold front about seven A.M.; Red Bluff doubtful; Fresno open and expected to remain so, available for emergency landing."

In the gray of the morning Al picked up the Reno beam, and turned the plane to its new course.

In the first dim light of dawn the cloudburst was unloosed over all the tangled foothill country of gully and ravine and deep-cut canyon where rise the feeders of the American. Under the covert of pine and live-oak and manzanita millions of oozing trickles converged and grew larger. Muddy streams ran brawling; over rock ledges they poured in waterfalls. The steep slope of each canyonside shed water like a roof. Gulches and gullies converged into ravines; the water foamed downward in torrents. Creeks flowed like forks, and forks like rivers.

At Yankee Jim's two inches of rain fell in ten minutes. Brushy Creek was rolling boulders. From Shirttail Canyon the waters gushed out in a wave three feet high. The rise of the North Fork was so sudden that for a moment it backed up into the Middle Fork. Weber Creek took out two bridges. The South Fork went over the flats at Coloma. And on Folsom gauge where the united river swept out into the plain the red-brown water already swirled close to flood-level.

Flanges grinding, coaches swaying on the curves, the streamliner pulled up the steep grade toward the summit. No longer could it race at eighty miles an hour; such speed was for the plains; here, laboring tortuously up the pass, its rate was cut in half. On both sides of the track the piled-up snow was deep.

At every block-tower the green lights glowed through the gray of the dawn. Snow-encrusted track-walkers—their patrols just finished ahead of the streamliner—stood by the side of the track, and waved salutation.

Passengers were waking up—hearts pounding a little, ear-drums tight, from the sharp increase in altitude. Here and there a head popped out from between the curtains.

"Are we on time, porter?"

"Dis train *ah-ways* on time, suh!"

The two young men—early risers—were shaving. "Looks like a lot of snow out there," said one of them, trying to see through the corrugated glass of the dressing room.

"Don't worry. They may have to hold up the freights and the locals, but 'the streamliner goes through on time.' I'm quoting that pamphlet again."

The General's office was not so much of a mad-house as he had feared. Even before he had the reports from the Weather Bureau, he could tell that the cloudburst which had swept across Sacramento had not been very widespread; the long-distance calls plotted its course and extent almost exactly.

Except for the partially protected lands in the delta, the General was still optimistic. The timing and distribution of rainfall was such that the rivers would reach their hours of greatest discharge in regular order, one crest passing on before the next arrived. First of all would come the American, next the Yuba, then the Feather, and only after these were well out of the way would the full flow of the upper Sacramento arrive in the lower river. All this was assuming that the forecast of clearing weather was accurate.

The American was the immediate and worst problem. By the latest report Sacramento gauge was at twenty-five-point-nine and still rising. Already the red-brown backwater covered U. S. 40 between the bridge and North Sacramento. The Committee had loosed its pressure through the newspapers. And on the other side a sheaf of telegrams from the ranchers in the delta lands lay in one of the baskets on the desk.

The General set his jaw, and figured carefully on the reports which were already in. The flooding of the highway he dismissed from his thoughts. The balance was between the delta and the city. He decided he still had an outside chance of saving the delta without running too grave a risk for the city. *If* the Yuba crested as slowly as now seemed likely, and *if* the cloudburst conditions over the near-by foothills were not quite as bad as reports indicated, then he might—just possibly—squeeze through without opening the weir-gates. But if the gauge-reading at Sacramento crept up to twenty-eight-five, and on toward twenty-nine, he must act; for with the water slopping at the levee-top any unforeseen gust of wind might mean disaster to the city. For the moment he could only wait.

The telephone bell rang. His secretary was speaking. "Sacramento gauge at twenty-six-point-one."

That will put the water over the tops of the wickets, thought the General. Up two tenths in an hour! We can't stand *that* very long.

He again made some calculations. With water spilling through the weir the rate of rise against the levees would be cut down. But he thought of the cloudburst over the foothill country and of the water which was already pouring down the American. He shook his head.

The J.M. climbed to the roof, and picked his way among the skylights and ventilators. The wind gusts made him stagger. It was full day now, but the thick sweeping rain and low hard-driven clouds made the light dim.

"Go up and take a look at it," the Chief had said. "A well-defined cold front coming in from the Pacific is something to see."

The violence of the storm increased. The wind was hard from the south; the rain was thick before his eyes. In spite of the wind and rain he felt no sense of chill.

Then in a moment the wind seemed suddenly to come from all directions at once. He staggered this way and that against it. A few handfuls of hail rattled on the skylights. From far off came a boom of thunder.

And now the wind was a buffeting flaw from the west. Huge drops flying level, spattered in his face. Just as suddenly, there was no rain, and he was cold. Another windshift threw him off balance, and he caught himself with one hand against the parapet. The wind had veered forty-five degrees more and was a cold blast from the northwest.

The rain came again. A chilling shower, hard blown, but with smaller drops. He shivered beneath his oilskin. After a minute the shower was gone. For another minute the storm seemed more threatening than ever. Low-flying scud swept the tops of the higher buildings around him. The wind backed gustily from northwest to west, and then veered to northwest again.

All at once he was conscious that he could see better. From somewhere there was more light. The cloud-deck was higher and more sharply defined; beneath it he saw the bases of the hills five miles to the north.

As neatly as if someone drew curtains aside, a hole opened in the cloud-deck just above him and a patch of pure blue sky showed through for a moment. The clouds rolled over it again, but at the same time he saw another patch of blue to the west and a much larger one to the north.

Then another shower of cold rain enveloped him and clouds were close around. But the insistent northwest wind seemed dry even as it was driving the raindrops before it. The wind did not change; the shower lasted perhaps two minutes. Then it was gone into nowhere as quickly and unexpectedly as it had come.

Now he did not have to glance rapidly here and there to see bits of blue sky. Over all the north and west the clouds were broken. The dark low-hanging remnants of the stratus-deck changed while he looked at them. They contracted and piled up; the edges took on a touch of white fluffiness. High up they reflected a gleam of sunlight.

He looked eastward. Over the Bay he saw the slanting

lines of two rain-squalls; the Berkeley Hills were still veiled in cloud, which rose high enough to shut out the rays of the morning sun. But now even at the zenith blue sky was showing.

He looked at his watch—only fifteen minutes. But he felt as if he had passed from one world into another. Already the wind was licking up the water, and dry spots showed on the tiles of the roof-floor. Now he could make out, clear across the Bay, the white shaft of the tower on the University campus. Any moment now the sun would shine over the top of the cloud bank, fast receding to the east.

His fingers were numb, and his damp feet were like ice-blocks in the chilling sweep of the northern air; but he felt a fine sense of exhilaration. The shock of dropping humidity and the rising pressure gave a sharp stimulus to his body and mind. He indulged in a vigorous, awkward tap-dance which served to get the circulation started in his feet again.

Then the sun came out, and he was suddenly too warm. He stripped off his now dry slicker. The northwest wind was still chilly, but it seemed to generate an excess energy which made the chilliness pleasant. He wanted to take a long walk on some wind-blown hill.

Reluctantly he turned to get back to work. The front was only a low blur of cloud on the horizon of the upper bay. The sun shone brightly in a clean blue sky, scattered with drifting high-piled masses of white cloud. The northwest wind again possessed the city.

The Chief Service Officer, backing his car from the apartment-house garage, stuck his head out the window and looked toward the rear to see where he was steering. Thus he got the whiff of the northwest wind full in his face. He felt reassured; more than any other phenomenon of the atmosphere, he was inclined to trust that particular wind. To him it meant stable air flowing steadily, not likely to shift without warning.

But as he drove toward the airport, he felt his usual wariness returning. The front must have passed by; off to the northeast he could make out what was probably the last of the vanishing rain; the air was still full of big but harmless-looking clouds.

He began to notice evidences that the last flick of the storm had been even more severe than he had realized. The sun was shining, but while he had been asleep something might have been happening. Here was a small branch blown from a tree and lying still in the street; a newly planted sapling had broken its stake, and now flopped over in a helpless curve; a telephone gang was repairing wire. Of course a cold front must have passed in, and its attendant line-squall would be enough to account for all this. But where was that cold front now, how violent was it, and were any planes in its path? Unconsciously, he began to drive faster. He noticed that little deltas of sand and gravel lay on the pavement at street-corners and driveways. "Act of God!" he thought viciously, and at the thought stepped hard on the accelerator.

Overcoat still flapping about him, he strode into the dispatching room at the airport. "What's happening?" he snapped at the meteorologist.

"A little patch of unstable air from somewhere—doesn't show up well on the map—too small. Seven o'clock reports showed she hadn't got to the summit yet. Weather-bureau reports at four showed a lot of local thunder-storms, and—"

"Thunderstorms!"

The CSO turned on his heel, and made for the radio-room just across the hall. At the doorway he met his assistant; reading the face he did not waste time on salu-tations.

"What's the matter?"

"Trip one-sixty-five. The air went bad over the sum-mit all at once. I was going to order it down at Reno, and suddenly we can't make contact. Some electrical disturb-ance blanketing everything out—nothing but static."

The assistant said other things, but the CSO did not listen. He concentrated on the problem for a moment with such violence that perspiration broke out upon him. No solution!

"Keep on trying," he said to the radio-operator.

He took off his overcoat and sat down to wait limply for news, hoping it would not be too long delayed or too bad. Deep and bitter cynicism smoldered inside him. Years of accumulating experience, hundreds of men, sci-entific experiment, unfailing vigilance, instruments of precision, teletype circuits, radio, beacons, beams, emer-gency landing-fields—and yet the air could still pull off a trick like this! And what had you left? Only a plane and a pilot in wild air over the mountains.

"Fire and hail," he thought. *"Snow and vapors, stormy wind fulfilling his word. Well—"*

He lighted a cigarette, and his hand did not shake—not even when the telephone rang. Every man was tense, but it was a call of no importance. Too soon to be hearing anyway. He blew a smoke ring.

There had been disasters before in this business; he had been in on some of them. There would be still more disasters before men beat the storms. He thought bitterly again, *"Act of God!"*

In the silence he heard the clock tick; it was seven-twenty-three.

Pablo, the Mexican, finished patrolling his stretch of track. The plows had passed already; he knew that the streamliner would be along in a few minutes.

Pablo was mountain-born, on the bleak slopes above Toluca where corn fails and men harvest thin fields of barley. Also he was patient and enduring by virtue of his Indian ancestry. So even the intensity of the storm as it had blown up in the last few minutes did not disturb him.

He stepped aside as he heard the streamliner drawing near through the falling snow. After the last car had sped by and gone out of sight around the curve, only the sound of the wind in the trees was left upon the mountainside, and in that seeming hush Pablo heard the plane.

Impulsively he crossed himself. "Jesús de mi vida!" he said. Pablo was used to the planes; hourly, east and west, they passed over him; he saw them sharp-cut against the sun; he saw them even at night as gleams in the moonlight or moving shadows against the star-lit sky.

This plane he did not see. But somewhere low in that close-hanging cloud he heard it. He judged that it was coming from the east, but it did not pass on quickly and steadily out of hearing. Now the roar of engines was loud;

now it was dimmed out. Even Pablo knew that the plane was in trouble, buffeted here and there, fighting, lost, beaten down until it was low over the mountain-tops.

Pablo had the secrecy bred of long generations of slavery. He did not stare about as an American would have done, eager to be the first to report even a disaster. Instead, he walked stolidly along the track through the storm, not looking around. He could not shut the noise out of his ears, and he knew craftily that the plane was moving off northward. But he did not wish to be mixed in the affair. If anybody should ask him about it, he was ready to think first, "No se nada!" and then translate this into "Don't know nothing about it!"

At French Bar Power-House the snow had melted under the warm rain, and now everything was awash in the cloudburst. The gang was out tending to some lines. Johnny Martley, half-drowned under the downpour, was trying to do a dozen things at once to control the water. It was gullying the road in a half dozen places, threatening to flood two basements and the garage, and in general looking as if it might wash the whole place over the edge into the canyon.

When his wife whooped at him from the porch, he knew that the L.D. had called, and he was also pretty sure what the call was about. They had been caught with the dam nearly full, and now this cloudburst would send the water over the top unless the sluice gates were opened—maybe it would go over anyway. He had been waiting for orders.

"Yes," he said to the L.D. "The water's close up to

the top, and all the streams are coming down a-boiling. She'll spill in no time. I'll go right away."

"How's everything else?"

"The boys are away on that job still. Everything loose around the place is washing down the canyon. I've been out with a shovel busier than a monkey, and wet as a trout."

Just as he opened the front door, his wife yelled that there was a leak in the living-room.

"Set out a pan," he yelled back.

He hurried along the narrow trail at the lip of the canyon. A dozen rivulets were rushing across it, and then a few feet beyond cascaded off into space. Ten, twenty, or fifty feet they dropped as little waterfalls until they hit some rock ledge or the sloping wall of the canyon, leaped out in spray, gathered for another fall, and so at last reached the bottom, three hundred feet below.

Martley picked his way along the trail. He went quickly, but his footwork was as neat as a lightweight boxer's. It was not a healthy time or place for a slip. The wind came in great gusts, taking him off his balance. The rain was in spurts—now merely a spatter, now a deluge as if someone were throwing buckets of water. When rain and wind struck together the man had to brace himself against them, crouching, steadying himself with his right hand against the rocks on the upper side of the trail. A few feet to his left was the void of the canyon. The little rivulets, as he crossed them, hardly slopped his ankles, but if he should slip and fall their rush of water might be enough to carry him downward before he could catch himself.

As he neared the dam, he saw that the water was almost level with the top; the wind was upstream; even so, an occasional wave was slopping over. It was an old-fashioned dam, not well designed to spill; if it went at all, it went along the whole crest; that was why the L.D. always watched the sluice-gates. But this time, thought Martley, the L.D. for once had missed. The gates should have been opened twenty-four hours ago; now the water was coming in faster than the sluices could carry it off; but anyway no harm was likely to result.

He unpadlocked the little steel door just below the overhang of the dam, went in, closed it behind him, and snapped on the lights. He was in a cramped passageway inside the solid concrete of the dam. He went along it a few yards until it ended at a round hole just large enough for a man to descend. Far down the hole one electric light after another, far apart, glowed with a dull, wet gleam.

He lowered himself into the hole, found with his foot a steel rung projecting from the concrete wall, grasped an upper rung with his hands, and began to descend. The hole was so small that he brushed against the concrete with hips and shoulders. Everything was wet with the seepage of water through the dam. The farther he went the more water dripped upon him from above. He descended steadily without hurry, knowing that he had two hundred thirty feet to go.

Usually he made the descent with a companion, and now even his well-trained nerves felt the isolation and the almost physical inward pressure of the monolithic concrete. He was an ant crawling through some minute crevice of a great rock. Each light, yellow in the dripping atmosphere, seemed a friend as he drew near it.

As it receded he felt a touch of primitive panic. But still he descended steadily from rung to rung, taking care that neither hand nor foot slipped on the wet rounds of steel.

U.S. 40 was open again, and this day was not so bad as the Superintendent had feared. At the lower levels there was a cloudburst, but it was falling as rain. The cloudburst was so violent that it exhausted itself on the lower and middle slopes, well to the west of the summit; above six-thousand feet, heavy snow-squalls alternated with lulls when only a little spit of snow kept falling. In between the lower and upper levels was a belt of blinding snowfall, but it extended along only a few miles of road, and so the Superintendent had been able to throw plenty of equipment into that short stretch and easily keep it clear.

He had just talked to a rotary-operator and was getting back into his car; then he heard the mutter of a plane. He glanced upward involuntarily, but of course saw nothing. If you could hardly see across the road, you couldn't see any higher into the air.

"Must be like flying through the water in a washing-machine," he thought.

He was used to hearing the planes overhead even in what seemed to him impossible flying-weather. Still, he wondered. Where he stood, he was somewhat sheltered in a thick forest of spruce and cedar; even so, the wind came in great gusts and swirls. And the noise of the engines seemed loud, as if the plane had been forced too low. Might be just a trick of the wind. Still— He noted mentally just where he was on the road. If a man offered information (or testimony) it ought to be accurate. He looked at his watch. Seven-thirty-six.

When Big Al had passed over Reno it had been full daylight, but the visibility was getting rapidly worse instead of better. He went on, following the Reno beam. Ten minutes later he was getting close to the summit, and things looked so doubtful ahead that he fully expected to be ordered around any moment and told to land. Reno would have been fair landing when he passed over, but might be hard by the time he could get back to it.

Then inside of a minute, things had got bad. He could have turned around on his own responsibility, but he did not like to seem to lose his nerve—and maybe Reno had been buttoned up too. He was at eleven-thousand, leaving a good two thousand feet of room to get over the near-by peaks. The air was rough, and the plane was in thick cloud; a little ice was forming. Any moment he hoped to come out into one of those long clear spaces with stratus banks above and below and maybe a mountain top just showing through the lower bank. Then suddenly Jerry yelled at him:

"Bay trying to contact us; got the signal, but she faded —static."

At that moment Big Al saw the whole picture. He was just about to make headlines, perhaps. Maybe the headlines would keep running for several days until someone spotted the crashed plane and the charred bodies. He felt coldly calm, and decided to go ahead. Bay was just as likely telling them to keep away from Reno as to turn back and land there. Half a minute later, he knew that he had made the wrong decision.

He'd have done better to try for some emergency field or even take her clear back to Elko on the reserve gas. A side-swipe took the plane, and then she went into a down-draught. He fought to regain control and get back altitude. (He hated to think what was happening among the passengers.) By the time he had control he was off the beam over in the N-sector somewhere. For the moment it was more important to get back some altitude than to hunt the beam. Just then he went into a thunderstorm, and even the N-signal disappeared. All he could do was to fight for control. If he kept moving west, he would gain altitude as the slope of the mountains fell away. Already he felt the drag of the ice; the de-icers couldn't handle it; the weight was not so much as the distortion which the ice made in the flying-surfaces; the plane was getting hard to handle.

And then, almost at his level, a mile away perhaps but looking close enough to touch, some black fangs of crags seemed to drift by—too steep for snow to rest on. There was nothing like them along the air-lanes. The Sierra Buttes, maybe, he thought. If so, he was already miles off his course, to the north. He fought for control, and to keep to the west.

Blue Boy, the big boar, decided that he would get back to his dry shed. With the rain still sluicing down in torrents he trotted stolidly along the semblance of a trail which the feet of animals and men had worn on the steep hillside. When he came to the gully, he paused a moment, hesitating. Usually the gully was dry; even during most of the storm it had flowed **an insignificant** amount of water; but now, such was the cloudburst, the stream rushed six feet wide across the ledge. Above and below, it was a series of waterfalls.

Blue Boy plunged ahead. He was almost across, when his long, low-hung body began to act like a dam. The water piled up in a wave against his upstream side; its buoyancy suddenly neutralized his weight; at the same moment his left hind-foot slipped.

He was rolled over, kicking, ten feet downhill to the next ledge. He squealed shrilly, as a root scraped his tender snout. He struck the ledge more or less on his feet, and indignantly started to scramble out almost as he lit. But to scramble he had to crouch first, the buoyancy of the water tricked him again, and its sweep carried him away.

This time he went farther, and hit on his back with a crash. For a moment he had another chance, but he was already bruised, half-stunned, and completely confused. His feet pawed the air uselessly for an instant; then a new wave slewed his forequarters around, washed him off the ledge, and dropped him head-foremost. Six feet down, he hit with a thud, all but smashing one shoulder; the shock took all the fight out of him. Convulsively sucking in for another squeal, he sucked water instead of air.

From then on, he was an inert mass. The torrent hurled him end over end, and cracked his rump on a boulder. Where the water might have grounded him, his momentum as a falling body carried him on; it hurled him downward through bushes and vines. For the last thirty feet he rolled, spinning like a log. At the bottom he crashed through the barbed-wire fence, rolled three times more, and came to rest as his midriff suddenly crushed against something solid.

His whole descent had not occupied ten seconds. He had hit against the place where the two big pipes of a culvert came together. The culvert passed under the railway; his forequarters sagged limply inside one pipe; his hindquarters inside the other.

He was not yet dead, but he was too battered to save himself. The position of his body obstructed the flow; the water quickly rose higher, covered mouth and nostrils, and drowned him.

Opening the sluice-gates unaided was something of a job; when Martley had finished, he was tired. He listened for just a moment to the water sweeping through beneath him. Then he thought of the leak in his living-room, and the road washing away, and a dozen greater emergencies which might arise any moment. He turned and went rapidly along the narrow passageway leading to the hole up which he must climb. "Gotta hurry," he thought. "Sure is a busy day!"

The passageway was just high enough for a man to walk; now and then his shoulders brushed the sides. Seepage water dripped from the top and oozed through the walls; the air was so wet that he half seemed to be breathing water; he coughed. From above, from the sides, the concrete of the great dam—millions of tons— pressed in upon him.

Ahead in the passageway as far as the bottom of the hole one electric light after another sent out a feeble yellow gleam. Then—without a warning flicker—they all went out. Black as Hell's basement and the fires out!

The darkness stopped the man in his tracks like a blow. The unexpected loss of his best sense brought momentary panic, but he suppressed it so quickly that he hardly missed the time of two strides. In the narrow passageway there was no chance of getting lost; he knew the distances and the hazards. He remembered where he was when the lights went out; as he walked he methodically counted his paces to know when he should expect to arrive at the end of the passageway. What worried him was why the lights had gone. In the storm anything might happen from the breakage of a local wire up to some major disaster. He hurried even faster; his men would need him; the L.D. might be calling. "Sure is a busy day!"—And this time he unconsciously spoke out loud for company and courage; he started as the voice reverberated hollowly from the concrete walls.

Reaching ahead with his left hand he felt the end of the passageway. With his right hand, groping in the blackness, he found a steel rung—wet, cold, and slick. He began to climb upward into the narrow hole which he could not even see was there; it was as if he forced his way by will-power right into the concrete.

Not for nothing had he been Superintendent at French Bar for eleven years. He knew every detail of the dam. He had to climb upward two hundred thirty feet, and the rungs were ten and a half inches apart—two hundred sixty-nine rungs.

One—two—three—four. Counting to himself, he climbed by feel in the darkness—hand over hand, foot following foot. The water spattered upon him; he coughed in the dank air. Twenty-eight—twenty-nine—thirty—thirty-one. He was climbing as fast as he dared. Forty-five—forty-six. His heart began to pound. His feet grew heavy. Sixty-six—sixty-seven. The hole was too small to give him free action. He felt cramps in his loins. Eighty—eighty-one—eighty—! (His left hand missed a grip and threw him out of rhythm.) Eighty-two—eighty-three. There was a pain across his chest and his ankle tendons were numb. He kept on grimly. *One hundred!* Then he rested. He took the next hundred again without halting. On rung two hundred, as he rested, he saw the dim little circle of half-light still high above him.

His feet were heavy from the start, but he took the last sixty-nine rungs with a rush. He was wondering what had happened to his power-house. Were the dynamos still purring steadily like sleek happy cats? Had something smashed? Had the L.D. called? Exhausted, like a man finishing a race, he pulled himself out of the hole. Leaking in from the closed door was a dim halo of light. He stumbled toward it. He was suddenly conscious of some unusual roaring noise. He flung the door open; the flood of light blinded him for the moment; he put one foot out—and then paused. There was no wind, but only the strange roar, and spray—not like rain —in his face.

In half a breath his sight came back to him, but for the moment he was not sure that he saw aright. There was no canyon wall, no swirling rain—only a solid wall of falling water. The dam was spilling; he was trapped.

Perhaps it was the mere inrush of water from the streams swollen by the cloudburst; perhaps a wind-shift had piled water against the dam instead of the other direction. As he had feared, the opening of the sluice-gates was not enough; but he had not realized that it would be so soon.

Because of the overhang there was a space of five feet between the doorway and the falling water. He looked one way and then the other, seeking escape. To the left his view ended against the solid wall of a concrete buttress. To the right his glance ran far along the sheer front of the dam with the water pouring over it; a few feet from where he stood the ground fell off and disappeared into the canyon.

He reached out, picked up a stone, and threw it. From long experience with flowing water he knew from the way the stone disappeared that the solid-looking wall could not be more than an inch or so thick. It was falling only fifteen feet from the top of the dam. Given level and sure footing, a man could rush through such a waterfall, and no harm done. But here he had only a rough trail on a sloping rock-face and the precipice a few feet to one side. The best man in the world would be swept down. Courage would be only foolishness. If he stayed where he was, he would be safe; eventually the boys would come and pass a life-line through to him, or the dam would quit spilling. The storm wouldn't last much longer.

But not for a moment did Martley consider staying where he was—tamely. He remembered his leaderless men, his dynamos, the leak in the living-room, and the L.D. "I'm too busy to stay here," he thought.

He cast about for some means of escape. A few bits of junk lay in the passageway. They were useless. But just outside the door he saw a worn and rusted half-inch cable. Some construction boss had cast it aside as no longer trustworthy; but even if it were nine-tenths rusted through, the steel would still hold the weight of a man.

Martley grabbed the end and pulled. The cable extended through somewhere beyond the wall of water. Martley dragged it in, hoping that the other end was stuck firmly. But it yielded; he pulled the loose end through the water, and found himself with thirty feet of cable.

"I can't stay here; I'm too busy," he thought again.

Martley looped one end of the cable around upon itself. He pounded it with a stone for a hammer. The rusty projecting ends of wire tore at his hands, but he fabricated a loop about three feet in diameter.

Just outside the doorway he dug his heels in for a firm footing. He was so close to the falling water that he could reach it with his finger-tips. Like a cowboy on foot making ready to rope his pony, he stood with the awkward steel loop in his right hand. He cast it at the wall of water.

It struck flatways, and was flung back. He corrected his aim. This time it disappeared neatly through the water. He pulled hopefully, but the loop came back to him without much resistance. He gathered it to his hand, and stood for a moment judging distance and direction.

In eleven years he had come to know every detail about his dam. He knew that just beyond the water stood three rocks close together. If he could cast the looped cable among them it might stick.

The third attempt did not pierce the water. The

fourth went through, seemed to stick, and then yielded as he pulled a little harder. He tried again and again—now with no luck at all, now with enough hint of success to keep him trying.

He was a methodical man and kept his count. The eleventh and fourteenth throws stuck momentarily. By now he knew exactly where the rocks must be. But the fifteenth try was a complete miss; his arm was tired.

On the sixteenth throw he was careful. He pulled in; the cable ran freely for a foot and then stuck with a sudden jam. He was sure he had it! He pulled hard; he rested a moment, and then strained with his full weight. The cable was solid.

There was, of course, a very good chance that, when he swung through an arc of more than a right angle, he would slip the loop off whatever projection held it. "I can't stay here all day," he thought.

He grasped the cable at a point which he knew was about eight feet from whatever (presumably the rocks) the loop was caught on. He did not plunge at the waterfall. He merely stuck his head and shoulders into it, and felt the rush take him from his feet. He held his breath and gripped the steel strands. The sluice of the water swept him across the sloping rock, but he knew that holding the cable he must swing in a circle. Beneath his left foot was nothing; he felt the void of the canyon sucking him down. He knew that he had been too reckless, but he gripped the cable.

Then, still gripping the cable, he was lying on the sloping rock with water rushing against his face and shoulders. The loop of the cable was holding. Under his feet was empty space. He raised his face above the foaming rush, and heard the thunder of water plunging into the canyon. He panted a moment before daring to move. Then he bent both elbows, and hunched himself half a foot forward. He pulled up his right knee, and felt the roughness of rock beneath his foot. Only then did he dare to loose one hand and move it up on the cable for a fresh grip. (Even at that moment he felt, more than heard, the hum of the dynamos, and knew that the failure of the lights inside the dam had been purely local; the water going over the dam must have caused it.) The rest was easy.

"Did the L.D. call?" he yelled at his wife from the doorway.

"No!" she yelled back from where she was washing the breakfast dishes. "What made you so long?"

"Oh—nothing much!"

He was glad she did not come to look at him. His face and hands were scraped and bleeding; his pants-knees were both torn out. He grabbed the shovel from where he had left it on the porch, and hurried off to see about the road.

At the airport they waited. Waited. The radio-operators were listening. Now and then they tried to make contact. Minute passed by minute. Seven-fifty-four; seven-fifty-five. In the air, minutes count like hours on land or sea. The CSO sat there. He said nothing. There was nothing to say. Or to do! "Act of God!" Seven-fifty-six. No contact.

Eight o'clock. Big Al due in at eight-thirty-five. Outside, the sun was shining. To the south the airways fine as silk. A Los Angeles plane taking off. Keep things moving—as if nothing has happened. Maybe nothing *has* happened. Maybe.

Somebody came in. "Lottie's out there!" he half whispered. Al's wife—married six months. Used to be a stewardess. They all knew Lottie. Nice little thing. The guys joking Al about a baby.

Who's the best bluffer? Send him out. Let him kid along with Lottie. Don't *say* anything. Not yet. (Pretty hard to bluff a stewardess.) Buy her a drink. No. She'd think that was funny. Buy her a coffee. God, why'd she have to come so early?

Only eight-two! You mean—eight-two already! People will be coming to meet the passengers. They won't be worrying. Sun shining. You wouldn't think things could be so bad inside of two hundred miles. Would you now? Really. "Act of God!" "Prince of the power of the air!" Eight-three.

A half dozen men had gathered in the lounge-car just after eight o'clock. The conductor came in.

"Good morning," said a passenger, "On time—"

Just then the brakes went on with a grab that shook the whole car. One passenger went right down in the aisle; the others flopped half over in the chairs. By the time they pulled themselves up the conductor was gone.

"God! Emergency stop!"

"Anybody hurt?"

The train was standing still. The men peered out. The rain was falling by bucketfuls. On one side the train was close against the steeply sloping wall of a canyon. On the other side—across the up-track—the canyon-wall dropped off fifty feet more to a roaring stream. The clouds were drifting in so low that they covered most of the opposite wall of the canyon beyond the stream.

"Nasty place! Glad we didn't go off the track!"

They waited five minutes—ten minutes. They speculated what the trouble might be. The porter had no idea; no trainmen showed up.

"We'll not get in on time anyway. Tough! Here we hit every stop on the nose all the way across, and get held up just at the end."

"Come on," said a young man to his companion, "let's go out. Maybe there's been an accident."

The sheets of rain made them hesitate, but once they had their overcoats on, neither one wanted to be the first to back down. They hurried along toward the engine, where the trainmen gathered about.

They saw, not fifty feet ahead of the engine, water flooding across the tracks. Already it had washed out a lot of ballast, and the outside track was hanging in a long sag; even the inside track was much too doubtful-looking to risk the passage of a train.

The conductor was shaking his head. "Look at that track!" he said. "The track-walker just found it in time to stop us—lucky he did, too! But not even a crew here to work on it yet. It'll be two hours if it's a minute. Lucky if we get away under three."

Only by a narrow margin was the whole train not lying a crumpled tangle in the brawling torrent of the North Fork. "Tough steel, aluminum alloys, resplendent chromium, satiny copper, crimson leather, shining glass—miracle of modern engineering and art"—the streamliner stood still, balked in its course. All the cunning of wires and clockwork, of lights and semaphores, was as nothing before some trick of the storm.

Just then a draggled little track-walker came slopping up-track through the water. He had mud and slime all over him, and his language matched the slime.

"What you know!" he blurted. "That one pipe clogged so tight she not running water—just a little mud. I crawl up through there; think I see what's wrong. What you think jammed in there and blocked the pipes—drowned—*a great big hog!*"

Minute by minute Big Al fought the storm. He could feel the drag of the ice. Lightning crackled all around; the radio roared with static. Now and then the whine of the beam came through or some blurred words—Bay trying to get them. But it was no use trying to follow a beam. He tried to keep to the west. Once an air draft dropped him so fast that he thought he was gone; he looked ahead for the mountainside that would come crashing through the mist. But nothing came through the mist, and he fought for altitude with his logy, heavy plane. Side gusts tossed him back and forth. (He didn't dare to think what was happening to the passengers.) He himself was tired as a dog. In the air minutes count like hours. What kept him going was the thought that it couldn't be so bad as it was, and last very long. Then suddenly he knew that he had wished it would be over pretty soon—one way or the other. That was his first touch of panic.

He tried to think of the plane itself. The engines were sweet as you ever heard. Everything else was fine. Just a little heavy with ice, and that didn't seem to be getting worse very fast. But the machine's being so fine, strangely, didn't make him feel better. It only made him feel that the man, by contrast, was the weak part that was going to pieces. Already he knew that he didn't trust his instruments, and when a pilot doesn't trust his instruments, he's going bad. But just the same, he began trying to look for the ground to know where he was. But there wasn't any ground—naturally. He was tired; he was going bad; he knew it.

The worst blast of all struck him. He was sure it was the end. He bit his tongue to keep himself alert, and just managed to keep her under control.

And then—so suddenly that he blinked and looked again—there, just ahead was blue sky—blue as water. The moment he saw it he felt rested. He knew he was all right. He'd flown right through the front. That last wallop had been the final wind-shift. There might be more squalls, but he'd be all right. He saw more blue sky, and then a glimpse of ground—foothill country. Just then the Bay operator came through as clear as if he were on a direct wire.

Five minutes later the plane was heading south over the Sacramento Valley. (The passengers were getting hold of their stomachs again.) Off to the southwest Big Al was watching two showers, but they didn't amount to much. He'd been blown miles out of his course, northward; but he'd be landing inside of an hour.

4

Through eleven days the storm had flourished and been strong. Tyrannical, it had drawn power to itself from the north and the south. From the Arctic to the tropics, in great circuit, it had ruled the air, and troubled the sea, and warred against the mountains.

It had been as a conquering king who boasts in bronze —I was great and increased more than all that were before me; I gathered silver and gold, the treasure of kings and of the provinces. It had been as a firm-founded nation—vigorous in youth, virile in prime, knowing no doubt of the future.

The king and the nation seem unassailable, but within them breeds decay. Time is a strong warrior.

While the king sits enthroned, the generation of worms makes ready. To everything there is a season—a time to be born and a time to die. There is a time for the breaking of nations. Of storms also it is written, "This too shall pass away."

Far off, the sun at a certain angle with respect to the revolving earth had for a while shone favorably for the continuance of this particular eddy of air. Now its existence was becoming no longer possible. The storm had seemed some emperor of the air; actually it was only a puppet-king.

The storm was dying, but even in death it was great. The last front, close to a thousand miles in length, revolving like the spoke of a wheel about the storm-center far at sea, hurled itself against the mountains. Great pines tossed wildly as the fierce wind-shift took them aback; thick branches snapped; whole trees went down. Then the front had passed on, and the steady cold wind from the northwest was scattering the clouds.

Onward moved the front, still revolving about the far-distant center. It burst in snow-squalls upon the saw-toothed desert ranges; on the high plateau it powdered the sage-brush with shining crystals; the quick snap of its wind-shift whipped the desert junipers. But its stores of moisture drawn from the tropical sea were already exhausted upon the mountains. As midday neared and passed, the wall of the front ceased to advance so vigorously; the snow-flurries were fewer.

Hour by hour over thousands of square miles, from the solid surface of the earth upward to the quiet of the stratosphere, the air acknowledged a new dominion. The great storm was dying.

THE STORM during its life had traveled a third of the way round the world; at its height, it had encompassed an area larger than the United States of America.

By mixing in gigantic proportions the northern and southern air the storm had helped adjust the inequalities of heat between equator and pole.

Next notable of its actions was the transfer of water from ocean to land. One inch of rain falling upon one square mile totals a weight of seventy thousand tons. Rain and snow from this single storm had fallen over a land area of more than two hundred thousand square miles, and the average precipitation of water was several inches.

Of all this water a little had already been reabsorbed into the dry air following after the last front. Another small amount had been impounded behind man-made dams. Somewhat more had passed through natural channels and returned to the ocean. Much remained as snow —attaining a depth of many feet—upon the higher moun-

331

tains. Much was contained in the flooded streams, and was somewhat violently engaged in flowing toward tide-water. Another large part was held within the now saturated earth. Still another had gone into vegetation, for in many places the grass had grown an inch during the storm.

The third notable work of the storm was its lowering of the land-surface. Here by landslide, there by less spectacular erosion, the water had carried millions of cubic yards of earth a greater or less distance toward the ocean.

Beside these cosmic effects, the direct influence of the storm upon men seems small and secondary. *Good* and *bad* lose their meaning, and exist only according to point of view, within a limited range of vision.

"Sixteen dead by storm," declared the *Register*. This would doubtless be rated a bad effect, but perhaps the world was better off because of these deaths. And even the accuracy of the headline can be impugned. (Does the match or the powder cause the explosion?) The sixteen died not because of the storm but because of their own mortality. The storm was merely the occasion; after a few years they would in any case have died.

But if the editor was to hold the storm responsible for sixteen deaths, why not for hundreds? Many invalids died during the days of the storm, their deaths precipitated by chills and heart-depressions, attributable to the weather. Some healthy persons suffered wet feet which led to colds, pneumonia, and death within a few weeks. Other colds resulted in weakened resistance which opened the way to various fatal diseases.

"Million-dollar rain," was another headline in the *Register*. This, doubtless, would be rated a good effect.

But the saving of a crop in California might quite possibly lead to bear raids in Chicago, foreclosures in Oklahoma, suicides in Florida, strikes in Massachusetts, and executions in Turkey.

As with the so-called bad, the so-called good was often far removed and difficult to appraise. Only a few entomologists realized that the rain, falling just when it did, destroyed billions of grasshopper eggs, and prevented a plague six months later.

Even aside from its cosmic effects the storm had thus vitally affected, in one way or another, the life of every human being in the region. It had accomplished all this without being itself catastrophic or even unusual.

2

The particular storm known as Maria to the Junior Meteorologist in San Francisco had rained, snowed, and blown chiefly upon California, secondarily upon the neighboring states. But there was in the nature of this storm nothing peculiar to that region alone.

Maria was dead. But on the eighth day of her life she had begun (after the strange manner of storms) to give birth to a new storm which the Junior Meteorologist had called Little Maria. Now four days old, no longer little, having swept the southeastern states, this storm centered over New York City.

In the Appalachians as in the Sierra Nevada, wires were down. The Peedee and the Santee, like the Sacramento, rolled flood-waters seaward. Snow-plows fought drifts in the Catskills as in the Siskiyous. Trains and buses ran late; planes were grounded.

In New York City the Department of Sanitation

mobilized fifteen thousand men to clear snow from the streets. The Commissioner announced that mechanized equipment at work included 177 rotary brooms, 377 flushers and plows, 619 crosswalk plows, 46 sanders, and 1,246 trucks with plows attached; he added that he was ready to call out further reserves of men, and was making ready 268 additional pieces of equipment.

The wind howled a hundred-mile gale atop the Empire State Building. Pedestrians, jack-knifed against the blast, slipped and fell on the snowy sidewalks. A woman, losing balance and blown against a stone buttress, went down with a fractured skull. Wind gusts swept a workman from a scaffolding, and he broke his neck. Falling signs injured seven. Accidents were so numerous that hospitals reserved ambulances for the more severe cases. An emergency squad of police roped several squares for safety, and the few passers-by clung to the ropes as if to life-lines.

Station WKY reported twenty-one interruptions to service between five and ten A. M. Williamsburg Bridge was closed to traffic while the sweepers cleared it. Pulaski Skyway was blocked for two hours.

In the harbor a freighter broke its moorings. A South American liner was held up in the lower bay, and docked four hours after announced time. A coast-guard cutter went out to rescue a fishing-boat. From fifty miles beyond Sandy Hook a tanker radioed: "Steering gear carried away; helpless in full gale; all ships close by please help."

In Queens the power company reported ninety poles down and two thousand families without lights. In Bronx Park a freak twisting wind snapped hundreds of branches. Four elevated lines in Brooklyn suspended all traffic for forty minutes of the morning rush-hour, marooning thousands of passengers. La Guardia Field cancelled all flights.

His Honor the Mayor whimsically stated to some reporters that he used to be able to enjoy snowstorms, but now he had to worry about what the cost of snow-clearance did to the budget. While His Honor happened to be looking from one of his office windows, the flagpole in City Hall Park—fifth to stand there since the original liberty pole of the Revolution—snapped off and fell.

In the midst of disaster there was rejoicing. The Water Department announced gleefully that the heavy snowfall up-state would do much to make up a critical deficiency in the City's reservoirs. Five hundred public-school children received a holiday because some heating equipment was disabled. Rena Carey, a declining Hollywood star, broke into all the picture sections with a photograph which showed her on a slippery sidewalk skidding into the arms of a tall policeman.

But at least there were no deaths from cold. The storm had moved from the southwest, bringing only gales and sticky snow. "This snow follows necessarily," commented a learned writer of editorials, "from the fact that our ancestors chose to locate this city in a rather snowy part of the snowiest of all continents."

3

And now a line of linked storms across North America blocked the outflow of polar air southward along that easy route in the lee of the Rocky Mountains. In China and across the Pacific also the storms drove hard against the North. So, along that broad ocean passageway between Norway and Iceland, the overflow of the Arctic poured out.

Fiercer than Pict or Caledonian, more furious than the Northmen, it swept upon Britain. On Grasmere and Windermere, the ice was like steel. On moor and down and heath hard-driven crystals flecked the gorse and bracken. Cold wind upon warmer land, it swept the mist from the gray cities by the northern firths; and cleared the smoke from the great towns of the Midlands; and drove before it the yellow pall of London, covering six counties. Even in sea-girt Cornwall, men whiffed the dry air of the North, sharp upon the cheek-bones, biting the nostrils.

Still onward drove that wind. It buffeted ships in the Channel. It swept the lands of Scheldt and Seine and Loire. Still on! For, when the sun rides deep in Capricorn, what power shall withstand the North?

4

The General had jumped from bed at four-thirty Friday morning when the cloudburst suddenly beat against his windows. During the night when Friday passed into Saturday, he did not consider the question of bed.

As he looked from his office windows in the still hours of the morning, he felt a curious sense of unreality. The full moon was brilliant; street lights shone upon dry asphalt; branches of trees and shrubbery swayed in a steady breeze. It was no night to imagine floods and disaster. Apparently the inhabitants of the valley felt a similar sense of safety. Few long-distance calls came in from panicky ranchers and business-men demanding the news and asking advice.

The storm was over. But for the General the crisis had not yet passed. Far and wide, he could feel those billions of cubic feet of water, penned in behind the levees, pouring toward the Bay. The water-level in the rivers stood far above the valley floor, high as the roof-eaves of the cottages in the river towns, high as the second-story windows in Sacramento. Along hundreds of miles of levee-top, in the bright moonlight, his patrols walked their beats, back and forth. The men needed no slickers tonight; each carried a shovel on his shoulder. On one side each man looked far down the slope of the levee, and saw the street-lights of some little town still burning or perhaps only the wide stretches of the valley where the scattered houses showed no lights. On his other side, the patrol looked out almost on his own level, and saw the brown backwater among the leafless willows of the stream-margin; beyond the willows flowed the swift water of the channel.

At one o'clock word was telephoned from Kennett, far north under the peak of Shasta, that the upper Sacramento had crested at twenty-four-point-six, and was falling. This crest was high enough to be dangerous, but it would not arrive in the lower river for several days and could be disregarded for the moment.

The critical stream was still the American. Although the rain in the foothills had ceased twelve hours previous, the crest had not yet had time to descend to the plain. Every fifteen minutes the General had a telephone call from his deputy at Sacramento gauge where the American poured into the main river. Hour by hour the water rose—twenty-seven-point-seven, twenty-eight, twenty-eight-point-one.

By now so much water was flooding from the American that it almost monopolized the main channel below its mouth. The water from the upper river had topped the wickets of Sacramento Weir, and was flowing across in streams two feet deep. At either end of the long weir a man stood on guard; the moonlight glinted upon the star of a deputy sheriff and showed the bulge of the pistol at his hip. There were many people who might like to have those wickets opened, and the General was taking no chances.

Between two and three, the gauge held steady. Perhaps, thought the General, the crest had arrived; perhaps he had held the American. But then the gauge crept up—twenty-eight-point-three, twenty-eight-point-five. Beyond twenty-nine it must not go. The trouble, the General suddenly realized, was with the Sacramento itself. Under present conditions the four miles between the weir and the mouth of the American should be practically still water. But now the outlet through the weir was not sufficient, and the water still pressed down against the outflow of the American and rose against the levees around the sleeping city. The telephone rang, and the deputy reported twenty-eight-point-seven. On top of that was another call—police headquarters; a patrol-car just reporting, three inches of seepage water covering a street. Again the telephone—northwest wind freshening, waves slopping at the top of the American levee, we're holding it with a row of sand-bags; not dangerous—yet.

The General shrugged his shoulders. Like a good

soldier he had held his lines until he could retreat with honor. He gave his orders.

Men hurried along Sacramento Weir. They knocked out the pins holding the wickets in place. An eight-foot wall of water swept through.

Then occurred what might seem a miracle. Along four miles of its course the great swirling river grew still, and then reversed its flow. Water which had passed the weir on its way to the sea, now turned and flowed back up-stream. The suck of the suddenly opened wickets seemed to annul the power of gravity. Even the American felt the pull; part of its waters continued down the main channel, but part took the up-channel, and flowing through the weir entered the by-pass. The level at Sacramento gauge fell half a foot in ten minutes.

The General started home to bed. As he drove his car along the dry streets under the bright moon, he again felt that sense of the unreality of disaster on such a night. Yet the opening of the weir was sending down water which would flood thousands of acres in the delta. Already he had sent out the warning.

He had lost both his fights. First he flooded the highway, and in the end he had to open the wickets. Flooding the asparagus country was a nasty business, but at least it saved the city—like sacrificing a platoon to save a battalion. And somebody had to take the responsibility. The next few days might raise some excitement. But barring accident, the levees and by-passes would carry the run-off; the rivers would crest successively, and the storm was over.

Yet other storms would come; again the brown water would rise against the levees. In the end the levees would go down—a hundred years, a thousand years; but in the end they would go, and the men who built them.

Perhaps it was only that he had lost a night's sleep; he felt old. He sensed a great weariness, of storms that came and went, of water that fell as rain and rushed through the rivers, only to return again as rain. He knew there was a quotation, not Bret Harte this time, something more ancient. What was it all about—this ceaseless, ineffective activity of storms, and of men? Then he found the quotation somewhere back in his mind: "All the rivers run into the sea; yet the sea is not full; unto the place from whence the rivers come, thither they also return again." The cold northwest wind eddied about the General's neck, and he shivered.

5

The Old Master was dead. A drenching, a chill—and he had never rallied.

"Gosh!" said Whitey. "It won't be like the same place without him dropping in to see what the map looked like. As long as I remember, he was so old he never seemed to get older."

The Chief and the J.M. bent together over the map. It looked much the same as it had during the weeks before the coming of Maria. The Pacific High, rearing like some sea-monster, thrust itself against the California coast and joined with a continental high over the Great Basin. Far to the north lay the storm-track. Over New York City was Little Maria; the new storm which had brought the chinook to the northern plains was moving across Manitoba; Victoria, magnificent in maturity, held the Gulf of Alaska.

But neither the Chief nor the J.M. was really thinking of the map.

"He was a good weather-man—for his day," said the Chief. "You know, I can't help liking the way he went— with his boots on. The barometer rose a little, and he forecast clearing; he left his umbrella in the rack, and went out on his own convictions."

"Crazy," said the J.M.

"Bad judgment at least," said the Chief. "He was an old man. Probably he was a little gone. I don't mean to say he'd have done a thing like that when he was at his best. In those days he had a real feeling for weather. Without the instruments and reporting-service we have today, I've known him to make some amazing forecasts. I don't yet know how he did it."

"Luck, maybe," said the J.M.; he talked more boldly to the Chief now.

"Well, in this world who doesn't need luck? Hn-n? And forecasting will be a mighty dull business when it's no guessing and all slide-rules."

In the pause the J.M. knew that he should say something; he felt the glancing reference to himself and all the new meteorology; but he did not think of any words, and the Chief went on. Somewhere in the Chief, the J.M. realized now, there was a vein of poetry.

"Storms or men," he was saying. "Hn-n? They get born, and they grow up, and they get old and die. (Some of them die before they grow up.) Everything is always changing, and always it comes back to what it was before. Storms come and go, but there's always weather. I've seen a lot of them—storms and men. Each one is different. There are the big bluffers, and the sneaks, and the honest dependable ones. Some of them will sulk for days, and some will stab you in the back, and some walk out on you between night and morning, and some do exactly what you expect of them."

"It's all a matter of air-mass properties and relationships," said the J.M. stubbornly, still remembering that remark about the slide-rule. "And in men, doctors say, it's glands working."

But the Chief did not seem to notice. "Storms and men —they're all different, and yet they're all the same. Each little storm starts out hopefully, but until it's all over, you can't say whether it was better than the ones that went before it—or as good."

The J.M. felt the implication of that remark too, but there was nothing to say.

"And in the end," the Chief went on, "it doesn't seem to make much difference. Every storm mixes up the air a bit. Sometimes it raises quite a hullabaloo. Then it's gone, and there you are in a high-pressure area just where you were before, with maybe another storm showing up on the edge of the map. Month in, month out, a lot of wind blows, but at the end of the year everything is just about where it was before."

The Chief moved on to other work. The J.M. still looked at the map.

Maria was dead—completely vanished. Perhaps off the Olympic Peninsula or Vancouver Island there might be areas of drizzle and shower, but no ships were there to report. The air which had composed Maria twenty-four hours before had now turned to new courses and revolved around other centers of activity. But she had been a good storm—Maria!

He turned back over his charts. He told himself that it would be a good idea to study, scientifically, the history of that storm. Actually, he realized that he was sentimental about Maria. Twelve days back he found that first little closed isobar shaped like a football which he had drawn half way between Titijima and Hatidyosima. Day by day, in twenty-four hour jumps, he followed Maria across the Pacific. She grew larger; her fronts became more sharply defined, her winds more violent. He saw her on the day when she smashed the *Byzantion*. The great outburst of polar air drove her to the south, and then blocked her passage inland. From her sixth to her eleventh day she had brought rain and snow to California. She had given birth to Little Maria. Then, with a rapidity remarkable even for a storm, she had died.

From south of Kamchatka the Junior Meteorologist followed the long blue line of a cold front southwestward along the chain of the Kuril Islands and across the Sea of Japan. Somewhere along that line a new wave should be forming—a wave which might develop into a great storm like Maria. But now no ship happened to be at the proper location.

6

The Captain was spruce in his uniform of the Highway Patrol. He drove into the garage at Donner Summit, and talked with the Superintendent.

"How's everything?" he asked, noticing that the Superintendent was heavy-eyed and tired-looking.

"Quiet enough today. We were blocked eight hours, the other night."

"Tellin' *me?* We had our own time with the traffic that you—that couldn't get through."

"Well, she beat us; that's all. We lost the road."

"Tough! Yes, that sure was tough!—But, say, that's not what I stopped in about. Maybe you can help us. A fellow and a girl left Frisco the first night of the storm—driving for Reno. Haven't been located since. D'you hear of it?"

"Haven't had time for papers or for radio—except weather reports."

"A service-station man we talked to last night in Auburn is pretty sure they were the ones he sold some gas to. So they're probably along this road all right."

"Yes, they would be."

The Superintendent thought back through the days of the storm. He knew every foot of his road; he could remember for weeks a detail which another man would not have noticed in the first place.

"Come on," he said. "There's a spot we'll take a look at, just down from the crest of the Pass here. I noticed a broken snow-stake there, back about the beginning of the storm; it didn't look just like snow-plow work."

At the place, they got out of the car. The day was cold on the Pass after the storm—a steel-sharp wind from the north, close to zero. They found the broken snow-stake, and floundered through the snow-wall toward the edge of the cliff. (There had been no snow-wall on the first night of the storm.) They peered over the hundred-foot drop; even through the snow, jagged rocks stuck out.

"Look!" said the Superintendent, pointing.

During the last night it had not snowed, and now on

the shining white surface far below them the two men made out an intricate criss-cross of delicate markings.

"Coyote tracks—he must have smelled something!"

They went back to the Maintenance Station for a shoveling crew. The truck had to go down around the curve of the road, and then the men went in toward the base of the cliff on skis.

After fifteen minutes digging, they found the car. It was badly smashed.

The Captain looked upward toward the top of the cliff. "Blinded in a snow-flurry, probably," he said.

They wrapped each body in a blanket, made sleds by fastening two skis side by side, and dragged them across the deep snow to the highway.

7

Once again the clipper was well upon its course. Day after day the flight had been postponed, through that week while the storm held dominion. Now once more, the great and gentle swirl of air which men call the Pacific High lay above the far-reaching ocean between the Hawaiian Islands and North America. Northeast by east, the pilot laid his course, until at a point calculated in advance by compromise of distance and wind-conditions, he must turn more toward the east.

Ten days before, the same pilot had flown toward Honolulu. Then he had skirted to the south of the center of high pressure. Today, men skilled in the ways of the air had charted his route farther north, so that for two-thirds of the distance steady southwest winds might aid his flight.

The sky without clouds, the unfeatured ocean, gave no

points of reference. Once again poised between sky and ocean, the great clipper seemed to hover motionless.

8

On the Pass, where old trapper Greenwood and hawk-nosed Elisha Stevens first led the way, a golden sun in a blue sky shone dazzlingly on the fresh white snow. The cedars were dark green columns, powdered with shining crystals. Cars lined the highway. Costumed in red and blue, dark-goggled against the glare, the skiers moved swiftly across the snow. Where the violet-gray shadows of the firs lay upon the whiteness, the skiers pulled their jackets close, but in the sunshine they cast back their jackets and rejoiced in the brisk air. In the ski-tracks the light of the sun, refracted among the snow-crystals, gleamed in ethereal blue.

In that world as clean and beautiful as mortal man can ever know, the skiers came to play; but along the highway the men in the plows still worked on. The road between the ten-foot snow-walls was like a deep-cut trench. With cutter-bars deep in the snow-wall, the spouting rotaries cast their white fountains far among the trees. The storm was over, but the storm would come again. All must be ready. The road was safe and two lanes wide. But the plows would keep working until the snow was thrown back clear to the line of the orange-painted snow-stakes; then, when the next storm came, there would be a reserve and margin of safety laid up against its attack.

On the railroad the trains moved freely, but there too the plows were busy. The rotaries and the flangers must pass back and forth until all was clear and clean. The railroad must fight the storm not only while it was present, but also after it had gone and before it came.

Where the washout had halted the streamliner, a track crew, prying with crow-bars and hacking with axes, had dislodged the carcass of Blue Boy from the two pipes. Now they had re-ballasted and re-aligned, and were finishing off. Downstream, in the still tumultuous waters of the North Fork, the fragments of the dismembered boar, hourly growing more bloated, rolled toward the sea.

Back and forth along the highway shuttled the green trucks of Telephone. In the shadow, snow still clung heavily, but in the sun the spans were unloading—*slu-ush, slu-ush;* the wires vibrated sharply for a few moments and then were still. The linemen inspected the work done hastily in the storm. Where the tree-bole had gone through the Transcontinental Lead, they set a new pole, strung wires of bright copper, and then gathered up the duplex which had served for the emergency.

The chipmunk whose burrowing had removed gravel from beneath the tree-bole had not been disturbed when it rolled away; but with the tree-bole gone, cold had penetrated to his tiny hibernaculum, and he had stirred for a while uneasily in his sleep. Now the snow had drifted deep above him. He was warm, and had again sunk into a death-like slumber.

At French-Bar Dam the water was no longer spilling over the top. Mrs. Martley mended the torn knees of her husband's pants, wondering what in the world he could have scraped them against.

High above the Pass a plane moved from the east. Its metal glittered in the sunlight. It followed the steady hum of the Reno beam. The pilot looked down upon the far-stretching, snow-covered mountains—quiet, beautiful. Like twisting furrows in the snow he saw the highway and the railroad; as straighter lines he made out the faint trace of poles and wires. He passed the air-beacon on the crag. Over Blue Canyon he picked up the Oakland beam, and—turning—set his last course for the airport on the Pacific.

9

The words of Hamlet, Prince of Denmark: *If it be now, 'tis not to come; if it be not to come, it will be now; if it be not now, yet it will come; the readiness is all.*

10

Again the northwest wind possessed the City. The flowers flared, yellow and blue, from the stands. The air was fresh; sunshine filled the streets. Above the tall buildings the proud flags of the great companies flaunted against the clear blue sky.

From those citadels the commanders against the storm reviewed the last combat and planned the next. The General Manager read the report on the blocked culvert, and ordered some construction to prevent its happening again. The L.D. thought of his thousands of miles of dipping and rising wires; he looked over reports from dams and power-houses, checking storm-damage, searching for weak points in construction and personnel. In the Telephone Building the District Traffic Superintendent reviewed the storm—"That one nearly missed us; not much damage or interruption of service, taking the system as a whole; hope we do as well next time." At the airport the Chief Service Officer had everybody on the carpet to see just why trip one-six-five had got into that unstable air; somebody was likely to be out of a job.

High above the City—blue, blue and white, maroon, crimson and black—the great banners stood out stiffly, rippling in the steady northwest wind.

11

The words of the Preacher, the son of David, king in Jerusalem: *The wind goeth toward the south, and turneth about unto the north; it whirleth about continually, and the wind returneth again according to his circuits.*

12

Steadily the great sphere of the earth spun upon its axis, and moved in its unvarying course around the sun. From far-off Venus a watcher of the skies (if such we may imagine) viewed it as a more brilliant planet than any to be seen from the earth. It gave no sign that storms or men disturbed its tranquil round. Bright against the black of midnight, or yellow at the dawn, it hung in the sky— unflickering and serene.

BIOGRAPHICAL NOTE

George Rippey Stewart was born in Sewickley, Pennsylvania, in 1885. He received degrees at Princeton, Berkeley, and Columbia, then taught for two years at Michigan—where he married the university president's daughter. Subsequently he had a stable if undistinguished teaching career at Berkeley. Chafing at slow academic advancement, he began writing, first on Bret Harte, whose work is alluded to in *Storm*, then on the Donner Party.

Storm is by no means the only Stewart book that has remained part of our California legacy. His *Ordeal by Hunger* (1936) is one of the best books on the ill-fated emigrants who perished at the foot of Donner pass because they would not accept edible roots from the local Indians, did not know how to make snowshoes or camp in snow by snuggling up together in buffalo robes, and could not otherwise adapt to the challenges of winter in the Sierra Nevada.

Before *Storm,* Stewart published two novels, *East of the Giants* (1938) and *Doctor's Oral* (1939), a satire on university life. *Storm*'s success gained him a national name. He followed it with the less successful sequel, *Fire*. After that, he became prodigiously productive in a variety of genres, and in 1947 persuaded the university to let him teach half-time—an unprecedented arrangement.

As *Storm* makes clear, Stewart was fascinated by place names and the sometimes imaginative, sometimes painful, sometimes ludicrous processes by which they are bestowed. *Names on the Land* (1944), though national in its coverage, is full of wonderful California names. As we learn in a book-length interview done for the Bancroft Library's Regional Oral History Project in 1972, Stewart regarded it as his best book.

In 1950 he published *Year of the Oath,* an account of the struggle by a handful of brave Berkeley professors, including Stewart himself, against the state legislature's imposition of a loyalty oath during the McCarthy period. Stewart and his defiant colleagues, though in some ways conservative, were fiercely libertarian. As free citizens of the West, they loved their country and were deeply insulted by being forced to swear loyalty to it.

Earth Abides (1949), Stewart's other long-lasting novel, is an apocalyptic story of a mysterious worldwide plague that suddenly kills almost all human beings, and of a tribelet that somehow manages to survive in the San Francisco Bay Area. It won a science fiction award and is still in print. Like *Storm*, it is anthropological in its understanding of how humans inhabit the landscape, organize themselves, and try to maintain a culture. And like *Storm*, it is a melancholy book.

Stewart came from a Scots Presbyterian family, which may have something to do with this overarching melancholy as well as with his precision of expression. He liked to work with his hands, building brick walls and doing carpentry, and he wrote with pencil and paper on a large board. When *Sheep Rock* (1951) was being readied by a New York publishing house, its famous editor offered only one change: he wanted to delete a comma in the opening sentence. Stewart acceded, but after turning the sound of the sentence over and over in his mind during the night, he retracted. The editor gracefully let the comma stand.

Sometimes criticized for not dealing with characters in psychological depth, Stewart knew he shied away from "emotional involvements." Reacting in his craftsmanlike way, he developed types of writing in which this was a virtue. Indeed, in *Storm* he was proud of achieving a whole in which the people became auxiliary to the storm, instead of the usual vice versa. He was not altogether modest; he knew his strengths and relished his tremendous curiosity, delighting in writing about things "so you can look at them." His books were not really documentary novels, as some said at the time they were published, but were instead like Conrad's novels and Griffith's films: they made us see.

After retiring from teaching, Stewart moved to San Francisco and continued writing until his death in 1980.

Ernest Callenbach

A California Legacy Book

Santa Clara University and Heyday Books are pleased to publish the California Legacy series, vibrant and relevant writings drawn from California's past and present.

Santa Clara University—founded in 1851 on the site of the eighth of California's original twenty-one missions—is the oldest institution of higher learning in the state. A Jesuit institution, it is particularly aware of its contribution to California's cultural heritage and its responsibility to preserve and celebrate that heritage.

Heyday Books, founded in 1974, specializes in critically acclaimed books on California literature, history, natural history, and ethnic studies.

Books in the California Legacy series appear as anthologies, single author collections, reprints of important books, and original works. Taken together, these volumes bring readers a new perspective on California's cultural life, a perspective that honors diversity and finds great pleasure in the eloquence of human expression.

Series editor: Terry Beers
Publisher: Malcolm Margolin
Advisory committee: Stephen Becker, William Deverell, Charles Faulhaber, David Fine, Steven Gilbar, Ron Hansen, Gerald Haslam, Robert Hass, Jack Hicks, Timothy Hodson, James Houston, Jeanne Wakatsuki Houston, Maxine Hong Kingston, Frank LaPena, Ursula K. Le Guin, Jeff Lustig, Tillie Olsen, Ishmael Reed, Alan Rosenus, Robert Senkewicz, Gary Snyder, Kevin Starr, Richard Walker, Alice Waters, Jennifer Watts, Al Young.

Thanks to the English Department at Santa Clara University and to Regis McKenna for their support of the California Legacy series.

SCU

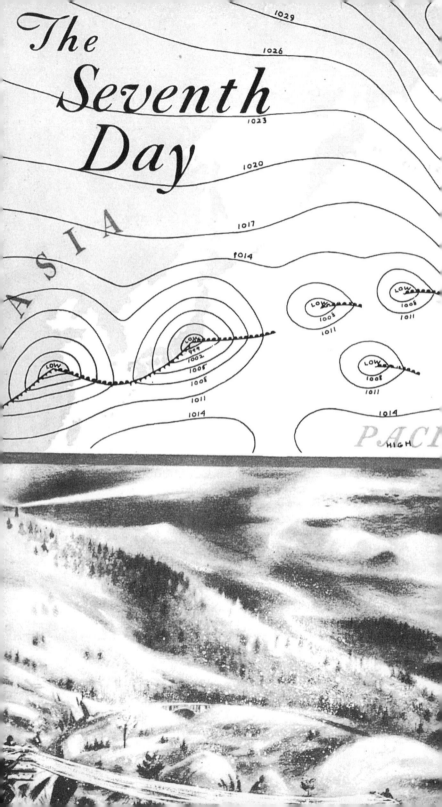

The Seventh Day